W9-CHB-525

ALSO BY
ELIZABETH DAY

The Party

Paradise City

Home Fires

MAGPIE

. . .

Elizabeth Day

Simon & Schuster

New York London Toronto Sydney New Delhi

Simon & Schuster
1230 Avenue of the Americas
New York, NY 10020

This book is a work of fiction. Any references to historical events, real people, or real places are used fictitiously. Other names, characters, places, and events are products of the author's imagination, and any resemblance to actual events or places or persons, living or dead, is entirely coincidental.

Copyright © 2021 by Elizabeth Day

Originally published in Great Britain in 2021 by Fourth Estate

All rights reserved, including the right to reproduce this book or portions thereof in any form whatsoever. For information, address Simon & Schuster Subsidiary Rights Department, 1230 Avenue of the Americas, New York, NY 10020.

First Simon & Schuster hardcover edition May 2022

SIMON & SCHUSTER and colophon are registered trademarks of Simon & Schuster, Inc.

For information about special discounts for bulk purchases, please contact Simon & Schuster Special Sales at 1-866-506-1949 or business@simonandschuster.com.

The Simon & Schuster Speakers Bureau can bring authors to your live event. For more information or to book an event, contact the Simon & Schuster Speakers Bureau at 1-866-248-3049 or visit our website at www.simonspeakers.com.

Interior design by Lewelin Polanco

Manufactured in the United States of America

1 3 5 7 9 10 8 6 4 2

Library of Congress Cataloging-in-Publication Data is available.

ISBN 978-1-9821-8760-6
ISBN 978-1-9821-8762-0 (ebook)

For Justin,
plot consultant extraordinaire

MAGPIE

PART I

1.

The house was perfect. Well, not perfect exactly, because houses never are, but the imperfections were ones Marisa could live with. The flooring, which had clearly been bought in bulk by the developer, was a shade too light, the wood laminate a touch too smooth to pass for real. The plantation shutters were plastic and layered with thin spores of dust. Someone had made the odd decision to put a bathroom on the second floor with doors that led out onto a roof terrace. Marisa stood on this terrace, her sandals shadowed on biscuit-colored patio stones, and she looked down to the garden below, which had a strip of lawn lined with potted plants, the soil newly turned. She noticed the quiet, which was rare for London, especially when you were this close to a main road. When she commented on this, the woman who was showing her around nodded.

"Yes, it's got a lovely sense of calm to it."

It was this that ultimately persuaded her. Marisa's own childhood had been studded through with noise. In her memories, it was always the sound she remembered first. The discordant hesitations as her father attempted to play the piano. The slamming of an oven door, the jangle of an overloaded dishwasher shelf. The raised voices of her parents' arguing. The shrill caterwaul of her newborn sister's crying. And then, when Marisa's mother had left, baby clamped to her, the house in the countryside had fallen silent. There had been little explanation.

Her mother had hugged Marisa tightly before leaving, whispering into her ear that she would return for her just as soon as she'd "got back on her feet." Marisa remembered how she looked down at her mother's shoes, wondering what was wrong with them. They were a pair of penny loafers, the coin glinting through the oxblood leather. She had tried, once, to winkle out the penny with stubby fingers, but it hadn't come loose. Marisa wanted to know why her mother was going. Most of all, she wanted to know what was going to happen to her and why she was being left behind. She was seven.

Her father had worn pajamas and slippers for a succession of long, stuffy days and his stubble had grown out into a patchy beard. In those sludgy, ill-defined weeks after her mother had left, Marisa tried to load the dishwasher the way her mother had liked, rinsing off the plates and putting the knives in handle-first. After a while, she grew tired of the domesticity and left the dirty crockery piled up in the sink. And then, four years later, she had been sent to boarding school and there had been a whole different set of noises to contend with.

This house was the antidote to all of that, she saw now. She had examined it online, zooming in to look at the gray front door and the steps leading up to it. The brick was the color of toasted hazelnuts. The road was, in the parlance of estate agents, "leafy" and in a prime catchment area for the local school that had been rated "outstanding" by the Office for Standards in Education. That was important, because they were going to get pregnant as soon as they moved in together. That had been the plan, and thinking back to her discussions with Jake, she felt an unspooling of tension, as if a warm stone had been placed in the palm of her hand.

Jake was her safety, her berth, her rock, her anchor. She had used all these words to describe him, albeit not to his face, as he wasn't given to shows of emotion. This was partly what had drawn her to him: his solidity was uncompromising. He showed her how much he loved her through the things that he did, rather than the words he said. She knew Jake mistrusted overt displays of affection because he found them insincere. After Marisa's childhood, where passion was deployed by her mother like heavy artillery in a battle with no clear end, she was relieved by Jake's undemonstrative nature.

The house felt right for them: a sanctuary of sorts, but light-filled and blank enough to imbue with their own character.

The kitchen was in the original basement, every possible dividing wall knocked out so that the room stretched outward like a beach. There was a midcentury walnut table with eight spindly legged chairs, and low-slung lights with pale enamel-blue shades over the island unit. An industrial-sized cooker that looked like it could be used to launch a rocket. A fridge buffed to a perfect metallic shine, with a built-in water system that dispensed ice cubes when you slotted your glass into place. A vast television hung on the white wall, an inky-black square with a dot of red light in the corner as if it were a painting that had just been sold.

The woman said she felt Marisa was just the right person to move into the house. Marisa smiled.

"These things can be so . . ." Marisa searched for the right word. "Instinctive, I guess?"

"Instinctive." The woman nodded. "Exactly."

It was when the woman opened the glass doors into the garden that the bird flew in. It swooped in low and fast so that neither of them had a chance to stop it.

The woman ducked, shielding her head with her hand. Marisa winced. She hated birds. The flap of their wings. The sharpness of their beaks. The smallness of their dead pebble eyes.

A magpie. Black and white with petrol-streak purple across its feathers. The bird flapped around, panicked by its sudden incarceration. It was large, almost the size of a crow. It seemed to stare right at her. For a moment, Marisa panicked that the bird was going to launch itself at her face, but then it darted up into the corner of the ceiling farthest away from where they were standing.

"Shoo!" the woman shouted, walking toward the bird, raising her arms up and down by her sides to scare it off. "Shoo!"

"I don't think—" Marisa started. She had been going to say that she didn't think it was wise to scare it, but the bird shot off before she could finish the thought. The tip of its wing crashed into a small, intricately painted vase on the top of the bookshelf. The vase teetered and then fell, splintering into pieces on the floor, shards of it gathering along the skirting board.

Then, as if some spell had been broken, the bird seemed to understand where it was. It flew in a straight line out of the open doors, passing so close to Marisa's face that she could feel the atomic weight of its movement in a gust of displaced breeze. It smelled mossy and slightly rotten. She imagined for a moment that she could sense the tickle of a feather, as if the magpie had grazed against her cheek in the mad flurry of flight.

"Good riddance!" the woman shouted after it, sliding the doors swiftly shut. The doors slotted into place with a sucking sound, and the muted noises of faraway traffic were cut off. The woman and Marisa existed once again in the centrifugal force of their glass-and-concrete bubble. It felt peaceful but also unnatural.

"I hope that didn't put you off," the woman said.

"No." Marisa smiled. "Sorry about the vase, though."

The woman waved her hand as if to show it was of no great significance. "These things happen."

They shook hands warmly and Marisa told the woman she would have a think and then she would be in touch.

In truth, she didn't need to think about it. Jake was happy to leave decisions like this to her. He was unfussy about where they lived, he said; he just wanted her to be happy and for there to be enough room to start a family as soon as they moved in. He saw it as her domain, and although Marisa should have felt indignant at this retrograde parceling up of the domestic, she secretly liked it.

On the street, she took out her phone to message him.

Seen the house. Love it. Feels right.

She did not add kisses. This was not their way.

She wasn't sure if she'd hear back from him straightaway, as he was in meetings all day. "Back-to-back," he had said, warning her there might be a delay and not to worry about it.

Jake worked for a consultancy firm in the city. Beyond that, Marisa had no clear idea of what he did, except she knew it was about making companies more streamlined and efficient, and there was a lot of travel involved, although not always to glamorous places. Recently, he had spent several weeks in Nottingham working for a pharmaceutical firm.

"Surprisingly good midcentury furniture shops," was all he'd said.

"How are the books?" he'd ask, and she'd tell him about the orders she'd got that week via her website from doting parents or aunts or godmothers wanting personalized storybooks for their little darlings. Marisa had a range of seven stories you could choose from online—there was the sleeping-princess story, the dragon-slaying prince, the fearless adventurer, the naughty jungle monkey, and so on. You could type in the name of your child, upload a recent photograph and provide some defining characteristics, and Marisa would illustrate each book accordingly.

Her website was called Telling Tales, and when it had launched last year, it was featured in some of the major glossy magazines. The Instagram account had several thousand followers and a blue tick. Marisa enjoyed the work because it was repetitive enough not to have to think too much and yet creative enough to be stimulating.

It didn't make her a fortune, despite what her carefully filtered Instagram tiles might have had people believe, and over the last few months, orders had slowed and she'd struggled to pay her rent. Which was why, when Jake suggested they move in together, she had jumped at the chance. That, and the fact she was in love with him, obviously.

"Whoa, Ris, where did you find him?" her friend Jas had asked when she had first told her about Jake.

"Online," Marisa said. "I know, I know! You don't need to say. It's a miracle."

Jas had been single for even longer than Marisa. Both of them had spent lengthy evenings over consolatory glasses of Pinot Noir on Marisa's sofa bemoaning the lack of decent men, and both of them had got a great deal of enjoyment from the clichéd pose of being two women in their late twenties drinking wine while bemoaning said lack of decent men. They had signed up to dating apps at around the same time, the ones named after imperative verbs that were linked to preexisting social media profiles and required Marisa to set about creating a personality for herself.

There were lists of favorite films and music and food. Endless questions to test compatibility over areas including religion and love and sexual predilection (polyamorous or gender fluid or "sapiosexual," which Marisa had to Google to find out that it meant being turned on by intelligence) and whether you'd consider dating someone in debt and whether it was more romantic to go camping in the woods or be whisked away for a dinner in Paris.

All the answers went into some mysterious algorithm that determined, down to the closest percentage, whether you were a match with Peter, the director of a graphic design company with a nine-year-old son who meant the world to him, or Wez, a tennis coach from Crawley looking for a woman with warm eyes and a sexy smile.

Marisa became numbed to the stream of men who posed shirtless with motorbikes or German shepherds or who said they were six feet when they were actually five feet ten or who took spooky selfies in hotel room mirrors so that the flash rebounded and illuminated the walls in dirty white like some budget horror movie. She was unmoved by Gareth, who posed with a young girl holding a teddy bear and who had written in his potted biography "Girl is my niece" while linking to his favorite Spotify tracks. He had Fleetwood Mac on there, like everyone else. She messaged him anyway and they went on a date and it was, like all the others, disappointing. Not terrible.

She had texted him to say thank you for the date, and she had watched as the WhatsApp tick turned from single gray to double gray and then to double blue, signifying that he had read her message. She kept looking at her phone to see whether he would reply, looking out for the telltale typing ellipsis, but there had been nothing.

After Gareth, she had told Jas she was giving up the apps altogether.

"I hear you, babe," Jas said, wincing as Marisa recounted the evening.

"It's like they think I'm . . . weird or too much or something," Marisa had said. "I can see it in their eyes."

"You're reading too much into it." Jas twiddled a small diamond hoop in her earlobe. "Like I always say, it's math."

Jas had read an article online about the fact that there were fewer men than women on dating apps, and she cited it frequently.

"And when you're a Black woman, it's even worse," she said. "Trust me. Hardly anyone swipes right on me."

"Racists," Marisa said.

"Yeah, but honestly, though." Her face was serious and Marisa felt bad. "It's everywhere."

"I texted Gareth."

"Again?" Jas looked at her.

In fact, Marisa had texted Gareth several times. At first, she simply wanted to tell him he owed her an explanation, but then she had got angry and accused him of being a misogynist prick. Her last WhatsApp had simply said "Fuck off." He'd stopped reading her messages. Or perhaps he had blocked her. That kind of thing had happened before.

Jake had been different from the start. For one thing, he always responded to her messages. They had met at a theme party, organized by the online agency she had signed up to that prided itself on "finding your perfect match." It was a dreary, fancy-dress affair and Marisa drank too much. She had chatted briefly with him at the bar and he had insisted she take his number.

She had woken up with a fuzzy head the next day, but there was already a text from Jake on her phone when she reached for it. He messaged her consistently for about two weeks before he asked whether she'd like to meet up for a date.

Instead of drinks or dinner, Jake had suggested a cafe in the middle of the day, which Marisa liked. It meant there would be no tipsy awkwardness at the end about whether to kiss or not. It was unthreatening and uncomplicated.

He was already sitting at a table by the window when she got there, a cup of coffee in front of him with a small shortbread biscuit on the saucer. His blond-brown hair was short and unfussy, swept into place with a moderate amount of gel. His clothes were freshly pressed and unexceptional: a gray T-shirt with no logo; chinos worn in at the knees; a dark belt with a burnished brass buckle; a watch with a dulled silver strap.

When she walked into the cafe, Marisa felt a strange sense of peace settle just underneath her breastbone, as though a bird's wings had stopped their fluttering.

"Hi." He stood.

She wasn't sure how to greet him, so she held out her arm to shake his hand, which he did while looking her directly in the eyes. He made no motion to lean forward and graze her cheek, and she was relieved when he sat back down on his side of the table, and she took a chair opposite him with just the right amount of distance between them.

He smelled of freshly washed laundry. No cologne. His face was uncomplicated: A defined chin and boyish cheeks. Kind eyes. A smattering of sandy-colored stubble. He had looks you could imagine aging well and at the same time you could see instantly what sort of a child he had been. Underneath his T-shirt was a ripple of muscle, but it was muscle that didn't like to announce itself. It was not gym-obsessive muscle but the understated strength of a man who could, if required, be counted on to push a car whose engine had given out.

In the cafe, Jake took quiet charge. He asked Marisa what she'd like to order and then conveyed this desire to the waitress as if Marisa might find it too much bother to do it herself. She liked that. She could imagine Jas rolling her eyes at her lack of feminist outrage. Her tea arrived in a glass pot on a wooden tray with a rectangular egg timer.

"I don't know if you've had our tea before," the waitress said. She had a tiny gold stud on the side of her nose. Marisa shook her head. "Right, ok, so you need to let it brew for three minutes to get the full flavor." The waitress turned the egg timer upside down. Inside, the fine, black sand started to trickle down.

"Wow," Jake said as soon as the waitress had left them to it. "That's a complicated cup of tea."

Marisa laughed.

"I'm more of an English Breakfast man myself," he said.

"Yes, I can see that," she replied, playful but not too much.

After that, the conversation came easily, passing between them fluidly like the egg timer grains. Jake spoke about his upbringing. He was the oldest of four, with three younger sisters, he told her. He was close to his mother, raised in Gloucestershire, "and still a country boy at heart."

"Do you go in for all those country pursuits?"

He laughed. "I don't think I've ever heard anyone actually *say* 'country pursuits.' I mean, outside the pages of a Victorian novel, that is." He looked at her, unblinking. "It's very quaint."

She flushed.

"Don't worry—it's charming. And no, not really. I've been to the odd pheasant shoot but fox hunting is not really my thing. I quite like . . . foxes."

He caught her eye and Marisa was left with the distinct impression that he meant to refer to her when he spoke the word.

He brought up the subject of children. It was unusual for a man to mention it, even more so on a first date and given their age difference—Marisa was twenty-eight and Jake eleven years older.

"But, you know, I want to be able to play football with my kids," he said. "I don't want to be the only dad at the school gates getting his hips replaced."

"You're not that old!" Marisa said.

"Well . . ."

Jake stretched back, resting one arm on the table and placing the other on the back of his chair. He had an effortless capacity to inhabit a space.

The cafe was beginning to fill with the thrum of the lunchtime rush: mothers pushing buggies and businessmen in suits and young women in glasses and cropped jeans carrying laptops in rucksacks. Jake and Marisa had to raise their voices to hear each other over the clattering of chrome chairs and hissing of the espresso machine.

"To be honest, I've always wanted kids young," Marisa said. "I think I told you my mum was twenty-one when she had me and . . ." She let the thought drift, annoyed with herself for having said something she did not particularly want to share. She couldn't remember what she'd told him on their first meeting and Marisa did not want to reveal too much. Her mind ballooned with an image of her beautiful but disheveled mother, dungaree dress unbuttoned so that her breast could slip out to feed the mewling baby, and Marisa had to make a conscious effort to remove the memory so that she could return to the conversation in the cafe with Jake. Don't go there, she told herself. Come back. You are here, right now, with this man. Do not fuck this up like you have done before.

She took a breath and smiled and fiddled with her teaspoon.

"I just think it would be great—a couple of kids, a dog . . ." Marisa said, and as she did so, she took a risk. She leaned forward casually and grazed his wrist with the tips of her fingers. She felt a crackle of energy, a fissure of some sort, as if two molecules had collided and meshed and sparked into a new thing.

Jake looked surprised. She removed her hand quickly and carried on talking as if nothing had happened, while all the time suspecting that everything had.

Later, he would tell her that he knew from the moment she reached across and touched his arm that Marisa was "the one." She'd always thought the phrase was only something that belonged in her hand-drawn fairy tales, but it turned out to be true.

II.

She moved into the house on a day Jake was at work. She didn't mind doing it by herself. She set up her studio in a small spare room at the back of the house, overlooking the garden. The previous tenant had used it as a makeshift gym, and when she unpacked her desk and her paints, she noticed a circular weight on the floor of the cupboard that must once have been affixed to a barbell. She used it as a doorstop.

Marisa had ordered cardboard boxes and Bubble Wrap online, and she had packed all her possessions with fastidious care, ensuring each one of her favorite mugs was insulated from damage and hanging her clothes in the special containers sent by the removal company. Jake had told her not to bother with crockery. "We've already got everything we need," he said, and she noticed the casual possessive pronoun with delight.

They had been seeing each other for a little over three months. The house move had been smooth as soon as they'd set their minds to it. She had rented her little flat and it was easy to talk the landlord into letting her leave before her lease ended because he wanted to charge higher fees to someone new. It all felt to Marisa as if some benign deity had finally decided to smile on her.

"It's your time now," she imagined this kindly-faced bearded man saying to her (because God, in her imagination, was always the cartoon childhood version, a version of Father Christmas but more serious and without the red clothes). "You deserve it."

Jas was less convinced. She had come over to Marisa's flat for a farewell dinner of take-out pizza and gin and tonics with not much tonic.

"It seems very soon," Jas said, sliding a slice of pizza out precariously with two hands, threads of cheese stretching like saliva strings in a giant opening jaw. "You barely know each other."

Marisa, who wasn't eating much, refilled her drink. "Yeah, but it turns out all those people who said it were right."

"Said what?"

She looked at Jas, at her short, peroxide hair, at the glare of her eyes, the slant of her arrow tattoo along one pronounced collarbone, and she felt something she'd never felt for her before. She felt pity.

"That when you know, you just know."

It was the sort of thing that both Marisa and Jas would have rolled their eyes at in the past. Their bonhomie had been forged in the shared experience of being single in a world geared up for couples. But meeting Jake had changed things for Marisa. She had realized lately that her friendship with Jas was based on shared bitterness—the resentful cynicism of the overlooked masquerading as brittle humor—and now that she had found the person she wanted to spend the rest of her life with, there was less common ground.

In the flat, Jas glanced at her skeptically but then, sensing something in Marisa's face, she broke into a smile.

"Girl! You've got it bad!"

Jas had grown up in Lewisham, but she often broke into an easy American patter, as if she'd watched too much nineties TV.

Marisa downed the rest of her gin. She shook her hair back, the ends of it landing with a soft tickle on her bare shoulders. She felt the absolute rightness of this moment, of the exact movement she had chosen to execute. She felt her beauty, the power of it.

"I suppose I do," Marisa said. "You'll be next."

Jas shrugged. "I'm not that bothered anymore," her friend said.

"I've decided I like my own company, my own space. Why invite someone in to mess it all up, you know?"

Marisa didn't press it. She would never feel the same as Jas. Her sense of completeness relied on finding another to fill in the blanks. She sat on the floor, cross-legged, taking the smallest slice of the pepperoni pizza and chewing slowly.

"I just . . ." Jas started, then hesitated. "You fall hard for people. Remember . . ."

"This is different," Marisa snapped. She stood up too quickly and felt dizzy, her vision pixelating. She took the remaining pizza slices still in the box and threw the whole thing decisively in the rubbish bin.

"Hey," Jas protested. "I hadn't finished!"

"Whatever."

"I'm just looking out for you, Ris."

Marisa turned away from her, washing her hands in the sink. Her flat was made up of one big room divided into three smaller ones so that the kitchen and lounge bled into each other. The cold water calmed her, breaking off the sprig of fury she had felt begin to blossom inside. When she turned back to face Jas, she was calmer.

"I know." She put the kettle on. "I appreciate it."

The evening ended earlier than nights with Jas usually did, and Marisa realized, when she hugged Jas goodbye, that their friendship might not survive the next iteration of her life. She felt judged by Jas and she was uncomfortable under that level of scrutiny. It wasn't anyone's fault, not really. It was just that things moved on. People changed. Besides, she had Jake. She had the house. She had their future children.

In the house, the studio began to take shape. Marisa hung two framed original sketches from her first Telling Tales book. It had been written for a boy called Gabriel, and she had given him a knightly quest to complete, filled with princesses in flowing pink gowns and dragons breathing fire from inside hidden caves. She put her brushes in jam jars, and on the shelves she lined up the lever arch files where she kept track of her orders and invoicing. Jake told her she should computerize everything and that he would show her how, but Marisa preferred the tangibility of paper. It was a way of proving to herself that she existed, that she left a trace.

As a child, she had always felt so ephemeral, a will-o'-the-wisp expected to contort herself like smoke to fit in wherever necessary. She didn't have a single earliest memory, but rather a jumble of images of walking into rooms and her mother jumping when she realized Marisa was there.

"I didn't see you, darling!" was the refrain. She was always too quiet to be noticed.

Her younger sister, by contrast, was determined to make herself heard from the outset. She would cry throughout the night and Marisa got used to the sound of her mother padding across the hallway to get to the baby, rocking her back to sleep with soft tuneless songs. The next morning, Marisa and her father would sit opposite each other at the breakfast table and share conspiratorial looks as he prepared her toast, doing it badly and leaving gaping holes in the bread where the fridge-cooled butter made stubborn dents. She was always late for school, and Marisa felt cross about this, blaming her sister, this unwanted intruder with her furious, crumpled red face and balled-up baby fists. It was astonishing to her how someone so small could create so much havoc.

Marisa was simultaneously fascinated and horrified by the baby. It seemed strange that this alien being had been squashed up in her mother's stomach and had emerged, bearing only the vaguest of resemblances to a proper human, with skin so thin and stretched it seemed almost translucent. The baby's fingers were tiny as maggots, her eyes cloudy like apple juice. And all the grown-ups were mad about her, this squalling newborn, who had no personality as far as Marisa could see.

"You need your nappy changed, don't you, sweetheart?" Marisa's mother would say, cooing and smiling and lifting the baby high in the air so she could sniff her bottom and then make a great show of wrinkling her nose. "Ugh. What a stink! You need a clean nappy, don't you, darling? Yes, you do. Yes, that's just what you need."

On and on it would go, with Marisa skulking on the sofa watching it all unfold with degrees of embarrassment and disgust. She couldn't understand why her mother was talking to the baby in the first place, when it couldn't understand.

Once, when the baby was a few months old and down for her afternoon nap, Marisa had conducted an experiment. Her mother had been sleeping on the sofa downstairs, limbs flung out gracefully, her patchwork skirt riding up her thighs. Her father had been at work. The house was silent, apart from the deliberate ticking of the grandfather clock in the hallway.

In the nursery, the cot was pushed against one wall, with a mobile of brightly colored elephants and beach balls twisting in the breeze above the child's head. The window was fractionally open, and a ribbon of sunlight unfurled across the floor.

Marisa knelt down by the cot so that she was level with her sister. The baby's eyes were closed, its nostrils dark and mysterious like minuscule caves, the flesh around them frilling delicately as it took shallow rock-pool breaths. Marisa always thought of the baby as an it, but her sister was actually called Anna. Anna and Marisa, joined by the pretty vowel sound at the end of their names, so that if you said them quickly, one after the other, it sounded as if you were laughing or singing.

In the cot, she was stirring; her pudgy arms started to wave slowly, the peony-pink hands clenching and releasing. It was as if the baby could sense she was being watched. Marisa waited. She wanted her to be awake. She needed it, for the experiment.

The baby's eyes opened. They were dark blue and had lost their earlier cloudiness. Her pupils swam and then locked into focus on

Marisa's face, and then she smiled, pushing her cheeks up so that they dimpled at the top.

A few weeks before, the baby had been in her mother's arms, peering over her shoulder. The baby had smiled at Marisa and Marisa had pointed it out in delight.

"Oh, that's not a real smile," her mother had said confidently. "It's wind."

Sitting cross-legged on the floor of the nursery, feeling the roughness of the carpet imprint itself on her ankles, Marisa was not sure if this was a real smile or a windy one. She wanted to see if her baby sister was like her. If she felt things in the same way as Marisa did, if she too was confused and lonely and cross at being misunderstood. She seemed so alien, with her bald head and tiny fingernails, that Marisa thought there was little chance she did.

In the cot, Anna was starting to grizzle next to her toy bunny, her fingers crunching closed, then open. Marisa knew it was time. She slid the pin out of her dress pocket; she'd taken it from her mother's sewing kit earlier that day.

Marisa leaned toward the cot, slipping her hand through the bars, the pin pointing outward from the grip of her index finger and thumb. Anna was still looking at Marisa, gurgling and wriggling. Her eyes were fixed on Marisa's face. Above, the mobile shivered and elephants with jaunty bow ties cast their dancing shadows across the ceiling.

Marisa selected the softest part of the baby's flesh, on the upper part of her arm. The skin there was plump, like the freshly baked loaves of bread her mother used to leave out for Marisa when she got back from school. Swiftly, before the baby could move, Marisa stuck the sharp end of the pin into her arm.

For a split second, the baby looked at Marisa with confusion. In that moment, she looked older than anyone Marisa had ever met, as if she understood everything in a single instant. Marisa drew a sharp breath. She wondered if she had been right all along, that this wasn't, in fact, her baby sister but a life form from a different dimension sent to spy on them and ruin Marisa's life.

But then the baby screamed. It was a howling scream, not like the usual cries of hunger or tiredness but a catastrophic shriek of what Marisa recognized immediately as pain. Pain and upset and mistrust. The baby was screaming so loudly that Marisa felt a lurch of panic. She checked Anna's arm. The pin had not drawn blood. There was instead a full stop of red, unnoticeable unless you were looking for it. Marisa put the pin back into her dress pocket. Her chest was tight.

She reached back into the cot, but the baby flinched and Marisa realized that she was scared of her now.

"Shhh, shhh, shhh," she said, hopelessly trying to copy her mother's intonations. "There, there; it's fine. I'm here. We're here. It's ok."

But the baby would not be pacified and after a few more seconds, Marisa thought she was going to throw up. What if she'd ruined the baby forever? She only wanted to see what would happen. Anna was red-faced now, her eyes scrunched, tears blotting the blanket beneath her.

"What on earth is all this?"

Marisa looked up to see her mother rushing into the room, already unbuttoning her blouse in readiness to feed the infant. Her mother still had that half-asleep look and her cheek was wrinkled where the edge of a cushion had pressed into her face.

"Shush now, darling, shush. Mummy's here."

She lifted Anna out of the cot and kissed her cheek with excruciating tenderness. Marisa started to cry.

"I'm sorry," she whispered. "I just wanted to see . . ."

Her mother looked at Marisa absentmindedly. "Why are *you* crying?" she asked briskly, before lifting her breast out of her bra. She squeezed the nipple into the baby's mouth but Anna wouldn't settle and kept twisting her head out of the way.

"What happened?" she asked Marisa.

"I wanted to see . . ." Marisa started. And then she realized, quickly, with a child's certain intuition, that there would be no way of explaining the experiment. That, in order to preserve the sliver of maternal affection she still felt worthy of, she would have to lie. She stopped crying and the last two tears stilled and dried on her cheek as if she had commanded it.

"Anna was crying and so I came to see if I could make her stop so we wouldn't wake you up," Marisa replied, the mistruth coming with frightening ease. It was the first lie she ever told.

"That's so thoughtful of you. Thank you, darling."

But she said it in a distracted way that meant it didn't really count. All her focus was now on getting the baby to feed. Her mother sat in the nursing chair by the window, holding Anna close. Marisa watched the baby crying loudly, then more quietly, then hiccoughing to a stop and greedily taking the nipple between her lips, and she thought how strange it was that two separate people could be so connected, as if they were just one big human, pulsing with a life that did not involve her.

She left the room without saying anything and then she placed the pin back in exactly the right compartment in her mother's sewing box. No one had noticed it was gone.

III.

They decided to start trying for a family straightaway. Marisa stopped taking birth control. When she saw the metallic rectangular packets of her pills, unpopped in the bottom of her toiletry bag each morning, she felt a sense of rightness, a twinge of satisfaction that she was doing something so grown-up.

"I can't wait to have a baby," Jake blurted out one night over dinner. "I know that sounds weird." He swept back his hair and left his hand resting at the back of his neck.

"It doesn't," Marisa protested. "Why would it?"

"Blokes aren't meant to say stuff like that."

"That's silly."

She had made macaroni and cheese because he had told her once that it was his favorite childhood meal, and she had a recipe that used four different types of cheese and salty lardons sizzled up in the frying pan. She picked one of the lardons up with her fingers and popped it in her mouth, licking the grease off.

"I can't wait either, and I don't care if that makes me sound weird."

She smiled and reached across to stroke the top of his hand. He slid it away to pour her some more wine and their fingers bumped awkwardly against each other.

"Sorry," he laughed. "Clearly I'm far too excited."

He tipped the wine bottle toward her glass, but she covered it with her palm.

"No. Thank you. But . . . if we're serious about this . . ."

"You're right. You're right. Of course."

He placed the bottle back on its coaster and she could tell he was pleased. He was still in his work suit, although he had taken the jacket off and it hung from the back of the dining chair. He had loosened the tie as soon as he came through the door. The corners of his eyes were creased with tiredness. There had been a new deal going through at work, she knew, and the whole process had been stressful and liable to collapse, but he never liked to talk about his job, instead asking Marisa how her day had been.

"How's the new book commission coming along?" he asked, rolling up his sleeves before tucking into the food.

"Yeah, great. You know, it makes such a difference having that room to work in—the light is just gorgeous."

"What's the kid's name for this one?"

"Moses." She rolled her eyes. It was a source of amusement to both of them how the monied upper classes had turned toward the Old Testament as inspiration for their progeny's names.

She told him about the latest panel she'd been painting—a complicated scene involving twists of the princess's braided hair. He forked pasta into his mouth as she talked and held her gaze, as if she were the most important person in the world to him, which, Marisa realized with a jolt of pure love, she was. It was an unfamiliar sensation: she had never been anyone's priority.

"It's difficult to get the texture right. Hair's tricky to paint."

"This is what I like about you," Jake said. "You introduce me to a whole new world I wouldn't have a clue about otherwise. Hair being complicated to paint. Huh. Who'd have thought it?"

Despite Jas's warning, Marisa enjoyed the fact that she and Jake were still getting to know each other in this intimate way. Every day under the same roof was another layer unpeeled. With every stripping back, their oneness felt more solid, as if revelation were also fortification.

Marisa cleared the plates, stacking them on top of each other. His was wiped clean. Hers still had remnants on it. She'd been talking too much.

"You don't need to do that," Jake said. "Let me." And he lifted the plates from her, stroking her hand as he did so.

He was not a tactile man. Jake did not like to walk arm in arm while strolling down the street or even to kiss her at home when there was nobody watching. Still, she thought, as she watched him bend to load the dishwasher, she would rather have the straightforwardness of his love than any amount of superficial tactility.

He put the kettle on. She took pleasure in watching him move, the reassuring heft of his broad shoulders and the stockiness of his legs, the hardness of his muscular thighs. Her mind wandered to them making love, her legs wrapped around his back and him thrusting into her, biting the lobe of her ear as she felt the undiluted force of him inside her. She had never felt such a physical connection with any man. Her previous lovers had, she now realized, been too pliant and unsure of themselves. She had an image in her mind's eye of Jake's head, dipping down between her legs, his tongue circling her clitoris, intently focused on the task of making her wet. She thought of him flipping her over onto her front and guiding his way into her from behind so that her insides felt stretched and complete, as if everything had slotted into place.

"Penny for them," he said, standing behind the kitchen island.

"Mmmm?" Marisa glanced toward him. "Sorry, miles away. I was just . . ."

"Yes?" Jake cocked his eyebrow flirtatiously and she knew he was imagining exactly what she was.

"Thinking." She grinned.

"Come on. It's getting late."

The next morning, Jake got up early to go to work. She slept in so she didn't see him at breakfast. She padded downstairs and put a capsule in the coffee machine, which gurgled and spat out an espresso. Light filtered through the sliding doors, and on the lawn outside were two magpies, strutting around each other, pecking the grass with jittery movements as if they knew they were being watched. She remembered the first time she came to see the house and the bird that had flown indoors.

One for sorrow, Marisa thought, two for joy. It was a sign, she told herself. She might be pregnant already, the glowing seed of it unfurling in her womb. For a long time after her mother left, Marisa had thought she didn't want children of her own. She felt so lonely with her father and confused by the unpredictable nature of his domestic routine that she nurtured a spiky resentment against her sister, Anna, blaming her for everything that had happened. It had all been fine before the baby came along.

She had once tried to talk to her father about it, but although he was a kind man, who loved her in his own way, he had been undone by his marriage ending and pottered around the creaking house with a permanently distracted air.

"Daddy," she said in bed one evening, when he shuffled into her bedroom to say good night. He was wearing a dirty bathrobe tied with a colored length of rope and on his feet were a pair of red knitted socks that she remembered her mother using every Christmas for stockings left at the end of her bed.

"Yes, darling?"

"Did Anna make Mummy leave because she wasn't happy with us?"

Her father looked startled and his watery eyes widened.

"What a strange question," he said as he sat on the edge of her bed, too far away for her to touch him. "She's just a baby. Anna couldn't make your mother do anything she didn't want to do." And then, in a quieter, more defeated voice, he added, "No one could."

Marisa actually wanted a reply to a different question altogether, one she was too afraid to ask. She nodded her head in what she hoped was a grown-up way.

"I understand, Daddy," Marisa said, even though she didn't.

He pressed down on the mattress to lever himself upward. As he walked toward her bedroom door, she experienced a late surge of courage.

"But, Daddy," she said.

He stopped, resting one hand on the doorknob, and waited.

"Do you . . . Do you . . . miss them?"

She felt a sob rising up her gullet and had to swallow hard.

"I do," he said, without turning round. "Do you?"

"Yes."

She thought her father would come back and comfort her but instead he said, "Humph," like the sound the sofa would make if you sat on it too heavily, and he walked out of her bedroom. Moments later, she could hear him brushing his teeth and running a bath.

She lay awake for a long time, feeling the slug trail of tears on her face, and she made a promise to herself that she would never talk about it again. She would pretend not to mind, and in this way, she would grow strong and careless and no one else would ever be able to hurt her.

So, Marisa had never wanted to be a mother. But then, at some point in her midtwenties, without any explicit reason for a change of heart, she realized that having her own baby would be a way of reclaiming the past and making it better. It became something she wanted very much indeed.

And so she had signed up to every single app and website and forum she could. She was strategic, choosing only to pursue the people who had openly stated their seriousness about having children. Everyone had been a disappointment until Jake.

She drank her coffee, and then, invigorated by caffeine, Marisa went upstairs to the studio. She took out a fresh sheet of watercolor paper. She'd forgotten to stock up on the 110-pound paper, so each morning she had been undertaking the laborious task of stretching sheets for the next day's painting. She took her plastic tray, walked up to the master bathroom, and filled it a few inches with water, holding it gingerly as she walked back downstairs to the studio.

She set out the wooden board on her drawing table and cut the tape to size. She pressed the sheet of paper down to the base of the plastic tray, feeling the coolness of the water lapping at her wrists. Stretching paper like this was time-consuming but Marisa liked the meditative process of it. It was a task that took exactly as long as it took. There was no rushing it.

She returned to the scene she'd been working on, with the princess high up in a gray-bricked tower, her blonde hair tumbling down to the ground in a long plait. She flicked her brush in the jam jar of water and dropped the tip into pink paint and started with the princess's expression: her mouth an *O* of surprise and anticipation as she waited for Prince Moses to climb up and save her. Marisa gave the princess blue eyes and freckled cheeks. The prince was trickier and had to be painted with brown, curly hair, tufts of it sticking out at angles. She had a photo of Moses propped up on her desk and tried as much as possible to make the prince look like an idealized version of him. Real-life Moses was plump, with an unfortunate overbite that Marisa glossed over as she worked.

It was as she was painting his left eye, making it look ever so slightly less bulbous and staring than it did in the photo, that the doorbell rang. She sat up, startled. The doorbell had never rung before while she'd been in the house. Her shoulders tensed. Marisa didn't like to be interrupted midflow. She listened intently, wondering whether whoever it was would turn and go away. It must be charity canvassers, she thought, or Jehovah's Witnesses trying their luck or . . . The doorbell sounded again.

"Fuck," she said out loud, dropping her brush into the water pot where wisps of brown paint stained the liquid. Prince Moses would just have to wait.

She ran downstairs in the sandals she always wore when she worked—comfortable, Germanic things with molded soles that fit into the exact shape of her foot. The front door had a spy hole three-quarters of the way up the wood. Marisa pressed her eye to it and blinked. She could make out the shape of an older woman with her back turned to her.

She opened the door.

"Yes?" she said.

The woman turned around. She was tall, elegant, probably about sixty. Her face had the delicate sheen of expensive skin care. She was wearing discreet makeup: a touch of mascara, a dusting of blush, and a pinky-red lipstick. Along each eyelid, a contour of shimmery beige powder.

"You must be Marisa," the woman said, unsmiling.

"Yes," Marisa said for the second time.

"I'm Jake's mother, Annabelle." She held out her hand with such grace that Marisa almost expected her to be wearing gloves, despite the warm spring weather. Marisa shook her hand, feeling the bright, hard pressure of a signet ring on her little finger.

"Oh! It's such a pleasure to meet you at last!"

Marisa was a flurry of exclamation. Annabelle assessed her coolly from the doorstep.

"I wasn't expecting you . . ." Marisa continued, and everything she said sounded foolish and unnecessary. Stop speaking, she told herself. Just shut up. "Were you in the neighborhood, or . . . To what do we—I mean, I—owe the honor?"

Why was she talking like this? She realized she was nervous. Jake was close to his mother but evasive about her in their conversations.

"Things with my mother are a bit . . ." he had said on one of their first dates. "Let's just say she's a tricky character."

"How so?"

He had hesitated. "She struggles to see things from other people's points of view."

She hadn't pressed it. She and Jake existed in such a bubble that she supposed it made sense she hadn't yet met any of his family. It had all been so quick.

"I was in the area," Annabelle was saying. "Are you going to invite me in? I'd be most grateful."

"Of course, of course. Sorry. Forgetting myself there."

She ushered Annabelle in and gestured down the tiled hallway.

"The kitchen's in the basement," she explained. Annabelle walked down the stairs with her shoulders pressed back, one finger on the banister as if assessing it for dust. Marisa followed in her wake, her sandals feeling ugly compared to Annabelle's chic espadrilles.

"I just fell in love with the original features," Marisa said, lapsing into meaningless chitchat to counteract the unsettling silence. "The cornicing . . ."

"I shouldn't think that's original," Annabelle replied, glancing at the light fitting. "It's most likely a later addition made to look old. I suppose a developer did the whole place up for rental, did they?"

"Um . . . I don't . . ." Marisa stuttered.

"Looks like it. These floorboards aren't real wood."

Annabelle walked deeper into the kitchen, toward the glass doors giving on to the garden where she paused and stared at the patch of lawn.

"Needs watering." She turned and assessed the stove. "Goodness gracious, what on earth is that?"

Annabelle was pointing toward the mirrored backsplash.

"It's . . ."

"What a very strange idea, to want to look at yourself while you're cooking."

Annabelle smiled, lips parting to reveal large teeth. Marisa was reminded of the wolf dressed up as Red Riding Hood's grandmother.

"Are we sitting here?" Annabelle pointed at the kitchen table, which now looked shabby and pockmarked with mug rings. There was a scattering of breadcrumbs at one end where Marisa hadn't cleaned up properly after Jake's breakfast.

"Yes. Can I get you a cup of—?"

"Coffee. Black." Annabelle sat down, unwinding her printed Indian shawl from her shoulders. "Thanks."

The mirrored backsplash Annabelle so despised gave Marisa the chance to assess the woman she already thought of as her mother-in-law. Under the shawl, Annabelle was wearing a white linen shirt, unbuttoned to reveal papery, tanned skin and a long gold necklace threaded with semiprecious stones. Her pale trousers stopped just above her ankle and were frayed at the hem in a way that looked fashionable rather than ragged. Her hair was whiteblonde, swept back into a chignon kept in place by a tortoiseshell clip. Her profile was that of a ballerina in repose: jutting nose, chin tilted upward, taut cheeks, and an alertness that suggested a woman used to being looked at. She must have been very striking, Marisa thought, but there was something that stopped her being fully beautiful, some sense of unease or defensiveness that you could just about make out in the vertical frown lines between her eyebrows or the discernible clench of her jaw. It was as if Annabelle had learned how to be beautiful from the pages of a book but had never quite got the hang of it.

Marisa busied herself with the espresso machine, placing a cup under the nozzle.

"Do you like those things?" Annabelle asked from her seat.

"You mean the coffee—?"

"Yes."

"I do, actually. It makes it all so easy. No coffee grounds to clean up and—"

"I never think it tastes as good."

"Mmm," Marisa said and she felt like a child who had just been slapped down.

"Sorry," Annabelle added, perhaps aware that she had been too brusque. "I'm sure it'll be delicious."

This was all it took for Marisa to experience a surge of hope. Perhaps she had read the signals all wrong—she had a tendency to do that, to misread people and to believe they were judging her—and perhaps she and Annabelle were going to get along famously. She imagined Annabelle saying just that to her impressive friends: "Oh, I adore my daughter-in-law. We get along famously." Perhaps they simply needed to get to know each other better, to learn the quirks and hidden charms of their individual behaviors. Perhaps, perhaps, perhaps.

"Here we go."

Marisa set down two cups of coffee, each one on a saucer they never normally bothered using.

Annabelle took a sip of coffee, her mouth twisting as she did so.

Then she crossed her legs, leaning back against the chair, her hands loosely clasped around the cup.

"So," she said. "We meet at last."

"We do." Marisa smiled. "I've been so looking forward to it."

Annabelle looked mildly astonished.

"Really?" She grimaced. "I can't imagine why. I shouldn't think Jake would have had any reason to talk about me."

"Oh . . . no . . ." Marisa slid into silence. She had nothing to say to this.

"But there we have it. I suppose children never tell their parents what they're up to. Not really."

Annabelle placed the cup back on its saucer. It was still almost full. Marisa knew that, however long she chose to stay, she was not going to drink any more.

"Nice garden," Annabelle said distractedly. "So," she said, propping one elbow up on the table and leaning forward, her face cupped by long fingernails painted a dark shade of plum that was precise in its tastefulness. "When did you move in?"

"Two, three weeks ago? No, actually, maybe it's been a month."

Annabelle nodded. "You'll have to forgive me, but I'm quite old-fashioned about this kind of thing. I don't entirely approve."

It was Marisa's turn to nod. "Living in sin, I suppose you'd call it," Marisa said.

"Well, no," Annabelle said, taken aback. "I wouldn't call it that. That wouldn't be the right phrase. It's just . . . in my day, things were done more *traditionally*." She placed great emphasis on the final word. "One always faces challenges, doesn't one?" She stared at Marisa, her blue eyes steady and shrewd. "But if it's what nature intended, then it's what nature intended. There's no point forcing it. One must go at the pace dictated to us."

Marisa's breath quickened. It was strange to feel so offended by someone whose good opinion she also craved. Annabelle lowered her head slowly. In her right earlobe was a twinkle of studded gold. It probably cost more than Marisa's entire outfit.

"It might seem like we're moving too fast to you," Marisa said, "but it feels right to us, and that's all that matters, isn't it?" There was no reply from Annabelle. Marisa coughed. "I hope you can understand." No response. "In time, of course. We don't mean to rush you."

"We?" Annabelle gave a short, sharp bark of laughter. "You're very possessive, aren't you?"

Well, why wouldn't I be? Marisa thought. He's my bloody boyfriend. Just because you're his mother and you've never thought any woman would be good enough. If you cared so much about him, perhaps you shouldn't have sent him away to school when he was seven fucking years old.

Of course, she didn't say any of this. Her fury lodged in her flesh like a piece of buckshot. Her mouth set in a mutinous line.

"Thank you for the coffee," Annabelle said, pushing the cup and saucer farther into the table with such force that the coffee spilled out onto the wood. "I was only passing by. I have a lunch to get to."

She wound the shawl back around her broad swimmer's shoulders and gathered herself up to her full height. Marisa, watching her, was reminded of a giant bird. A pelican, maybe, or an ostrich. A bird with beady eyes and an intrusive beak and an edge of malicious intent.

She followed Annabelle back up the stairs and neither of them spoke. At the front door, Annabelle turned and shook Marisa's hand again.

"Nice to meet you," she said.

In the distance, a siren sounded.

"You too," Marisa lied. "See you again soon, I hope."

Annabelle took a pair of dark glasses from her handbag and slid them onto her face. Her eyes disappeared behind shellacked black ovals.

"Oh, I shouldn't think so," she said. Her voice, as she uttered this, was as polite as if she'd been observing the weather.

Annabelle walked down the steps into the street and Marisa watched her go: a tall silhouette in white. She shivered in the doorway. Even though it was a hot day, her arms were trailed with goose bumps.

IV.

She didn't tell Jake about his mother's visit for several days. She convinced herself it was because he was busy at work and she didn't want to bother him. She claimed to be tired and went to bed before he got home. In the mornings, she waited until Jake had left for the office before going downstairs for her coffee and toast and then starting work, stretching out the paper methodically to calm her thoughts.

But it was not his preoccupation that stopped Marisa from saying anything. It was her own humiliation. She had so wanted to make a good impression on Jake's family when she met them. She had hoped an invitation would be issued at some point in the near future, perhaps to Sunday lunch in the house in the country or to some family gathering—a birthday or an anniversary—where Marisa would be able to wear a pretty dress with just the right amount of flounce and cleavage and she would insist on buying a bouquet of flowers, or perhaps a potted plant because it would last longer, and she would ask Jake what kind of wine his parents liked and he would laugh at her, kissing her forehead affectionately, and he would tell her there was no need to go to so much effort. "They'll adore you," he would say. "How could they not?"

And when they got to lunch, his mother would embrace her warmly and say they'd heard so much about her and Marisa would offer to help with the cooking, which "smells delicious, Mrs. Sturridge."

"Oh please, call me Annabelle," Jake's mother would say, patting her arm conspiratorially and telling Marisa that she was a guest and absolutely must not lift a finger but that she must sit down and look gorgeous, and "Would someone please get this darling girl a strong gin and tonic?" Annabelle would say and her voice would be serious but her eyes would twinkle and Jake's father would do the honors and pass Marisa a crystal tumbler, rattling with just the right amount of ice, and he would lower his voice and say to her, "You're already a vast improvement on all the others."

"Dad," Jake would say, catching Marisa's gaze and smiling with fondness. "Stop! You're embarrassing her."

"No, no," Marisa would laugh. "It's fine! I'm having a lovely time."

That was how it was meant to happen. That was what she had hoped for: to make herself indispensable to both Jake and his family—no faults to be picked over, no reason for anyone to leave her behind.

"I don't know what we'd do without you," his parents would say. "You're the best thing that's ever happened to this family."

Wasn't that how it was supposed to be? Wasn't that the appropriate plot climax? Wasn't that going to be Marisa's redemption, where she set to right all the wrongs that had been inflicted on her, all the bad things she might unwittingly have done to send her mother and baby sister away? Wasn't that how this was going to end?

Apparently not.

So she didn't tell Jake until the weekend, when the two of them were in the garden. Jake, stripped to the waist, was in loose-fitting gym shorts. He liked to work out on Saturday mornings, ears plugged with headphones streaming angry hip-hop as he did goblet squats and push-ups and held a plank for at least one minute, sweat dripping off his torso and leaving damp dots all over the yoga mat. Marisa was sitting on the bench, her face partially obscured by the wide brim of a straw hat. The book she was reading was facedown next to her, the spine of it flexed so that she kept her place. It was a bestseller, a book that everyone seemed to know about before they'd actually read it, but Marisa couldn't get into it. The cover was a modernist painting, depicting a woman's head with no eyes, nose, or mouth so that the only way you knew it was female was by the hair: a severe, fringed bob, sensibly cut to just below where the ears should have been. Marisa's hair was long and golden: light brown that went lighter in the sun to caramel blonde. It had been so sunny lately that her skin was tanned, a spray of freckles across her nose.

She took off the hat and lifted her face up to the warmth, closing her eyes for a moment and thinking of what she had to paint before the end of next week in order to meet the deadline for Moses's sixth birthday. After a few moments, a coolness crept over her face and she opened her eyes to see Jake standing above her. He was glinting with sweat and breathing hard. He wiped his face with the crumpled-up T-shirt in his hand.

Seeing him postworkout made her think of him just after they'd had sex: his skin shining, muscles taut, the smell of his body in its purest form.

He sat on the bench next to her but left a gap between them. She took her book and folded it shut, placing it on her lap in case he wanted to shuffle up, but he didn't.

"Mum said she came round," Jake said.

"Oh, yes," Marisa said, her heart leaping. "I was going to tell you but . . ."

"It's ok; you don't have to. Not your responsibility. Anyway," he said, rubbing the hair by his right temple in that way she loved. "I'm sorry if she was rude to you."

She wasn't sure what to say to that. She let the realization sink in, that Jake must have spoken to his mother to know that Annabelle had visited. Would his mother have called him, Marisa thought, or would it have been the other way round? Or—even more worryingly—would they have met for lunch? What would they have said about her? She couldn't imagine Annabelle would have been warm or flattering. Would Jake have changed his mind?

A small panic began to rattle around in her chest like a loose marble. She looked at the back of the house, the window frames painted white, the roof tiles ordered and straight. She could just about make out the edge of her desk in her study if she squinted. Marisa felt, with unexpected acuteness, the fragility of everything, the ease with which it could all be taken away from her. She told herself that she needed to redouble her efforts to do better. She could give Jake no reason to end their relationship. If it ended, she thought miserably, she would be undone.

"Was she rude to you?" Jake asked.

She tried to laugh. "Why do you ask?"

"I just . . . I know that she can be . . . intimidating."

She wondered if this was some sort of trap. Was she meant to say Annabelle hadn't been rude and lie in order not to criticize his mother? Some people were funny about their own families. They would carp and bitch about them to their heart's content but if anyone else did so, they would claim instant offense. Or was she meant to acknowledge what had happened and show that she was on Jake's side?

She settled for an indeterminate middle course.

"Yes. I mean, no. It was fine. She is a very impressive woman."

Jake laughed. "That she is." He put the nozzle of his water bottle between parted lips and tilted it upward to drink. "Very diplomatic, Marisa."

He looked at her tenderly.

"Listen, she's entitled to her views," Marisa said. "It's just not necessarily how I would have chosen that meeting to go."

"I know. The thing is, she's very particular about how things are done. She's traditional and—don't tell her I ever said this—a massive snob. She's never going to understand how things are with us. And I don't give a fuck whether she does or not. She—they—are irrelevant to me. To us, I should say."

He wiped his eyes with the hem of his T-shirt.

"This," he said, gesturing toward the house and Marisa, "is the family I've chosen."

"Thank you," she said quietly. "That means a lot."

She felt so lucky then, so blissfully content to be with a man who understood the safety she wanted before she understood it herself. If Marisa could have stopped time right there, she would have. They were perfectly happy on that bench, in the sunshine, sitting next to each other with an unread book on her lap and the faint smell of jasmine in the air.

But nothing stayed perfect forever, did it? It was a lesson she had been taught as a child and she had promised herself never to forget it, until Jake came along, and then, stupidly, she had let herself be carried along by unfounded faith that everything was going to keep on getting better. She had allowed herself to fall in love.

Looking back, Marisa would see this interaction on the garden bench as the last moment of bliss before everything changed. Before their little, protected world slid on its axis and sent them spinning into blackness. She was foolish to have believed in their future. Because happiness was transient. She would find this out when the lodger came.

V.

It turns out Jake's work has been going less well than he'd let on. The deal that had threatened to fall through eventually did collapse, he explains. It's as if the exchange of vast sums of money has acquired a physical dimension.

She can't remember when the idea of a lodger was first raised, but soon, it shifts from a discussion of ifs to a confirmation of whens. Marisa was opposed to it at first. She hates the thought of a stranger in their home, filling up the fridge with food she doesn't recognize and watching television in the evenings when they would want their own space. But she doesn't feel she can say this to Jake, who had put down the deposit for the house with money she didn't have and who continues to pay the lion's share of the monthly rent. She knows he wants her to feel like an equal partner, but she doesn't. She is always aware of the precariousness of her situation, as if she were a Victorian governess forced to live off her wits, surviving on the charity of richer people. The study in which Marisa paints becomes, in these fevered imaginings, a sort of storage cupboard that she has to fold herself into, taking up the least amount of space and creating the smallest amount of bother so that Jake will never have a reason to break up with her.

Jas always told Marisa that she went to one of two extremes with men she liked.

"Either you're the baddest bitch, who doesn't give a single fuck," Jas said, "or you lose yourself completely in the idea of them."

"I don't think that's true," Marisa had protested. They'd been getting their nails done in her local salon at the time. Marisa was having a pedicure. Jas was getting sparkly purple gel on her fingernails, having each one filed to a clawlike point.

"What about Matt?" Jas said, recalling Marisa's most recent fling with a singer-songwriter who never seemed either to sing or to write. "You lost your shit over him."

Matt had been extremely, unavoidably handsome. He was prone to sending Marisa lyrically composed texts and links to songs he had heard that reminded him of her. She had been smitten and only later had she thought to question the fact that "smitten" came from the verb "to smite," something more often associated with angry deities meting out dramatic lightning bolts of punishment and that, when she Googled the original etymology, actually meant "to smear or blemish" and wasn't romantic at all.

For the first couple of weeks, this devotion had been ardently reciprocated, and then Matt had disappeared for several days, causing her spirals of anxiety. She kept calling him and WhatsApping and there would be no reply and the messages would be left unread until, finally, after a whole week of silence, he had texted her with "Whatcha doin'?" She had been so happy to hear from him that the previous torturous bout of sadness and self-doubt was entirely forgotten, and they began the whole cycle over again. This lasted for five months, until Matt fell out of her life without a single word of goodbye and promptly blocked her from his phone. She knew this because her messages turned green when she sent them. They also turned green when someone owned a mobile that wasn't an iPhone, but she also knew he was so pretentious about technology that he would only ever have the latest Apple gadget.

"What *about* Matt?" she had said as the nail technician rubbed her feet with a rectangular file.

"You were never yourself around him. You let him walk all over you."

"No I didn't."

But when she thinks back, Marisa realizes Jas was right. She had misinterpreted his unpredictability for passion, mistaking her anxiety for the butterflies you were meant to get at the beginning of love. And so she kept trying different tactics to keep his interest. If she could just need him a little bit less, Marisa would think, if she could stop issuing demands or ultimatums when he wouldn't listen to all the other ways she had attempted to express her desires, if she could just cut off this part of herself and then this one and then that one, occupying an ever more limited space so that she would barely be any trouble at all, *then* she would be rewarded. Then she would be worthy of his undivided attention.

So she says yes to taking in a lodger and she tells herself it will alleviate pressure on Jake and that, as a result, he will be more present for her. The lodger, he tells her, will stay in the spare room in the attic extension, which has its own en suite bathroom. The Wi-Fi works up there, so there is no need for a TV because most people tend to watch on their laptops, don't they? He suggests getting a microwave and a kettle and a minifridge so that the lodger can be relatively self-sufficient. Marisa goes along with all of it.

And then Kate is there. Kate who, at thirty-six, is older than Marisa. She has a job in the publicity department of a film company. She is soft-spoken with a lively, sharp face and brown hair with an unruly fringe falling to just below her eyebrows so that the first time they meet to assess her suitability, Marisa notices that Kate keeps blowing it out of her eyes. She is petite and bony, with flat breasts, and wears denim dungarees and T-shirts that Marisa can't help but feel are inappropriate for a woman of her age. Still, she is relieved that Kate wouldn't physically appeal to Jake, who has always made it clear his type is blonde with curved and dimpled flesh and light eyes and honeyed skin that went freckled in sunlight. Marisa, in fact.

Plus, Kate has an office to go to, which means that she will be out of the house during the day and Marisa can work in peace.

"I appreciate you doing this for us," Jake says to Marisa that evening. "Truly."

"Don't mention it," she says. He has decided to do the cooking for once and has made an elaborate dish involving duck and cherries. It is too rich for her, the sauce too sticky, but she *mmm*s and *aah*s and tells him it's amazing, and later, when they go to bed, she is confident they have made the right decision.

Time passes and Marisa gets the fanciful notion that Kate has visited the house before, in a past life. She makes herself at home without any self-consciousness. She puts her toothbrush right there in the master bathroom, on the shelf next to theirs, ignoring the perfectly good sink upstairs. She places a mug in the kitchen cupboard, its insides stained mushroom brown and with a stenciled picture of a black horse on the front, accompanied by the phrase DARK HORSE in block sans serif capitals. She leaves her running trainers by the front door—"Mind you don't trip over them," she says to Marisa, sliding them against the skirting board every morning and trailing clods of dried earth across the doormat.

She possesses an assurance Marisa has always yearned for. She tells herself this is a good thing. It means they can coexist efficiently without having to become friends. They can keep their relationship distant and practical and then they will have saved up enough money not to have to house a lodger anymore, and Marisa and Jake can get on with their life. It is temporary, she keeps reminding herself. It will be over soon.

The weeks pass. Marisa makes good progress on her commissions. Prince Moses has been dispatched. She's immersed in a new project for a set of twin girls called Petra and Serena. The parents have asked her to paint a fairy tale with a feminist moral, so she has decided to make the twins into feisty princesses who dress up as boys to prove that girls can rule the kingdom just as well as their male counterparts. She is calling it *The Girls Who Run the World*, with a nod to Beyoncé, and she is enjoying storyboarding the adventure. Her favorite panel depicts the twins wearing plaid shirts and straw hats, chewing on matchsticks as they pretend to be a couple of farm boys. Their curly blonde hair is tied up tightly at the napes of their necks.

As she sketches out the panels, Marisa thinks briefly of her own sister, of all the companionship Marisa missed out on growing up. She comforts herself thinking about how, once she has a baby with Jake, she'll never feel that way again. After all, when you are a mother, you are never truly alone.

She works steadily until lunchtime, and then the stiffness in her back forces her to stand up and crick her neck, twisting it this way and that. Yesterday, she had seen a sign advertising a 1 p.m. prenatal yoga class in the window of the local newsagent and she decides, spontaneously, to go along.

Marisa had read somewhere that it was good for women trying to conceive to be around expectant mothers. Apparently the hormones rub off on you, or your body responds to the pregnancy pheromones or something like that—she isn't sure of the science.

She changes into tracksuit bottoms and an old T-shirt, slipping her feet into flip-flops and tying back her hair. She slings her yoga mat over her shoulder and leaves the house, locking the door behind her.

The studio is high ceilinged with a parquet floor, recently converted from an old chapel. Some of the windows are still patterned with stained-glass diamonds and there seems to be a faint smell of incense in the air. Her mother had always taken her to church for midnight mass on Christmas Eve. It was the one time of year they went, and Marisa loved it because she was allowed to stay up so much later than usual. She had liked the singing and the feeling of togetherness, and afterward, the vicar would offer her a tin of

Quality Street and invite her to pick a chocolate and she would always winkle out the silvery-green triangle that tasted of hazelnut and something her mother called "praline."

"Is it your first time here?" the instructor asks Marisa as she unrolls her mat in the front row.

"Yes."

"Lovely." The instructor is a tall woman with a deep tan and a tattoo of roman numerals all the way up her left forearm. She wears star-printed leggings and a tank top with INHALE. EXHALE. REPEAT. written on the front. "And how far along are you? Just so I know for the modifications."

"Oh," Marisa stumbles. She hasn't thought this bit through. "It's very early days. Six weeks," she blurts out.

"Congratulations," the instructor says with a beaming smile. "I'm Carys."

"Marisa."

"Beautiful name," Carys says. "Welcome, goddess."

Marisa scans the instructor's face for signs that this is a joke but finds none. Goddess it is, then. Carys tells everyone to sit cross-legged at the front of their mats and to use any props they need to make themselves comfortable. The other women are all in varying stages of pregnancy. Some of them have neatly packaged bumps underneath the expanding waistbands of their leggings. Others, in the later stages, move their limbs around with graceful heaviness, as if swimming through swamp water.

"Breathe in," Carys says, and her voice acquires a performative edge. "Breathe out. And again."

The instructor plugs her phone into a cable by the windowsill and the room is filled with the plinkety-plunk of strings, offset by the rhythmic beat of a tribal drum. The music is too loud for Marisa to hear what Carys is saying, but everyone else seems to know what to do through an unspoken herd instinct, so she follows as best she can and crouches back into a wide-kneed child's pose.

She has always struggled with yoga, with the idea that you have to be in the present moment and concentrate on what you're doing rather than on anyone else. Marisa can't help but compare herself to the other women here. The one next to her, whose mat has been positioned slightly too close to Marisa's, is one of those skinny, glowy women whose body hasn't much changed since adolescence. She has elegant shoulders and slim hips and her baby bump is as discreetly scaled as the rest of her, in a way that accentuates her thinness rather than masking it. That is how I want to look when I'm pregnant, Marisa thinks.

"Today, I slept through my alarm," Carys is saying. "And it meant I was a bit late for everything. I left my flat without eating breakfast. I forgot my umbrella. The first tube was too busy to get on. We've all been there." Carys laughs gently. "And I just felt so . . . *disconnected*, you know? Unrooted from Mother Earth and, like, not in my own skin. I was getting frustrated and anxious. And then, yogis, I remembered what I say to you every single week. I did what I tell *you* to do. I closed my eyes. I looked inward. And I found my breath. Because breath is life. And as you are in charge of bringing beautiful new life onto this earth, we need to free our breathing now more than ever. Let it float! Liberate it!" On the mat, Marisa is trying to liberate her breathing. The skinny blonde next to her is making a noisy, rasping sound. Marisa tries to emit a slightly louder rasping sound just to prove that she can but then her throat constricts and she realizes her competitiveness is distinctly un-zen.

At the front of the room, Carys is still proclaiming. "As the teachers tell us," she says, and then she launches into something that sounds like Sanskrit, by way of Chelmsford: "Sarva karyeshu sarvada. Please make my understandings free of obstacles."

Please make my yoga class free of Carys, Marisa thinks. She is already sweating and they haven't even started properly yet.

There follows an hour of side bends and gentle pigeon poses. The music rises and swells and then drops off again for the final resting pose, when Carys shares a meandering disquisition on the nature of creation ("What does it *mean* to create, to be fertile, to open your heart up to the wonder of the universe?"). After it is over, Marisa rolls up her mat. The blonde woman next to her catches her eye and smiles.

"You new?"

"Yeah," Marisa says, loosening her ponytail so her hair falls around her shoulders.

"Thought I hadn't seen you before. She's great, isn't she? So in tune."

Marisa looks over at Carys, who is midconversation with a heavily pregnant mother-to-be, nodding intently while keeping her hands clasped in prayer at her chest.

"Mmm," Marisa says, knowing that she will never come back to this class. There have to be easier ways to trigger pregnancy hormones, she thinks.

"I always feel so much better after coming here. How far along are you?"

Marisa can't remember what she told Carys, so she fudges it.

"Oh, it's still early days for me," she says and doesn't elaborate.

The woman raises her eyebrows but, when the silence draws out, says, "Well, good luck. See you next week."

"You won't," Marisa utters under her breath and then she turns to walk out of the studio as quickly as she can without making eye contact with Carys. It's only when she is right at the back of the hall, about to push the door open into the street, that she catches a familiar shape out of the corner of her right eye.

It takes her a minute to focus. Dark hair. Fringe. Gray harem pants and—of all things—a crop top sporting the logo of an expensive athleisure brand. And when it all slots together into one human form, even then Marisa has to blink to ensure it is actually her. The lodger.

"Kate," Marisa says. She is astonished to find her here. She has the uncomfortable realization that if Kate took the class, she would have been able to watch her throughout the class from her vantage point at the back of the room. Surely she can't be pregnant . . . can she? And then, quickly, Marisa remembers that she isn't pregnant either, and that she can't ask the question without facing uncomfortable questions of her own.

"I didn't see you here."

Kate grins, revealing slightly crooked front teeth. "I was at the back!" she says. Her yoga mat is one of those expensive padded ones. It is mottled gray with a swirling pattern of palm leaves, and Kate has it neatly rolled up and slung over her shoulder with a purple strap.

"Did you enjoy the class?" Marisa asks, placing a certain emphasis on the final word.

"I did! I saw you coming and thought I'd join in at the back. Thought it would be nice to do it together, you know?"

Kate's manner is relaxed and comfortable, as if it were totally normal to follow one's landlady out of her house to a pregnancy yoga class without explanation. Kate is looking at her frankly, as if expecting Marisa to be appreciative. Marisa is stunned by the sheer entitlement of this.

"Except we didn't."

"Didn't what?" Kate says, holding the door open for her.

"Do it together. You skulked at the back."

Kate laughs. "I wasn't skulking. I just wanted to give you your own space."

Funny way of showing it, Marisa thinks. They walk out into the street.

"Do you fancy a coffee?" Kate asks. "It would be great to chat."

"No, I'm sorry," Marisa says, flustered and then annoyed with herself for being flustered. "I mean, I've got a deadline. Work stuff."

"Ah yes. The painting! How's it going?"

How can I get rid of her? Marisa wonders. Why all these questions? They are standing on the pavement now, facing each other,

Marisa with her arms crossed in an attempt to create some physical boundary between them.

"It's going well, thanks."

"That's great. Do you like working from that room?"

She's just trying to be friendly. It is not how Marisa would have gone about it, but she must try not to judge. She calms her breathing as Carys would have advised. Inhale. Exhale. Empty your mind of anxious thoughts.

"Yeah. The light's amazing."

"I'm so glad."

Why are you glad? Marisa thinks. It's my fucking house.

"Ok, well, that's a shame about the coffee but let's do it another time." Kate reaches out to squeeze her arm. "I'm so happy we're living together."

She looks at Marisa with such intensity, and although Kate is smiling, the smile doesn't quite reach her eyes, which remain dark and narrow and slanted. Marisa pulls the sleeves of her sweatshirt over her hands.

"I'd better go."

"Sure thing," Kate says.

As Marisa walks away, she knows without looking that Kate hasn't moved. She crosses the road at the lights and turns left by the cafe that has faded gilt lettering in the window, and when she turns back, Kate is still there.

Kate lifts one arm and waves.

"See you back at home!" she shouts across the street.

Automatically, Marisa raises one hand in response. Then she quickens her pace until she gets back to the house and when the door shuts behind her, she realizes she has been holding her breath.

VI.

Back in her study the next day, Marisa can't concentrate. She stares at the photo of Petra, one of the nine-year-old twins she's painting. It has been taken at the beach and Petra is wearing a blue swimsuit, imprinted with orange pirouetting dancers. She is standing there, unsmiling, in the middle of wind, sand, and sea, staring straight at the camera, calmly waiting for the photograph to be taken.

When the twins' parents had emailed Marisa the photos, she had printed them all out as she normally did. But this particular image, she had blown up to double its original size and pinned to the corkboard. She was drawn to it—to the child, rather. What must it feel like to be so calmly confident about one's place in the world? To not have to try to make people love you?

It is difficult to translate all of this into a series of brushstrokes. Marisa can get the physical attributes down—she finds the other twin, Serena, much easier—but she knows there is something missing, some vital intimation of Petra's character that remains lacking so that the paintings remain flat and lifeless.

She tries with a different flesh color, mixing in a dab of orange with the pink, and then she tries putting her in skirts rather than dresses, and then shorts rather than skirts, and nothing works. She has been in here since six this morning, sneaking out of bed before Jake was awake and before Kate left for the office. She had barely slept and her dreams had been scattered and fragmentary. At one point, she had sat bolt upright in the bed, convinced that Kate was bending over her, closely examining her face.

She didn't want to see her this morning, not after the awkwardness at the yoga class. She will tell Jake about it later. But for now, she needs to concentrate on getting this commission done. Telling Tales has no orders lined up for the next few months. She knows from last year that summer tends to be quiet before the Christmas rush, and although Marisa should have put money aside to see her through, she has had to use her savings for moving costs. When they moved in together, Jake's salary had been more than enough for both of them to live on, but now finances are more precarious and every outgoing expense has to be carefully monitored. Lately, he has been stressed and distracted, even less affectionate than normal. It worries Marisa, but she tells herself not to be stupid. She reminds herself that he loves her, that their love is strong enough that it does not need daily reassurance to bolster it.

Whenever she recognizes the gradual slow-motion descent into her usual panic, she reminds herself to focus on things as they actually are. She counts off the points on her fingers. He wants to have a baby with her. He has encouraged her to download an app on her phone to keep track of her cycle. He is so happy he met her. They are living together. These are the facts. And beneath all of it is another, unassailable truth that Marisa keeps buried deep within her, plucking it out from the earth only when she needs to hold it and feel the certain weight of it in her hands: Jake is not her mother. Jake will not abandon her.

When she was seventeen, Marisa had run away from her boarding school for the weekend. She had typed a letter, forged her father's signature, and informed her housemistress that he had been diagnosed with prostate cancer and that he wanted her to come home for the weekend.

“We’re trying to stay positive,” she said to Mrs. Carnegie when she was called into her office. “I’ve looked into it and I think it’s quite normal for men his age. There are good recovery rates.”

Marisa was pleased with herself for the flourish of this detail. She had decided that the most convincing attitude would be one of hard-won courage. Tears would be too much, although she knew how to cry on demand. But with Mrs. Carnegie, she wanted to imply that she was shocked by the news yet coping with it in a practical way and not allowing herself to imagine the worst. Mrs. Carnegie, a jolly-hockey-sticks type, would appreciate that.

“Quite right, Marisa,” her housemistress said, right on cue. “It’s good to keep positive.”

She took off her glasses and let them hang across her generous chest on a colorful plastic chain.

“Will someone be picking you up?” Mrs. Carnegie asked.

“Well, it would normally be my dad,” Marisa said. “There’s just the two of us, as you know, but . . .” And here, Marisa allowed her voice to falter slightly. “He’s not really in a fit state so I’m going to get the train.”

Mrs. Carnegie nodded and said, “Very good, very good,” and signed the permission slip.

Her father had been fine, of course. He never knew that Marisa had claimed a terminal illness on his behalf and when he appeared at the end of term, seemingly healthy, if a touch absentminded, Marisa had told her housemistress that their prayers had been answered and her father had made a full recovery.

“He doesn’t like to talk about it, though,” she had said. Mrs. Carnegie had smiled and placed a supportive hand on Marisa’s shoulder.

“Of course not, dear. I won’t breathe a word.”

With Mrs. Carnegie’s permission slip in her blazer pocket, Marisa was granted magical access to the outside world. Her school had been built right next to the town’s railway station, so it was a short walk to catch the train to London, and once she had found a seat, she took off her blazer and replaced it with a denim jacket from her bag. She rolled up the waistband of her navy school skirt four times until the hem lay a couple of inches above her knees. She untucked her white blouse and tied it in a knot by her belly button and then she unclipped her hair, shaking it out over her shoulders. She did her makeup in the train lavatory and had to reapply her eyeliner when the carriage juddered and her hand slid across her face, leaving a smudged kohl mark across the top of one cheek.

Marisa had learned how to do makeup by reading girls' magazines. There had been a cut-out-and-keep guide called "Makeup for Your School Prom" in one of them, and she had bought or shoplifted all of the products suggested. Now, in the blurry mirror, she brushed her lashes with two coats of Maybelline mascara: "Heavy lashes are totally having a moment!" the magazine had informed her. She dabbed cream blush on her cheeks at an angle, underlining them with sweeps of bronzer. She slicked her lips with pearlescent gloss and then stood back, assessing her reflection. She looked older than she had thought she would and her face seemed detached from the rest of her, briefly unrecognizable as her own. But then she got used to it and she began to smile. She looked sexy, she thought, and mussed up. A bit like Britney Spears in that video or an old photo of Brigitte Bardot her dad had once shown her.

When the train drew into Paddington station three hours later, it was already midafternoon. She had a carefully mapped-out plan and she knew she needed to get the Circle Line tube from Paddington to King's Cross, and then to change and board the Northern Line branch to High Barnet. There were two branches to the Northern Line, she knew, so she would have to be careful to get the right one. Although apparently you could always change at Camden Town if you made a mistake. Her destination was Kentish Town.

A few months after her mother had left, Marisa overheard her father on the phone, talking to an unknown person. It had been late at night and she was meant to be asleep, but Marisa could tell from the lowered, urgent sound of her father's voice that the matter being discussed was important. As a child, she had been finely attuned to the gradations of every conversation.

"No idea," her father was saying as Marisa crept out of bed and crouched by the upstairs banisters in her nightdress, kneeling quietly so as not to creak any of the floorboards and pressing one ear between the varnished wood roundels.

"As I say, she never left an address."

There was a long gap as the person on the other end of the line spoke. Marisa knew, without any prompting, that he was discussing her mother.

"It's so fucking irresponsible—you're right. But what did I expect, really?"

Marisa had never heard her father swear before. His words were slurring. He sounded angry.

"Oh, I don't know. Last I heard it was Kentish Town."

The name slotted into a gap in her mind and locked itself away for Marisa to take out later and examine more closely.

"Ha! Quite. Yes. Well, quite."

Another long silence.

"All right, then. Yes. You are kind to call; I do appreciate it. Sorry if I've been maudlin. It's just—"

Marisa started tiptoeing back to her bed, aware that the call was about to end and that her father would probably come up and check on her.

"Marisa?" He sounded surprised to be asked. "Oh, she's fine, fine. Taken it like a trooper. No trouble at all."

She felt proud, then, that she had been no trouble. It was only years later that she came to realize she should have caused a lot more of it.

She arrived at the Kentish Town tube shortly after 4 p.m. It was autumn, and dusk was already edging into the sky. It was only as Marisa got to the top of the escalator and tapped her Oyster card at the turnstile to exit that she realized this was as far as her plan went. Kentish Town was the sum total of her knowledge. There had been no other clues as to her mother's whereabouts over the intervening years, no matter how many phone conversations she had strained to overhear or how many drawers she had rifled through at home, hoping to find meaningful scraps of paper and only ever coming across old shopping lists or stray paper clips.

She had imagined Kentish Town as a small country village. But there was no village green or pub and not a single pretty cottage. When she emerged from the tube, she found herself standing on grimy pavement, next to a rush of traffic separated from her by only a thin gray railing.

A bus screeched past, burping exhaust fumes into the air. She felt acutely aware of her not belonging, of the purposeful rudeness of everyone who strode past her knowing where they were going while she did not. A woman in a red trouser suit. A man with a small dog on a leash. A teenage boy on his mobile phone—a Nokia, the same one she had—shouting at someone that he didn't want to do the fucking interview and could she stop going on about it, please. They were all half walking, half running, these people, and she noticed them looking at her with impatience for standing there without understanding what she had to do next.

And still, she had faith. A peculiar, illogical sense that if she only walked around a bit, she would eventually see her mother. It had been ten years, but she knew she would recognize her immediately, that she would turn a corner and see a familiar silhouette, shoulders pressed back, raggedy hair, a slight heaviness around the hips, and it would be her. She would be able to smell her, the trail of vanilla and the undertone of the single Silk Cut cigarette her mother allowed herself every day. The soap she used, which came in patterned packets, the paper stuck together by a gold circular disc that looked like a medal. Yes, Marisa thought, she would know her mother anywhere.

Anna she was less sure about. It would be harder to imagine what kind of ten-year-old her baby sister would have grown into, but she would probably look like Marisa did at that age. It stood to reason, she told herself. They were siblings, even if they had been apart for so long.

She walked up the pavement from the tube station, the street turning into a gentle hill. There was a pub on the corner and when she glanced in through the windows, it looked warm and inviting, the beer taps shiny in the buttery light. Although she was still only seventeen, Marisa had been to pubs plenty of times before. Being at boarding school gave you a remarkable amount of freedom. They were allowed to frequent one bar in town, as long as they only drank nonalcoholic drinks, which was a rule they ignored. At weekends, Marisa and a group of her friends would sign out and tell Mrs. Carnegie they were going to the sanctioned bar, and instead they would catch the train to Worcester and present their fake IDs to the bouncers at Cargo's, which was a trashy nightclub that played something the DJ called "club classics" every Saturday night. They would drink rum and Cokes and dance and Marisa would throw her head back and forward in time with the beat and dance a little bit closer to the boy she fancied at any given moment. She was a good dancer and picked up moves quickly from studying music videos. She knew that, while she might not have been the prettiest girl in her year, the dance floor was her element. In the prismatic glare of a strobe light, with a shuddering bass line reverberating against her rib cage, she knew she could have anyone she wanted.

There were only four other customers in the pub in Kentish Town: two men sitting at the bar and an older couple holding hands at a table, nudging the salt and pepper shakers to the edge with their arms. She was reassured by the couple and held her head high, pushing her shoulders back the way she had been taught in a one-off deportment class the school had arranged to help graduates with job interviews.

"What'll you be having?" The barman looked at her with a smile.

"Rum and Coke, please."

She watched the barman's back as he prepared her drink. He was younger than she had imagined looking in from the outside, and she could see the ripple of his shoulder blades underneath his checked shirt. The sleeves were rolled up, and he had a strip of muscle running down each forearm, the indent of it catching the overhead lights.

"There you go," he said, presenting her with a glass that looked fuller than it should.

"Thanks." She detected an Australian twang to his voice. "How much is it?"

He flipped a towel he had been using to wipe down the bar over his right shoulder. "On the house."

"What? But . . ."

"It's a midweek offer. First drink free." He winked at her. She reddened.

"Ok," she mumbled. "Thanks."

She sat at a table by the loos because she knew no one else would bother her here, in the least desirable part of the pub, and she wanted to be alone. She took a sip of her drink, feeling the bite of the alcohol and the sweetness of the Coca-Cola jostle for space on the back of her tongue until finally the Coke won out and it stopped tasting like rum at all. She took a gulp. Then another. Soon, half of it was gone and she could feel the incipient haze of light-headedness that she craved. She took out her phone and began, halfheartedly, to play a game of *Snake*. She just needed to sit here for a few more minutes, finish her drink, and then she'd go and find her mother. She knocked back the rest of the rum and Coke.

"Another?"

The barman was beside her. She jumped at the sound of his voice.

"Oh. I thought I had to order at the bar," she said, immediately hating how pathetic it sounded. If she were truly a grown-up, she would know exactly how to behave, Marisa thought. Play it cool, for fuck's sake.

The barman winked again. Marisa had never thought anyone actually winked unless they were actors in soap operas or characters in bad spy novels.

"For special customers, I come out from my cage."

The way he said "cage" made her shiver.

He patted her back. "Only kidding. What'll it be? Another rum 'n' Coke, yeah?"

She nodded. One more couldn't hurt. She would just have one more, she told herself, just to take the edge off her nerves, and then she would stand up and leave and it would all be fine.

But the barman, who she soon learned was called Kevin, kept bringing her drinks and Marisa worried it would be rude to say no. Her anxiety was mounting that she wouldn't be able to pay the bill but then she remembered her dad's credit card, which he had given her for emergencies and to pay for her driving lessons, and she relaxed. After the fourth rum and Coke, she began to feel very relaxed indeed. She started laughing at something Kevin had said, something involving a horse with a long face who'd ordered a drink and there was an ostrich in the joke because he started talking about a bird with legs all the way up to her arse, and Marisa found it so funny that she couldn't stop laughing for a full minute.

At some point, the older couple and the two men left the bar—she couldn't remember seeing them go—and then it was just her and Kevin, who had now drawn up a seat to sit next to her, and when she asked him whether he should be working, he shrugged and said, "Shift's almost over anyway," and she saw that he had brought the bottle of rum with him, or maybe it had been there all along, she couldn't recall, but he kept filling up her glass so that it was all rum and no Coke and she kept drinking it, not because she was anxious now, but because she wasn't and wanted to preserve the precious sensation of having nothing to worry about. She would have one more drink and then she would leave. One more, and then pay the bill and then walk out and go and do what she came here to do, which was . . . What was it, exactly? There was something important . . . and yet . . . why couldn't she remember? It eluded her, slipping out of her grasp like a heavy necklace spiraling to the bottom of the sea as her fingers unfurled. Oh yes—that was it. She was here to find her mother.

"I'm here to find my mother," she said to Kevin, and when the words came out, they were oddly cheerful.

"What's that, babe?"

When had he started calling her "babe"? She wasn't sure, but as she made her way to the loo, she saw that the pub wasn't welcoming and safe like she'd thought but was dingy and grubby and the toilets stank of stale urine and Red Bull, but she didn't care. It was fun. She was having fun. Wasn't she?

Out of habit, she checked her reflection in the mirror. She looked bleary but fine. She applied some more lip gloss because you could never go wrong with more lip gloss, and when she came back out, she saw that Kevin was holding out her denim jacket, waiting for her to slide her arms into the sleeves, which she did without asking why, and then he led her out onto the street, which seemed to wobble beneath her feet so that, all of a sudden, she had trouble finding her balance and this was even funnier than Kevin's joke, which, now that she thought about it, wasn't that funny at all but more creepy than funny but that didn't matter because he had been so nice to her, bringing her all those drinks.

"I haven't paid," she said, the words bouncing off each other like bumper cars.

"Told you, babe. On the house. Now let's get you home."

"Have to find my mother."

Kevin laughed. "Ok, babe. This won't take long. Then you can go and find whoever you want. Deal?"

She nodded. "Deal," she said, because she trusted Kevin. He was Australian, wasn't he? Like the boys on *Home and Away*. And he was wearing a collared shirt and he was kind of handsome when he turned his head into profile. She felt his arm tightening itself around her and was reminded of a boa constrictor she had been taught about in biology, its cold flesh contracting and flexing until it squeezed hard enough to stop a rat's blood pressure and heart function.

"Are you a snake?" Marisa asked, raising her head to his. She noticed that he was carrying her backpack where she had placed her phone after the second or maybe the third drink and she realized then that she had no way of telling anyone where she was. In fact, she did not know where she was because Kevin was guiding her through dark, unfamiliar streets and it was a ten-minute walk or maybe fifteen or maybe a couple of hours, she couldn't be sure, and then he was in front of a door and he took out a bunch of keys and she saw a tattoo of an anchor on the inside of his wrist as he pushed the door open and then she was in a hallway and he was turning on the lights, guiding her up a flight of stairs to another door, which he also pushed open, and then he started taking her clothes off and nudging her to the carpet and her knees buckled with the pressure and then he was spreading her legs with his hands—physically placing them wide apart as if she were a doll—and at that point, she tried to struggle and say no but it was too late and she was too drunk and too weak and too young and, suddenly, too scared. He loomed over her, so close that she could read the label on the inside of his shirt collar and this is what she chose to focus on, the two words spelling out RIVER ISLAND stitched white on black, while he pinned back her right arm and loosened his jeans with his free hand. She went quiet. Her muscles, betraying her, slid into compliance. There was a second of absolute silence and absolute stillness.

Then he raped her.

After it was over, after she had left Kevin's flat the next morning, she couldn't tell anyone. She had lied to her school to get the time off. Her father didn't know what she'd been planning, and they weren't close enough for her to confide in him anyway. She hated herself for having stayed the night, but there had been nowhere else to go. She had positioned herself at the very edge of Kevin's double mattress so that he wouldn't touch her again, but she needn't have worried. He had lost interest as soon as he had withdrawn. He had seen the spots of blood on the carpet and said, "Fuck. You could have told me," and Marisa had never worked out whether he meant that she should have told him she was a virgin or whether he had assumed it was her period.

She had stood up, feeling the trickle of him down her inner thigh, and she had gone to the bathroom, where she sat on the toilet, hunched over in an attempt to halt the brutal, slicing pain in her lower abdomen. She knew that tomorrow there would be bruises. She bruised easily, she reminded herself, still trying to make light of it, still trying to convince herself that she had wanted it to happen.

Later, much later, she learned that survivors of sexual assault talk of things being "snatched away" from them—their dignity, their identity, or even, as in her case, their virginity—but Marisa always felt the opposite, as if something unwanted had forced itself into her, like shrapnel, and her entire self had to grow around it over the years that followed, warping the muscle and the skin out of shape until the scar became a misshapen part of her, something she simply had to live around.

She has never told anyone, not even Jake. Although she thinks about it every day, she only ever lets the memory skim the surface of her mind. Everything changed after her rape, and there was no option but to accept the new reality wholesale. This she did. And when she started dating men in her twenties, she did so with a ferocity of intent. She was determined to plaster over the cracks Kevin had left in her with new experiences of intimacy.

She has never found her mother. But with Jake, she has found someone who accepts her as she is without too many questions, and when she fell in love with him, it was not accompanied by fireworks and a surging feeling of roller-coaster stomach leaping. It didn't feel like a thunderbolt. It felt like something more beautiful than that. It felt like relief.

VII.

Kate is cooking dinner. She "insists" and says it is "the least I can do" and "you've been so generous" and would Marisa please just let Kate show her appreciation? This last line is delivered with a laugh that requires a lot of comic pouting and a playful, semisarcastic tone that grates. She barely knows me, Marisa fumes. Jake is delighted, especially when Kate says she's cooking "his favorite" macaroni and cheese.

How would she know? Marisa thinks, but she doesn't say anything and then has to endure the spectacle of Kate in the kitchen—*her* kitchen—moving around as if she owns it.

"Now, where has Jake put the paprika?" Kate says, as Marisa observes her from the sofa.

"Cupboard to the right of the sink," Marisa says, just to prove the point that she knows the location of condiments just as well as Jake does.

"Oh yes! Sorry." Kate looks at her oddly. "Didn't know I was speaking out loud."

Marisa is pretending to watch the television evening news. Onscreen, a politician with a florid face and narrow eyes is being interviewed about his plans for international development spending while the newscaster, sporting a blue-and-green tie, is interjecting with mounting incredulity.

Normally she'd switch it off, but she wants to be able to see what Kate's doing without making it obvious. So she stares at the screen, trying to zone out of the argumentative pitter-patter and slide her gaze discreetly toward Kate, bustling around the stove and taking out an unnecessary array of pots and pans. Kate is humming a tune under her breath, and it is this—the humming—that Marisa finds most objectionable for reasons she cannot fully express, even to herself.

Kate empties a kettle of boiling water into a pot and mixes together paprika and something that looks like egg yolk into a bowl. What on earth is she doing with paprika and egg yolk? Marisa wonders. Well, at least her macaroni and cheese won't be as good as mine if she's putting all that gunk in it, she thinks with satisfaction.

Since the yoga class, this antipathy toward Kate has crept up on her, like a fog over an incoming tide, and now there is no escaping it. Also, she's about to get her period, so her hormones are making her spiky and intolerant. In the kitchen, Kate fishes around in her pocket, removing a hair clip. Marisa watches as she scoops up her short dark hair into a tiny twisted coil, placing the clip at the highest point so that strands fall from its grip around her flushed cheeks. She is wearing a striped Breton top and flared jeans, which Marisa could never wear without looking absurd and out of proportion. But Kate's narrow hips and boyish figure lend themselves to fashionable clothes. Marisa assesses her own clothes: a faded ocher sundress brought back from a Greek island holiday that is baggy and comfortable and paint-spattered from an afternoon's work. She is wearing no makeup and her hair is held up with a paintbrush and needs a wash. On one wrist, she wears a silver charm bracelet she never takes off, the loops hanging with lucky horseshoes and miniature compasses. It had been a twenty-first-birthday gift from her father, and although she had moved out by then and barely made the effort to keep in touch, he had sent it to her in a padded envelope, inexpertly wrapped in tissue paper, with a card written in his familiar copperplate saying that the bracelet had once been her mother's and she would want Marisa to have it.

In each of Kate's ears, she has several piercings, but the earrings she wears are delicate golden hoops, occasionally lined with tiny sparkly diamonds so that the overall effect is muted and elegant. Around her neck, she wears three thin chains in the same burnished gold and on the third chain—the longest—is a bulbous locket engraved with a single K. Marisa wonders what she keeps inside it. Paprika, probably.

"Sorry, what was that?" Kate looks over at her and Marisa realizes that she had accidentally snorted out loud at the thought.

"Nothing. Just something this guy said," and she waves at the TV screen.

"Oh God, he's such a fuckwit," Kate says, nonchalantly lobbing the swear word into the room, which is gradually filling with steam and the smell of melted cheese.

Again, it's not that Marisa is particularly prudish and it's not that she doesn't swear herself, but still—if she were a new lodger in someone else's house, she is not sure that she would do so with quite such a lack of self-consciousness. Maybe she's being unfair. Maybe.

"Jake should be back at about seven thirty p.m.," Marisa calls over from the sofa.

"Yeah, I know," Kate says, not raising her head from the stove.

In the end, they hear the key rattling in the front door lock at twenty to eight, by which time Kate has put the macaroni and cheese in the oven, laid the table with napkins and wineglasses, and filled a jug with water and sprigs of mint from the herb pots in the garden. "I just find it tastes fresher," she explained, "don't you think?"

Marisa, who has no strong opinions about mint in water, had murmured a noncommittal assent.

"I'm back!" Jake calls from the hallway.

He walks downstairs into the kitchen and goes straight to Kate, seeming not to see Marisa as he strides past.

"Oh my God, Kate, that smells fantastic." He peers into the oven.

"No opening the oven door until it's done, please," Kate says, playfully smacking his hand away.

"Ok, ok, I promise."

"Hi," Marisa says. She watches the two of them, side by side, and she gets the most curious feeling that she is the odd one out.

"Oh, hi, Marisa." Jake grins at her, raising one hand in greeting.

He doesn't even move toward her. She knows that if she doesn't leave the room, she will embarrass herself by crying. She makes a bolt for the door and rushes upstairs, heading straight for her study, where she closes the door behind her and leans her back against it. The tears come, as she had known they would, and she doesn't wipe them away. She allows herself a moment of mawkish self-indulgence, because she knows there is no reason to cry, not really, and it's simply that she's feeling frayed and anxious and tired. So tired. She's been feeling tired for days now and can't seem to shake it.

There is a knock on the door.

"Marisa?" It is Jake, his voice concerned and pleading. "Are you ok?"

"Yes, truly—I'm fine. I just needed a moment."

There is silence on the other side of the door.

"Ok, well, if you're sure." She hears his intake of breath and can imagine the expression on his face that she knows so well: loving and concerned and worried he's made a mess of things without knowing how. In many ways, he is still the seven-year-old boy who got sent away to boarding school. He needs as much parenting as loving, she thinks. And so does she. It's why they are perfect for each other.

"Don't worry, Jake. Nothing's wrong. I'll be down in a second, just after I've . . . I've . . . finished . . . answering this email," she concludes weakly.

"All right. We'll see you downstairs. No rush."

She hears his footsteps recede and slumps to the floor. She is so exhausted that the last thing she feels like is making polite chitchat with Kate in her perfectly judged smart-casual Breton top. She'll give herself a couple of minutes to regroup, she thinks, and then she'll go back. She walks to the bathroom and splashes cool water on her face, and it's then that she sees the pregnancy test in her toiletry bag. She thinks about her period, which was due days ago, and the fact that she's been feeling so tired, and she thinks about how they've been diligently trying to get pregnant, and she's astonished then that it has taken her so long to realize what the explanation could be.

She sits on the toilet and when her bladder begins to empty, she angles the lip of the pregnancy test into the stream of urine. After she's done, she slides the pink plastic cap back on and places the test on the edge of the sink where it sits for the allotted number of minutes, and once her watch tells her it is time to check, she allows herself to look at the aperture, which reveals two lines—two clear vertical purple dashes that tell her with incontrovertible certitude that she is pregnant.

She screams with joy and it is loud enough that Jake comes running back upstairs. This time, she lets him into the room.

VIII.

After the initial thrill has subsided, Marisa finds the early weeks of pregnancy tiresome. She is shattered and heaviness oozes through her veins, settling slowly into the pit of her stomach where it gurgles and splutters at inopportune moments. The first trimester is a constant disconnectedness, as if she is not quite inhabiting her body. Her normal food proclivities shift overnight. The thought of a green vegetable makes her want to throw up. She can eat hummus and bread and anything else beige and that's about it. She does not feel the inner calm she had anticipated from all the baby books and the health magazines that talked about pregnancy glow. Instead, she is overwhelmed by the admin: the leaflets that appear through the letter box as soon as she has informed her GP, the pamphlets in Comic Sans advising her to book prenatal classes and proselytizing the merits of breastfeeding. She dutifully attends all the requisite hospital appointments, Jake sitting next to her, puppyish in his enthusiasm. She goes back to the pregnancy yoga class and grits her teeth as Carys talks about Mother Earth and maternal energies and the goddess within all of us.

At home, she spends a lot of time in bed or reclining on the sofa. She watches daytime television and subscribes to an internet streaming service that means she can get the latest reality shows from America. There is one, following the lives of the cabin crew on a luxury yacht, that she becomes inexplicably involved in and she finds herself opening up her laptop over breakfast to catch up on the latest romantic entanglements between the male and female deckhand or the chef's travails after being presented with a preference sheet listing the no-gluten dietary requirements of the next oligarch client.

"I don't know how you can watch that stuff!" Kate says one morning. She says it jokingly, but Marisa hears the judgment underlying it. Kate watches *Newsnight* and listens to Radio 4. Kate eats a single piece of toasted rye bread spread thinly with Marmite before heading to the office each morning. Marisa can't face anything other than croissants for breakfast. She worries, stupidly, about putting on weight.

She works for a bit every day but her paintings lack energy. She can't seem to wield the paintbrush in a way that brings the children to life, and she gets frustrated, ripping up more than she keeps and tossing fistfuls of paper into the wastebasket.

Jake goes to work as usual and when he comes home in the evenings, he brings her treats: a perfectly ripe nectarine one day that she doesn't want, so he eats it instead and she watches the juice trickle down his chin and feels rage that he is so clueless and so entitled in his cluelessness. Imagine just being able to eat a nectarine and not even wipe the juice away! An American classmate of hers at school once described an overweight uncle as "lummoxy," and this is the word that comes to Marisa's mind as she watches Jake move solidly around the house, leaving a trail of unwashed mugs on coffee tables and sink tops, safe in the knowledge that she will be the one to put them in the dishwasher. He is used to people doing things for him, she realizes. He belongs to that cadre of Englishmen who have never had to worry about learning the rules, because they are the ones who make them.

At night, in bed, she is filled with self-loathing and remorse about her unkind thoughts. Jake is lovely, she reminds herself. He is kind. He is good. She can trust him. He is supportive and excited and wants to have this baby with her. She catches him sometimes looking at her from across the room, his face suffused with pleasure.

"I think your tummy's poking out a bit," he says as they drink coffee in the garden one morning. She allows herself only one coffee a day now and sips it as slowly as she can to make it last. The late-summer sunshine is eking out the last of its pale light and the patio stones are the yellow white of a once-clean flannel.

Marisa looks down at her stomach. She sees no difference, and it adds to her feeling of unreality. How can she possibly be building a person inside when there is no external evidence? She glances at Jake and can see he is willing a pregnancy bump into existence. He is so desperate for it to be happening. He has never been good at waiting. Impatience, he had once told her, was his most obvious flaw. On the bench, she smiles, places her coffee cup on the ground, and then rearranges herself, subtly jutting out her stomach slightly.

"Yes," she lies. "I think it is."

Jake leans forward, putting his lips close to her belly button.

"Hello, my little darling," he whispers. "I can't wait to meet you."

She looks down at Jake's head, tracing the feathery point where his hair neatly meets in a V at the nape of his neck, and she can smell his soapy freshness and she feels a cresting of love for him.

"I love you," Jake tells her tummy.

"Love you too," she whispers.

So then everything is all right again, and when he leaves for the office, Marisa has a spurt of motivation and completes the twins' princess fairy tale by lunchtime, forgetting for five straight hours that she is pregnant at all. Part of her is worried that things will change when they have a baby, and that Jake won't have enough bandwidth to love her as much as he does now. She is anxious, she realizes, that in giving him the thing he most desires, he will have no use for her.

"You're being silly," she says out loud into the empty room, and the certainty of her own voice is comforting.

Downstairs, she hears the front door slam shut. And then, unmistakably, she hears Kate's voice.

"Hello?"

Marisa walks onto the landing, her paintbrush still in hand.

"Kate," she says. "I wasn't expecting you."

In the hallway, Kate stands silhouetted against the tiles. She is wearing a polka-dot jumpsuit, the sleeves rolled up to reveal her thin wrists. A leather belt with an oversized gold buckle sits tightly around her slender waist. Marisa has never been able to wear belts. They look strange on her, as if she is trying too hard to be someone she isn't. She would never wear polka dots either, being wary of patterns and the way they accentuate her curves, making her feel lumpy and oafish when she wanted to be girlish and light, drinking cocktails in rooftop bars with stylish friends as the sun went down. Like Kate, in fact. Kate would look just right at a rooftop bar.

"No," Kate is saying, ruffling her hair so that her fringe shakes itself out at an angle across her left eyebrow. "I had a meeting and wanted to pop back to change. These"—Kate points at her shiny black shoes—"are not conducive to walking quickly. Not conducive to walking full stop, to be honest."

On Kate's feet are strappy heels with pointed toes. She doesn't normally wear smart shoes and Marisa is struck again by how chic she looks.

"Cool," Marisa says, immediately regretting the choice of word. "I'm just in the middle of something, so . . ."

"Fancy a coffee?" Kate looks up at her, a pleading quality to her face.

"Oh. Well." The worst part of working from home is that you can never come up with a suitable excuse. "I've already had my one coffee of the day, so . . ."

"An herbal tea, then?"

There is a tiny pause.

"I'd love a chat," Kate continues. "But I totally understand if you're busy. Sorry."

She starts taking her shoes off with abrupt movements, one hand on the wall to keep her balance, and Marisa can see that she has upset her.

"No, that would be nice. An herbal tea it is. I'll just put this away." She gestures at the paintbrush, which is now dripping a trail of greenish water into the palm of her hand.

Kate grins. "Oh good! I'll put the kettle on."

Back in her study, Marisa places the brush back in the water jar, unties her painting apron, and hangs it on the hook on the back of the door. Best get this stupid cup of tea over with. Pretend to have some girly bonding time and smile and nod and then hope Kate leaves more quickly than she would have done otherwise.

Downstairs, Kate is sitting on the barstool by the kitchen island. She's made herself a French press coffee and is slouched across the marbled surface, flicking through a Sunday newspaper supplement. Her raincoat is slung over the back of the sofa, arms thrown out like a police corpse outline. She is humming.

Make yourself at home, why don't you? Marisa thinks. Her irritation has become more marked since her pregnancy, the heat of it rising like sap at the most trivial thing. Yesterday, she had been furious at a pedestrian crossing when the traffic light took too long to turn to red.

"Oh, hi," Kate says, sitting up straighter and sliding the magazine away. "I didn't know what tea you'd want."

"Camomile is fine. I'll get it."

"No, no—let me."

Before she can stop her, before she can protest that this is her house and she's perfectly capable of making herself a cup of tea, Kate is bustling around the kitchen, taking a tea bag out of the jar, removing a mug from the cupboard, and waiting for the kettle to steam and click. Marisa hauls herself onto a barstool, her limbs woollen. She observes Kate as she pours the water into the mug, noting the economy of each action, the litheness of each movement. She has a dip between her shoulder and the top of her bicep,

Marisa has noticed. You can't see it today because she's wearing long sleeves, but Marisa knows it is there: the tidy compactness of her muscle, the self-assuredness of it. When Kate claps, there is no swinging loose flesh under each arm. There is no excess flesh to her. She looks as if she has been molded from light-pink clay.

"Here you go," Kate says, passing the tea to her. "So," she says, leaning forward and looking at her straight on. "How are you feeling?"

"Fine." Marisa sips the tea, which burns her tongue.

"I mean, with the pregnancy and everything. How's it going? I want to know *everything*."

Marisa laughs. "Really?"

But Kate's face is open and expectant. It is odd, Marisa thinks, how invested she seems to be in their pregnancy. They had to tell her on the evening they found out because Kate had been waiting downstairs with her macaroni and cheese and the table laid for her special dinner and she had heard the screaming and wanted to know what was up. When they told her, Kate was almost as thrilled as Jake. At one point, her eyes had filmed over and Marisa had thought she was going to cry.

There is the same sense of emotion now, in the kitchen, over their cooling mugs.

"What's it like?" Kate asks. "Being pregnant, I mean."

Marisa feels sorry for her then. Her annoyance recedes. How sad it must be to watch a younger woman get pregnant and be in love, she thinks, when Kate's own life seems so dominated by work.

"It's amazing," Marisa lies. "It's what I've always wanted. I suppose I feel, in some way, that it's the reason I'm here. As a woman, I mean."

Kate blinks.

"Not that you can't be a real woman without being pregnant," she adds hurriedly. "I didn't mean that."

"I know." Kate smiles but it doesn't reach her eyes.

"It's weird feeling that there's something growing in your body that you have no control over. I feel a bit out of sorts."

"Like you're detached from yourself?"

Kate plunges the cafetière.

"Yes, exactly that," Marisa says, surprised at the perspicacity of the question. Jake hasn't been able to grasp this concept at all.

"It must be a bit scary. It's you doing it but at the same time . . . I suppose . . . it's not you? Sorry, that was so badly expressed—"

"No, I mean, don't get me wrong—I love it," Marisa interrupts. "I love knowing I'm bringing new life into the world and seeing how happy Jake is."

"I am too!" Kate says and she leans over and squeezes Marisa's hand. "It's so special."

This is it, Marisa thinks. This is why Kate is so uncomfortable to be around. It's because she has no boundaries. She is constantly trying to insert herself into situations that have nothing to do with her, to assert an intimacy that doesn't exist. There's a desperation to her closeness.

She withdraws her hand.

They make meaningless chitchat for a while longer.

"Thank you for the tea," Marisa says. "I'd best be getting back . . ."

"Yes, yes, of course. And I need to get to work. I'll tidy up down here—you go up."

Kate gathers the mugs, taking them to the dishwasher. And Marisa might have imagined it, but she could swear that she saw Kate's eyes fill with tears. I can't take this on as well, Marisa thinks as she goes back upstairs. Kate's emotions are her own business. She sits at her desk, picks up the paintbrush, and instructs her thoughts to settle. She takes a deep breath and regulates her exhalation to the count of four. But for the rest of the afternoon, there is a shadowy disquiet crouching like a cat in the corner of the room and she cannot ignore it, no matter how hard she tries.

IX.

Later, when Jake is back from work, she talks to him about it.

"So Kate turned up in the middle of the day while I was in the study," she says as he's unpacking his briefcase.

"Oh, that's nice."

He is distracted and she has to talk to his back as he moves around the room, taking off his jacket and loosening his tie before dropping down onto the sofa. Almost instantly, he starts scrolling through his phone.

"Yeah, it was a bit unexpected, actually. It totally messed up my concentration."

He looks at her, surprised. "I'm sorry," he says, his phone still in his hands but lowered now, its screen black.

She waits, her silence pointed. Jake shifts in his seat.

"That shouldn't happen," he says. "This is your home. You need to be able to work undisturbed. I'll have a word with her."

"No, don't," Marisa says. She doesn't want Kate to know they have discussed her. "I'm probably making too big a deal of it, you know. I guess, what with the hormones and stuff . . . well, maybe I'm losing perspective."

"Yes. How are you feeling, Marisa?"

"I'm fine. All going well down there."

She glances at her stomach, which still lies flat against the waistband of her tracksuit bottoms.

"I'm glad to hear it," he says, returning to his phone. She is losing his attention. He starts tap-tapping at the screen, fingers moving with smooth fury against the glass.

"Can I ask you something?"

"Mmm," Jake says, not lifting his head.

"Is it just me, or is Kate a bit . . ." She searches for the right word—one that will be accurate and yet not too critical, because she knows that Jake hates bitchiness and that she has to pitch her sentence carefully. "Needy?"

At this, he drops the phone onto the sofa cushions, stares at her, and crosses his arms. A crinkle appears just above the bridge of his nose. He pauses before answering.

"What makes you say that?"

His voice is cool and Marisa immediately knows she has misjudged it. Once, she had asked him what he most disliked about his work and he had replied, without having to think about it, "Office gossip." She had taken a mental note at the time, reminding herself not to say anything to him that could be construed in the same vein.

"Something she said earlier," Marisa says, trying to sound nonjudgmental and calm. "It was like she was trying to get in my head—asking me all this stuff about how it felt being pregnant, and it was just . . ."

"Yes?" He is sharp now.

"Maybe I misread it."

She backs down.

"You probably did," he says. "Like you said, hormones do crazy things."

That wasn't quite what I said, Marisa thinks to herself, but to Jake she simply nods. His mouth is a flat line.

"If you gave her a chance, I'm sure you'd find that Kate is a really lovely person. She's concerned for you, that's all. We both are."

The casual "we" slices through her.

"What do you mean 'we'?"

Anger fizzes around her solar plexus.

"It hasn't escaped our notice . . ." he starts. Jake's language becomes more formal when he is upset or angry. "That you're behaving a little . . ." He stops and looks at her. His shoulders soften. He walks over and pats her shoulder.

"Irrationally?" she asks.

"Not irrationally—I wouldn't say that."

"You just did."

He laughs, then takes a step back. "No, you did. I said *not* irrationally," he repeats, with the emphasis on the negative, "but maybe a bit . . . erratically. And we're worried, that's all. For you and for the baby."

She stiffens. "I'm perfectly fine."

"Yesterday," he continues, seeming not to have heard her, "I came downstairs and a pan of milk on the stove was boiling over."

"What?"

"A pan of milk . . ."

"No, I heard you; I just don't drink milk, so why would I be boiling it?"

It's true. She uses almond milk for her muesli because she prefers the taste. It's Kate who buys semiskimmed from the supermarket.

"Ok, well, neither Kate nor I were boiling milk either, so . . ."

"So it must have been me?"

Her voice is shrill.

"I don't want to upset you," Jake says, holding out his hand, fingers splayed as if he were trying to calm a wild animal. "But it's not the only thing that's happened, is it?"

He looks at her. "Remember all that unpleasantness with the music?"

The weekend before, Marisa had been trying to paint. She had been unable to concentrate because of loud music playing from downstairs. She had shut the door and closed the window and, eventually, twisted pieces of newspaper and put them into her ears like makeshift plugs but still the music was shatteringly loud. There was a screeching guitar and a thumping beat and the floor seemed to be reverberating beneath her sandals. When she could take it no longer, she went downstairs and found Kate and Jake in the sitting room. Jake was leaning against the mantelpiece, laughing at something Kate had just said, and Kate was standing too close to him, so close that their heads were almost touching.

"Do you remember this one?" Kate was shouting over the music. "Such a fucking classic."

Jake was nodding in time with the beat. "Yeah," he said. "Love it."

Marisa was taken aback. Jake almost never listened to music. He always preferred podcasts and 5 Live for sports. She got the impression he was trying to be cool and ingratiate himself with Kate, which was pathetic, really. But most of her ire was reserved for Kate, who was now bopping around the room, arms flailing as if she were at a gig.

"Guys," Marisa said, directing her comment to Jake. He didn't hear her. "HELLO?" she shouted.

Kate stopped dancing abruptly. She was wearing leopard-print ballet pumps and skinny jeans and a T-shirt with CIAO, AMORE splashed in sans serif across the front.

"Oh. Hi," Kate said, her cheeks shiny.

Jake smiled at Marisa standing in the doorway as if nothing were amiss.

"Could you turn the music down? I'm trying to work."

Two pairs of eyes gazed at her, uncomprehending.

"The music?" Kate asked.

"Yes." Marisa glanced at Jake meaningfully, trying to make her frustration understood.

"It's really not that loud," Kate said.

Marisa gasped. How dare she.

"It's loud enough that I had to put in earplugs."

"Ooookaaaaayyy," Jake said, drawing out the vowels unnecessarily. "Sorry about that."

He went over to the speaker and stopped the music.

"Thank you," Marisa said.

Kate had not moved from her position in the middle of the room. She was looking at Marisa, almost startled, as if Marisa were scaring her, as if she were the one being unreasonable.

When she had left, closing the door behind her, she had waited and listened at the door. Nothing. But when she reached the stairs, she could hear muffled female laughter and the sound of Jake shushing her. The music started up again, this time more quietly.

"Remember?" Jake is asking now. "When you asked us to turn it down?"

"Of course."

He raises his eyebrows, his expression one of intense understanding, as if he is trying—really, truly *trying*—to be sympathetic to this pregnant woman's needs. His eyes are so clear and blue they look unreal. "It was . . . disproportionate, wouldn't you say?"

She wants to tell him to fuck off. Instead, she mutely buttons up her fury.

"I'm sorry," Jake says. "Perhaps that was out of line."

"Yes," she replies, rigid with annoyance. "Yes, it was."

He sighs, and it is this—the audible exhalation intended to emphasize his ability to be infinitesimally patient—that finally pushes her over the edge.

"Why are you taking Kate's side over mine? It's so unfair! I told you I didn't boil the milk. The music was really fucking loud."

"It wasn't . . ."

"It was!"

She can hear how petulant she sounds and yet she can't stop herself. Her throat constricts and for one terrible moment she thinks she's going to throw up, right there in the kitchen.

"Sorry," he says. "I definitely don't want you to feel ganged up on. That's terrible. We'll be more considerate."

"Stop saying 'we.' You're not my parents."

He laughs. "That we are certainly not."

His eyes are kind again, crinkled at the corners. "As long as you're ok, and you have everything you need . . ." he says. "It's difficult for me to understand what it's like being pregnant. I'm just a fairly hopeless bloke, when it comes down to it."

It is her turn to laugh. "You're not. You're a great bloke."

"Not sure about that."

The light in the kitchen begins to turn. The end of their garden is overlooked by the neighboring council estate. On the other side of the fence is a tall, dark tower that houses the connecting stairwell for a series of flats. The windows are small plastic apertures that only open a few inches—slanted, at an angle—so the tower has the unsettling feel of a checkpoint. Sometimes Marisa imagines men with guns, angling their barrels through the single-glazed slivers, training their crosshairs directly at the house.

She shivers.

"Cold?" Jake says.

She shakes her head. "Can I have a hug?" she asks.

His eyes widen. A flush appears on his cheeks. So she *can* still embarrass him, Marisa thinks. She still has that power. He's so English and so upstanding and decent and so bloody repressed. She's not asking him to strip off naked and take her over the kitchen counter, is she? A few more seconds pass. He makes a great show of considering her request. It is a joke they share, and like all private jokes between couples, it is never as funny as it first appeared to be.

"Of course," he says.

She folds herself into his chest, inhaling him, and he crosses his arms around her back, holding her close. She closes her eyes, allowing herself to feel safe. She fits into him exactly—his chin propped on top of her head as if their sizes had specifically been designed to dovetail.

"Everything's going to be all right," he murmurs, and she allows herself to believe him and wraps her arms around his waist, placing her hands in the lower curve of his back. She presses herself closer and then she hears someone cough.

Jake pulls away from her. A strand of her hair gets tangled in his shirt button and she yelps as he jerks away. It takes her a moment to realize what is happening.

"Sorry," comes a voice from behind Marisa's left shoulder. It is Kate. Of course. Kate. Always there.

"Marisa was just—" Jake is spluttering over his words. "She was a little upset so I—" He brushes back his hair. "We were hugging." He swallows drily, the lump of his Adam's apple moving stolidly down his neck.

"I can see that," Kate says.

Marisa giggles. She can't help it. Jake is so unnecessarily flustered.

"He's really not great with public displays of affection, is he?" Marisa directs the question to Kate, deciding generously to include her. And then she asks, "I thought I'd get Vietnamese for dinner if you want to join?"

"Sure," Kate says with no enthusiasm.

"Great. I'm just going to finish up upstairs and then I'll order."

Marisa turns to wink at Jake as she leaves the room. He looks away, trying not to smile. She feels like a naughty schoolgirl, caught in the act by a disapproving teacher. She wonders how long Kate had been standing there before they heard her cough.

▪ ▪ ▪

The twelve-week scan. They get an Uber to the hospital and when the sonographer prods at her, a pixelated black-and-white image appears on the screen. The outlines of the image are shaped in an attenuated semicircle that gives Marisa the feeling of vertigo when she stares at it. And there, in the center of the monochrome curve, is a fuzzy shape studded into the darkness like some alien constellation. On the screen, the white dots pulsate and flicker and the blob contracts, amoeba-like.

"There's the heartbeat," they are told.

Jake is hypnotized and as he stares at it, his eyes film over. Marisa feels nothing and is surprised and a little scared by that fact. She wants to experience the same emotions as Jake, and yet the grainy cells on the hospital screen seem so far removed from the idea of a living, breathing, squalling baby. She knows she is pregnant, and yet she doesn't feel it. When she moves, it is as though there is an invisible layer of Bubble Wrap around her and she cannot move without there being a barrier between herself and the rest of the world.

"Well done, you," Jake says, looking at her fondly.

Once again, she feels patronized, but she chews the inside of her cheek and forces out a smile and Jake doesn't seem to notice. She can see the idea of himself as a father expanding to fill all the available space in his mind. There is no room left for her. Marisa has become a vessel. It is her worst fear: that, once she's had their baby, she will become expendable.

Pretend everything is fine and it will be, Marisa tells herself. She wishes she could talk to Jas about it, but the two of them have lapsed into silence and the distance feels unbreachable. Marisa had been so insistent she was making the right decision that to admit to any uncertainty, however minor, would be a humiliation.

Back at home, she tells Jake she's tired and goes to bed, slipping under the duvet without taking off her clothes. He asks if he can get her anything and she shakes her head. Lying there, she can hear him humming happily as he walks around in the room below her, floorboards creaking under his weight. The sounds of his presence calm her and her tiredness pools around her as if she is sliding into a cool, dark lake. Then, she sleeps.

She dreams of having to catch a flight. She knows she has not done enough packing, and yet she can't find time to put all of her belongings into the cases before the plane takes off. She misses flight after flight after flight, and she keeps feeling relief that the deadline has passed but then realizing that she still has to get on a later plane, and the time keeps running out and her possessions keep proliferating and she cannot pack them all and so she is forced to choose between the things she most needs and those she is willing to lose forever.

She has almost managed it when, in her dream, Marisa spots a pair of knitted pink bootees under the corner of a heavy rug. She lifts the rug and frees the bootees and holds them up to the light and then she knows, with a lurch, that these are her sister's and she drops them and zips up one of the cases, which has too much in it already, the zips buckling and warping as she forces it shut. It is only when she gets on the airplane and is finally seatbelted in that she is struck with fear that the bootees were not, after all, her sister's but belonged to her own baby whom she had forgotten in the rush to get everything together.

Marisa wakes with a gasp, air slamming into her lungs. She is sweating, the back of her T-shirt sticking to her lower back.

"I'm awake, I'm awake," she keeps saying.

She brushes the hair off her forehead and presses her fingers under her eyes to blot away any mascara that might have run. Outside, it is dark. She had not drawn the curtains, and beyond the window frame, the stammering light of a streetlamp bulb casts narrow rectangles across the duvet. She shivers, exposed.

She gets a cardigan from the wardrobe—one of those chunky, baggy affairs with big pockets—and wraps it tightly around her. The nap seems to have had no discernible effect. If anything, she is more tired now than she was before. Her throat is dry and her stomach is lightly cramping. She stretches out flat on her back and the cramps go away. She is weak but doesn't want to eat. And yet she must or Jake will be worried.

"You need extra energy now you're building a whole new human," he has started saying. "We need to feed you up!"

She can't bear the thought of him hovering over her at dinner, looking worried as she fiddles with the vegetables on her plate. Lying in bed, she runs through a mental inventory of various foods that don't make her feel sick. All vegetables are out. Tomatoes too. Avocados make her want to throw up.

Cornflakes? She can't stomach the idea of her usual almond milk.

Toast? Too dry. The idea of honey repels her.

Eventually she lands on a baked potato. Plain. Maybe she could put some hummus in it? But no butter. No cheese. Perhaps some salt if she dares.

Buoyed by the thought, she rolls to the edge of the bed and levers herself upright. Yes, a baked potato, she thinks. That will make her feel stronger and more herself. In addition to the cardigan, she is wearing a faded gray T-shirt and the same leggings she wore to the hospital, with the Lycra sagging at the knees. She hasn't washed today and there is a metallic fustiness emanating from her armpits. Her face is slack from sleep but she can't be bothered to check her reflection in the mirror before going downstairs. It is unlike her, this casual approach to her appearance. In the early days with Jake, she had set an alarm on her phone and put it on vibrate under her pillow so that she could get up half an hour before he woke to brush her teeth and dab cream blush over each cheek.

Lately, she has been having odd thoughts about what would happen if her hand slipped while she was curling her eyelashes. Weird visions of her lashes being sliced off with the guillotine pull of the metal. She hasn't been able to cut her nails for the same reason. What if she stabbed herself with the sharp point of the scissors?

What would it look like if she gouged into the soles of her feet and allowed the blood to pool on the tiled bathroom floor? These images are so vivid they bring her to the edge of fainting and then she has to sit down and put her head between her knees.

The last time she fainted . . . But she doesn't want to think about that. She refuses to think about the downward spiral, the sensation of being sucked into quicksand. She is fine. She has Jake. She is happy. They live in a perfect house. They are having a baby.

These are the solid things, the hooks of clarity onto which she can hang her feeling of dread. These are the good, decent facts. They are all that matter.

Jake isn't in the sitting room anymore, so he must be in the kitchen. Marisa turns onto the staircase that leads to the basement. Her mind is still fogged by sleep, by the lingering aftermath of the dream, and so she doesn't pay much attention when she walks in and hears a rustling sound coming from the sofa. Fleetingly, she thinks of the magpie and wonders if a bird has gotten into the room again.

"I thought I'd have a baked potato," she announces, turning toward the island where she imagines Jake will be standing, preparing dinner or even pouring a glass of wine in readiness for her appearance. He will have missed her, Marisa thinks. He will want to talk about the scan and baby names and what color they'll paint the nursery and when they should tell his mother now that twelve weeks have passed. But as her mind snaps into focus, she notices that Jake is not where she thought he would be and that the rustling from the sofa was not, in fact, a stray bird but the sound of two people huddled together rapidly separating themselves. Out of the corner of her eye, she sees what looks like two embracing shadows contract and release, pushing each other away. She thinks of the scan, of the black-and-white blobs tightening then unfurling.

"Shit," she hears Kate mutter. Kate scampers to the farthest edge of the sofa, putting distance between her and Jake.

"Great," Jake is saying, standing and smoothing down his hair in one swift motion. "About the baked potato, I mean." He tries to smile at her and Marisa's chest tightens. There is a whooshing sound in her ears. She feels like a cartoon figure she had watched as a child: a coyote whose legs whir as he runs off a cliff edge, the intensity of the motion ensuring the coyote stays suspended in midair for several seconds until reality catches up with him and he drops onto the ground below.

Beneath her chest, her heart knocks and beats. There is a light fluttering in her throat, as if a space has opened up in her gullet.

Jake is blushing. He is actually fucking blushing. His eyes are flicking to the left and right and he is unable to look at her. His shirt is untucked, four buttons undone from the neck.

Kate, wild-eyed, is now cross-legged on the sofa in the half gloom. She stares at Marisa and the way she looks at her feels like a challenge. The light is so dim that Marisa can't make out the individual features of her face, just the sparkle of her blackened eyes and her lips, blurry and pink, as if something has been pressed against them. As if someone has been kissing her.

Marisa, standing by the stove, wonders if she is still, in fact, dreaming. If this is part of a nightmare. Or one of those violent, surreal visions that have been creeping up on her lately. Whatever it is, the truth—if it is indeed the truth—of what might have just happened is too big for her to digest. She will leave it for later, she thinks. She will deal with it then. For now, she just wants things to be normal. To be as they were before she walked down the stairs. After all, she hadn't seen anything. She has simply imagined the worst. Yes, she thinks, that's all that has happened. Her imagination has run away with her. That's it.

"Yeah," she says. "It's the only thing I feel like eating."

Jake walks over to her then, his face beaming.

"Wonderful," he says. "Then a baked potato you shall have."

Kate stays sitting on the sofa. Marisa meets the lodger's gaze and smiles at her. It is a lethal smile. Kate looks away, and in that single moment she knows.

I'll fucking destroy you, Marisa thinks.

X.

She starts following her. At first, it is almost a joke. Marisa tells herself she'll do it once, to set her mind at rest. She is aware of the absurdity of it, and yet this doesn't stop her on the first day from putting on a beanie hat, pulling it low over her eyes, and wearing a pair of plain-glass spectacles and an oversized army jacket bought from a charity shop for just this purpose. She feels swaddled in the anonymity of her new clothes and when she glances at the hallway mirror on the way out, she is satisfied with what she sees. From a distance, it would be hard to make out any distinguishing features.

She listens from the study for the sound of Kate's footsteps and the click of the front door as the lodger leaves the house. Jake, as ever, has gone to work hours before either of them, so there is no one to ask Marisa what she's doing as she runs down the stairs and into the street. She spots Kate about six hundred feet away, walking toward the Vauxhall tube. She waits until Kate gets to the end of the road, turning right through the council estate housing, and then she follows, walking briskly but not too quickly. She trails her across the pedestrian crossing on Fentiman Road and into Vauxhall Park, where Kate cuts across the grass.

At the exit from the park, Kate stops and checks her shoe. Marisa, several paces back, also comes to a halt. She pulls her hat farther down over her ears. She is breathing heavily. Excitement twists in her chest. She hasn't felt this energized in weeks.

They get on the same tube but in different carriages. Marisa sits near the glass so that she can watch where Kate gets off. The intersecting window has been pulled down and she faces the breeze, grateful for its coolness under the warmth of her beanie.

After four stops, Kate stands and holds on to a railing as the tube shudders into the station platform. Oxford Circus. Marisa steps onto the platform, zigzagging in and out of the crowds, keeping sight of Kate's bobbing head in the melee. Kate's hair is shiny and freshly cut and she has tucked it behind one ear and it stays there, obediently, as if advertising itself as particularly good hair.

Beneath the beanie, Marisa's forehead is sweating, her hair sticking to her scalp and frizzing at the ends. She hasn't showered for a couple of days. Kate's neatness seems an affront.

Marisa stands to the right on the escalator, hunkering down behind a meaty-shouldered man in a high-vis jacket. Kate is standing a few steps ahead of her, but then she decides to walk the rest of the escalator. Marisa can't risk walking too. She'll be noticed immediately if Kate decides to turn around.

Instead, she stays on the escalator, feet planted wide because she notices now that she feels dizzy and off balance. She grabs hold of the railing.

"Are you all right, darling?"

The woman behind her, a grandmotherly type carrying a rumpled Sainsbury's bag, is looking at her with concern.

"Yes, fine," Marisa says, turning to face her. "Thank you so much."

"You want to be careful. I remember that stage."

The woman points at Marisa's stomach and when she looks down, she realizes the pregnancy has started to show. Her jacket has flapped open and her tummy protrudes from the gap: a tiny, swelling mound.

"Don't worry. You'll feel better in the second trimester."

Marisa tries to smile. They're at the top of the escalator now and the woman seems intent on making conversation.

"Thank you. I should—" She gestures toward the ticket barriers.

"I used to be a midwife, you see."

Marisa nods. "Oh, how interesting! Well, anyway . . ."

By the time she has shaken the woman off and emerged onto Oxford Circus, Kate is nowhere to be seen. But then she squints and makes out the familiar outline of Kate's trench coat. She has crossed the road onto the other side of Regent Street. Marisa surges forward, pushing people out of her way to make the crossing before the traffic lights change—"Oy, watch it!" she hears one man shout angrily—but it's no good. She watches from the curb as the red turns to green and the cars and buses start streaming past. People crowd around her, jostling for space, and she sees Kate disappear into the busy London morning.

The next few days follow a similar pattern. She gets a little bit farther each time. On the third day, she trails Kate to an office block in Soho that has tinted glass and a reception area with a neon sign that spells out DO WHAT YOU LOVE in aggressively bright blue. By the following week, she has taken to spending the morning sitting in the cafe opposite, a healthy fast-food place that serves baked eggs in cardboard bowls and small tubs of hummus. Their straws are paper, ringed red and white like candy canes. She checks her phone, sends the odd email. She has started to keep a diary. When she gets bored, she takes out a notebook and starts to write: observations, thoughts, anxieties. She finds the process cathartic. At midday, she waits to see if Kate will come out for lunch, but she never does, and by midafternoon, Marisa makes her way back home, dejected.

Her work suffers. A backlog of uncompleted commissions piles up. Jake tells her she seems distracted and asks if anything is wrong.

"Not at all," Marisa says. "Just, you know, pregnant."

The pregnancy becomes her excuse for everything: for early nights to avoid three-way conversations; for not having sex with Jake; for no longer cooking his favorite meals because raw food makes her feel nauseous. In this way, she effectively removes herself from the discomfiting atmosphere of the house when Kate is in it. Jake has been attentive ever since the incident in the kitchen, and she notices that he stands at the opposite end of the room when Kate is nearby, casting frequent glances in Marisa's direction. Kate, by contrast, is quiet and calm in the evenings, reading her book or watching television with the volume turned down.

"Is it ok if I watch something?" she will say, settling herself into the kitchen sofa area, and Marisa shrugs.

"Why wouldn't it be?"

"I guess I just thought . . . you know . . . you might prefer to watch something else," Kate will reply, biting the edge of a thumbnail.

"No."

"Ok, then," Kate will say, and there is always something passive-aggressive in her tone, as if it's Marisa being the unreasonable one.

She watches the interactions between Jake and Kate with morbid fascination. She tells herself she doesn't want to find any further evidence of their closeness and yet, at the same time, she is compelled to do so. She wants her suspicions proved right, while at the same time knowing that this will undo her. It will smash apart everything she has ever wanted. It will destroy the only relationship she has ever been able to trust. But she keeps returning to it, a freshly formed scab that she starts to pick at with the tip of her finger, worrying the edges as if to test the strength of the rust-dried platelets, the web of fragile new skin.

Perhaps I truly did imagine it, she tells herself. After all, it had been dark, and she had just woken up. She was making a fuss out of nothing, winding herself up because of all the pregnancy hormones running amok inside her. Her insecurities are heightened. That's all it is.

But then again. There was the incident with the music—the two of them together like teenagers just one floor beneath where she was working. There was Kate's easy intimacy with Jake, that strange possessiveness she'd had from her first moments in the house, the way she assumed this place was hers and had taken up space in it, leaving her belongings scattered around different rooms. She sees Kate brush the back of Jake's hand as she walks past him in the corridor. Out of the corner of her eye, she watches as Kate squeezes his arm when he brings her a cup of tea. They think she doesn't notice but she does. Marisa lets them believe she doesn't suspect. She allows time to pass until she can work out what to do next. She watches. She takes notes. It feels as if she is putting together a case and that, one day, she will be called upon to present it.

At night, she stays up while Jake and Kate go to bed. She says she wants to get ahead with work before the baby comes, but instead she sits at her desk and writes furiously in her notebook. *I think he's having an affair with Kate*, she writes, over and over again on a single page until the paper is dense with scrawling and she feels better for having stated it so plainly. The idea, in its transference, has lost some of its power to hurt her.

During the third week of trailing Kate to work, there is an unexpected burst of sunshine. By the time she gets to Oxford Circus, Marisa is so hot that she takes off her beanie, sweeping back her hair so that it sits smooth against her scalp. She unbuttons the army jacket and ties it around her waist. Kate, as usual, has got off the tube before her. Marisa watches her walk up the escalator. She waits on the side as usual because she knows, by now, that this gives her just enough time to catch sight of Kate before she leaves the station.

At the top of the escalator, Marisa steps onto the concourse. She walks toward the barriers, fumbling in her bag for her phone, when someone grabs her by the arm, twisting it with such force that she spins on her heel and yelps with pain.

"For fuck's sake!" she says, trying to shake herself free. When she lifts her head, she sees Kate, inches away from her face.

"Why are you following me?" Kate is saying, her mouth so close that Marisa feels spittle against her cheeks. Her breath is warm and smells of coffee. "Why the fuck are you following me?"

Marisa is too shocked to think. She has become so used to her routine that she has forgotten to justify it to herself, let alone Kate. She has nothing to say to her, no way to explain.

"I want you to *stop*—do you understand?" Kate's eyes are blazing, the skin around her lips puckered with anger. Kate is still gripping her arm, fingers pressing into the tender flesh above her wrist so tightly that Marisa imagines bruises beginning to form: pink then bluish then purple indentations.

"It's *enough*."

Acid rises in Marisa's throat. She can see now how easy it would be to make it seem that she was the one overstepping boundaries rather than Kate. It was another trap, and there was no way out of it.

"Yes, ok, yes," Marisa says quietly. "Sorry."

"You're lucky I haven't called the police."

"Please don't do that."

Kate lets her hand drop. Marisa shakes her arm, letting the blood back in. When she looks back up, she sees that Kate's face has softened. Her eyelids are powdered dark brown with shadow at the corners and she has perfectly applied kohl and mascara that is smooth of any clumps. Kate isn't wearing any lipstick. This morning, Marisa had slicked her mouth with gloss and now strands of her hair are sticking to it. In comparison to Kate's distilled elegance, Marisa feels stupid and unwieldy. The baby is heavy in her belly, twisting her own self out of shape.

"Please don't tell Jake," Marisa whispers, blinking back tears she had not known were there. Her voice constricts. She sounds whispering and pathetic.

Kate sighs. Behind her, a uniformed man collecting for a military charity rattles his collection tin. The sound jangles, indistinguishable from the noise in Marisa's head.

"I won't," Kate says, belting up her coat. She brushes down the coat fabric with the palm of each hand, as if ridding herself of dust.

As if ridding herself of me, thinks Marisa. "I wouldn't want to bother him with it."

Marisa bites her cheek until she tastes blood. Tears are replaced with fire in her veins. Fury draws itself back within her, a tightening sling ready to slam its shot into its target. She nods, then turns and goes back down the escalator, unsure whether her anger or her humiliation will win out.

But by the time she gets onto the tube, she knows. Anger.

Anger always wins.

XI.

She doesn't sleep that night. Again. The traffic noises, which she had never noticed before, have grown louder. She begins to think that sleep is an affectation, that she can function perfectly well without it. She wonders why she wasted all that time unconscious under the duvet when she could have been busy doing other stuff. Imagine the paintings she would have produced, the commissions she could have completed. She might have written a children's book of her own. Her work might have been exhibited in the world's best galleries. There would be champagne toasts to her on white-walled private-view evenings where the chatter would be polite and murmured and she would glide easily past other people's glances, knowing that they were talking about her and looking at her and marveling at her talent and her success.

"See," she would have said to her mother, standing in front of an abstract work of splattered reds and oranges, dripping across the canvas like butcher's blood. "I *am* someone."

She spends the early hours at her desk in the study, waiting for the sun to rise over the garden so that the council estate stairwell will cast its morning shadow over the grass. She takes out a sheet of paper and tapes it down, but instead of painting as she had meant to, Marisa scrawls words across it in black Sharpie. She wants to experiment with a different form. She wants to use typography in her pictures, in the same way as she had once seen an American conceptual artist cut out red-and-white strips of text and stick them across grayscale photographs of women with their eyes closed, of empty houses on dilapidated streets, of rough seas and glowering skies and prostitutes in urban doorways.

She remembers her father had a girlfriend once—the first of many. It was four years after her mother and sister had left and just before she had been sent to boarding school. He had brought her home late one night, when he must have thought Marisa was asleep. But she heard the car drawing up outside, the slam of the driver's door and then the passenger's, and then she heard the key in the lock, the clink of glasses in the kitchen, and eventually the whispered footsteps leading upstairs, tracing a path across the landing.

The smell of cigarette smoke. Her father's gentle cough. His stumble as he reached the bedroom, which told her he was drunk.

She heard them through the thin bedroom wall. An unfamiliar female giggle, bubbling and muffled from the other side of the plaster, and then her father's steady bass-line chuckle. What could the woman have said to make him laugh like that? Marisa thought, and why couldn't she do the same? Why was he always so sad with Marisa, when he could be this happy with someone else?

From underneath her duvet, she heard sighing, followed by the shuffling of bedsheets, the creak of a headboard, the low groans of adults trying to be quiet and failing, and then a high-pitched shriek and Marisa's father shushing the shrieker.

The next morning, she got dressed in her school uniform and went downstairs for breakfast. Her father was sitting as usual at the pine table, the well-worn wood ringed with imprints of long-ago mugs, and he turned to her as she entered.

"Marisa," he said, his voice formal. "Good morning, darling."

He was wearing a shirt and tie and a knitted cardigan waistcoat and it was this—the effort he had made to appear normal—that alerted her to the other presence in the kitchen. Marisa's gaze turned toward the other end of the room and came to settle on an aggressively thin woman sitting on the red armchair by the radiator. She had fine dark hair, piled high on her head and held into place with a velvet scrunchie. Her mouth was masked with red lipstick. She was clasping a coffee in long pale fingers, hunched over the cup as if seeking out the weak plume of steam for warmth.

"Hello, lovey," the woman said.

"Marisa," her father said. He was standing now and the napkin that had been on his lap slid to the floor. "This is . . . um . . . well, this is my . . . friend, Jacqueline."

"Jackie, please!" she said with a whoop of last night's laughter.

"Hello," Marisa said, dipping her eyes so she didn't have to look too long.

Jackie put down her cup and moved toward her, opening her thin arms widely.

"I'm a hugger," Jackie said, emitting a throaty smoker's laugh. "Come here, darling."

There was no escape. It felt like hugging a rotatory clothesline.

"There, there," Jackie was saying, patting Marisa's back. "I'll be seeing a lot more of you, I should think."

Marisa pulled away.

"I don't have time for breakfast," she said. "I'm late for school."

"It's only eight fifteen," her father protested.

"God, they work them hard these days, don't they?" Jackie said. "I feel sorry for you, sweetheart."

Marisa turned to Jackie then and smiled.

"Fuck you," she said, the words landing cleanly in the silence between them. There was a moment of shock. Jackie took a step back, stumbling against the armchair. Marisa's father opened his mouth, about to say something that she already knew would be irreparable. She ran out of the house before she could hear it.

She never saw Jackie again.

Over the years, Marisa had set herself up in competition with every single girlfriend her father had introduced to her. She would always win and in the end, her father had stopped dating altogether. The last time she had seen him, he had come to visit her in her flat in London wearing a battered raincoat and a tie pockmarked with food stains. His eyebrows were wiry and overgrown. He was slight—slighter than she remembered—and, despite the food stains, looked malnourished. His eyes were rheumy and unfocused as he looked around her tiny one-bed in an ecstasy of insincere appreciation. She could smell gin on his breath. She had made him tea and he had drunk it sitting on her sofa, without taking his coat off.

"Are you sure I can't take that for you?"

"Oh, no no no. I don't want to be any bother."

He seemed so weak and so old. She realized he would probably die quite soon and when she thought of it, she felt a pang of incipient loss. Not because his death would leave an absence in her life, but because his existence had.

After that, she hadn't contacted him again. She had ignored his phone calls and his sad "To My Daughter" birthday cards and he had stopped trying. Then Marisa had moved in with Jake and left no forwarding address.

In her study, she watches the sun rise. The clouded sky goes nicotine yellow. Her desk turns sepia in the light. It is too bright. She takes the roll of masking tape from her desk and starts sticking strips of it across the panes of glass. Better. The central heating starts up, pipes clanking and creaking like stretched sailing ropes.

Her belly pushes outward over her tracksuit bottoms. She rests both her hands on her four-month-pregnant stomach, pressing lightly with her palms in a bid to feel something. The websites tell her that "Baby could be sprouting hair" and "Baby can use her facial muscles to grimace or smile" and "Baby is about the size of a lemon or your clenched fist."

She clenches her fist, placing it underneath her navel, and leaves it there, her knuckles white against her skin.

"By now, fully developed genitals will be making their grand entrance."

She visualizes a miniature penis and vagina arriving at some glitzy black-tie ball, walking down a red-and-gold staircase to the elegant strains of a string quartet.

She goes downstairs to make herself an herbal tea. Her head feels heavy. She drops it down toward her chest, massaging the back of her neck with her hand. As she does so, her eye catches on a flat gray square on the seat of one of the kitchen chairs. It is Jake's laptop. He normally takes it to work but he's clearly forgotten today.

She reaches into the pocket of her dressing gown for her phone. But then, just before she calls him, she changes her mind. Marisa lifts the laptop onto the table, its edges sleek, the surface slightly granular to the touch. She flips open the computer. She knows Jake's password. She had watched him once type it into the keyboard as she had been standing behind him, pretending to busy herself with the washing up.

She taps it in: 143Richborne. It is their address. Maybe it still means something to him—this house, their home, their baby, her?

The screen fires up and a picture of a Renaissance painting flashes into place. A rosy-cheeked Virgin Mary, with long golden hair twisting around her collarbone, and a fleshy baby Jesus placed against an Italianate landscape. He has a thing for devotional art.

Marisa is not sure what she's looking for. She tells herself she's logged on because she wants to check the news. Having been so insulated over the last few months, so distracted by her necessary involvement in establishing their own joint life, she has lost track of what is happening in the outside world.

But before she has a chance to visit the BBC website, an alert pops up in the right-hand corner of the screen. She sees Kate's name flash up, black sans serif font against a gray rectangle.

Did you see her this morning?

It takes a beat for Marisa to understand. But then she works it out. The laptop is connected to Jake's text messages, and she is witnessing his communications in real time. At the bottom of the screen is an icon consisting of two overlapping speech bubbles, one blue, the other white and containing an ellipsis. There is a red circle with the figure "1" pulsing like an eye above the larger speech bubble.

Unread message.

Marisa clicks on the speech bubbles and there they are: text after text from Kate to Jake and Jake to Kate.

The first thing she notices is the amount of kisses. Jake never signs off affectionately to the texts he sends her—she had thought it was one of his quirks. He was businesslike because he had to be, because he had so many other demands on his time at work. That is what she had told herself.

But she was wrong. When he texts Kate, his messages are festooned with lines of "X"s, as if his finger has slipped, as if he is composing nonsense poetry. The lines are so dense it is almost as if he were redacting paragraph after paragraph of a top-secret document.

There are hundreds of messages. She scrolls back and back and back to see where they started, but the screen keeps offering to "load more." Her heart collapses in on itself. Her chest empties.

I love you, Kate wrote on June 2. That would have been a few weeks after she moved in, Marisa calculates. But the messages go back far longer. They already knew each other. This whole thing—pretending she was a tenant, telling Marisa they could no longer afford the rent without outside help—has been a sham. She has been set up. Jake has exploited her unquestioning love for him to move his mistress in. How could she have been so stupid?

Her throat fills with a metallic taste. She swallows, then gags. She hasn't eaten for hours, maybe even days—who knows? Who fucking cares? The dry heave of her stomach does not release anything. She covers her mouth with her hand, keeping it all in, tamping down the fear like coffee grounds in a filter.

Baby I can't stop thinking about you, Jake had written on July 15. Wear that lingerie tonight. He'd signed off with a winking face and an eggplant emoji.

Haha ok but what about Marisa?

We'll find a way. Another winking-face emoji.

Just want to make sure she's ok.

She's fine, Jake had typed. Trust me. We don't need to worry.

It is so clichéd—that is the worst part. She had thought more of Jake. She had believed him to be different: honest, plainspoken, straightforward. Not passionate, but dependable. It turns out that she doesn't know Jake at all, this man she was supposedly in love with. It turns out he is an overgrown adolescent schoolboy in the throes of illicit passion and that he communicates with crude sexual innuendo and emojis. It turns out he is patronizing Marisa, in the foulest way possible. He is treating her like a fool because she has been acting like one, blinkered and uncomprehending, as he continues shagging their lodger. What Marisa has taken to be Jake's buttoned-up English propriety is actually just deception. He has been deceiving her for months. Maybe even from the moment they met.

What is the point of it? To show that it can be done? To use her as a broodmare while he gets his kicks elsewhere? Perhaps he is a psychopath—she had read a book about them once and knows that one of the signifying factors is a lack of empathy and glib, superficial charm. That is Jake. She had believed he was so deep. But he is a hologram of a person. A fake. A fraud. A phony who doesn't care who he hurts.

Her wrist is aching. When she looks down, she sees she has been scratching at it with fingernails from her other hand and has drawn blood. Automatically, she stands and goes to the cupboard underneath the sink where there is a box of tissues. She presses a tissue to her wrist. Red-brown dots appear through the white. At the sight of her own blood, Marisa feels a pure, violent rage. In front of her is a fruit bowl, containing four lemons, the ceramic painted and intricately patterned. It had been brought back from one of Jake's backpacking trips to Morocco as a student and she knew he adored it.

Without thinking, she lifts the bowl and throws it toward the opposite wall. The lemons fly out and bounce on the floor. The ceramic slams and breaks, making a noise like a scream but then she realizes the scream is coming from her. She is shouting, but there are no words. She screams, clutching her distended belly, feeling the weight of her pregnancy against her hands, and then she screams again, until her throat is ragged with the effort of it, until all she can hear is the ringing of her grief in her own ears. Grief for the love she had so foolishly believed in. Grief for the child she is carrying who will not now be born into the embrace of two loving parents. Grief for her own ridiculousness in believing she was worthy of Jake's love, in believing any of it. She understands it now—the lesson that life has been trying to teach her. It is that she will never be enough. The world is laughing at her for thinking, however briefly, that she might be.

"You fucking cunt," she screams, drawing out the vowels of the final bleak syllable so that it becomes a caterwauling echo of the original sound. She doesn't know, when she screams it, whether the word refers to her or to Jake or to Kate.

Marisa leaves the shards of the fruit bowl scattered on the floor. She remembers the first time she had seen this kitchen and how impressed she had been by the largeness of it. She had been cowed by its grown-up beauty: the sleek surfaces, the light floorboards, the dishwasher that you knocked on twice, sharply, to open the door. Now it looks unreal, like a bad dream. The room is taunting her. The walls are closing in on her fevered thoughts, squashing them into a tiny, painful cube. A sharp bolting headache grips her temples. The wineglasses in the cupboard, bulbous and sparkling, are clinking their congratulations for having tricked her. And outside, the tall council estate stairwell is looming ever larger, blotting out the slivers of her internal light—those popping pixelations of hope studded against the darkness of her mind, each one extinguishing itself as the blackness leaks into her thoughts. Who was she to have hope? Who was she to believe that life was on her side?

She exhales, unclenches her fists, and begins counting to ten.

"When I get angry or upset or I think no one is listening to me, I count to ten," her mother had once told her. Marisa, who must have been five or six, was lying on her bed, breathing heavily with hot cheeks. "Try it, darling."

She imagines her mother now as she counts—six, seven, eight—and as she pictures her face, undimmed by age in her memory, she becomes calmer.

She returns to the laptop open on the table. Her fury has been replaced by numbness. Her actions are now governed by a shocked coolness, and she finds she can examine the texts more dispassionately, almost as objects of historic curiosity.

Did you see her this morning?

Kate's last text, hanging in the ether. And then: three dots, appearing one after the other in quick succession. Jake is typing.

No. She was in her room. Didn't want to disturb. X

Even when he's being unfaithful, Jake is particular about his full stops and grammatical sensibility.

Then: three more dots, shimmying across the screen like a caterpillar. Jake is typing again.

Don't worry, Jake texts. It's all going to be fine. And soon we'll be a proper family. Love you xxxxx

She feels sick. So this isn't just a fling. Clearly Jake and Kate are planning for the future as a "proper family." But how, exactly? She's the one pregnant with his child . . . unless . . . No . . . The thought is too vicious. They couldn't be thinking . . . Could they?

Can't wait, Kate replies. Love you too x

Unless . . . they are planning to wait until Marisa has given birth and then get rid of her? They wouldn't. It would be too cruel. After everything she has told Jake about feeling abandoned by her own mother, the idea that he could willingly enact the same on their unborn child makes her want to rip off his scalp. What a callous fucking bastard.

Think. She has to think. Think, Marisa. Think, think, think.

But again and again, she keeps being drawn back to the text messages.

July 5

Jake: You're amazing and I love you. Whatever happens, please remember that.

Reading his words, her heart seems to start pumping and squeezing in the pit of her stomach.

August 20

Kate: Going to be late tonight. Don't wait up.

The casual proprietorship is what strikes Marisa. The idea that he'd be waiting up so that, what—they could have a quickie on the downstairs sofa while she was sound asleep upstairs?

September 12

Kate: Worried about Marisa. She seems edgy.

Jake: It's all under control. You worry too much. Xxxxx

Kate: Ok

October 15

Kate: Jesus, Jake. She just turned up at my work.

Jake: WHAT?

Kate: So freaked out.

Jake: Going to call you.

Marisa scrolls down until the last messages. She stares at the screen, waiting to see if those three dots will emerge again. She thinks of Kate, her narrow hips and her slight figure, the way she looks like a ballerina from certain angles. Kate is all discipline, from the amount of food she eats to the rigorous nature of her exercise routine and the way she insists on going through her diary every Sunday night to run through her meetings and appointments.

What is she going to do? In a cheap film—the kind that she watches on cable channels in the afternoons lying on the sofa when she should be working—the wronged woman would pack her bags and leave the house in a fit of righteous indignation. But Marisa has nowhere to go. Her rented flat was given up as soon as she moved in with Jake. She hasn't been paid for weeks because she has neglected her work. Tracking Kate's every move has taken up so much of her time, and what little she has left over she spends napping or staring into space, thinking.

She has lost touch with Jas, although maybe she could reach out and ask to stay. Jas would probably say yes. But the humiliation of having to explain everything that has happened is too much for her. She hasn't spoken to her father for years.

And yet, she can't stay with Jake, can she? She will have to confront him and they will have a screaming row and . . . then what? What if he calls her bluff and tells her it's over and that he sees a future with Kate? Marisa will be a single mother, in a shitty little flat, with Jake visiting every other weekend. She and Jake aren't even married. He pays the rent. She has no legal rights.

"Count to ten," she imagines her mother saying, leaning over Marisa in bed so that a strand of her long blonde hair—hair just like Marisa's is now—falls forward and tickles her collarbone. "Count to ten, my darling, and then see how you feel."

That is what she will do, Marisa decides. She will count to ten, over and over again, until she works out what to do next.

PART II

XII.

Kate gets back first. The house is dark when she turns her key in the door, its windows blank. Inside, the temperature is cool. The central heating hasn't kicked in yet. She has to remember to tell Jake to reprogram it now that winter is approaching. He's good at that sort of stuff.

The first thing she does when she gets across the threshold, before she even takes off her coat, is to draw the curtains in the sitting room. She doesn't like the thought of passersby being able to peer into her home from the street.

She hangs her parka on one of the hooks lining the hallway. She still hasn't turned on the lights. It is as she is removing her scarf and ruffling her hair free of her beanie hat that she hears it: a scuffle and then a creak.

Kate stills, halting her breath, listening as the darkness tunes her ears in to a higher frequency. A faraway car horn sounds. Outside, someone has turned on a radio and she can just make out its tinny jingle.

No more noises come. Probably just the clatter of an old house, she thinks. She's still getting used to it. Before, she had lived in new-build apartment blocks with concierges at the door. She hadn't liked the sterility of the interiors, but she had felt safe there.

The Richborne Terrace house, by contrast, has history built into its brickwork. She had researched it once, using the online census to discover that in 1901, it was occupied by J. Humphrey, a retired lighterman, and his wife and three children and—surprisingly—another family of four, headed by one Patrick Lancton, a postman. Kate doesn't believe in ghosts but she doesn't not believe in them either.

In the hallway, she shivers.

Outside, the sky has leached itself of color. The clocks went back last month and though it's only 6 p.m., it feels like midnight. Even the moon, which she can just make out through the glass above the door, is dulled by gray wisps of cloud.

She drops her bag on the floor and slips her phone out of her pocket, checking to see if she has any messages. Jake has texted, saying he misses her and he'll be back by half past seven. She feels a small, familiar thrill seeing his name there. She unlocks the home screen and starts typing back a response.

Ok xx. She uses thumbs to text, her shoulders hunched over the phone. She sends the message, slides the phone back into her trouser pocket, and then Kate turns and feels along the wall for the light switch.

Her eyes, confused by the brightness of the phone, struggle to adjust to the darkness and the switch isn't where she had thought it would be. She gropes along the plaster, stumbling slightly.

The phone vibrates against her thigh. She reaches into her pocket, and then she sees it: a ball of shadow, tumbling toward her, expanding like an ink blot. She has no time to raise her arms to defend herself. She understands, too late, that the scuffling noise she had heard was not just the creak of ancient pipes or the residue of half-formed ghosts, but a thing that wishes her harm.

Before Kate has a chance to react, a heavy weight is thudding against her skull with such force that her neck cracks and slackens and her head drops forward. Her thoughts atomize then coalesce into a bright, dazzling white. She crumples to the floor. She had always thought she would scream if she were attacked. But in terror, it turns out Kate is silent. As she passes out, she thinks of brown, gloppy water, rising up over her face. She imagines the dim light of a slow-moving boat receding into the silty darkness and she tries, in vain, to reach for it as the current sucks her to the bottom of the riverbed.

When she comes round—she has no idea how much time has passed—her right leg is numb and pressed against a hard, cold surface. Her eyelids are sticky, and opening them requires effort. Her vision is blurry, and she realizes one of her contact lenses has slid around her eye, the edges of it scratchy and dry. She blinks—once, twice, three times—and it slots back into place. A kaleidoscopic pattern comes into focus, brown-and-white mosaic pieces that jiggle and then solidify into a tiled floor. Her cheek is raw and cold. She is lying on her side, her face against the tiles, her right shoulder twisted uncomfortably underneath her chest. Her left ankle is splayed back at an awkward angle. Her head is throbbing. She has the unpleasant sensation of liquid coagulating at the nape of her neck. The thought of blood makes her feel faint and she blinks her eyes shut for a minute, to rid herself of the image.

"Kate."

Her name.

"Kate."

There it is again, spoken in a voice she recognizes but can't yet place.

"Open your eyes, Kate."

Her head is still fuzzy. Someone has upended a snow globe and scattered her thoughts like glitter.

"Kate."

It is a female voice. It is one she knows, but not intimately. And then, suddenly, it comes to her. Marisa. Thank God. Marisa is here. She must have come in after her and disturbed the intruder and found Kate lying here.

"Mrsssa," Kate slurs. A tooth has loosened in her mouth. Her tongue is swollen. She tries to say she's glad Marisa is here but it comes out as "Sgld wwhhere."

"Don't speak," Marisa says.

Kate opens her eyes fully. She sees the edges of Marisa's slippers: fluffy beige bootees Kate has always hated. They look so matronly, and Marisa is so young. She doesn't make the best of herself. But why is she thinking this now? She needs to concentrate. She needs to get up off the floor and get some medical attention. Marisa will have called an ambulance, she is sure. But why is Marisa wearing slippers if she's just come in from outside?

Kate tries to untwist her shoulder and to press her hand against the floor so that she can lever herself into a sitting position against the skirting board. Even this sends an electric eel of pain slamming into her ribs and swimming down her spine.

"Arrrghh," she cries out. The loose tooth comes away entirely. It floats in her mouth, lodging underneath her tongue. Kate gags. She spits out the tooth. It lands on a white tile, amid a spatter of blood.

She rests her cheek back on the coolness of the floor, allowing the nausea to pass. Why is Marisa just sitting there? Why isn't she trying to help her?

"Sit up, Kate."

Marisa's voice is monotone, almost robotic. Perhaps it's tough love, Kate thinks. Perhaps she thinks this is the best way to snap her out of her shock.

"Ambulance," Kate says. Without the tooth, it is easier to make herself understood.

"You don't need an ambulance, Kate. You're perfectly fine. I just want to talk."

That is the first odd signal that reaches Kate's jagged synapses. Oh, she thinks, Marisa is not going to help after all. Marisa is not acting as she thought she would. Oh, she thinks. Oh.

Then Kate notices that she can't move her legs. They seem to be fused together, impossibly heavy to lift. She lowers her head. Looking down along the hallway floor, she sees there are coils of rope wound tightly around her thighs. She recognizes the rope as one of Jake's at-home fitness purchases. On weekends, he loops it behind the back garden gatepost and slams the rope up and down from a squatting position to burn belly fat. Now, the rope is still, the woven weight of it heavy against her legs. Kate follows the rope with her gaze across the hallway floor. In the split second before she sees, she understands that it will be Marisa holding the end.

"Hello there."

Marisa is sitting on a kitchen chair, erect and poised in the half gloom, the rope twisted several times around her hand and wrist. Her blonde hair is loose around her shoulders. She is wearing a gray cardigan and a grubby T-shirt and no bra. Her pregnant belly sticks out. Her legs are spread apart. There is a strange nonchalance to her stance. It reminds Kate of a portrait of the Virgin and Child she had seen on Jake's laptop.

"How long have you and Jake been sleeping together?"

Marisa asks the question calmly but there is a flush on her cheeks. Kate is so surprised by the question, so utterly taken aback by the surreal weirdness of the situation, that it takes a moment to register what is being asked. For a second, she forgets about being scared.

"What?"

"You heard me."

Kate laughs. She tries to haul herself upright once again, and this time, she manages it. She bends both her arms to the deadweight of her legs, half pushing, half carrying, until they lie at an approximate ninety-degree angle to the rest of her. She sits with her back slumped against the wall, exhausted by the effort. Sweat drips from the end of her nose. She wipes it away with the back of her hand and when she draws it away, it is smeared with blood.

"What . . . have you . . . done to me?" Kate asks.

Marisa raises an eyebrow. "Oh, Kate, Kate, Kate. Whatever I've done to you pales in comparison to what you've done to me."

"I don't know what you mean." Kate starts to cry. She hates herself for it. "Why am I bleeding?"

"Don't worry. You'll live. It's just a minor blow to the head."

She has never seen Marisa like this—cold and distant. Even her language has acquired a medical gloss. Usually Marisa is so chaotic and rumpled and earth motherly. Kate has always believed her to be a bit hopeless. Strange, yes. Lately, her behavior has been erratic and worrying. But this—*this*—is beyond anything she had imagined.

She looks directly at Marisa and then down onto her lap, where Marisa appears to be holding something in her hands. The hallway is still gloomy, but light is filtering out from an open door farther down the corridor. The light reflects weakly from a tiny glimmer between Marisa's hands and Kate realizes it's a knife. She's holding a knife.

Panic scrabbles in her chest. She swivels her head, trying to make out an escape route, but there is none. No windows. No way of moving with her legs tied. A warmth seeps into her trousers and she realizes she has wet herself. She is still crying, sobbing now, her throat raw. She starts to scream, hoping someone will hear. But she knows the walls in this house are thick. They have never heard any noises from their neighbors.

The screaming seems to unsettle Marisa.

"Shush, Kate, shush."

But Kate carries on because the noise of it reassures her she is still alive. That there is still hope. She screams. No words, just sounds, and the more she does it, the more she realizes Marisa becomes agitated.

"Kate, please stop. Shush, shush, shush now. You're ok. You're fine. It's ok. I'm not going to hurt you. I promise."

Marisa shifts forward in her chair, placing the knife carefully onto the floor. Kate registers that it's a knife from the wooden block in the kitchen, one of the ones that needs sharpening. She had used it the other day to slice into a tomato and the knife was so blunt it had been difficult to dent the skin. This calms her. Marisa can't hurt her with this knife. It is for show, nothing more.

"I just want to talk," Marisa says. Her voice is different now, less flat and more fevered. "I feel like I'm going mad and I just want to talk."

You are, Kate wants to say. You are going mad. These are not the actions of a sane person. For months, she's been worried about Marisa, about the way she barely sleeps or eats, about the way she slinks around the house as if she's stalking Kate. There had been that time, a few weeks ago, that she'd found Marisa following her in the tube station at Oxford Circus. She had been spooked enough to tell Jake about it.

"It's like she's obsessed with you," he had said, stroking her hair out of her eyes. "A girl crush or something."

But she had known, even then, it wasn't a harmless crush. It was something darker. It was as if Marisa actually wanted to *be* Kate, to inhabit her form, to stitch together clothes made of her skin.

"It can't be good for the baby, all this," she had said to Jake. "I'm really worried about her. And we both know it's more important than just her. The baby's my main concern."

They had plans, the two of them, of what would happen when the baby arrived. What they would do. How happy they would be once Marisa had left their lives.

"I know," he had said. "I'll talk to her." And Kate had trusted him to do so. She always had.

XIII.

Then

They had met six years ago. He always joked that she could never remember specifics. It was Jake who recalled anniversaries and Valentine's Days with small gifts and cards referring to long-held private jokes, but she knows they met six years ago because it happened at her thirtieth birthday party. She had, at the time, been working on the publicity for a low-budget independent film directed by one of her friends—it was a favor, really, she wasn't making any money on it, but she believed in the movie, which was interestingly shot and told an important story, about a twelve-year-old girl who was taken into foster care and sexually abused by one of the counselors. Kate had persuaded a couple of newspaper critics to come to a screening, and they had loved it and given five-star reviews that made them seem edgy and helped the film expand its distribution to more than a handful of cinemas. Kate's friend Ajesh, was now being courted by the bigger studio heads, one of whom had shown interest in developing a script about a teenager who discovers she has been born with no sense of morality. The working title was *Badolescent*.

Ajesh came to her thirtieth birthday, which was held in the upstairs room of a Wandsworth pub within walking distance of her flat, and he brought with him a couple of men Kate had never met. This was typical Ajesh. He hadn't asked if he could come with anyone but he was so likeable that you could never begrudge it. It was how he persuaded people to do things for him.

"Katie!" he bellowed from the other side of the room. Ajesh was also the only person allowed to call her Katie. She was drunk on champagne, wearing a tight blue satin dress bought for the occasion from Topshop, and heels that were higher than usual because it was her party and she was allowed to dress like a slut. She beamed at Ajesh, handsome in a corduroy jacket and his familiar tortoiseshell-framed spectacles, and made her way over to him.

"Happy birthday, darling," he said, hugging her. "Fuck me. You look fiiiiit."

They had slept together once, back in university. It had been good but not good enough to pursue, and it seemed not to have damaged the closeness of their friendship, although occasionally she still thought of him, and the thought of him turned her on sometimes, which she had never told him. He smelled of tobacco and Red Bull.

"Thanks," she said, standing back to do a little curtsey and losing her balance. She was drunker than she had realized. He put his arm around her waist to steady her.

"Meet my mates." Ajesh ushered the two men forward. They were both in suits.

"You're both in suits," Kate said stupidly.

"That's because they're very important, and—unlike us—proper grown-ups with proper jobs, isn't it, fellas?"

The taller suited man bent forward and gave her a bright-yellow box containing a brand of expensive champagne.

"I hope you don't mind us gate-crashing," he said. He had a nice face and his smile reached the corners of his eyes, which wrinkled in a satisfying way.

"Thank you. This is much better than the stuff I normally drink."

"I told you, Katie. They're classy as fuck."

"So how do *you* know them, then?"

Ajesh still had his arm around her waist and was stroking her hip with his hand. She was enjoying it, knowing that she looked good, that this was her night.

"Well, Jake and Steve"—here, the shorter suited man winked at her—"are financing my next film."

"Not all of it," Jake said, still smiling. "Just enough of it to get invited to a beautiful woman's thirtieth birthday party."

She raised her eyebrows. She felt herself loosen, as if all her muscles were relaxing under the steady weight of Jake's gaze. Carefully, in case the moment broke, she took Ajesh's hand in hers and removed it from her hip. She took a single step forward, moving toward Jake. She needed, she realized, to be close to him. His suit, which she had previously thought was black, turned out to be a dark navy. He wasn't wearing a tie—she would discover later that he had taken it off and folded it into his jacket pocket. The top two buttons of his shirt were undone, revealing a triangle of skin she wanted immediately to lick. She wanted to reach up on her tiptoes, lean into the big, safe bulk of his body, and press her lips against every inch of him. She had never felt such a conspicuous physical urge and in that single quick moment, Kate realized that all of the sex she had had up to that point, all of the flirtations and relationships and kisses, had been a superficial precursor to this. She had been doing it wrong all this time. She had been playing in the sandpit, when there was a wild expanse of beach to explore.

The odd thing was, they didn't even talk that much. It was as if there had been a tacit agreement as soon as Jake walked through the pub door and into her party that this was simply how things would be. It was inevitable.

She couldn't remember much after that initial burst of excitement. The rest of the evening came to her in flashes. The two of them dancing to "Mr. Brightside," jumping up and down, sweaty and grinning, Jake's shirt half untucked from his trousers, the suit jacket long ago abandoned. Drinking the champagne he had brought from the neck of the bottle, Jake tipping the bottom up so that she could get the final dregs, his eyes meeting hers over the yellow-labeled glass. She made a speech and welled up when she saw all her friends in front of her, but really, she had just wanted to impress Jake as he stood at the very back of the room, tall enough to see over everyone else's heads. Ajesh handing her a tiny plastic packet of powder as she licked the tip of her finger and dunked it in. The lights and the music and the feeling of utter rightness. And then, when everyone was high or drunk or both, the sensation of Jake grabbing her hand and pulling her out into the corridor, pushing her against the wall, and holding the back of her head in his large palm as he kissed her, his tongue deep, pressing the weight of his body into hers.

The kiss was long and when he pulled back, he cupped her face with his hands, running the tips of his thumbs across the soft skin underneath her eyes.

"There you are," he said. "Hello."

He spent a lot of time at her flat. She lived in a one-bed and there wasn't really room for a six-foot-four man to move in permanently. He said he didn't mind, and he left his clothes in a neat pile at the bottom of her wardrobe, never complaining that his shirts would be creased when he lifted them out each morning to get dressed for work. She would watch him put on his trousers, do up his belt, and shrug his arms into his jacket before looping his tie into a perfect Windsor knot, and she would be amazed at how adult he seemed.

There were only three years between them, but Kate's work did not require her to wear formal clothes or act like a grown-up. Quite the opposite, in fact. In film, it was a positive asset to seem as though you were perpetually in your early twenties. Her offices were in the heart of Soho, and most nights of the week, she would still go out for drinks with her colleagues. Once or twice a week, the drinks would turn into all-nighters, and a ragtag group of them would end up in the Groucho in the early hours, eyes glittering, noses twitching as they piled into a single toilet cubicle and shared out lines of coke despite the sign hanging on the wall that said THIS CLUB OPERATES A STRICT NO-DRUGS POLICY.

Afterward, they would stagger through the streets arm in arm. They'd wait for the night bus as street cleaners started clearing the pavements, and they would go home, get a couple of hours' sleep, and then go back into work, wearing dark glasses and leopard print and eyeliner, still out of it from the night before. Speckles of last night's glitter on their faces, sticking like burrs to the hem of a skirt.

They were inviolable. They were having fun—so much conscious, declarative, necessary *fun* that it seemed the only way to live. They pitied the men in suits, the "fat cats," the chief executives, the wage slaves, the bankers, and the management consultants and defined themselves in opposition to them. Never mind that they got paid less, that they had no pensions, that their bosses used them as glorified student interns. It was the principle of the thing that counted, whatever that principle was. The personal was political, they would say to each other, nodding fervently but not really sure what it meant. They were anarchists, rewriting the rules of work, of life, of the world their parents had inherited. Except they were also just producing movies and marketing the make-believe and going to free private screenings with miniature bottles of mineral water and triangular sandwiches from Pret on plastic trays where they would ask journalists to sign nondisclosure agreements and email them afterward to ask them their thoughts. But the moral worth of their work or the inherent contradictions in their position never seemed questionable as long as they voted Labour and did their recycling.

Part of Kate's role when she had first joined the company was to help organize the junkets where a hotel suite would be booked for two days and the actors, accompanied by their entourage of assistants and trainers and scented-candle lighters, would sit in an overstuffed armchair, enveloped in a mist of unlikely glamour, as interviewers from newspapers and magazines and radio and television would come and ask the same questions over and over again.

"What was it like to work with so-and-so?"

"How did you prepare for the role?"

"Why did you and [insert name of celebrity spouse here] break up?"

And, exclusively to the women with children, "How do you manage to juggle it all?"

And, exclusively to the women without children, "Do you want a family?"

At first, she had been swept up in it. But after a few years, she hardened. She lost her love for mainstream film and forgot about her previous beliefs in the power of art to change people and she became cynical about the publicity stunts and the gross expense of the junket hotel suites and the endless lobbying at film festivals and the stupid requests from Hollywood A-listers to find a macrobiotic chef at 3 a.m. in Soho. Which was why, when Ajesh had asked her to help with *Badolescent*, she'd leapt at the chance. She had enjoyed caring about something, working late into the night in the front room on the foldaway table that doubled as a desk. She had stopped going out as much with her colleagues and found that she didn't miss it. She was older now and lacked the energy, and the coke was getting tiring and she was ready for something to shift, as if she were playing a computer game and waiting for the next level to unlock. When Jake had walked into her thirtieth birthday party, she knew. She knew that this was the thing she had been waiting for. It wasn't just him. It was everything he represented. Adulthood. Togetherness. Settling down. Opting out.

He was so sincere, and this is what she liked. He didn't operate in her world, didn't understand it. He was not swayed by the glitz or impressed by the names. He liked numbers and spreadsheets and mathematical sums that made sense. But he also liked her a lot—this much was obvious. After three months, he asked her to move in with him. Her flat was only rented, but Jake, being sensible, had bought his before the property market boom. It was a split-level in a mansion block in Battersea near the park. The old Kate would have turned her nose up at it, believing it to be far too posh an establishment: a part of South West London populated by young men who seemed to exist for the express purpose of one day managing their family estate. But thirty-year-old Kate decided not to be as judgmental as twenty-five-year-old Kate would have been. Besides, Jake's salary dwarfed hers and he was offering to pay most of the mortgage, asking for only a nominal contribution from her.

The flat itself was nicer than she had imagined: low ceilings but big windows; two bedrooms and one en suite bathroom; the floors strewn with Moroccan rugs; a kitchen with floating white shelves filled with patterned crockery that Jake's mother had given him. The main bathroom had a huge shower, which Jake called a "wet room."

"It's a shower, Jake," Kate insisted when she moved in.

"It's a wet room," he said, grabbing her lightly by the shoulders and pressing his thumbs into her back, massaging the knots loose. "That's what the estate agent called it."

She laughed. "Oh, well, in *that* case . . . I mean, estate agents always tell the truth, so . . ."

He bent his head down and kissed her and she pressed herself against him, feeling the hard warmth of him and the dependable beat of his heart.

"I love you," she said, and she had never meant it so much.

The sex was good. It wasn't, if she were going to be brutally honest, the best sex she had ever had, but contextually, it worked. The context being that this was a good man who loved her. When she'd had amazing sex in the past, it had always been with unreliable narcissists who prided themselves on their performance and showed little interest in emotional attachment. She had mistaken the bubbles of anxiety in her stomach for a simmering romantic passion, wrongly believing that love felt unsettled, like a half-packed suitcase awaiting a trip that never comes.

Jake, by contrast, was home. He felt safe. He was solicitous in the bedroom, always asking what she wanted, always concerned in case he was hurting her or making her uncomfortable or in some way not pleasing her, whereas really what Kate wanted was to be dominated and fucked, cleanly and without any conversation. She had too much conversation in her normal life. She was so sick of negotiation, so sick of people not knowing what they needed. But she felt this was shameful of her, and her feminist self was appalled by her secret desires. So the normality of sex with Jake turned into its own kind of relief.

The biggest turn-on about Jake was that he wanted her so much and this made her feel sensual and desired. The sex got better the more time they spent together. Jake began to learn how her body responded to his touch and Kate tried to switch off her thoughts until she existed as much as she could as a pure physical entity, and in this way, it worked. For a while, at least.

XIV.

Looking back later, after their life imploded, Kate would try to pinpoint the exact moment when it had started to go awry. She eventually came to the conclusion that it was when she had met Jake's mother. That was the first time there had been any tension between them, and it had stayed there, this discomfort, like a speck on the kitchen floor from a long-ago broken glass: unnoticeable until you stepped on it with your bare morning feet and the sharpness of it lodged under your skin.

They had been together for six months when Annabelle issued her invitation. Jake's mother called him every Sunday night at 5 p.m. for "a catch-up." Kate could hear the strident tinkle of her voice through the phone when he chatted to her on the sofa. Jake would sound different when he talked to her. Needier, somehow.

Kate found it odd that a grown man should have such a regimented yet cloying relationship with his mother. On the rare occasion that Jake would forget the 5 p.m. slot, Annabelle would be hurt. Once, Kate and Jake had been to the cinema on Sunday evening and when they emerged into the night, he had turned on his phone to four missed calls and three messages from Annabelle, each one increasingly frantic.

"Fuck," Jake had said. "I better call her. She'll worry otherwise."

"Ok," Kate replied, removing herself from his arm. She wasn't going to interfere but she still wanted him to know it was weird.

Annabelle had been mollified by his call, but he still sent her flowers the next day, which Kate definitely thought was overkill.

"I guess I should be glad that the only other woman in your life is your mother," she joked halfheartedly.

"You're the only one I want to have sex with."

It wasn't quite reassuring enough. He hadn't, she noticed, criticized Annabelle or sought to distance himself from her.

Instead, Jake explained that Annabelle relied on him because he was the only boy, and the eldest. But it seemed odd she didn't turn to her daughters or to her husband. "Oh, Chris isn't much good at that sort of thing," Jake said with a matter-of-factness that suggested he was parroting someone else's long-held view. He called his father by his first name when he wanted to diminish him. "I mean, he's very affable and nice and all that, but Mum's the strong one."

"I thought he was a doctor."

"Retired GP. He was never exactly a highflyer."

"What about your sisters?"

He flinched. "It's tricky. Two of them live abroad and Millie never calls . . ."

"Your mum could still call them."

"She does. But we've always been close."

He had turned back to whatever he was doing, and that was that. He never seemed to sense any subtext or ulterior motive to Kate's questions. It was part of his unconscious charm, she knew, and she couldn't have it both ways.

So his family was a topic best avoided. Besides, Annabelle and Chris lived miles away in Tewkesbury, and as long as Kate didn't have to spend time with them, she supposed she was fine with it.

But then the invitation came, via one of the Sunday-evening phone calls. Jake was sitting on the sofa as usual and Kate had moved to the bedroom to flick through one of the newspaper supplements. She heard him talking.

"Yes, Mum . . . All good, thanks . . . Oh, not too busy this week, actually. The deal went through, so that's good . . . Yes . . . . Mm-hmm . . . Oh. Ok. Yup . . . Well, she's not with me, actually. Let me ask her."

He had walked through the door toward the bed, phone outstretched.

"It's my mum," Jake said. "She wants to talk to you."

Kate had the strangest feeling she was about to be told off, as if Annabelle were going to inform her in no uncertain terms that she was not good enough for her much-adored son. She didn't take the phone but put up the hood of her sweatshirt, burrowing her head deeper inside the soft cotton like a child. She didn't know why she did it. Jake shook the phone at her, mouthing, *Take it!*

She reached out and pressed the phone to her ear. "Hello?"

"Hi. Kate?" The voice was clear, imperious.

"Yes."

"It's Annabelle here, Jake's mother."

"Yes. I know."

Annabelle laughed sharply and Kate realized she had been rude.

"How are you?" Kate said, her voice assuming a faux cheeriness. "It's lovely to talk to you!"

"It's nice to talk to you, too, Kate, and to put a voice to the name I've been hearing so much about. I suppose you and Jake have been"—there was a slight but meaningful pause—"*courting* for, what, three months or so now?"

"Actually it's six, but . . ."

"Six! Goodness!"

Kate looked at Jake, who was leaning against the door frame, arms crossed, a light frown across his forehead. She wondered if he had deliberately shortened the length of their relationship so as not to make his mother feel threatened.

"And you're spending so much time together," Annabelle continued. "You always seem to be at his flat when I call."

"Well, I . . ." So Jake hadn't told his mother that they were living together. "Yes," she concluded weakly.

"Listen, I've got to dash as there's a paella on the stove, but I was just saying to Jakey that we'd love to have you guys down for lunch one weekend. Whatever suits you. I know how busy you young people are, so you choose a suitable date and we'll work around you. Except the twentieth. I can't do the twentieth because of the Choral Society. And actually, not the thirteenth either, but any other date would be *wonderful*."

"Thank you," Kate said, even though this was her least favorite kind of invitation. There was no way of coming up with an excuse unless someone offered a specific date. "That would be lovely."

"Great. Looking forward to it."

The silence stretched out between them for slightly too long. Kate looked at her feet at the end of the bed. She was wearing knitted brown socks. Beyond them, she could make out the tops of the trees in the park and a thin trail of reddish-pink cloud.

"Could you pass me back to my darling boy?"

"Oh yes, of course, sorry."

She handed the phone over. Jake raised his eyebrows, but she turned away from him and pretended to read her magazine. Kate hated having to meet the parents. It was why she had never suggested a similar thing to Jake. Her own parents were perfectly nice, quiet, Tory-voting, semi-detached-house kind of people, but they were largely irrelevant to who she was now. They didn't understand her and she didn't understand them and both parties were respectful of this. She mistrusted adults who could not invent themselves away from their family units. She didn't see why she had to obey the rules of convention by traipsing to the countryside and paying her dues to posh Annabelle and mousey Chris simply because she chose to pursue a relationship with their son.

The bed dipped as Jake finished the phone call and came to lie next to her. She felt his body slot into hers, his knees bending into the backs of hers. He kissed her neck.

"Is that ok?" he asked. "I know it's the kind of thing you loathe but I really appreciate it."

Her shoulders softened.

"Mum will love you. I just know it."

She turned to him and kissed his mouth. "I'll do it for you."

And she was as good as her word.

Three weeks later, they drove to Tewkesbury. The car had been their first serious joint purchase, with Jake scanning the AutoTrader website for days before he found a suitable option: a silver Volkswagen Polo with a reasonable number of miles on the clock being sold for £2,000 because of a scratch on the front, which neither of them cared about. The description had alerted them to the fact that the car had only ever been handled by "women drivers," which Kate found hilarious.

"Can we email them and ask what *kind* of women they are?" she said, scratching the back of Jake's head in the way he liked.

"What sort of woman would you refuse to buy a car from?" he asked, smiling.

"A fallen one. A loose one. One who wears too much Lycra and smokes fags out of the passenger side of her best friend's ride."

Jake laughed, without getting the reference to TLC's "No Scrubs." He never really listened to music, preferring sports commentary and talk radio, but the one thing they agreed on was Oasis.

"We shall examine the women in question," Jake said, pulling her over his lap so that she was sitting astride him. "And if we find them wanting, we shall refuse to buy their car."

They kissed, and when she pulled back and looked at his handsome, open face, Kate thought to herself that she had never liked anyone this much. She loved him, of course, but often being in love with someone did not translate into liking them.

When they turned up to a low-rise 1950s apartment block in Lambeth to buy the car, there were no women in sight. It was a man who took their money and handed them over the keys.

"And that, my friend, is how the patriarchy works," Kate had said, sitting in the passenger seat as Jake reversed out of the parking space.

"Is it ok for me not to care about the patriarchy for just one day if it's got us a good deal on a car?" Jake asked, letting the steering wheel spin back on itself.

"I'm not sure it is, but I won't report you this time."

She had traced her fingertips along the line of freckles on his bare forearm, and later, they'd had sex and she imagined herself sprawled across the car bonnet, feeling the heat from the engine against the small of her back as she came.

She thought of this again on the drive to meet Jake's parents. They had never actually had sex in the car. It would have been too small and uncomfortable, she knows, but still she liked the idea. She would be embarrassed to suggest it to Jake in case he laughed at her and thought her perverted. His attitude to sex was similar to his outlook on life, which was the fewer unnecessary complications, the better.

She turned to look at Jake in profile in the driving seat—he always drove because he was better at it. His face had caught the sun from yesterday's picnic in Battersea Park when they had taken a blanket, a bottle of rosé, a baguette, and a tub of supermarket hummus and got tipsy through the warmth of the afternoon.

Kate switched on the radio. A pop star's voice, heavy on the reverb, snaked into the car. Although she didn't feel nervous, she had taken great care with her clothes. It's not that she needed to impress

Annabelle, but rather that she wanted to feel as confident as she could, and for this reason, she had worn her favorite cropped jeans, dressed up with a pair of block heels, and a silk mustard-colored shirt, unbuttoned to reveal a chunky gold necklace. She used the hair dryer this morning, so her hair was smoother than usual, the familiar choppiness now tamed into a sleeker bob. Red lipstick, dark mascara, a hint of blush on the apple of each cheek, and that was it. She knew Jake liked red lipstick. He said it made her look Parisian and every time he said it, she laughed at the blinding obviousness of male desire.

It took them three hours to get there, through the Chiltern Hills and the endless roundabouts of Swindon and then into the mottled buttery houses of the Cotswolds before finally Jake indicated and they turned off into a short driveway, emerging into the courtyard of an imposing redbrick house. When Jake talked about his childhood home, he referred to it as a farmhouse, but looking at it, Kate realized it wasn't a real farmhouse as much as a posh person's version of what they believed a farmhouse to be. She could count four chimneys on the roof and there were stone carvings around each of the windows. The front door had two perfectly pruned miniature trees on either side of the entrance, the leafy branches obediently cut into glossy green spheres. The gravel on the driveway looked so clean it seemed staged. The house was surrounded by fields and woodland and Kate emerged from the car to the sound of birdsong.

"You are joking," she said.

"What?" he said, getting out of the car and extending his hand to her.

"This is beautiful."

He blushed. "Thank you."

She hadn't meant it warmly. "Beautiful" was the wrong word, she realized. It was intimidating and she hated herself for being intimidated.

The door opened before they had pressed the ornate Victorian bell button.

"Darling!"

Annabelle swept out and hugged Jake close, burrowing her head into his neck. The clinch lasted for several seconds before she let him go.

"And this must be Kate."

Annabelle stepped forward, taking both Kate's hands in hers.

"Let me look at you," Annabelle said, and she allowed her gaze to travel over Kate's body. "You're very *thin*, aren't you?"

Jake laughed. "Mum, stop! You're so obsessed with weight."

"Oh, I'm only joshing. It's a compliment for us girls, isn't it, dear?"

She forced Kate into a bony hug. Kate had to close her eyes to prevent herself from rolling them.

"It's so lovely to see you," Annabelle said. "Come in, come in."

The hug ended abruptly and Annabelle walked into the house.

"Lovely to meet you too," Kate replied to her receding back.

In the dim half-light of the hallway, she was able to look at Annabelle properly for the first time. She was a tall woman, upright and elegant. Her body was strong rather than willowy. She had large hands, with long fingers encircled by thin gold rings. She was deeply tanned and on the right side of her face, two livery splotches had formed a pale-brown archipelago. Her eyes were the clearest blue, like shallow seawater you can see sand through. She was wearing a white floaty linen cardigan over a sage-green camisole, white linen trousers, and pale-purple Moroccan slippers, the leather folded down at the back so that her ankles were exposed.

"Hi, Dad," Jake said, and Kate noticed a slight figure emerging from a doorway. Chris shook his son's hand and then came across and kissed Kate lightly on both cheeks. He had kind eyes and wore a burgundy sweater with elbow patches.

"Nice of you both to make the trek," he said, his voice immediately getting lost in the echoing gloom of the house. He beckoned them into the sitting room, which was light and floral, the plump sofas upholstered in a lily-of-the-valley pattern. "Now: drinks."

Chris pottered off to the drinks cabinet beneath the wall of bookshelves. Kate spotted a copy of *Civilisation* by Kenneth Clark and several silver-framed photographs of mop-haired children. Jake sat down and she realized she was still holding the bunch of tulips she had brought from the local Battersea florist in her hand. The stems had pressed against the brown paper ends and made them soggy.

"Oh, I meant to say, Annabelle. These are for you."

Annabelle looked at her oddly. She reached across in her billowing linen and took the flowers, holding them out slightly as if they might stain her. She smiled, but the smile didn't quite reach her eyes.

"Kate, thank you," she purred. "I was going to tell you we don't stand on ceremony round here and you must call me Annabelle, but I'm so glad you felt comfortable enough to do it straightaway." She lowered her head to breathe in the scent of the flowers. "You are clever to find these. I don't normally bother with cut flowers—we've got so many beauties in the garden, you know. Oh!" She gave a short burst of laughter. "Of course you don't know. You've never been here before, have you? Forgive me, darling, I lose track of all of Jakey's friends." The way she said "friends" implied quotation marks. "I'm such an idiot. We'll have to show you around later, won't we, Jakey? You can see the little cottage we've just done up in one of the outbuildings. Yes. Lovely." She lifted the bunch of tulips, wilting now under the pressure of her gaze. "But these are just . . . *gorgeous*. Now I must try and remember where the vases are."

She slid out of the room, giving Jake's shoulder a squeeze as she went and kissing the top of his head like he was a toddler. Kate caught Jake's eye. He winked at her. She inhaled slowly. Just a couple more hours and then they could get out of here.

"Here you go." Chris pressed a giant tumbler of gin and tonic into her hand. She took a large sip just as Annabelle reentered the room with a glass of white wine. She ushered Kate into an upright armchair and then launched into an impromptu toast. Kate swallowed her gin as quietly as she could.

“I just wanted to say what a *treat* it is to have Jakey home and to meet the ever-so-stylish Kate.”

“Hear, hear,” Chris said, raising an even bigger glass of gin toward the center of the room and smiling with a vagueness that suggested this drink had not been his first of the day.

Annabelle sat on the sofa next to Jake, placing her free hand proprietorially on his knee. Kate, on the other side of the room, watched as Chris bent to sit on a battered leather stool by the fireplace. He was interrupted by Annabelle saying, “Nuts, darling!”

“Oh yes, my mistake,” Chris said, straightening up from his half squat, bones creaking as he did so. He walked back to the drinks cabinet, took out a jumbo-sized packet of peanuts, and poured a measly handful into a tiny crystal bowl, which he brought back with great ceremony and placed on a low coffee table filled with back copies of *House & Garden*. The table was too far away for Kate to reach, so she drank her gin and her head became light. Chris had made it exceptionally strong.

“So,” Annabelle said, leaning back on the sofa, her legs crossed at a graceful angle. Kate had read somewhere that high-society women crossed their legs in this way so as not to leave red patches on their skin. “How did you two meet?”

“I gate-crashed Kate’s thirtieth birthday party,” Jake said, looking over the room at Kate and grinning at her.

“Goodness,” Annabelle said. “How rude!”

“It was fine, Annabelle. He came bearing champagne, so I let him in.”

She decided she was going to use Jake’s mother’s name as much as possible in conversation.

Chris tittered. “Sensible,” he said.

Annabelle did not laugh but gazed levelly at Kate, a slight smile shadowing her mouth. She said nothing more, and there was power in her silence. Kate felt the back of her neck prickle. She drank more gin and didn’t try to move the conversation on as she might usually have done. She sensed Annabelle was testing her, and Kate refused to give in. The silence stretched outward until Jake reached forward for the nuts and walked around to offer her some.

"You can't get at them from over there," he said, and Kate was happy he'd noticed.

They had lunch in the kitchen ("No point in the dining room when it's just the four of us, don't you agree?" Annabelle said) at a long pine table laid with a lavender-colored tablecloth that Kate was told had been brought back from one of their many trips to Provence. The crockery was even more floral than the sitting room had been, and the granary baguette was served already sliced in a bowl with BOWL written around its rim. The knives and forks had faded ivory handles, nicotine yellow in color.

Annabelle made a great show of clipping up her long blonde-gray hair and putting an apron on before removing a steaming dish of chicken thighs and preserved lemons from the AGA. It was served with mashed potatoes that still had a few lumps in it and overboiled broccoli.

"Red or white?" Chris asked, proffering bottles of each. "The red's fairly good plonk. The white's a crisp little Sancerre . . ."

"Or rosé. I know some people like rosé," Annabelle added, as if it were an odd and slightly distasteful foible.

"Red, please," Kate said and then watched as everyone else had a glass of white. The conversation was dominated by Annabelle asking Jake interminable questions about his work and how so-and-so colleague was doing and what his plans were for the future and how was the flat and had he bought that bookshelf he liked and so on and so forth, all of it designed, Kate felt, to show how well she knew her son and how intimately involved she was in every aspect of his life and how there was no room for anyone else.

Jake, who always thought the best of people, who couldn't spot an ulterior motive even if it ran straight for him and wrestled him to the ground, chatted away easily and then helped himself to seconds while Annabelle commended his appetite.

"Will you have some more, Kate?" she asked, pushing the chicken dish toward her. "Please." She gestured with her hands. "You could do with some feeding up."

"I'm fine, thank you, Annabelle. It was delicious, though."

Annabelle drew herself up, shoulders pushed back, and slid the dish back along the table. "Such a shame to have leftovers. I'll give you some to take back with you, Jakey."

"Mmm, yes, please. Thanks, Mum."

Under the table, Kate clenched a fist and dug her nails into her palm.

"More wine?" Chris asked, and he started to pour even before she'd said yes. Kate quickly understood that her relationship with Jake's mother would be made palatable by alcohol and wondered how long it had taken Chris to reach the same conclusion.

They had coffee in the drawing room accompanied by a musty box of chocolates, presumably fished out from the back of a cupboard where they kept household presents they didn't much care for. Kate picked up a praline truffle to be polite but noticed it had a coating of white sediment around the outside, suggesting it was several months out of date. She swallowed quickly.

Annabelle continued her conversational assault, while Chris, who had by now graduated from wine to whisky, nodded his head at various junctures to show he was listening. Annabelle outlined their plans for summer (Provence, then maybe "a jaunt" to Seville, although it was very hot at that time of year) and gave a comprehensive rundown of what Jake's sisters were up to (Millie had just been promoted, Julia was enjoying Hong Kong more than she'd expected, and Toad was heading up her university department in Dublin).

"Why's she called Toad?" Kate asked.

Annabelle, apparently taken aback to be interrupted in full flow, gave a little cough. "Well, it's her family nickname and we've never called her anything else, have we, Jakey?"

"To be fair, I do tend to call her Olivia now."

"Whatever for?"

"It just sounds odd if you call your sister after an amphibian in polite company."

Kate laughed.

"It's affectionate!" Annabelle protested. "Anyway, Kate, in answer to your question, it's because as a baby she used to make the strangest sound when she burped. More of a *ribbit*, really, and Julia was still so young she couldn't say the name Olivia, so 'Toad' seemed easier and quite sweet . . . You know how these things are."

Annabelle waved her hand, showing that what she meant by "these things" could encompass all or none of the room's contents.

Kate didn't actually know how these things were at all. She had never met a family willing to call their adult daughter Toad. It was a peculiar privilege of the posh to be able to give their progeny the most unflattering nicknames and for it not to affect their life chances. Kate had never had a nickname and found them infantilizing. She even shuddered when Jake called her "babe."

The after-lunch chat dragged out for two more hours during which Annabelle asked Kate precisely one question about her job, then talked over the answer. Eventually Jake found a gap in the conversation to say, "We'd best be going. It's getting dark," and he walked over to Kate, took her hand, and when she stood, he kissed her briefly on the lips right there, in front of his parents. "Thank you," he whispered into her ear.

He didn't let go of her hand as he led her into the hallway. Annabelle was fussing over Jake and handing him an old Waitrose carrier bag filled with leftovers boxed up in Tupperware while Chris smiled benignly in the doorway. He was probably seeing double by now, Kate thought as she smiled back at him.

"Darling," Annabelle said, as she pressed Jake to her in a lingering hug. "It was so wonderful to see you." Her voice started to break. "I miss you, you know. You must come home more often. I don't like thinking of you up there in London all on your own."

"I'm not on my own," Jake said, pulling away. "I have Kate."

"Of course you do, but it's not quite . . ." Annabelle stopped herself. She dutifully gathered Kate up in an embrace. Kate could feel the locket of Annabelle's necklace jut into her collarbone. She barely came up to Annabelle's shoulders.

"It's been lovely to meet you, Kate," she said and sounded more sincere than she had for the entire day up to that point.

"Thank you. It's been really . . . nice to meet you, too, Annabelle."

"Take care of my boy, won't you?"

"Oh, I will. You can absolutely trust me on that."

They got into the car and waved out of the windows all the way back along the driveway. Jake indicated and turned left into the road.

"Thank you. You were amazing," he said. "I've never seen my mother be so . . ."

Vicious, Kate thought. Cold. Patronizing. Possessive.

". . . impressed."

She looked at him to discern a smile on his face, or a twist of the mouth indicative of held-back laughter or some discreet sign that he wasn't being serious. There was none. "What?"

"I knew she'd adore you."

"Wait, are you saying . . . you think . . . your mother acted in that way because she *likes* me?"

Jake turned to her briefly, surprised.

"Yes. She definitely likes you."

Kate was about to make a joke, something to puncture the absurdity of their conversation that would make Jake admit he'd only been winding her up, and yes, wasn't his mother awful, and no, they never had to do that again. But she stopped herself. The set of Jake's profile warned her against it. He was simply stating the facts as he believed them.

"Oh," Kate said finally. "I'm glad. I wasn't sure that she did, to be honest." She chose her words with unfamiliar caution, trying to feel her way through the fog.

"I think she can sense I'm serious about you and she's not used to it."

"No?" Kate asked, placing her hand on his knee where a few hours ago, she had seen his mother place hers. "What about all those many *friends* you've brought home and shown around the garden?"

He winced. "I don't know what she's talking about. I've only ever brought a couple of girls home and they pale in comparison to you."

"Do they?"

He tilted his head to look at her. "They do."

He turned his eyes back to the road, and they drove for some minutes in companionable silence. She leaned forward to turn the radio on, but just before she pressed the button, Jake spoke.

"I love you and I want to spend the rest of my life with you," he said.

She stared at him and her heart thudded with hope.

"I know you don't want to get married," he added hurriedly. It was true. Kate had told Jake from the outset that she did not want to be trapped in a patriarchal tradition, given her lack of religious faith and her feminism. He had laughed at her seriousness.

"Fine with me," he'd said. "As luck would have it, I've never had ambitions to be a religiously zealous patriarch. It'd look rubbish on my CV."

Now, in the car, he said, "I want to have a family with you. Our very own."

She leaned her head against his arm, feeling the smoothness of his shirt against her skin. "I want that too."

Kate marveled at the truth of it: she wanted to have Jake's children. It was a new sensation, and yet it felt as if it had been in her bones for a lifetime. How she felt about Annabelle or how Annabelle felt about her was irrelevant. She and Jake were the family unit now.

Back then, it truly seemed as simple as that.

XV.

They planned it all meticulously. Kate would wait until the end of the year to come off birth control. By then, a couple of big movies would have come out and work would be less busy. They would start looking for a bigger house once Kate got pregnant.

They went for walks through the park at weekends and talked about names they liked (Matilda for a girl, Oscar for a boy) and how they would be different parents from their own mothers and fathers and what they thought about private schools—Kate was vehemently against them, and Jake believed that if they had enough money, they should obviously try and give their children the best education they could, but they agreed to disagree for the time being.

It felt so good having this joint project, something that they could always revert to discussing when conversation ran dry, a picture they could paint together, adding in details in the foreground here and there, choosing a different color for this patch of sky and a thinner brush for the tiny figure that awaited them. It reassured Kate to be in a relationship with a man who was unafraid of long-term commitment, who believed in partnership and sharing and communication. He had never once let her down, not even when his mother tried her hardest to separate them.

After that strained Sunday lunch, Annabelle had subjected Jake to a barrage of phone calls, asking if he was sure about Kate, and how much he truly knew about her, and weren't they moving a bit too quickly, and she was only saying this because she loved him, he understood that, didn't he, and so on and so forth until Jake, despite his tendency to always give his mother the benefit of the doubt, was forced to start ignoring her number when it flashed up. So then Annabelle began calling Kate, leaving voicemails inviting her for coffee the next time she was in town: "I'm popping up to Peter Jones and I'd love to see you. Just us girls."

Kate replied with noncommittal texts and gradually the communication eased off.

"She just doesn't like the thought that she's losing me," Jake said one evening as they sat on the ledge of the open kitchen window, drinking Aperol Spritz and looking out over the London rooftops.

"Mmm." Kate thought this was an inappropriate way for a mother to feel but she didn't say anything.

A pigeon was pecking at a roof tile a few feet away. She watched as it realized there was no food there, then puffed out its chest as if embarrassed and stalked off.

"She'll love you—just you wait. There's part of her that already does. It's just that you're both actually quite . . ."

"Don't say it, Jake."

"What?"

"You were about to say we're both actually quite similar."

He laughed, brushing a hand through his hair, fluffing it up like the pigeon's feathers. "I was."

"Which is (a) not true, and (b), if it were true, it would make you into some kind of creep with a serious Oedipal complex."

"Fair point." He held out his glass to cheers her. "Here's to us."

"To us."

"We don't need anyone else," Jake said, looking straight at her in that way he had.

"We don't."

They cheersed, taking great care to maintain eye contact because everyone knew that otherwise, it was seven years of bad sex and they intended to be doing a lot of it from that point on.

She came off the pill in January, after a boozy fortnight of parties and work lunches and a particularly drunken Christmas Day, with just the two of them in the flat opening bottles of Cabernet in front of the television and eating too much brandy butter. It had been bliss. But back at work, the familiar New Year lethargy seeped in. She decided to do Dry January just as the temperature dropped to below freezing and the nights were drawing in. She reminded herself that she was detoxifying her system for a good reason, but the days felt long and her sleep patterns too short.

When she wasn't pregnant by February, she didn't think much of it. Her hormone levels were rebalancing after a year on the pill, Kate told herself, and January had been exhausting. In March, she reassured herself by searching online for the average amount of time it took a woman of her age to get pregnant and realized she'd been setting her hopes too high. Apparently, you had to give it at least a year.

April came and went. Then May. In June, she felt angry when blood stained her underwear and she had to retrieve the tampons from the bathroom cupboard. When she got her period again in July, she cried. She hadn't realized how much she had wanted to be pregnant until she started trying. But they'd talked about it for so long and had made all their plans, and now she was frustrated that her body was holding everything up. She didn't talk to Jake about it, and he didn't ask.

Instead, she bought ovulation sticks from Boots and dutifully pissed on them every morning to check her HCG levels in order to monitor when she might be releasing an egg. HCG stood for human chorionic gonadotropin, she learned on the internet. The internet also revealed that rubbing the trouser bulge of a Parisian statue, piercing the left side of her nose, and having sex on the Cerne Abbas Giant would all potentially help her to get pregnant. She laughed at the suggestions but remembered them in spite of herself.

In August, they went on holiday to Mykonos and she gave herself a month off. "Just relax" was all anyone ever said when she confided that they were trying for a baby. "You'll go on holiday, get drunk one night, have sex, and you'll be pregnant before you know it. You just need to stop stressing."

But Kate was tense all holiday, and when Jake asked what was wrong, she didn't want to tell him. She felt ashamed of herself for not getting pregnant and believed it to be her fault.

Back home, they fell out of the habit of having sex regularly, and September and October passed in a flurry of opportunities missed. She worked late, but without any passion for what she was doing. In November, Kate was determined that she would initiate sex at all the most fertile moments in her cycle, but it was difficult to do this in a way that seemed natural or sensual because she was in her head so much of the time they were actually making love. Would this be the time they conceived, she would ask herself as Jake fucked her, and would she know, would she feel any differently, would there be some cosmic sign that this was it? And should she stay lying down for half an hour afterward as she had read you were meant to, so that the sperm had time to make their way up your cervix? And should she put her legs up to help them along? Except that would look ridiculous and still she didn't want to let on to Jake that she cared so much. She didn't want him to be as obsessed as she was, and yet at the same time, she worried that he was fixated on a baby and she was letting him down. All of this whirred through her mind when they had sex, and when Jake was on the verge of coming, she sometimes pretended she was too, so that it would be over. After all, what did her own pleasure count when she was failing so conspicuously to do the thing other women did without thinking?

Then it was December again and almost a whole year had passed, and they had agreed to go to Annabelle and Chris's for Christmas and Kate was dreading it, but they packed up the car and made the trip to the farmhouse-that-wasn't-a-farmhouse and when they arrived, Kate was so shattered she made her excuses and went straight to bed. She knew Annabelle would prefer to have her out of the way anyway.

She fell into a deep sleep, waking half an hour later when there was a knock at the door. Jake walked in, with a cup of tea in his hand. He placed the saucer down on the bedside table and came to sit next to her. He stroked the hair out of her eyes and his hand felt cool against her hot forehead.

"It's going to be ok," he said. "I love you, whatever happens."

She believed him. She always had.

Christmas was not as bad as Kate had feared. Annabelle's cooking was as atrocious as ever, but her conversation seemed less aggressive, as though she had run out of fight. She asked Kate a handful of questions about herself this time, including what her favorite book was, and when Kate said *Middlemarch*, Annabelle dissolved into ecstasies of agreement.

"That bit when they're on honeymoon," Annabelle said, cheeks glowing from her after-dinner brandy, "and Dorothea says she thought love was going to be like an ocean, but it turns out to be nothing more than a basin . . . oh, it's *perfect*."

Chris, who was sitting in his usual corner of the drawing room letting the conversation wash over him, was suddenly roused.

"Steady on," he said.

They all laughed and Kate was surprised, not just by Annabelle's literary taste but at the warmth she felt in that moment.

Of course, Annabelle played all her usual tricks too, insisting on placing Jake next to her at every meal, recalling long-ago family anecdotes that excluded Kate in their retelling, and at one point getting out an old photograph album filled with pictures of Jake and his ex-girlfriend.

"Oh, how funny—I'd forgotten we had so many photos of you and Charlotte," Annabelle said. "I only wanted to show you the funniest picture of Toad . . . Now, where is it?" She placed the album on the dinner table, angled so that Kate could see it clearly, and she continued to flick through the pages, stopping occasionally to say, "Charlotte was such a sweet girl, wasn't she?" and "Jakey, you look so young and handsome and happy there!" and "What happened to Charlotte? Are you still in touch with her?"

Jake shook his head. "No idea, Mum."

"Shame. I'd love to see her again."

Underneath the table, Jake squeezed Kate's hand.

But Kate found it funny more than hurtful. Annabelle's jabs were so unsubtle that it would have felt almost churlish to get upset.

When the two of them left for London, laden down once again with Tupperware packages of turkey and an old tub of cream repurposed to contain a dozen devils on horseback, Kate was astonished to find that she had quite enjoyed herself. More than that, she was relaxed.

"That wasn't too bad," she said to Jake on the drive back.

"Told you. Mum thinks you're great." Then he grinned. "She just can't admit it to herself yet."

XVI.

Months passed and still she wasn't pregnant. In April, her period was a few days late and she bought a test from their local pharmacy and sat on the toilet seat, trying not to let herself get excited, trying not to allow herself to believe that this, surely, was their time. She placed the cap back on the test and waited for the lines to appear. The minutes passed, and she stared at the small oval aperture. One line made itself visible, a pale mark like a charcoal stroke on blotting paper. Her breath caught in the top of her throat as she waited for a second one to join it, but it never came and instead the single marking grew darker and darker until its presence seemed to taunt her with the indisputable absence alongside it, like a tree on a sunlit street that doesn't cast a shadow. It looked so wrong, Kate thought. She kept checking the packet the test came in, which had a visual key denoting that one line meant not pregnant, two lines meant pregnant, and she wondered if, in her haste to unwrap it, she had misread the instructions. She hadn't.

She started to cry and was consumed by her own perceived stupidity for believing it would be different. What was the point of hope when it existed only to be extinguished, month after painful month? She threw the test in the bin and didn't tell Jake. The next morning, her period came. She got drunk that night, on tequila mixed with premade margarita mix, the alcohol hitting the back of her throat like a well-landed punch.

When Jake found the pregnancy test in the garbage can, he held her in his arms and stroked her hair, but she felt numb.

Slowly but perceptibly, Kate cloaked her emotions in cynicism. It was a form of self-protection. When another friend announced their pregnancy, uploading blurry twelve-week scans to Facebook, she groaned and cracked a bitter joke with Jake. She crossed the street to avoid women walking with toddlers, their dimpled fists held in bigger, adult hands. She started to complain about babies crying in restaurants and to avoid social gatherings where she knew there would be newborns that Kate would be expected to coo over and interact with. It was all too painful.

It was Jake who suggested they start looking for houses, as a way of taking their mind off it.

"We shouldn't put our lives on hold while we wait to get pregnant," he said. "It's causing way more stress than it needs to be."

"It's pretty desperate if you genuinely think buying a house is going to be *less* stressful than this," she said blankly.

But she agreed, and they spent a few weeks going on viewings, assessing the relative size of bathrooms and gardens and asking each other whether they really needed a separate office space and whether they should investigate the catchment area for local schools, and finally they found somewhere that they loved and the sale went through with barely any hitches or delays and then they moved in and unpacked and chose a color scheme and bought a purple velvet sofa and the whole process took just over four months and then they had nothing else to distract them.

Kate would walk up and down the stairs of the new house, unaccustomed to all the space, and she would go into the room they intended to use for the nursery and sit on the floor, imagining the mobile they would hang from the ceiling and the framed animal alphabet they would put on the wall and she would imagine, too, being greeted by the smile on their baby's face when she came in at night to feed him or her.

Still nothing happened. And then another year had passed, and they made an appointment to see their GP, who took blood from Kate's arm that, a few days later, revealed nothing of note but because it had been two years of trying to conceive (or TTC, as the internet forums called it), they were referred to their local hospital to discuss their options with a consultant called Mr. Cartwright.

When she first met Mr. Cartwright, Kate liked him. He spoke kindly and had wavy gray hair and was handsome in a weathered way that made him look like a TV detective. He told them about the further tests they would do, the sperm samples and the internal scan and a procedure that would involve putting dye into her womb.

The tests came back and nothing was wrong. Mr. Cartwright said their infertility (it had a name now, her failure to get pregnant; it was diagnosed as an issue) was "unexplained." He talked through their options and they decided to try IVF, which Kate did not realize involved self-administering daily hormone injections to fool her body into thinking it was going through menopause.

"That's the suppression phase," Mr. Cartwright said matter-of-factly. To Kate, it felt as though her natural reflexes needed taming as if they had misbehaved for too long.

Then there were more injections to stimulate the ovaries, tickling their underbellies like trout until they produced the requisite number of eggs. Except when Kate went in every other day for her internal scans, she was told by the soft-spoken Portuguese nurse that there weren't as many as they'd like to see.

And still she was not crying. The hormones made her fuzzy rather than emotional, as if she were experiencing the world at one remove through smeary lenses. She produced one egg.

But for whatever reason, it wasn't the right egg. It did not fertilize with Jake's sperm in a petri dish. It was a nonstarter. It did not proceed to the much-fabled blastocyst phase when success rates for implantation were so much higher. It did not contain the right stuff. It had promised so much, but it had failed to deliver.

That night, they sank two bottles of wine between them.

"We'll try again," Jake said.

XVII.

They did a second cycle with Mr. Cartwright. This time, he retrieved seven eggs. A single embryo was transferred into her womb, and for a glorious twelve days after that, during which the nurses encouraged her to take things easy and put her feet up and not do any strenuous exercise or take hot baths, Kate felt indisputably pregnant.

"Because you are," Jake said, kissing the tip of her nose. "Clever thing."

On the thirteenth day, she started bleeding. Not a lot. A rusted spotting in her pants that she chose to ignore. It got slightly heavier in the following hours, so Kate turned to the internet, obsessively scanning fertility forums for the stories she wanted to find and discarding all the ones that warned her of bad news. It could be an implantation bleed, she read, and a sign that everything was progressing positively. She clung on to this notion through the sleepless night that followed, but in the morning there was a red stain on the sheets.

Jake, sleeping beside her, would be oblivious until the alarm woke him an hour later. When he opened his eyes, he was facing her. He knew instantly—she could tell he knew—and the fact that he didn't have more faith in her made her angry.

"It hasn't worked," she said, and then she turned away from him, lying on her side, facing the wall. She thought he would move toward her and take her in his arms as he usually did, but Jake made no movement. Minutes passed. A muffled sound from the other side of the bed. She turned back and realized, with a lurching heart, that Jake was crying. He was pinching the top of his nose with his thumb and forefinger, trying not to make a sound, but when she took him in her arms and said, "I'm so sorry. I'm so, so sorry," he started sobbing—big, racking sobs that sounded like he was gasping for air.

He allowed her to comfort him, and then he reached for a tissue from his bedside table and blew his nose.

"This is shit, isn't it?" he said after a minute. She nodded. It was the first time his optimism had flagged, and she realized he had been putting on a brave face for her all this time.

She felt so bad for not having been able to hold on to their baby. She felt, again, that it was her fault.

Across the mattress, he grabbed her hand.

"I love you, Kate. We'll have a baby, even if it takes us longer than we expected. And when we do have our baby, we'll love it so much because of everything we've been through to get there."

His hand grew hot over her own. Outside, there was the sound of a puttering exhaust as a motorbike started up. The sun slid through the gaps in the blinds and she wished it would go away again, that it would rain and that the weather would be in tune with her thoughts.

She kissed his wet cheek, and then she kissed his lips. He returned the kiss with forceful passion, gripping the back of her neck and pressing her head into his. It was as if he were trying to prove something. But what that was, she didn't allow herself to question.

Mr. Cartwright told them they should take a few months off before trying again.

"Allow yourselves to recover. Go on holiday."

The walls of his office were covered with pictures of babies held in the arms of shiny-eyed women and tired but happy-looking men.

Mr. Cartwright was featured in several of the photographs, smiling broadly as if delighted with himself. In one, he carried twins, his checked shirtsleeves rolled up and an identical baby nestled into the crook of each arm.

"Is it worth it?" Kate blurted out.

In the plastic chair next to her, Jake looked surprised.

Mr. Cartwright met her gaze. "That's a decision for both of you," he said. "I can speak from my experience working with hundreds of patients and tell you that they definitely think it was worth it."

His voice was calm. The consultant's demeanor seemed designed to make Kate feel like an increasingly hysterical woman. His manner had changed from their first appointment, when he had cracked jokes and been breezily optimistic. Now, Mr. Cartwright was frustrated that she wasn't holding up her part of the bargain. He had done his bit, after all. More than once, he had told her that she was "failing to respond to the drugs," as if the drugs themselves could not possibly be blamed, let alone his efficacy in prescribing them.

"Thank you, Mr. Cartwright," Jake said. "We'll take some time to think about our next steps."

They went for a coffee in the ground-floor cafe. They didn't go on holiday but spent the next couple of months trying to occupy themselves with other projects. They had friends round for dinner. They went to the cinema and art galleries and restaurants. Annabelle came up and stayed for the weekend in the room that would eventually be the nursery. She was polite about the house and brought Kate a huge bunch of peonies to say thank you for having her. Only once did she revert to form, when she asked why they'd moved into such a big place.

"It's palatial," she said, even though it wasn't and certainly not when compared to Annabelle's own sprawling residence in the countryside. "You two don't need this much room, surely?"

They were sitting on the L-shaped sofa in the kitchen extension. Kate and Annabelle were sharing a bottle of Chablis, while Jake was drinking a Peroni straight from the bottle, despite his mother's protestations that he really should get a glass.

"Don't you like the house, then?" Jake asked.

"Oh, no, no—I didn't say that. It's lovely. And how you've done it up is very . . . well, it's very sweet. I just wondered if you ever felt like you rattled around a bit, that's all."

Annabelle tilted her face toward him. She was wearing another one of her floaty, thin-knit cardigans, her wrist weighed down with a chunky gold charm bracelet that shook every time she took a drink.

Kate refilled her glass, staying silent.

"We don't rattle around," Jake said. "And it won't always just be us anyway, will it?"

"I don't understand."

"Well, when we have children . . ."

Annabelle laughed.

"*Children*?" she said, enunciating the word as if Jake had outlined a preposterous conspiracy theory. "But surely you can't be thinking . . . You're . . . well . . . I hadn't . . . You're not even married, darling!"

Kate snorted. Jake's neck was mottled red.

"It's not the nineteenth century, Mother."

"No, I know, but . . ."

"Actually, we've been trying to get pregnant and it hasn't been easy, and I—we—would appreciate a bit more sensitivity on that front."

When he was furious, Jake's syntax became formal.

Annabelle looked as though she had been slapped. Beneath the peachy circles of blush, her face was pale.

"I'm sorry to hear that," she said, placing her glass on the coffee table. She stood up from the sofa and swept out of the room, leaving a trail of Christian Dior perfume in her wake.

Kate emptied her glass.

"That went well," she said drily.

Jake walked over to the kitchen counter, slamming his empty beer bottle into the recycling bin with such force she was surprised it didn't shatter.

The next morning, at breakfast, Annabelle sat with an uneaten slice of toast in front of her, very still and upright. She hadn't applied her usual makeup, Kate noticed. She looked old and pale and clearly wanted to demonstrate her hurt.

"Some coffee, Annabelle?" Kate asked.

Jake was sitting opposite his mother, ostentatiously reading a copy of *The Economist*.

Annabelle shook her head, resting a hand on her clavicle as she did so.

"I'm sorry if I spoke out of turn," she said finally, her voice clear. "I didn't realize . . . it was such a *difficult* subject for you both."

Jake didn't say anything, but he raised his head from the magazine and met his mother's eyes. Well, Kate thought, I suppose it falls to me to explain.

"The thing is, Annabelle, we've been having IVF."

Annabelle looked blank.

"I can't seem to conceive naturally," Kate said.

"*We* can't," Jake corrected her softly.

"Oh, I see. And what do the doctors say the chances are?" Annabelle inquired politely.

"Around thirty percent," Kate said.

"We've had two cycles," Jake added. "Unsuccessfully. They advise three."

Annabelle reached for the marmalade and started spreading it on her cold toast. She replaced her knife carefully onto the plate and took a small bite, chewing thoughtfully. They waited for her to swallow and for the next inevitable comment to slice into the room.

"I'm just worried about you both, that's all."

"We'll be fine," Jake said.

"I wouldn't want you to get your hopes up only for them to be dashed," she continued, frowning with concern. She reached across the table and rested her hand on Kate's arm.

"You know my dear friend Trisha? Her daughter had IVF five times and no luck. They don't know why. I suppose it's just one of those things. And it must be awful for you to go through, darling Kate. I worry that doctors suggest all sorts of medical procedures when maybe there's nothing to be done, and the procedure itself can be so draining, can't it? From what I understand, I mean. Of course, I've never been through anything like that myself."

Kate tried, as much as possible, to let Annabelle's words wash over her. A year ago, she would have been righteously indignant at the invasive nature of Annabelle's opinion, but now she no longer seemed to have the mental or physical capacity to make her case. And really, she told herself, it was none of Annabelle's business. She wished Jake hadn't told her.

"It is draining, yes," Jake said. "Kate's been heroic."

Annabelle blinked slowly, those clear blue eyes seeming to become even clearer as she spoke. "Poor Kate." She patted Kate's arm. "It must be so tough. I read somewhere that giving IVF to women who aren't able to conceive is a bit like giving chemotherapy to a terminal cancer patient."

For a second or two, Kate wasn't sure if she'd heard her correctly. She shifted her arm and Annabelle's hand dropped onto the table. She stood, pushing her chair back so quickly that it slammed onto the floor. Jake reached out for her but she didn't want his comfort.

"That's not helpful, Annabelle," Kate said quietly. Then she left the kitchen and walked out of the house, forgetting her coat, so that when she returned two hours later, she was cold and damp. Jake greeted her with a hug in the hallway.

"She's gone," he said. "We had a massive row. I'm sorry. She won't be speaking to you like that again."

Kate allowed herself to be hugged but didn't say anything. She marveled at how, even when enveloped by the man she loved, she could possibly feel so alone.

The third cycle produced nine eggs ("You're going up every time!" Mr. Cartwright said with a cheeriness that made Kate want to punch him). Four of them fertilized and two were placed back in her womb, so that now she was technically pregnant with twins, except this time she didn't feel pregnant at all. She accepted that the cycle would fail with a fatalism that seemed safer than the alternative hope, and when she started bleeding again, this time on the final day of the two-week wait, she wasn't surprised or even particularly upset. She had, over the preceding eighteen months, become immune to fluctuating emotions. She was like one of those robots she had once seen in the Seoul airport when traveling back from a film festival. The robots had scooted along the terminal floors, with a touch screen for a face you could press to find the right answers. This was what she became: at work, at home, with Jake. She answered questions and took part in conversations but she had no real feeling beneath the surface. If she allowed herself to feel the smallest things, Kate knew it would lead ineluctably onto the bigger things and then that would be the start of a fatal unraveling, like a single dropped knitting stitch that ruins the whole pattern.

They went to a private clinic. They thought that going private would be the equivalent of flying business class after economy, but the appointments still ran late and the consultants' offices were still cramped and papered with more baby photographs and thank-you cards Blu Tacked to the walls.

Their consultant—another man, this time an Israeli doctor called

Mr. Abadi—was matter-of-fact about their dwindling chances but said that they were in the right place to get "your preferred outcome."

For cycles four and five, she still did not respond to the drugs and Mr. Abadi upped the dosage so that she felt constantly on the brink of a weepy meltdown. These cycles didn't work and so they did more tests for things called natural killer cells and DNA fragmentation and uterine scarring and they put both of them on long courses of antibiotics during which they couldn't drink and became crotchety with each other.

And then—rejoice!—the sixth round of IVF produced a pregnancy. Kate wanted to feel uncomplicated joy but couldn't. She was too aware of what could go wrong. Every time she went to the loo, she checked for blood.

Mr. Abadi put Kate on steroids and blood thinners, which she injected into her stomach each morning just as she had done throughout IVF. The needles left pockmarked bruises either side of her navel like an astral map of some undiscovered galaxy.

She made it to week seven. Mr. Abadi asked her to come in for an early scan, and she was scared but hopeful. Jake was outwardly confident and told her everything was going to be fine, but she couldn't believe him. When Mr. Abadi placed the probe inside her vagina, she noticed the telltale seconds of silence before he spoke and she already knew it wasn't good news.

"There is a gestational sac," he said, pointing at the screen with his latex gloves. "But I'm afraid there is no embryo, Kate." He spoke with a gentle accent, his "t"s sounding like punctuation marks.

"We would expect to see an embryo at this stage, and what this means is the pregnancy has not developed as it should."

"Could it just be developing more slowly?" Jake asked.

"In the event of a natural pregnancy, yes, we could see that being a possibility. There is always some leeway around dates of conception. But in your case, we know exactly when we introduced the embryo, so . . ." He shook his head. "I'm very sorry."

"It's ok," Kate said, and then she didn't know why she'd said it. Because it wasn't ok. It wasn't ok at all.

He talked her through the next steps. Either she could wait to miscarry naturally, although there was no way of knowing when that might happen, or he could give her drugs to induce a medical miscarriage. She opted for the latter, wanting now to be rid of her false hope as quickly as possible. The idea of carrying a dead thing around in her for an unspecified number of days and weeks seemed inhuman. Mr. Abadi warned her the pain would be intense, that it would build to a climax in the first twenty-four hours, but then the worst would be over.

They went home and drank wine and the next morning, Kate prepared herself with a towel over the sheets and a series to binge on Netflix. She put her phone on airplane mode and she placed the first pills up her vagina, as instructed. Then she waited. She took acetaminophen. And waited some more. About two hours after inserting the pills, the cramping started. It was as if dirt were being excavated by an industrial digger from inside her womb. The pain was so severe she thought she might pass out. It came in waves, cresting and receding, and at one point she threw up into the sink. Jake, who had taken the day off work to tend to her, would come into the bedroom pale and worried, asking if there was anything he could do, but there wasn't, because Kate knew that to get through this, she had to go into a place where no one else would be able to follow.

The pain surged in peaks for the next hour and a half and then it went away, becoming milder with astonishing rapidity. The bleeding got heavier and she did not allow herself to look as she passed clots and scraps of what might have been into the toilet bowl. She did not allow herself to think of what it represented. Of the names they might have chosen. Of the child they might have loved.

It took a week for the bleeding and the pain to subside completely. The experience had been barbaric. She was appalled that no one had told her it would be like this and she knew, without doubt, that she could not endure this again.

Mr. Abadi gently suggested that they start thinking of alternative options. "It's been four years now, hasn't it, since you've been trying?"

"Yes," Kate said, thinking of how much had happened in that time and how little had been achieved. It seemed to have lasted forever but it also went by in a flash.

"Donor eggs might be something you would like to explore, although you have some scarring in the womb that suggests you will not be able to carry a baby, Kate."

Carry a baby. It was such an odd expression. You carried shopping. You carried burdens. You carried viruses.

"So, depending on what feels right for your particular circumstances, you might want to consider surrogacy. Or adoption."

Kate was appalled that her first feeling was relief. Relief that she wouldn't have to do it again, that she wasn't expected to keep trying and trying and failing. She glanced at Jake, who was massaging the back of his neck, his face blank. Adoption had always been their final option, the thing they would turn to last, and it felt strange to have heard it voiced out loud as part of the next stage.

After, they went to the overpriced deli next to the clinic and drank cappuccinos and ate the free amaretto biscuit that came with each cup.

"How are you feeling?" Jake asked. She was leaning on the table and he did not take her hands in his as he might once have. The procedures had drained him too. His face had lost its ruddy complexion and there were horizontal lines across his forehead she hadn't noticed before. The strain sat oddly with the rest of his body, which was lean and muscular. He had worked out more as a way of dealing with the emotional stress, lifting weights in the gym and going for long runs and boxing with a personal trainer every Thursday morning. He had invested in ever more sophisticated gym clothes: athletic brands that had to be ordered from America, with discreet yet noticeable logos, and mesh sneakers with light soles intended to recreate the experience of barefoot running through the Masai Mara. He drank protein shakes and ate chicken breasts, leaving the skin on the side of his plate so that when Kate swept it into the bin, she felt silently judged by its goose-pimpled presence. He looked great, objectively, but she missed the comfort of his softer chest.

Her own body had become alien to her. She had always been toned, with neat muscles in her arms from yoga and the faintest tracing of abdominals on the skin across her ribs. But now her belly felt flabby and filled with fluid. She was convinced her hips had spread more widely. She hadn't exercised regularly for months. She was sure that the effort of becoming pregnant and the shadow effort of losing each pregnancy had left a physical mark.

"Kate?"

She realized she hadn't answered his question.

"I'm tired," she said.

"What do you think about surrogacy? Or would you rather talk about it later?"

She began to cry then, without feeling particularly sad. He handed her a napkin and she blotted her cheeks with it. In a corner of the cafe, a baby started wailing, as if to echo her own unhappiness, and the mother unbuttoned her top and began to breastfeed. The baby, instantly calmed, suckled away intently. Looking at them, Kate was overcome with a mixture of jealousy and awe. She was desperate. She wanted nothing so much as she wanted a baby. She was incapable of seeing anything other than this. She felt she would die if she did not become a mother.

"I think maybe it's a good idea?" she said. "I just . . . I hadn't expected to feel so much grief for something I can't do."

"Oh, my love," Jake said. "I'm so sorry."

"And can we even afford it?"

"Of course we can. We can remortgage the house if it comes to it. This is more important, isn't it?"

She nodded, then said, "Do you still love me?"

His face broke. "Why would you even ask that? I love you more than anything. And we'll get through this. Together. Ok?"

"Ok."

Within two weeks, they had contacted a surrogacy organization, which invited them in for a chat. Carol, a competent, gray-haired woman in a plain cotton shirt and sensible pump shoes sat down with them and said, "I'm going to give you quite a lot of information here." She laughed in a way that reminded Kate of her old biology teacher. "Are you ready?"

She told them that it was illegal to pay for a surrogate in the UK, other than covering their expenses; that any surrogate would have to be acting out of an altruistic instinct to want to help; that there was then a three-month "getting to know you" period before anyone signed anything; that they would have to decide whether to use Kate's own eggs, or the surrogate's; that they had a website where potential surrogates could match with couples like them; that there were regular conferences and social events where prospective parents outnumbered potential surrogates three to one. They took home a dozen leaflets and read them in the kitchen, sitting across from each other, drinking strong mugs of tea. It was nice to have a project, to have something they were more in control of, rather than outsourcing it all to male consultants who spoke in a medical language designed to alienate.

The following month, Carol invited them to a social event at a hotel in Coventry.

"It's a theme party. *Bugsy Malone*. I don't know if that's your kind of thing. But if it is, you should come along. You'll meet a lot of couples with similar journeys to yours and it can be very healing to share stories with people who understand."

Both Kate and Jake hated themed parties, but they decided it was worth it and so they ordered costumes from Amazon: a cheap polyester flapper dress for Kate, accessorized with fake pearls and a cigarette holder; a baggy pinstripe suit for Jake. They drove to the Grand Eastern Hotel in Coventry, a two-story building in yellow brick with beige carpets patterned with burgundy diamonds. The room was sparsely furnished and sterile: a bed with a foam mattress; a kettle with individually wrapped packets of sugar and creamer; shower gel and shampoo mixed into the same plastic dispenser that was fixed to the tiled wall in the bathroom. The view out of the window was of the car park. They made vodka tonics from the minibar and drank them sitting on the bed, and then they looked at each other and started to laugh at the weirdness of the situation. It was the first time Kate could remember laughing like that in ages.

"Do you think we're drinking too much?" she asked Jake, and she wasn't sure how seriously she meant the question.

"If you can't knock back a couple when you've been through what we have, then when can you?" he said.

"I guess."

They got dressed in their costumes, and Kate put on a dark-red lipstick and Jake told her she looked so hot that she would have to wear the same outfit one night when they got back home. Kate, lightly buzzed from the vodka, felt beautiful again. They held hands as they walked along the corridor to the conference hall where the party was being held. It had been decorated with gold helium balloons and WANTED posters of Al Capone. The room was already half-full of guests. They headed straight to the bar. Kate was nervous, though she didn't quite know why. They asked for vodka tonics from the barman.

"Single or double?"

"Double," Kate and Jake said simultaneously.

An unfamiliar voice came from behind.

"I like your style."

They turned to find a woman standing there. She had tousled blonde hair held back with a feathered headband and was wearing a man's suit, with a silk camisole underneath. Her skin was tanned and she had a nice smile. She was pretty and approachable, the kind of person you would cast as the fanciable sister of a male lead in a mainstream movie.

"Hi," she said, holding out her hand. "I'm Marisa."

XVIII.

Now

"I feel like I'm going mad," Marisa says. "I just want to talk."

"Ok," Kate says, making her voice as soothing as possible. "I understand. Let's talk. I'll tell you everything you want to know."

Marisa's shoulders relax. She puts the knife onto the hallway table.

"Sorry about that," Marisa says. "I wasn't going to use it."

"I know."

She smiles at Kate, a cracked smile that makes the rest of her face look lopsided. Her hair is knotted and unwashed and Kate can smell the earthy bitterness of her body odor.

"Oh, Marisa," Kate says. "What's wrong?"

Marisa's chest is heaving suddenly and she is slumped in the chair, the tears streaming down her cheeks. She lifts her head, staring out from beneath her lank strands of hair. Kate presses herself against the wall as if she can make herself disappear through sheer force of will. But there is nowhere to go and her legs are still bound by the rope.

"Marisa, sweetie, please could you undo the rope? I promise I won't go anywhere; it's just that I'm a bit uncomfortable."

Marisa keeps staring at her, her mouth hanging open. Kate is not sure how much she has understood. She seems almost unreachable. *How?* Kate thinks. *How have we let it get to this? How did this happen?* Kate keeps up the soft patter, as though she is taming a wild horse.

"Please, just untie the rope, darling, and then we can talk. We can sit on the sofa in the kitchen with a cup of tea and we can sort all this out. You're not in trouble. I'm fine. I'm not angry with you. Please, Marisa."

After a few minutes of this, Marisa sits straighter in her chair and scoops up her hair with both hands, tying it in a loose knot at the back. Her face seems clearer somehow, the internal demons kept momentarily at bay. She stands, pressing one palm against her belly in a protective gesture. She bends to undo the knots in the rope, reaching for the knife to saw through when her fingers don't work. Gradually, the rope loosens and Kate can feel the blood rushing back to her feet.

"Thank you, Marisa."

"I don't want to go to the kitchen. We'll just sit here."

Marisa slides down to sit next to Kate, her back against the wall. She is so close that Kate can feel Marisa's loose strands of hair tickle her cheek and this is somehow more frightening than when she was looming over Kate with a knife. Kate tries to regulate her breathing. She closes her eyes briefly, gathering her thoughts.

"What is it, Marisa?"

"I know," Marisa says.

"You know what?"

"Stop it. I'm not stupid. I'm not a fool, even if you think I am, even if I've never been as clever as you. I already asked you once. So let me ask you again: How long have you and Jake been sleeping together?"

Kate is perplexed. "Six years," she says. "You know that."

"How can you say it so casually? We invite you into our home and this is how you repay me? By breaking up my relationship?"

"*Your* relationship?"

Marisa nods, and all at once, Kate gets an instinctive flash of understanding that she immediately wishes she could unsee.

"But . . . what . . . Marisa . . ." She stumbles over the words. Her voice is hoarse, almost a whisper. It can't be what she thinks, surely? "You're our surrogate," Kate says.

Marisa looks blank, as if she hasn't heard.

"You're our *surrogate*," Kate repeats. "Do you understand?"

Then Marisa does the most curious thing. She takes Kate's hand in hers and starts to laugh, slowly at first but then the laughter gathers pace and becomes a shrill, unstoppable noise.

"Oh, Kate," she says breathlessly between giggles. "Kate, Kate, Kate, you poor thing. You've got it all wrong. I'm Jake's partner. We're having a baby together. You're our lodger."

When Kate was a child, her father used to drive to a flea market on the second Sunday of every month. Sometimes, if she got up early enough, he would take her with him. They lived at the bottom of a valley and the drive would take them steeply up the road on one side of their house, and then back down toward the nearest village. There were few other cars at that time in the morning, so Kate's father used to speed up as they climbed the hill so that she would feel her tummy flip as the car careened over the other side.

"Tummy flip!" she would scream with delight. There was a sort of gleeful terror at the thought that the car could lose control, and when it didn't, her insides seemed to need an extra beat to catch up with the speed of the outside world.

Hearing Marisa speak to her now, Kate feels her tummy flip again, except this time it doesn't return to normal.

"Marisa," Kate says, trying to be as clear and concise as possible. "Jake's my partner. We've been together for six years. We couldn't conceive. We asked you to be our surrogate and move in with us. You're carrying our baby. Ours. Not yours."

Marisa doesn't say anything for a while. She turns away, huddling into herself, and Kate can see her picking at the ragged cuticles of her right hand. They sit in silence for several minutes before Marisa opens her mouth to speak.

"The thing is, Kate—"

She is interrupted by the sound of a key turning in a lock. The front door opens. Jake is home.

XIX.

Then

They couldn't believe it at first. No one could. Carol said that it took some couples years to find a suitable surrogate. It was very rare to match with someone on your first social event. But Kate and Jake had both felt an immediate affinity with Marisa. Looking back later, Kate would wonder whether their desperation made them find this affinity where there was none.

And yet, the three of them chatted easily that night about both the oddness and the comic potential of the setting they found themselves in. Marisa had asked a bit about their fertility journey, because everyone called it a journey, like some bad 1980s rock anthem, but her questions had not been intrusive or prurient. She listened and nodded and seemed genuinely empathetic. She told them that she had always wanted children but wasn't ready for her own quite yet. She said she knew firsthand from older friends and from her own mother how difficult infertility struggles could be.

"There's seven years between me and my sister," Marisa explained. "My mother had a string of miscarriages in that time. It was awful for her."

Kate looked at her and wondered if infertility could be genetically inherited. Marisa, as if reading her thoughts, said, "But I've had everything checked out and it all seems good, and I guess I thought this was something I could do for someone else, while I was still young, in the way no one was able to do for my mother, you know?"

She had that millennial way of speaking, littered with "like"s and unnecessary question marks that left sentences trailing upward.

"If it's not an impertinent question, how old are you?" Jake asked. He'd had four vodkas by then and was feeling looser than usual.

"I'm twenty-eight."

She spoke with such openness, such a complete lack of guile, that Kate was charmed. She was so used to dealing with cynical media types, their outlook on the world dulled after years living in a big city where being cool carried a higher premium than being enthusiastic, and Marisa came across as untouched, like a doll who had only just been removed from her cellophane wrapping. She had grown up in the countryside, she said, and to Kate, Marisa still seemed a touch old-fashioned, like a heroine plucked from the pages of a Thomas Hardy novel, with healthy bones and tawny hair and a glowing smile and a sense of oneness with her surroundings. There was a purity to her. Kate could quite easily imagine her with a baby.

Marisa left the party before they did, saying that she had to be up early the next morning, and Kate liked this about her, too: the fact that she was sensible and comfortable enough in her own skin to go when the party was just hitting its stride.

"I'd love to keep in touch with you guys," Marisa had said. "If you felt it was appropriate, of course. No pressure!"

Jake glanced at Kate, who gave a tiny nod.

"We'd like that too," he said. "Perhaps you could take my number?"

"Sure," Marisa said, and she fished out an old iPhone model with a cracked screen. She unlocked it and handed the phone to Jake.

"Wow," Jake said. "You must have dropped this from a great height."

Marisa laughed. "I've been meaning to get it replaced, but you know how it is."

Jake typed in his number and passed the phone back to Marisa.

"It's been lovely meeting you both," she said. She didn't make a move to kiss them on the cheek, and Kate was relieved. If this were going to go any further, the boundaries would have to be clear from the start.

"It's been so great meeting you too," Kate said, and she meant it. For the first time in four years, she felt a small bubbling of hope.

Carol told them not to get carried away.

"There's a long, long road ahead," she said. "You've got to get to know each other now, to check that you're really compatible and that you can trust each other with this incredibly precious thing. And Marisa is unusual—let's not forget."

"In what way?" Kate asked.

"Well, she's younger than most surrogates we get and she hasn't previously had a baby herself, which we do tend to prefer. It's not a deal breaker, obviously, but it's something to be aware of. She's also single, so she won't have the support of a partner. You need to be confident that she'll have a good support network going through this."

"But isn't her relative youth a bonus?" Jake asked. "Fertility-wise, I mean."

"It could be, yes. It's just something to be aware of," Carol repeated. "Have you had a discussion about whose eggs you are going to use?"

"I think we'll go for the surrogate eggs, if that's an option," Kate said.

She spoke clearly and tried to keep her voice from cracking. They were acting on advice from Mr. Abadi, who said this would give them the best possible chance of conceiving in the quickest time, and although Kate tried to tell herself that it didn't matter how they got there, that a baby was yours as soon as it was in your arms, she was also struggling to come to terms with the fact that her child would have no genetic link to her.

"All right," Carol said. "Then you'll also need to consider if you're ok with Marisa looking different from you, Kate."

"She looks like Jake," Kate replied.

"I know, but he'll be providing his sperm, so . . ."

"Yes, I realize that. I've thought a lot about it."

And she had. She had gone over it again and again in her mind, until she had come to the conclusion that all of Marisa's advantages outweighed this one rather solipsistic concern. She knew Jake was as desperate to be a father as she was to be a mother and she could no longer bear the idea of letting him down. She wanted to be fine with it, so she told herself she was. Gradually it became a version of the truth.

"I'm fine with it," Kate said to Carol.

In the chair next to her, Jake reached over and squeezed her hand.

On Kate's advice, Jake had kept in touch with Marisa regularly by text since the party.

"We don't want to mess up our chances with her," Kate said, half joking. "She was probably picking up digits left, right, and center that night."

They were sitting on the bench in the garden, admiring the hydrangea that had just started to flower.

"I feel like we're dating," Jake said. He poured her a glass of rosé.

She squinted at him. "What do you mean?"

"Just that I'm overanalyzing each of her texts because I want to show we're interested but I don't want to come across too keen."

She laughed. "You are silly."

The wine and the sunshine had given her a pleasant lightheadedness. She rested her head against his shoulder. "The only person you're dating is me."

He held her closer to him. "Thank goodness."

They arranged to meet Marisa in a cafe that weekend, the daylight rendezvous feeling appropriate and unthreatening. Kate dressed in clothes that were presentable but not too fashionable because she wanted to appear her most dependable and stable self. She settled for a white linen shirt and boyfriend-cut jeans with trainers. Jake wore a gray T-shirt and his favorite chinos. They arrived half an hour before the allotted time so that they could settle in and quell their anxiety, and they chose a table by the window so that Marisa could see them easily when she walked in.

When she arrived, she smiled at them and made her way over to the table.

"Hi," she said. Her hair was down over her shoulders. Out of fancy dress, she looked even more wholesome than Kate remembered. She was in a pink cotton sundress and the straps kept slipping down her tanned arms. The top button was undone, revealing a triangle of bright-blue bra. Looking at her, the one word that Kate kept returning to was "ripe." She knew, instinctively, that this woman would carry their baby, and this knowledge calmed her. It suddenly made a peculiar kind of sense that their struggles had led them here, as though their baby had been waiting to be born until Marisa came along.

"So nice to see you again," Jake said, shaking her hand.

Marisa ordered a tea, which came with all sorts of unnecessary paraphernalia including a tiny egg timer and a Japanese-style tray and a lengthy explanation of how long to let it brew from the waitress.

"Wow," Jake said. "That's a complicated cup of tea."

They laughed.

"I'm more of an English Breakfast man myself," Jake continued. Kate felt a twinge of affection for how he had taken on the difficult business of breaking the ice so that she didn't have to. She wanted to stay silent for a bit and simply observe.

Jake and Marisa talked about their respective families and their upbringings, and Marisa painted an idyllic picture of a contented childhood. Her parents, she said, were still happily married ("It makes it quite difficult to live up to, to be honest," she added) and she and her younger sister, Anna, were very close.

"And what do you do for a living?" Kate asked.

"I write and illustrate children's books."

"Oh, that's so wonderful!"

Kate was thrilled she was creative. That had been one of the things she had worried about: that her more artistic genes would not be passed on to the baby.

"Thank you! I mean, it's not like I'm Roald Dahl or anything. I get commissions from parents or family members to write personalized fairy tales for their children."

"How does that work?"

Marisa flicked her hair back over her shoulders. It was long and wavy, the kind of hair you see on models advertising suntan lotion on the beach.

"They send me a couple of photos and some key characteristics and I go from there."

She told them she called her business Telling Tales and they both commended her on the cleverness of the name. Under the table, Jake grazed his knee against Kate's and she clasped on to his thigh, not quite believing that this was going as well as it was.

They didn't mention the surrogacy until they had finished their drinks, and it was Marisa who brought it up.

"I know that we're at the very early stages of this, but I just wanted to put it out there that I really like you guys and would love to be able to help you by being your surrogate. If you wanted that, of course." She giggled and her face flushed. "No pressure!"

Kate's eyes filled with tears. "That's such a—" Her voice broke. "Such a generous and incredible thing to hear. Thank you. Excuse me."

She didn't want to cry in front of Marisa, so she made her way to the toilet, where she put the seat down and sat there for a few minutes, blotting at her cheeks with balled-up loo roll. She took some deep breaths. There was a sign on the back of the door for baby yoga. UNLEASH YOUR INNER MAMA GODDESS, it read, and there was a photograph of a broad-hipped woman in a kaftan holding a chubby baby up to the sky. Kate had seen the poster before and it had always enraged her. It seemed so smug, so tone-deaf, so badly misaligned with what she was going through that she had to stop herself from tearing it down. It was like those posts on Instagram of photogenic baby bumps and minuscule newborns that made Kate want to scream and wish there were a trigger warning for pregnancy content. But today, she stared at the poster and believed that one day this could be her.

She fished out her phone from her jeans pocket and texted Jake.

I think she's the one, don't you?

She pressed Send and waited. There was a rattling at the door, so she flushed and washed her hands, placing them under the dryer so that the person outside knew there wasn't long to wait. Her phone vibrated.

Sure do x

Kate left the bathroom, grinning broadly at the woman waiting outside.

"Sorry," she murmured. It was as she was walking back through the bustling cafe that she saw, in the flicker of a moment, Marisa reach out across the table and graze Jake's wrist with her hand. It was a quick gesture, as if to emphasize a conversational point, and Kate thought no more about it as she went back to her seat and told Marisa how lucky they felt to have met her.

XX.

They spent a lot of time together over the next three months, as advised by Carol. They went for picnics. They attended surrogacy conferences. They visited art galleries and museums and went on cinema dates, where Jake and Kate would sit on either side of Marisa so as not to make her feel awkward. They had dozens of conversations about what the surrogacy would entail. They thrashed out a surrogacy agreement between the three of them, whereby Marisa Grover would transfer legal parenthood to Kate Samuel and Jake Sturridge after their baby was born. Marisa always referred to it as "your baby." She knew all about the medical procedures that she would have to undergo to have her eggs retrieved and fertilized with Jake's sperm and reassured Kate that she wasn't daunted by the prospect.

"I just want to make sure you're ok with it all. Sorry for all the questions," Kate said one evening when the three of them were walking along the river, through Battersea Park.

"Oh gosh, I totally understand," Marisa replied. "But I guess I had thought long and hard about wanting to do this before I met you, so I think I do know what I'm getting into."

"That's good to hear," Jake said.

Everything Marisa told them was perfect. It felt, at points, as though they had invented her, as though she were too good to be true.

There was just one thing that Kate wanted to change, and that was Marisa's living arrangement. She had told them she rented a flat in North London, but when they visited her there, Kate was taken aback to find that it was more like a bedsit than a flat. The bedroom contained the galley kitchen, and the bathroom was barely bigger than a cupboard. It smelled of cooked food and bad plumbing. Kate could hear the thump of loud music coming from above. It was damp and poky and the front window looked out directly onto a main road. The glass was grimy from exhaust fumes.

"What if Marisa came to live with us?" Kate asked Jake later that evening. They were sitting on the sofa in front of the TV, drinking wine and watching a Netflix documentary about the doping scandal in cycling.

"Mmmm?" Jake didn't hear her at first. He reached for the remote control and pressed Pause. "What was that?"

She held her wineglass by the stem, gently swilling it so the liquid left a mark on the side. "I was wondering if it made sense to ask Marisa to move in with us."

Jake, who had reached to take a crisp from the bowl on the low table in front of them, halted the movement midair. He sat back and burst out laughing. "*What*?"

Kate looked at him levelly.

He realized she wasn't joking and his face became serious again.

"Um. Wow. Ok. I hadn't expected that. Ok. Let me just digest it for a second."

"I've just been thinking about it, and I don't really love the idea of her being so far away from us . . ."

"It's not *that* far."

"No, I know, but we both work long hours and it would be easier having her closer. That's the practical argument," she said, knowing how Jake's mind worked. "The emotional one is that I also don't love the idea of her being on her own, without a family support unit. They all live in the country, don't they? Besides, it would be much easier to keep an eye on her and check she's eating healthily and taking her supplements and all that stuff."

"But—"

"And given that it's illegal to pay for surrogacy, beyond reasonable expenses, anyway, this would be a way of thanking her for this enormous fucking thing she's doing for us."

Jake was quiet, but she could sense his mood had shifted from disbelief to logical assessment.

"We could give her the spare room and she could set up her studio there. There's more than enough space."

Jake went to pour himself another glass of wine but found the bottle was empty. He stood up and walked to the wine rack, removing a screw-top red, which he brought back to the sofa, offering her some as he sat back down.

"Thanks," she said, holding out her glass.

She was quiet, allowing the idea to percolate.

"Ok," Jake said.

"Ok?"

"I think it's a good idea."

Kate rolled across to him and kissed him all over his face.

"Oh, I'm so glad you think so too. Thank you thank you thank you."

Jake laughed and kissed her back on the mouth. He tasted of tannins.

"Assuming Marisa agrees," he said, holding her by the shoulders. "What do we tell everyone else?"

"I guess that she's a lodger?"

"Even my mother?"

Kate went back to her side of the sofa. "No, I think we should tell Annabelle the truth."

Jake shook his head. "She's not going to understand."

"She isn't," Kate agreed. "But she doesn't have to."

It was, in the end, quite easily decided. Kate mentioned it to Marisa the next day over the phone.

"Kate, oh my goodness—that's so generous. Are you sure?" Her voice was breathless, as if she had just been out for a run.

"We're positive. It would be lovely to have you with us. But we don't want you to feel under any obligation. Why don't you come round and see the house and your room and then you can make up your mind?"

"I'd love that."

They made a date for the following afternoon. Jake was unable to get out of a work meeting but Kate's hours were more flexible. She felt excited waiting for Marisa to ring the front doorbell, and she spent a couple of hours that morning cleaning and making everything look as inviting as possible. In the spare room, she changed the bed linens and put a selection of her favorite books on the shelves. Downstairs, she lit scented candles and wiped down the kitchen surfaces.

When Marisa arrived, they hugged and Kate invited her in and started showing her round as if she were an estate agent. She pointed out the double glazing, which made it quiet, the two bathrooms (which meant Marisa would have her own), and the fact that her and Jake's bedroom was on a different floor, for added privacy.

"Oh, it's so beautiful," Marisa enthused. "The light is just gorgeous."

In the kitchen, Kate opened the glass doors into the garden and a magpie flew in without warning so that Kate had to swerve and duck her head. In the flurry that followed, the bird caught its wing on a vase that crashed to the floor and then flew back outside. Kate, who had never liked birds and found them full of all sorts of sinister premonitions, tried to make light of it.

"Good riddance!" she said, as the bird flew higher into the sky before disappearing from view. "I hope that didn't put you off."

Marisa said it hadn't at all, and not to worry, and if Kate and Jake were really sure, then she'd love to move in for the next few months while they went on their surrogacy adventure together. Kate hugged her again, so tightly that she could feel the beat of the other woman's heart. When she pulled back, Marisa looked at her oddly, as though her eyes had lost focus, as though her mind had taken her somewhere else. It was a fleeting moment, and Marisa's face cleared almost as soon as Kate had noticed it.

She saw Marisa out, watching as the other woman walked down the street, taking out her phone to text someone on her way to the tube, and then Kate closed the door and stood for a while in the hallway, pleased with herself for how well it had gone.

▪ ▪ ▪

Kate helped Marisa move in, hiring a van and lugging boxes down the narrow stairs from her flat and piling them high in the back. They drove across the city with the radio on and Marisa seemed to know all the words to the pop songs. She had a nice singing voice, Kate thought, and this was another thing that made her happy about the genetic inheritance she would be giving their child. Marisa unpacked quickly and methodically and by that evening, it was all done and she was ensconced in their house, sitting across from them at the kitchen table, and it felt as though it had always been this way. It felt, Kate realized, like family.

Marisa set a slanted architect's table up by the spare window and worked long hours in her room, emerging for dinner with paint in her hair, wearing sandals and loose-fitting work clothes. She said she was sleeping better than she had done in years and her face filled out and the darkness beneath her eyes disappeared.

Jake and Kate, aware of this new presence in their home, did their best to make Marisa feel welcome. They were solicitous, always asking if she wanted cups of tea or the odd glass of wine, and they agreed they would not be "coupley" in front of her. They stopped being tactile or showing affection to each other so that Marisa wouldn't feel the odd one out. At night, they had sex quietly, not wanting her to hear.

It went on in this way for three weeks, maybe four. Afterward, Kate could never recall when exactly she got the first inkling that all was not as it seemed. It started with small things—gestures that would have been almost impossible to discern at the time but that in retrospect appeared all to be leading up to an inevitable end point.

There was the way Marisa moved her mugs to the front of the cupboard, pushing Kate's favorite coffee cups to the back, and the way she used the sink in the master bedroom to brush her teeth rather than the smaller one upstairs they had allotted her. She liked to take a lengthy soak in their tub before going to bed but she never cleaned the bath out after using it. She downloaded TV programs from their Apple account without asking. Once, Kate had found her in their bedroom, sitting at Kate's dressing table, trying on her jewelry.

"Oh, I'm so sorry, Kate!" Marisa had said. Her manner was light, as if it were no big deal. "I just love these particular earrings you have and wanted to see if they suited me. You don't mind, do you?"

And Kate felt there was no option but to say that she didn't.

Kate told herself she was being controlling. Why shouldn't Marisa treat their house as her home? Wasn't that what they'd encouraged her to do? Besides, Kate was wary of upsetting her. She was desperate not to lose this chance they'd worked so hard toward. Marisa was their perfect surrogate, she kept telling herself. Whatever Marisa wanted to do, and however she wanted to act, Kate would have to deal with it. The baby was the most important thing, and it guided her every action. Don't upset the status quo. Don't forget how fragile everything is just beneath the surface.

But Marisa subtly kept expanding her reach around the house. She asked if she could put some of her books on the shelves and Jake readily agreed. When Kate came down to the sitting room, she saw that Marisa had removed Kate's beloved collection of gray-spined Persephone novels and had left them piled untidily on the floor. The shelf was now taken over by weighty art tomes on photography and the female nude—the kind of books people displayed but didn't read.

Once, when Kate had a work meeting nearby, she had popped home in the middle of the day. She noticed as soon as she walked through the door that her running shoes had been moved from the hallway where she always kept them. Marisa came down the stairs, looking distracted.

"Oh," Marisa said. "I wasn't expecting anyone."

Kate tried to make light of it.

"I do live here!"

"I know. I just . . . I'm used to having my own creative space during the days, you know?"

Excuse me for breathing, Kate thought, as Marisa turned and went back upstairs.

"Hang on a sec. Marisa, sorry, but do you know where my trainers are?"

Kate wasn't sure why she was always apologizing to her. She was so worried about putting a foot wrong.

"Yes. I kept tripping over them so I put them in the cupboard under the stairs."

"Oh, ok."

Marisa smiled at her guilelessly. Her golden hair was lit from the landing window behind her, the sun encircling her head, halo-like. Marisa stood like this for several seconds, smiling at Kate, her eyes wide, her feet planted firmly hip-width apart. Kate got the distinct impression that she was being challenged but wasn't sure why.

"Thanks," Kate said eventually, hating herself for her own cowardice. *I could have just said I like having my trainers there*, she thought as she took her coat off. *Why didn't I do that?* But for all her hippieish appearance and unbrushed hair and baggy artist's overalls, Marisa could be intimidating. It wasn't that she was scary, exactly. It was more that you could never predict what she was thinking or how she would react.

Time passed. Kate didn't talk to Jake about it because, after all, it had been her idea for Marisa to move in and she felt she was making too much of relatively trivial things. So Kate stayed quiet, admonished herself for being unreasonable, and simply fished out her trainers from under the stairs and her favorite coffee cup from the back of the cupboard each morning until it became an automatic reflex.

Then Marisa started to cook for them. Kate had tried to dissuade her because, as much as she liked Marisa's company, she didn't particularly want her there every single mealtime. Marisa said it was no trouble and when Jake mentioned in passing that he used to like his mother's macaroni and cheese, Marisa took it upon herself to make it.

"My macaroni and cheese is legendary," she said airily. "Trust me."

When they had first met, Kate had been attracted to Marisa's sense of self. Now she wondered whether there wasn't a degree of overconfidence there. Occasionally, when talking about her work, she would refer to herself in grandiose terms as "an artist who works in paint and other media," and Kate felt this was a bit of an exaggeration, given that she illustrated twee little children's books and got most of her orders from parents sliding into her Instagram DMs. Kate had seen a couple of them, and the fairy tales consisted of simple pictures and plotlines. To Kate's untrained eye, all the children looked similar to each other. Jake had been more polite, asking Marisa questions about how she painted hair and what colors she would mix to get this particular skin tone and so on.

"You'll have to do one for our baby when it arrives!" he said cheerily.

"I'd love that," Marisa replied.

The macaroni and cheese, when it came, was very good. This was another thing that irked her: Kate thought of cooking as her domain and Jake complimented her on her ability to rustle up a delicious meal from any random leftovers, but now Marisa was stealing her thunder.

"Mmmm, this is so good," Jake said, eating laden forkfuls of the pasta.

"It's the lardons," Marisa said. "That, and four different types of cheese."

Kate noticed that Marisa directed all of her comments exclusively toward Jake as if she weren't there. Again, she told herself she was reading too much into it.

"It's yummy," Kate said, even though she thought the macaroni and cheese needed more salt. "Thank you."

Marisa smiled.

Jake, his plate now empty, leaned back in his chair and happily surveyed the scene in front of him.

"I can't wait to have a baby," he said out of the blue. "I know that sounds weird."

Kate met his eye and winked at him. Under the table, she reached for his knee.

"It doesn't," Marisa said. "Why would it?"

"Blokes aren't meant to say stuff like that."

"That's silly."

Marisa propped her elbows up on the table, resting her head in her hands. The V-neck of her T-shirt gaped open, revealing the tops of her cleavage. Kate was so close she could see Marisa's tan line left over from holiday sunbathing, the flesh turning white just above where her nipple would be.

"I can't wait either," Marisa said, "and I don't care if that makes me sound weird." She giggled.

Kate looked at her. The way Marisa had spoken felt so possessive, so nonchalant, as if this experience were hers to own, when it wasn't. It was theirs.

"We appreciate what you're doing for us, Marisa," Kate said, making the point.

Marisa, who had been turned toward Jake, acknowledged Kate with a slight tilt of the head in her direction. The atmosphere was heavy and Kate, feeling the weight of all that was happening between the three of them, said briskly, "It's going to be great," and got up to start clearing the plates.

In bed that night, Kate rolled across the mattress and slotted herself against Jake's back, wrapping her arms around his waist. He placed his hand over hers and they twisted their legs together. She pressed her face into the nape of his neck, feeling the softest part of his hair tickle her mouth.

"Love you," Jake said.

"Love you too." She closed her eyes and tried to sleep but she couldn't. "Jake?"

"Mmm."

"Do think everything's ok? With Marisa, I mean."

He turned to look at her, alert now. "What do you mean?"

"She's just . . . It sounds silly . . . but . . ."

"You're worrying me."

"Oh, no, sorry—it's nothing to worry about; it's just . . . she's made herself very at home, hasn't she?"

"Well, isn't that what we want?"

"I guess. It's just . . . she moves my stuff around."

He laughed quietly. "Your trainers?"

"Yes!"

"They were quite annoying right there by the front door, you know."

"Stop taking her side!"

He hugged her, adopting a jokey voice to say, "There are no sides! It's not a competition. We're all in this together, aren't we?"

She spoke into his chest, her voice muffled. "And you went on and on about her fucking macaroni and cheese."

Jake laughed. "Is *that* what this is about? Come on, Kate."

"Do you still like my cooking the best?" She knew she was being childish, but she couldn't help it. She wanted his reassurance.

"Of course I do. I love you the best. I can't wait to have a baby with you. I wish we didn't have to involve anyone else, but given that we do, we've found someone who seems great, and if her only annoying habit is moving your trainers, I think we can put up with it for a few more months, can't we?"

She snuggled closer to him. "You're right. I know you're right. Sorry."

"Stop apologizing." He drew back and kissed the tip of her nose. "I can't imagine how hard this must be for you. But we're meant to be doing the embryo transfer in a few weeks, aren't we? And I think we'll all feel a lot less tense then."

Kate was glad she'd said something. In voicing her fears, she could now see them for what they were: paranoia triggered by insecurity about her place in this unconventional family unit. The therapist recommended by the surrogacy agency had warned her she might feel like this. It was important to separate what her anxious brain was telling her from what was actually happening. Just because she thought it did not make it fact.

"You're still the mother," Jake said. "Don't forget that."

Jake was always good at calming her down and making her see things more logically. She closed her eyes again. It was quiet outside, and soon Jake was snoring. Kate was edging toward the brink of sleep when she heard a floorboard creak, followed by a padding noise, like the sound of footsteps retreating.

The next day, she wasn't sure if she had dreamed it or whether there really had been someone listening at the door.

XXI.

Annabelle's birthday was coming up and Jake suggested they take his parents out for a slap-up lunch in a good London restaurant and treat them to a night in a posh hotel.

"She loves that kind of stuff," he said when he outlined the plan to Kate. "And that way, she doesn't have to stay with us."

"She couldn't anyway, not with Marisa."

"I know. But this way we can dress it up as a present and she won't feel hard done by."

It was a Sunday morning and he was heating up croissants in the oven while rain lashed down outside, turning briefly to hail, which hurled itself against the glass doors.

"Sure, it's a great idea," Kate said. "Can we afford it?"

"I mean, not really, but I'd like to do something to mark her birthday. And then we'll have a chance to tell her about the surrogacy in a neutral setting."

Kate resented the way they had to "handle" Annabelle, as though she were an overly sensitive child. She'd been matter-of-fact when she told her own parents, who were supportive once she'd explained to them what surrogacy actually was and why they were doing it. Her mother's main concern had been what they were thinking of calling the baby and whether the child would have Jake's surname or Kate's, given that they weren't married.

"Let's cross that bridge when we come to it," Kate had said. "There's a long way to go yet."

"Don't leave it too late, love," her mother replied and then she had put the kettle on. "Cup of tea?"

But Jake had been worried about telling Annabelle ever since they started looking for a surrogate. Kate didn't understand why he cared so much what his mother thought of him, given that he was a thirty-nine-year-old man. She wondered if it was that, having been sent to boarding school at a young age, he subconsciously always felt that his mother didn't approve of him and that he had been trying to compensate for this lack ever since. Kate had mentioned this theory to Jake shortly after they met, but he had brushed it aside and told her to please spare him "the psychoanalytic bullshit about boarding school," and that had been that.

When the allotted Saturday of the birthday lunch arrived, Jake got dressed in a blue suit, Kate in a knitted dress and low heels. They walked downstairs and picked up the keys from the bowl on the hallway table. As they gathered up their coats, they heard Marisa behind them.

"Where are you two going?" she asked. She was holding a paintbrush in one hand and a jar of cloudy water in the other.

"Taking my mother out for her birthday lunch," Jake said.

"Oh. Well, have fun, won't you?"

"I very much doubt we will," Kate said.

"Kate," Jake said, mild admonishment in his tone. "We will, thank you."

Marisa stood there as Jake opened the front door, holding it for Kate to pass under his arm into the street.

"I'd love to meet her one day," Marisa said.

On the doorstep, Kate looked at her quizzically. It was an odd thing to say, wasn't it? Or was it perfectly normal for a surrogate to want to meet the mother of the soon-to-be legal parent?

"Be careful what you wish for," Jake said drily.

Kate shrugged her arms into the sleeves of her trench coat.

"See you later, Marisa," she said, keeping her voice breezy but marking the definite end of the exchange.

"Yes, see you! What time will you be back, do you think?"

"Not sure. We'll be a few hours, I imagine. Bye," Jake said, closing the door. "Have fun," he shouted through the letter box.

"Have fun?" Kate laughed as they walked through Vauxhall Park. There were workmen planting lavender bushes and creating a new tarmac path through the grass. "What did you say that for? She's not a child."

"I don't know. I just felt like I'd done something wrong by not asking her along. Did you get that?"

"Yeah. It was weird."

They scooted to one side to avoid a cyclist.

"Perhaps she's lonely? She doesn't seem to have any friends, does she?"

Kate shrugged. "She's got us."

"True."

They took the Victoria Line tube to Green Park, where they walked the short distance to the Wolseley. They were the first to get there, and the maitre d' showed them to their table in the central horseshoe where they sat next to each other on the banquette to people-watch. He offered them a newspaper to read and they said no. He left, returning with a jug of water, and Jake asked him for a Bloody Mary.

"Better make that two," Kate said. "Extra spicy."

Increasingly, these days, she found herself craving the carefully timed narcotic release of alcohol. She told herself that after all those months of not drinking through fertility treatment, she was owed it.

She examined the table. The menus were thick to the touch and the salt and pepper shakers were silver. There was a curtain around the door to prevent drafts from reaching the clientele, which Kate thought was always the mark of true class.

Jake's parents arrived fifteen minutes late, with Annabelle rushing toward the table looking harried. She was a billowing torrent of cerulean silk and apologies. Chris emerged a few seconds later having checked their coats in, sporting a tweed jacket and a vague smile.

"I'm so sorry," Annabelle said as Jake stood to let her slide into the banquette beside Kate. "The train was delayed by a trespasser on the line. It was awful! Every seat taken. People standing. Even in first class." She paused. "I did text."

"Oh, sorry, Mum. I wasn't checking my phone. Anyway, don't worry—you're here now. We've been having a lovely time."

"I can see that," she said, casting a glance at the empty Bloody Mary glasses.

"I'll have one of those," Chris said, summoning a waiter over. "Anyone else?"

Kate nodded gratefully.

"I'll have a glass of champagne, darling," Annabelle said, "given that it *is* my birthday celebration."

"Of course! We must order a bottle," Jake told the waiter.

Annabelle squeezed his arm. "Thank you, sweetheart. Treating your mother. Such a good boy."

Kate tried not to roll her eyes.

"And how are you, Kate?" Annabelle turned to her. "Sorry, I've barely said hello what with all the rush!"

Annabelle gave a sprinkling little laugh. She was wearing dangling sapphires from each earlobe and a discreet diamond on a chain around her neck. She seemed tense, and every time her head moved, the earrings wobbled with her.

"I'm good, thank you. It's nice to—"

"Darling, will you pass me my pashmina?" Annabelle gestured at Chris, who took out a pale-blue scarf from a tote bag embossed with a National Trust insignia. She draped it around her shoulders, shivering and huddling as she did so.

"I'm freezing, aren't you?" She clutched Kate's hand. "Feel how cold I am!"

"Oh dear," Kate replied. "I'm sure you'll warm up soon. Do you want me to get your coat?"

"No, no, no, it'll take far too long." Annabelle removed her hand, annoyed. "Let's order, shall we? I'm starving, aren't you, Jakey?"

When the food arrived, Annabelle added salt to her chicken salad, shaking it over the leaves for several seconds, claiming that the dish was "a touch on the bland side." She ate half the bowl, then left the remainder untouched. The conversation revolved around Annabelle's concern for Toad, who had recently been involved in some dispute with a student at the university she taught at in Dublin. The student in question had complained that Toad had made a transphobic comment in a lecture and now Toad was suspended from her job while the university authorities investigated.

"I mean, people are so *sensitive* these days. You can't say anything for fear of being lynched."

Kate groaned, pressing a napkin to her mouth to disguise it as a cough. "With respect, Annabelle, that's not the best metaphor."

Annabelle gazed at her, as though from a vast distance. "Oh, I suppose I'm using the wrong language now, am I? Well, you can't put a foot right."

Jake shot Kate a look but she pretended she hadn't seen him. She knew he would tell her later that his parents were products of a different age, that it was all to do with context, and that although he personally didn't support their casual racism, you couldn't hope to teach them new habits. Kate disagreed and felt an obligation to point out discriminatory attitudes. It was one of their long-running arguments and it would probably never be resolved. After all, Kate thought indignantly, Jake had only stopped voting Tory when he met her.

At the table, there was an awkward silence, which Chris broke by ordering a bottle of Picpoul.

The meal revived itself after that. Kate bit her tongue as Annabelle veered into the topic of Brexit, claiming she had met the most wonderful "immigrant cleaner" at her friend Trisha's house the other day who had "quite convinced me it's the wrong thing for this country to leave the EU. Hardworking people like her deserve a chance, I say. She's not claiming benefits, despite what Farage and his ilk would have you believe . . ."

Jake kept topping up his mother's glass so that she became gradually softer and tipsier as the lunch went on. By the time the dessert arrived, Annabelle had been successfully detoxified and was starting to ask Kate what films she'd recommend seeing at the cinema (this was always Annabelle's way of breaking the ice, as if she knew a single fact about her son's girlfriend's work and clearly intended to deploy it frequently to show how much she cared).

"We actually had something to tell you guys," Jake said, resting his spoon and fork on either side of a warm chocolate soufflé.

Annabelle, who had her glass of wine halfway to her mouth, placed it back on the table.

It dawned on Kate that Annabelle might think they were going to announce their engagement.

"We're not getting married," she blurted out. There was a stunned pause. Annabelle drew her pashmina closer to her.

"All right," she said. "What is it, then?"

"Sorry," Kate added, a few seconds too late. "I just . . ." She had no idea how Annabelle managed to make her feel so on edge all the time.

"We're not getting married," Jake said levelly. "But we do have exciting news. At least, we think it's exciting."

"You're pregnant!" Annabelle shrieked. "Oh, Kate, how absolutely wonderful. I know how much this means to you and I've been praying—*praying*—every night for this."

She put her arm around Kate's shoulders and pulled her into a hug. When Kate extracted herself, she was astonished to see there were tears in Annabelle's eyes.

"Annabelle," Kate said. "That's so lovely of you."

"I just know how wonderful it is to be a mother, and I want that for you so much."

This sincerity was so unexpected that Kate felt herself on the brink of crying. All the stress of the last few years, and the more recent tension of having Marisa in the house with them, churned up inside her and she had to press her fingernails into the palm of her hand to stop it from spilling out.

"I'm afraid I'm not pregnant," she managed to say. "But I—we—are hoping to be parents."

"Aha," Chris said, and then relapsed into silence.

The waiter came then, at just the wrong moment, to ask if they wanted teas or coffees. Jake asked him to give them a minute and the waiter stalked off, offended.

"I don't understand," Annabelle said.

"The thing is, Mum," Jake started out shakily, "as you know, we've been trying and nothing has worked, to put it bluntly. It's been a terrible strain on Kate, who has been a trooper—"

He caught her eye and she gave a minute shake of the head. She did not want him to go into how it had been for her.

"But, on medical advice," Jake continued, getting the message, "we've decided to explore a new option, which is surrogacy."

"Surrogacy?" Annabelle said, as if trying out a new foreign word for the first time.

"Yes. It's where another woman carries our baby—"

"I know that."

"And, extremely fortunately, we've found a surrogate!" His tone was breezy now, trying hard for nonchalance and not quite achieving it. "Her name is Marisa. She's very generously agreed to help us and we can't quite believe our luck, but there we have it."

Annabelle stared at Jake, as if she had been slapped. Kate had never seen her lost for words. Her cheeks were hollow, her mouth slightly agape. She sat perfectly still except for her hands, which fidgeted in her lap like small birds.

Chris took his napkin and, folding it up neatly, put it on the side of the table.

"Well, I think that's something else to celebrate, don't you?" Chris said, and it was the longest sentence he'd uttered since the meal began. He began filling their glasses and when he got to Annabelle's, he leaned across the table and smiled at her, nodding his head as though encouraging a young child.

"Thank you, Chris," Kate said.

"Yes, thanks, Dad."

"Can't have been easy," Chris was saying now. "I admire that you haven't given up."

"Are you all right, Mum?" Jake asked.

"What? Oh. Yes. Yes. Perfectly all right. I'm sorry. I'm just . . . taking it all in."

Kate reached out and pressed her hand softly against Annabelle's upper arm. The silk felt cool and slightly sticky beneath her palm.

"It does take a while to get your head round it," Kate said. "Sorry to spring it on you like this."

Annabelle turned toward her. "But . . . surely you can't be serious?" she asked, with those sharp, hawkish eyes. "How do you know this Marisa woman?"

"We met her through a surrogacy network," Jake answered, even though Annabelle was still looking directly at Kate, her distaste evident in the twist of her mouth.

"It's all aboveboard," Jake said. "We've signed an agreement and we will be the legal parents—"

Annabelle cut across him. "Legally, maybe, but what about genetically? These kinds of things are *important*. Especially for men.

I read somewhere that they need their babies to look like them so that they can bond . . ."

Kate almost laughed. Then she almost cried.

"It's not what we would have chosen," Kate said quietly.

"But it's where we are," Jake interjected smoothly. "Besides, nurture is far more important than nature." He paused and Annabelle lifted her fist to her mouth as if she were about to cough but no sound came.

"There are similarities where it matters," Jake continued. He told her a bit about Marisa's background, emphasizing the fact that she was an artist, which he knew would appeal to Annabelle's cultural snobbishness.

"An artist?" Annabelle shrieked. "She must be desperate for cash. How much are you paying her?"

"We're not paying her anything," Jake said, "because that would be illegal." He left a pointed gap in conversation before taking up the thread. "We pay her reasonable expenses."

"What, like her rent? How much is that setting you back?"

"Annabelle," Chris said softly. He made a shushing sound and motioned up and down with his hand, as though pushing a quiz show buzzer.

Annabelle took a deep breath. She exhaled impatiently, then poured herself some sparkling water.

"We're not paying her rent—"

"That's something, I suppose," Annabelle said.

"Because she's living with us."

Annabelle put down her glass so quickly the water spilled over the edges.

"She's *living* with you? Are you . . . I mean . . . Have you . . . Have you both taken leave of your senses? Surely that's far too close for comfort? This isn't parenthood; it's a ménage à trois! Is the idea that you'll have to"—her voice dropped to a whisper—"*impregnate* her?"

Kate could have hit her. Instead, she rose from the table and walked briskly to the loo. She almost lost her footing on the stone spiral staircase on the way down to the basement. She locked the cubicle door behind her and tried to regulate her breathing. When she emerged, there was an older woman standing at the sink, re-applying lipstick in a virulent shade of pink.

"You all right?" the woman asked her.

In the mirror, Kate noticed her cheeks were pale and that her mascara had run. "Yes, thank you. Sorry."

"Don't apologize." The woman finished putting her lipstick on and rubbed her lips together. "Family lunch?" she asked.

"Yes." Kate smiled as she washed her hands.

"They're the worst."

Kate dried her hands on a thick paper towel as the woman put the cap back on her lipstick and slipped it into her handbag, which, Kate noticed, was vintage Chanel.

"Good luck with it."

"Thanks," Kate said, calmer now. "I like your bag, by the way."

"Oh, you are kind. It was given to me by my daughter."

Then she asked the question—the question that Kate always knew was coming. Sometimes she could count the number of seconds it would take to be said out loud.

"Do you have kids?"

She shook her head. *No*, she thought, *no, I don't have children. But if you knew how much it cost me to answer that, you wouldn't ask.*

"I don't," Kate said, balling up the paper towel and throwing it in the circular hole cut into the marbled countertop.

"Ah well. There's still time."

She let the woman leave the toilets first so that they didn't have to walk back upstairs together. When Kate returned to the table, an impasse had been reached. Jake had probably told his parents what an unbalanced nutcase she was, Kate thought, and how she had been driven obsessive by the desire for motherhood and her failure to conceive. It was unfair of her to think like this, she knew. But she had to put her hurt somewhere.

Annabelle stood as Kate reached the table and walked toward her, arms outstretched so that the blue sleeves hung down like drooping crocus heads.

"Darling Kate. I'm so sorry for being insensitive."

Annabelle hugged her. The affection was administered like the bruising pain of a deep-tissue massage: uncomfortable but ultimately a relief.

"I'm very old-fashioned and ill-informed when it comes to these issues, and Jake's explained it all to me and I *do* understand—truly I do. I think it's tremendously brave of you to do this, knowing that the baby won't be genetically yours. I suppose I was just worried about you both, that's all. I apologize if I expressed myself badly."

Kate drew back but Annabelle wouldn't let go.

"Thank you, Annabelle."

"Can you ever forgive me?" Annabelle said, lapsing into hyperbole so that there was no option but to say yes, of course she did, and no, don't worry, she wasn't offended, and yes, she understood that it was an unconventional arrangement, and no, she mustn't worry, it was all aboveboard, and yes, naturally she was glad Annabelle was excited about becoming a grandmother.

Kate spent the rest of the lunch in a sort of daze, sipping her coffee and eating the accompanying chocolate truffles in a series of automatic movements. Chris ordered her a brandy, although she couldn't remember having asked for it, and she downed it in three gulps. Jake paid the bill and they went outside to hail his parents a cab to the hotel. She watched them go, standing at a distance from the world around her.

XXII.

It was Marisa, now, who was injecting herself every day with fertility drugs in order to stimulate egg production. It was Marisa who stored the little glass vials in the fridge, mixing the powder with the requisite amount of liquid, piercing the top with a needle and sucking it up inside the syringe. It was Marisa who would sit on the sofa in the kitchen, lifting her pajama top to slide the needle into a firmly held section of her belly and pressing down on the syringe. It was Marisa who put the used needles into the yellow-and-purple sharps bin provided by the hospital, which they stored on top of the fridge. Kate would catch sight of it every time she opened the door to retrieve the milk and she would be reminded of all the times she had tried and failed to carry out the same process.

It was Marisa who was the object of Jake's inquiries as to how she was feeling, and did she need any help, and could he get her anything from the shops? It was Marisa who was the golden one, the chosen one, the fertile one, the one who would make all their dreams come true, except their original dreams never involved a third person.

Kate tried in various ways to make herself a part of it. She told Marisa she wanted to be there for every injection, even offering to press the plunger down on the syringe herself.

"You don't have to do that," Marisa said. "I'm fine, honestly."

But I want to, Kate didn't say.

She asked Marisa if she was getting enough sleep or drinking enough water. She wanted to express kindly concern but Kate could tell that Marisa found it intrusive coming from her rather than Jake, so Kate began to censor herself. She was anxious about doing anything that would irritate Marisa. It meant that at mealtimes, Kate would often be almost entirely silent, while Jake and Marisa chatted easily. Jake was always so much better at that kind of thing.

He was in a good mood about it all, extremely hopeful and optimistic that they would have their baby soon. He took to whistling around the house and working out more in the garden, his chest lean and shiny with sweat as he performed Romanian dead lifts and lateral raises with ever-heavier dumbbells. As the weather got even warmer, Marisa would sit outside as he grunted and groaned, reading a book on the bench, saying she liked the company. Kate, observing them through the glass doors in the kitchen, thought how similar they looked: both blond and glowing and healthy and vital. In the mirror each morning, Kate was met by her own narrow face and darkened eyes. There was a gauntness to her collarbone and her jeans were loose around the waistband. Her natural slenderness had edged into skinniness and it didn't suit her. It made her look older. Her body no longer felt like hers. It had its own set of impermeable rules.

One day, she mentioned the pregnancy yoga class to Marisa, telling her she'd read an article about how being around pregnant women could boost fertility. Kate asked if she wanted to go.

"Sure," Marisa said, giving her the luminous smile that always made Kate feel she had imagined any previous strangeness. "I'll give it a try."

"Great. Let me know when you go and I'll come with you."

Marisa raised her eyebrows by a fraction of a millimeter, then smoothed her face out as if nothing had occurred. But Kate had already seen. Or she thought she had seen—she couldn't be sure. Marisa never did tell Kate that she was going to yoga. It was only by chance that Kate saw her leave the house one morning with a mat rolled up under her arm. She got changed into her tracksuit bottoms and T-shirt and tried to catch up with her but didn't make it in time. When she got to the class, all the other women were in situ on their mats and ambient music was playing.

It was a boring class, all the poses designed for the advanced stages of pregnancy, and Kate couldn't wait for it to be over. Marisa was at the front of the room, trying her best to follow the instructor, but she moved in a lumbering, inelegant way. Kate felt a glimmer of pride that she was better at yoga than Marisa. It seemed one of the only ways in which she was.

After the class was over, Kate waited for Marisa to roll up her mat and leave. She said hello to her and was surprised at how cold Marisa was, how taken aback she seemed to see her. Kate tried to make light of it, filling the awkward conversational gaps with small talk.

"Thought it would be nice to do it together, you know?" Kate said.

"Except we didn't," Marisa said.

"Didn't what?"

"Do it together. You skulked at the back."

Kate forced out a laugh. "I wasn't skulking! I just wanted to give you your own space."

They walked out into the street together and Kate asked Marisa if she wanted to go for coffee so they could catch up and have a chat. Marisa said no, that she had a work deadline, and that was that. Kate stood on the curb and watched as Marisa walked away from her, then turned back, looking over her shoulder.

"See you back at home!" Kate shouted. She raised her arm and waved, hoping she hadn't offended her.

▪ ▪ ▪

They did the egg retrieval on a Wednesday. They took the afternoon off work to go to the clinic with Marisa. She was in a good mood, the business about the yoga class apparently forgotten. She was wearing a bright-blue shirt tucked into baggy corduroys that had a white paint dot on one knee. There was always something about her that looked unmade, unfinished—as though she hadn't had time to get properly dressed. But at least, Kate thought, she hadn't worn those hideous sandals she usually clomped about in when she worked.

Mr. Abadi was pleased with Marisa's progress.

"Very good," he said, checking her charts. "That's looking very good indeed."

He beamed at Marisa in a way he never had at Kate.

Jake went into another room to provide his sample. He reemerged half an hour later, hands in his pockets. Kate couldn't meet his eye. As much as she tried to rationalize the process, it was still disarming to think of his sperm being used to fertilize another woman's eggs. What did he think of when he masturbated? she wondered. Was he thinking of her? Of someone else? Or was he flicking through the dog-eared porn magazines the clinic provided?

For the collection process itself, Kate and Jake were directed to a waiting area.

"I promise I'll come out and tell you how many we get as soon as possible," Mr. Abadi said, ushering Marisa behind a screen.

"Bye, guys," Marisa said as she left. "Here's hoping."

She crossed her fingers and they crossed theirs back.

"You're doing amazingly," Kate said, forcing herself to sound positive. She told herself to remember Marisa's generosity and not to focus on her own sad memories of this exact room in this exact clinic. This was how it had to happen.

Jake gripped her hand tightly.

"You ok?" Kate asked him.

He nodded, his jaw set in a rigid line.

"It'll be fine," she said, leaning in to kiss him on the cheek.

Marisa produced fourteen eggs. Mr. Abadi was ecstatic.

"It's a very good number. Very good," he kept saying. "Very good size."

Fourteen, Kate thought. It was excessive. It was as if Marisa were trying to prove a point.

Beside her, Jake's shoulders relaxed and he broke into a smile.

"That's wonderful," he said, standing to shake Mr. Abadi by the hand.

"Yes," Kate added quietly. "Wonderful."

The next day, Mr. Abadi called Kate to tell her that eight of the eggs had fertilized. She called Jake at work, and they both knew it was good news but that they would have to wait until they could be sure of it. The fertilized eggs now needed to divide and multiply their cells at the requisite rate for five days until they could be deemed worthy of transfer.

On day five, Mr. Abadi called again to tell Kate that they had "six perfect blastocysts." A blastocyst, she already knew, meant that the cells were starting to separate into those that would form the baby and those that would grow into the placenta. She knew that the blastocyst would have hatched, like a chick from an egg, sprouting from its protective shell to form the "zona pellucida." She had looked up the etymology of this term during their first IVF cycle and found that it meant a shining bright ring. She imagined this ring now as a flaming loop around their planet of three, a protective shield of light.

Mr. Abadi suggested transferring two embryos, "but with embryos of this quality, I warn you: you must be prepared for twins!" He sounded almost giddy on the phone, full of an avuncular good cheer Kate had never heard before. "And then we can freeze the remaining four, and you will be able to have more children than you can shake a stick at."

They followed his advice, as they always had. It was now a force of habit, as though, in their desperation to be parents, they had lost the power of critical thinking. Two embryos were transferred later that same day and the three of them got a black cab back from the clinic to Richborne Terrace. None of them talked in the taxi. The driver was listening to Magic FM so the back of the cab was filled with easy-listening pop tunes. Marisa, sitting next to Kate, leaned back with a sigh. Jake, perched on the jump seat opposite her, asked if she was feeling tired.

"A little, yeah. Must be the sedation. Mr. Abadi said it felt like drinking two gin and tonics and he wasn't wrong."

Mr. Abadi had used the same line on Kate, but she didn't say anything. Out of the corner of her eye, she saw Marisa cradling her stomach. Overkill, she thought uncharitably.

There was a fortnight's wait, during which Marisa was counseled not to take overly hot baths or to do any strenuous exercise.

"No more yoga,'" she said to Kate. "What a shame!"

"I don't think that class could ever be categorized as strenuous," Kate replied. "But you absolutely must rest."

Every day, Kate brought Marisa breakfast in bed.

"You don't need to do this," Marisa said, reaching for the hot buttered toast as she spoke.

Kate sat at the edge of the mattress, sipping her coffee as Marisa ate. They chatted a little, about how Marisa's painting was going, about the films Kate was promoting, about everything other than the thing that was actually consuming them. Kate felt closer to Marisa than she had in weeks. She began to allow herself to feel the slenderest filament of optimism. She felt like cooking again and made Jake his favorite dishes. Roast chicken with homemade bread sauce. Nigel Slater's classic ratatouille. A recipe for Moroccan lamb and prune tagine she had picked up in a free supermarket magazine.

And then: macaroni and cheese, which she cooked one night with Marisa sitting on the sofa watching TV. It was the thirteenth day of their two-week wait. Tomorrow, Marisa would take a pregnancy test in the morning, first thing after she woke up, when the hormone levels would be at their highest. That way, there would be no false positives.

Kate was nervous but also excited, and as she waited to hear the turn of Jake's key in the lock, she experienced a fluttery sensation in her stomach, as she had in the first days of their dating. She wanted to be close to him and to feel his arms around her. When he got home, he walked into the kitchen and smelled the melting cheese wafting from the oven and went straight to Kate's side, trying to open the oven as she swatted his hand away.

"No opening the oven door until it's done, please," she told him.

"Ok, ok, I promise," he said, shrugging himself out of his jacket and loosening his tie.

"Hi," Marisa said from the sofa.

"Oh, hi, Marisa," Jake replied, cheerfully waving toward her.

He turned to get himself a glass of water and as he did, Marisa dashed out of the room, her head lowered.

Kate slid her hands out of the oven mitts, leaving them on the counter.

"What was that about?" Jake asked.

She shrugged. "No idea."

"Something I said?"

She laughed at him, then went across and put her arms around his neck, kissing him deeply on the mouth.

"Probably," she joked. "It's probably all your fault."

He looked at her, tucking a strand of her hair behind her ear with the tips of his fingers. It was a familiar, proprietorial gesture and Kate liked it.

"I better go and check on her," he said. "See if she's ok."

"Yes, you do that. I'll finish up down here."

Jake went upstairs and Kate took out the macaroni and cheese, allowing it to stand and sizzle on the counter. She had just started chopping cucumber for a salad when Jake came back into the kitchen.

"All ok?"

"Yes, fine," he said, and he reached across to the chopping board and popped a piece of cucumber in his mouth.

A few minutes later, just as Jake was laying the table and lighting the candles, they heard Marisa scream. Jake dropped the knives and forks with a clatter and ran upstairs and Kate, heart beating wildly, followed close behind. As they reached the first-floor bathroom, the door swung open. Marisa, her cheeks wet, held a pregnancy test aloft.

"We're pregnant!" she shouted.

"What?" Kate said, feeling as though she might faint. "What?"

Jake's shoulders shook and he started to cry. "I can't believe it," he kept saying. "I can't believe it."

He went to Marisa, hugging her tightly, and then Marisa was crying, too, and Kate, pressing herself against the wall to steady the sudden shakiness of the world, sensed her knees give way as she slid to the floor. She clasped her head in her hands and wondered who was sobbing until she realized the sound was coming from her.

XXIII.

The three of them settled into a routine. The focal point was the pregnancy. Marisa had to sleep as much as her body told her she needed, so Kate and Jake were quiet in the mornings, leaving the house on tiptoes, gently closing the door behind them so it wouldn't slam. Kate bought new supplies of folic acid and pregnancy multivitamins, stacking them in the cupboard above the sink. She Googled the best foods for early pregnancy and cooked healthy, colorful meals full of leafy green vegetables and oily fish. Marisa, pale with nausea, couldn't eat most of it, so Kate ate for her, as if she could transmit all the necessary nutrients via osmosis.

For the first month, Kate wouldn't allow herself to believe in it fully. She kept asking Marisa to take new pregnancy tests and Marisa sweetly obliged.

"Here you go," Marisa would say, handing over the stick with the two pink lines or the digital aperture displaying the single word PREGNANT.

"Thank you," Kate answered.

Marisa hugged her. "I don't mind."

Kate built up a fairly substantial collection of positive pregnancy tests, storing each one in the drawer of the bathroom cabinet that stood by the sink. Sometimes she would open the drawer just to look at them, stacked neatly side by side, so that she could be reminded of this essential truth: they *were* pregnant. After so long, after so much yearning and loss, here the fact was.

Marisa took to her new condition with ease. She appeared calmer than she had for ages and Kate began to think it hadn't been fair of her to judge. They had all been living on frayed nerves for too long. Now the pressure lifted, and it felt like a cool breeze rustling through grass after a heat wave.

In bed at night, Kate fell asleep in Jake's arms, not waking until morning. Her sleep was dreamless and solid and she woke rested. Jake started texting her again during the day, little messages to say he was thinking of her or that he loved her or that he couldn't wait to fuck her later. Reading these texts at her desk, Kate hadn't realized how much she had missed them. When they made noiseless love, they did so urgently, as though they couldn't physically get close enough, as though they both wanted to consume the other.

In the second month, Kate started thinking again of baby names. It was a discussion she and Jake had had countless times before, but when her IVF cycles had started failing, they had shelved it. It was too painful. Expectation was the cruelest trick when you weren't expecting.

This time, with Marisa carrying their twin top-grade embryos, Kate was more confident. She and Jake agreed on Maya and Eva for girls and Leo and Oscar for boys.

"But really, we'll have to wait until we meet them," Jake said, "to see what they look like."

The thought of meeting their beloved children was almost too much to bear. After waiting for so long, seven more months seemed nearly impossible to endure.

They took to telling the babies they loved them, bending down to Marisa's tummy and whispering "I love you" directly into her belly. Marisa smiled benignly as she watched them, joking that her stomach had never had so much attention.

For a while it was perfect. It was important for Kate to remember that, later, after everything that happened. For a while, it was going so well.

At first it was the small things that edged uncomfortably into Kate's consciousness, like the distant slap of a wasp thudding against a faraway window.

At the weekends, Marisa stayed in her room until late afternoon. Kate would knock on the door, wondering if she wanted a cup of herbal tea, and there would be no answer. When Marisa came out, she was uncommunicative, responding to questions with single-word replies, eating her dinner without joining in the chat. They asked her if she was feeling ok, if she needed anything, and what could they do.

"I'm just tired," Marisa would say. "It's fine, honestly."

During the week, there was no way of checking up on her. Kate started ringing the house from her office in the middle of the day but Marisa never picked up the phone. The buzzing of the wasp got nearer and louder. Marisa spent longer and longer in her room, and when Kate asked her why, Marisa told her she was working, trying to meet a flurry of deadlines.

"I'd love to see some of your new paintings," Kate said, trying to start a conversation.

Marisa looked at her oddly. "I'm not painting as much. More writing at the moment," she said.

"Oh!" Kate continued brightly. "You're so clever to be able to do both."

It was true that she noticed Marisa writing more. When she was sitting in her usual place, on the far side of the kitchen sofa in front of the television as Kate or Jake cooked, Marisa would be scribbling rapidly in a notebook, the scratch of the pen providing an irregular rhythm to their conversation. Kate wanted to ask what she was writing but something about Marisa's mood left her too scared to do so.

"Am I being stupid?" she asked Jake one Saturday when they had gone for a walk in Battersea Park.

"No. I've definitely noticed the change in her." The sun came out in one of those unexpected bursts so familiar to London, and he fished out his Ray-Bans from his jacket pocket. "I've had a word with her about some of it."

"What do you mean?"

"Well, I didn't know whether to tell you this but . . ."

He looked out toward the river, refusing to meet her eye.

"What?" Kate said. "Come on, spit it out."

"Um. My mother paid her an unscheduled visit."

"Annabelle?"

Jake smiled. "I do only have the one mother."

"Thank goodness," she said.

He told her then about how Annabelle had turned up on the doorstep several weeks ago and Marisa had invited her in for coffee and Kate didn't know whether to be furious at the imposition or grateful that she'd taken an interest.

"I think," Jake continued, as they walked past the pagoda, "that she found my mother a bit forceful."

"I bet. Poor Marisa. I guess it makes sense she's been a bit jumpy since then."

Jake took a sip from his disposable coffee cup and when he lowered it, there was a thin trail of cappuccino foam lining his upper lip.

"I don't think it's anything to worry about," he said. "It's probably just hormonal, isn't it?"

"First-trimester stuff," Kate replied.

"Exactly. You're meant to go a bit loopy, aren't you? She's probably feeling sick and exhausted and not wanting to bother us with it."

"You're right." Kate was relieved.

"If anything," Jake said, putting his arm around her shoulders, "it's a *good* sign."

But back at home, the unease lingered. Kate had hoped that, by inviting Marisa to live with them, it would quickly become a normalized arrangement. Instead, it had begun to feel like living with a teenage lodger who had unpredictable mood swings but had to be indulged in order to keep the peace. When she asked Marisa what she had thought of Annabelle, Marisa seemed shocked.

"How did you know?"

"Jake told me."

Kate couldn't understand why Marisa had been so unforthcoming about it.

"I know Annabelle can be . . . a lot," Kate said, trying to gloss over it.

"I thought she was wonderful," Marisa replied. "I admired her a lot."

Kate didn't push it. She told herself it was a positive thing that Marisa should feel this way and that perhaps it would encourage Annabelle to support the arrangement too.

The weekend before their twelve-week scan, Kate and Jake had been in the sitting room reading the papers while Marisa was upstairs. It was comfortable, the two of them like this, just as it had been in their Battersea flat, and Kate wanted to put on some music that would remind them of those earlier years, before life had got so serious. She flicked through the playlists in her phone until she found an old Oasis album, then she plugged it into the speakers, turned it up, and allowed the drums to kick in.

She started singing the lyrics, jumping up and down and letting her hair fall over her face like she was at a festival, and then Jake was next to her, dancing with one hand up in the air as he always did, and they were both singing the chorus now, feeling the bass thrum up beneath their feet, sending a vibrating jolt through their bodies. It was so good to let loose like this, to allow the air into their lungs, to move like they didn't care, to forget their adult selves for a brief moment, and she was grinning wildly at Jake, and then the song stopped and there was a pause before the next banger kicked in.

They were both out of breath, so they leaned against the mantelpiece to recover, allowing the album and its memories to blaze through them as they nodded their heads to the beat.

"Do you remember this one?" Kate said. "Such a fucking classic."

They didn't see Marisa at the door. It was only when she shouted "HELLO?" that they realized she was there. Kate was startled and stammered, "Oh. Hi." They looked at Marisa, with her untidy hair falling snakelike over her shoulders, and Kate noticed an electric shimmer to her eyes that she hadn't seen before.

"Could you turn the music down?" Marisa said, her voice still raised, as though she couldn't control it, as though she didn't even notice herself how loudly she was speaking. "I'm trying to work."

Her hands were twisted together, the nails of one scratching the back of the other. She seemed jittery and unmoored, like a ball pinging against metal.

"The music?" Kate said.

"Yes."

"I'm so sorry. I hadn't realized it was that loud."

"It's loud enough that I had to put in earplugs," Marisa said.

Kate's throat constricted. She felt like a child who had just been told off by a teacher. She should be penitent, but instead she found herself on the verge of giggling. The dancing had unleashed something in her. She was free and young again.

She caught Jake's eye and saw he was also struggling to hold it together. There was something about the way Marisa was standing there, arms folded over her lumpy cardigan now, that made it even funnier.

"Ooookaaaaayyy," Jake said. "Sorry about that."

He stopped the music. Marisa stood there for a few more seconds, glowering at them both. Then she turned and left the room, closing the door behind her. Kate waited until they could hear her tread on the stairs and then she could hold it in no longer. She started to laugh helplessly until tears rolled down her face. She gripped her mouth in her hands, trying to stem the flow of it, and Jake was shushing her but he was laughing too and then their laughter stopped, just as unexpectedly as it had begun, and the room was empty and silent and the afternoon suddenly felt ruined, as if oil had seeped into clean water and slicked the feathers of all the swimming birds until they drowned.

At the scan, Marisa was back to her usual self: smiley and polite and so friendly to Mr. Abadi that it was almost flirtatious. Marisa's eyes shone as she talked and outlined all the early-pregnancy symptoms she'd been experiencing: tiredness and tender breasts and an aversion to green vegetables.

"Jake's been making me lots of lovely dinners," Marisa said, catching Jake's eye. "He's been a lifesaver."

Kate was taken aback. She was the one who did most of the cooking. Perhaps Marisa had misremembered.

"Good, very good," Mr. Abadi said genially.

Kate and Jake sat next to Marisa as she lay back in the reclining chair. They held hands as Mr. Abadi squeezed the ultrasound gel over her tummy, ever so slightly sticking out now if you knew what you were looking for, and then he placed the transducer to the left of Marisa's navel.

"Now then," he said, angling the screen so that Kate and Jake could see it more clearly. "Let's see what's going on in here."

Kate felt sick, and prepared herself for the bad news she had been given so many times in the past. She shut her eyes against the unbearable blackness of the screen.

"And there's the heartbeat."

She opened her eyes to see Mr. Abadi's smiling face.

"A strong, healthy heartbeat."

Her chest expanded and she whimpered, the sound escaping before she knew she was about to make it. She saw a beautiful pixelated beating white dot. She was engulfed by love.

"But," Jake said, "where's the second one?"

There was no second heartbeat.

Mr. Abadi told them that one of their twins had "vanished." This was the word he used, as if he were recounting a magic act involving sawn-through boxes and whipped-away silk curtains revealing empty spaces where previously there had been a whole person.

"Ok," Jake said. "Ok."

Of course, Kate thought. Of course there would have to be sadness too, piercing like a splinter into a moment of joy. That was what she had come to expect of fertility. There was never an uncomplicated reason to be happy.

On the chair, Marisa's eyes glazed over and she turned her face away from them.

"I'm so sorry," Mr. Abadi said. "But here"—he gestured to the screen—"there is a great deal to be cheerful about. This I am very pleased with."

As they left the hospital, Kate was surprised how sad she felt at the loss of one of the embryos, and at the same time, there was still a healthy pregnancy and that fact—a baby!—made her elated. *Her* baby. Theirs.

Strangely, it was Marisa who took it the worst. In the taxi on the way back from the clinic, she kept apologizing and saying how she felt she was letting them down. They reassured her as best they could, but when they arrived back at Richborne Terrace, she said she wanted to be alone and was going to take a nap.

Marisa went up to her bedroom where she slept for the rest of the day. Kate and Jake were worried, but they were also excited and they hugged in the hallway. Jake said they should open a bottle of champagne, but to Kate that felt too precipitous, as though they would be tempting fate, so they compromised on a vodka and tonic. Jake made them, pouring triple measures of vodka and barely touching it with the tonic. He squeezed fresh lime juice into each, topping the glasses up with ice cubes from the fridge dispenser, and then handed one to her and suggested they sit in the garden.

They took the drinks outside and were silent for a bit, not feeling the need to say anything and also aware that Marisa's room was just above where they were sitting so they shouldn't make too much noise.

After the first round, Jake made another two drinks and Kate began to feel fuzzy-headed and warm.

"This is one of the advantages of surrogacy," she said, holding up her glass. "Being able to drink."

"We've got to take our pleasures where we find them," Jake agreed. "We've been through a lot, haven't we?"

"We have."

At the end of the garden, the council estate tower rose high into the sky. Lights flickered on and off in the narrow windows. An airplane flew past, leaving a vapor trail across the dusk sky like unraveling cotton wool. As the light failed, they moved back indoors, taking their drinks to the sofa. Kate removed her shoes and socks, placing her legs across Jake's lap so that he would take the cue to massage her feet, which he did.

He started rubbing her toes, and then her ankles and then he moved up her jeans to her thighs and then her waistband and his breathing shifted and she felt a twinge of pleasure as she imagined what would happen next. He moved her legs apart, sliding in between them and lifting his face to press his mouth against hers. She grabbed hold of his neck with one hand and put her other hand over his cock, which stiffened obediently through his trousers.

"We shouldn't," she whispered. "Not here."

"You're right," he said, but he carried on kissing her and she carried on touching him and the weight of his chest made it impossible for her to move, so she kept kissing him back, knowing they shouldn't but being turned on by the shouldn't and then allowing the shouldn't to become a must.

They were kissing as Marisa came into the room silently. They were still kissing as she announced, "I thought I'd have a baked potato," at which point Kate pushed herself away from Jake. He tried rapidly to compose himself, standing too quickly and wobbling as he swept his hair back into place. He tried to act as though nothing had happened while Kate did the buttons back up on her shirt and smiled at Marisa, seeking to ease the mutual embarrassment.

But Marisa didn't seem embarrassed. She seemed disgusted, her face wan as she clutched at her stomach. Kate opened her mouth to apologize but stopped herself. It *was* their house, after all. They were a couple. They were allowed to show each other affection. They had been so careful, so considerate for months not to make Marisa feel excluded but they couldn't carry on like that indefinitely.

Jake was making polite chatter about baked potatoes and grated cheese, trying to gloss over the discomfort as he usually did, but Kate, fueled by the alcohol, was unrepentant. She'd had enough of Marisa making her feel like an unwanted visitor in her own home. So she sat there, meeting Marisa's eye, refusing to back down. She was astonished at the anger she sensed radiating from the other woman. Kate kept staring at her, waiting for Marisa to turn away first. It was important to Kate that she did this and that her power was reestablished as the owner of this house and as the mother of this baby. Marisa smiled. Kate blinked.

Jake, holding a baking potato in one hand, asked if she still wanted it.

"I'm not hungry," Marisa said, pausing at the door.

"You should eat something, Marisa," he implored.

"I told you, I'm not fucking hungry."

"Wow," Kate said.

Jake shook his head, uncomprehending.

She left, without apology.

"I guess today took more out of her than we realized," he said as he put the potato back into the fridge.

He had an everlasting capacity to think the best of people.

"Maybe," Kate said, wishing that he didn't always have to be so nice. There was a deep, silent part of her lying buried within that knew something was wrong. She poured herself another drink and ignored the creeping disquiet.

XXIV.

Now

Jake is home.

Sitting on the hallway floor next to Marisa, Kate has only just managed to calm her down, to get her to put the knife on the hallway table and to untie the rope around Kate's ankles. She has explained the situation as calmly as she can. Marisa, although distressed, seems to have accepted it. Kate does not want to do anything to upset this precarious equilibrium. Marisa is whimpering now, her shoulders hunched forward, her head curled in as if she is collapsing, like those buildings you see on slow-motion newsreels, imploding from the inside out. Kate's initial terror has passed. The most important thing is the safety of their baby. Everything else can be sorted out after that.

She stares at Jake, willing him to understand.

"What the fuck . . . ?" he says, taking in the scene: the two women sitting with their backs pressed against the skirting board, the kitchen knife, the rope, the damp patch leaking across the floor, the bloodied smear of Kate's face, her tooth on the patterned tile.

"Are you both ok? Kate—your face. Oh my God, oh my God. Is the baby ok? What's happened? I'm going to call the police."

He drops his briefcase and his keys and he is about to rush to

Kate's side when she says, "No, Jake," as coolly as she can manage. "Don't call anyone."

He stops, stunned by an invisible current.

"Look after Marisa," Kate says. "She's upset."

Marisa is sobbing now, but the sobs are melting into each other so that it sounds more like wailing. She is struggling to catch her breath because she's crying so hard.

Kate looks at Jake again in desperation, trying telepathically to convey the seriousness of what is happening.

He seems to get it. Or at least a version of it.

He kneels down beside Marisa and puts his arm around her.

"You're all right," he says to her. "You're safe. You're all right. It's all going to be ok."

Marisa leans her wet face against his shoulder and her hair comes loose from its elastic. Her grubby T-shirt gapes open.

"Oh, Jake," she says, gulping in air. "Why have you done this to me?"

"I . . . What have I . . . ?"

He looks at Kate over Marisa's head. She smiles at him shakily. *Trust me*, she mouths.

"Marisa thinks we've been having an affair," Kate says out loud, keeping her voice as firm and clear as she can. Her tongue slips into the gap left by her tooth.

"You *have* been," Marisa says, rocking against Jake's chest. "I saw the texts. I'm not stupid."

"Marisa is upset because I'm the lodger," Kate says. She has made the split-second decision to go along with Marisa's story in the hopes that it will keep her stable for long enough to get help. "That's why she followed me to work that time." She pauses, making sure Jake is with her. He gives a tiny tilt of the head and she knows that he is. "And I said we could sort it all out when you got back."

Marisa stops crying and raises her face to Jake.

"I just wanted to see you," Marisa says plaintively. "Because I'm having your baby."

"You are," Jake says.

Kate is relieved. He is going along with it, even if he doesn't yet understand why. His jaw is stiff, the tendons in his neck sticking out. He doesn't like it, but that doesn't matter. Their priority has to be the baby's safety and, by extension, Marisa's too.

"I'm going to get us all a cup of tea," Kate says. She slowly levers herself up to standing. One of her legs has gone numb and she has to shake the pins and needles from her right foot. She wipes the sweat from her face and when she looks at her hand, she notices blood. The blood seems almost totally removed from her physical self. She walks to the kitchen in a daze. She watches herself as she fills the kettle from the tap and presses the button to make it boil. She takes the garden keys from the top drawer and slides open the glass doors as quietly as she can. She steps onto the patio and slips out her cell phone.

She does not want to call the police or an ambulance or anyone in authority who will endanger the future of this pregnancy. What if Marisa is arrested? What if the stress causes her to miscarry? What if too many questions are asked and Marisa ends up keeping the baby? The agreement the three of them have signed isn't legally binding. It can't be until Marisa signs over legal parenthood to them after the baby is born.

Nor does Kate want to call Carol or the surrogacy agency in case they, too, insist on reporting what has happened. This needs to be dealt with quickly, calmly, and privately, with someone who has medical expertise and whose discretion they can rely on. And so she thinks of Chris. Retired GP. He would be able to advise them on Marisa's medical condition and check up on the baby, wouldn't he? He would know what to do. But to get to Chris, she knew she would have to call Annabelle and explain everything. It wasn't ideal, but it would have to do. She can hear the kettle coming to a boil behind her. She needs to act fast.

She holds the phone in one hand and dials Annabelle's number.

▪ ▪ ▪

After she makes the call, Kate mechanically puts tea bags in mugs and pours in boiled water and milk, adding extra sugar for everyone. She washes her face in the sink, patting it dry with the tea towel. She catches sight of her reflection in the mirrored backsplash. Her hair is sticking out at odd angles and her mascara has left the suggestion of dark trails across her face. There is dried blood at the corner of her mouth and a cut on her forehead she hadn't noticed before. She changes out of her wet trousers and reaches for a pair of leggings straight from the dryer. Then she places the mugs on a tray and limps back up to the hallway.

Jake and Marisa are still sitting on the floor. He has his arms around her and Marisa is no longer crying.

"Tea!" Kate says with a brightness she does not feel. She sets the tray down next to them.

"Thanks," Jake says. "Are we—?"

Kate shakes her head, the movement so small it would be missed by anyone else.

"Marisa," she says. "Have some tea. It'll be good for you. It'll make you feel better."

She holds out a mug to her, and Marisa takes it, looking up at Kate from the floor and tilting her head toward the light. She looks wary, untrusting, but she sips the tea as she is told, then turns back and rests her cheek back against Jake's chest.

"I'm so tired," Marisa says.

"Close your eyes for a bit," Kate says. "There's nothing for you to worry about anymore. You need to conserve your energy. Are you comfortable there or do you want to move to the sofa?"

"Here," Marisa says. "I want to stay here."

She slides her head down so that it rests on Jake's lap. He unfolds his legs, straightening them across the narrow hallway, his shoes touching the opposite wall.

Are you ok? he mouths to Kate above Marisa's resting head.

She nods. She reaches for her phone, trying to be quiet. She doesn't want to do anything to startle Marisa. She opens her Notes app and starts writing and when she is done, she holds it in front of Jake's face so he can read it.

> M attacked me when I got home. She's lost it. Properly crazy. Thinks that you and her are together. Thinks we've been having affair. I've called your parents. They're coming. Chris has sedatives. We need to keep her calm for next 3 hours.

Jake reads, his mouth setting in a grim line as he takes it in. Kate types again: Best to go along with her until we can discuss?

Jake reads the message, then nods. He grips Kate's hand. Kate squeezes him back and goes upstairs. She doesn't have time for emotion. She leaves Jake gently patting Marisa's shoulder.

She thinks then of that hackneyed line in airport detective novels or cheap made-for-TV films: that mothers will do anything for their children. There were those fabled stories about women finding superhuman strength to lift overturned cars off the wounded bodies of their progeny; about mums fighting for justice and campaigning for changes in the law after their beloved child died at the hands of a criminal on early release. But Kate has never fully understood this concept until this moment. She realizes, with undeniable conviction, that she will do anything for her child, even when her child is not yet born. It is this that saw her through those grueling rounds of fertility treatment. It is this that made her put up with Marisa's erratic behavior for so long, that will make her pretend that everything is all right now, even when she has been attacked, even when the side of her head has a dull, splitting ache, even when she has washed the blood off her face and seen the reddened water in the sink. The irrefutable clarity makes all decisions easy.

She goes to Marisa's room. She hasn't been in here since Marisa stopped wanting her breakfast brought to her. That had been weeks ago. Marisa mostly keeps the door closed. When Kate asked if she wanted the cleaner to give it the once-over, Marisa said that she would rather do it herself.

She turns the doorknob and walks into the room. The curtains are drawn, so at first she doesn't notice the smell. When she switches on the light, Kate gasps. The floor is covered with balled-up clothes and used tissues and cotton swabs and old fast-food cartons. A half-drunk mug of tea is growing mold across the surface. In the corner, by the plug sockets, is what looks like a thick beige snake. When she gets closer, Kate realizes it's a twisting clump of rotting take-out noodles. She gags. The room smells of turpentine and sweat and stale food mixed with an indefinable rotten sweetness. She puts a hand over her mouth, making her breathing more shallow. She picks her way across to the window and when she opens it, fresh air rushes in.

What has Marisa been doing? Kate wonders. This was the sign of someone profoundly unbalanced. This was a breakdown.

Then she sees the desk. On the old architect's table are several jam jars filled with paintbrushes in dirty water the color of silt. But there is no evidence of any painting. Instead, there are sheets and sheets of paper covered with scrawling handwriting in permanent marker. The words are so close together they make no sense at first. When Kate peers closer, she notices that they are not, in fact, words but names. *Kate* and *Jake* and *Marisa* written over and over again, looping through and under each other like a thicket of weeds, spreading their roots across all the available space until the paper was more black than white.

The corkboard above the desk, where Marisa usually pinned the photos of children she painted into her fairy tales, is covered with photographs of Jake. They are taken from a high angle, showing him working out in the garden, his chest slick with sweat, and she realizes that Marisa has been photographing him from her bedroom window. Another photo, at first glance, seems to be a picture of Marisa and Jake together, both of them laughing. On closer inspection, Kate notices a ripped edge and realizes that it is two separate photos that have been stuck together.

She rips the corkboard off the wall and, without thinking, throws it out of the window where it lands with a solid thud on the lawn below. She is angry. And at the same time, she is aware that this anger must be contained. That fucking crazy bitch, she thinks. And then: That fucking crazy bitch is carrying our baby.

How had they been so deceived? At first, Marisa had seemed so perfect. She had seemed sweet and willing to help—a pure rural milkmaid with a wide-eyed wonder about the world. She even wrote fairy tales for a living, for Christ's sake. Why had they not stepped in sooner, when she started acting oddly?

Maybe they hadn't questioned her motives as deeply as they should have. Maybe they hadn't done as much due diligence as the agency suggested. Maybe they hadn't wanted to listen to Carol when she kept sounding a note of caution about how quickly they were moving. But was that so wrong? With everything they had been through, was it so wrong to allow hope to silence any passing moment of doubt? Why shouldn't something be easy for once?

By now Kate is crying, wiping the tears away with her sweater cuff. She reminds herself of why she came into this room. She knows exactly what she's looking for. It's not on the desk. So Kate gets down on her hands and knees and turns her face to search under the bed. It is the most basic and obvious of hiding places, and Kate already knows it is where Marisa will have put her diary. For weeks, she has noticed Marisa writing furtively in a black Moleskine notebook and Kate is driven by a forceful need to know what the diary contains.

The carpet under the bed is covered at irregular intervals with dust balls. It is dark down there and Kate can't see clearly, so she reaches out her arm and starts to sweep it along the floor. Nothing. She is about to stand when she has another thought. This time, instead of sweeping her arm against the carpet, she repeats the same movement against the mattress and the bed frame. Her fingers brush against the soft edges of something trapped in between the bottom of the mattress and the wooden slats of the frame. Kate levers it out and it drops onto the floor. There it is. The notebook.

She takes it with her out of the room, leaning over the landing banister to check on Jake. He sees her and smiles. She gives him a thumbs-up sign and he nods. Marisa is still lying on his lap, and her breathing seems more regular. He is stroking her hair with one hand and although this is exactly what he should be doing, Kate feels a pang of jealousy so sharp it startles her. She brushes it aside, sits on the top stair, and starts flicking through the pages of Marisa's diary.

It starts, *The house is perfect*, and as Kate reads, she realizes Marisa is recounting the day that she came to visit Richborne Terrace and Kate showed her around, and they'd been interrupted by a magpie flying in through the kitchen doors. Except for this incident, Marisa remembers the event differently. She barely mentions Kate or the surrogacy, and does not use her name, as though Kate were little more than an estate agent. She looks at the date in the corner of the page: it had been written in the days and weeks after Marisa found out she was pregnant. It was a retelling of the story the way she wished it existed. Turning the pages, Kate sees the pattern repeating itself again and again: entire scenes from their life told from Marisa's warped perspective, where she has written Kate out of the narrative, referring to her as "the lodger" in her own home. Marisa has invented a whole relationship with Jake that doesn't exist. Their meeting in the cafe is depicted as though it were a date. Marisa has even written about Jake fucking her. Kate knows, without having to check, that every single night Marisa refers to in the diary, Jake was in bed with her, not Marisa.

The more she reads, the more Kate feels the ground disappearing beneath her. She is disgusted yet is compelled to read on. There is a ghoulishness to her fascination. She cannot believe the lengths Marisa has gone to in order to protect the integrity of her lies. Her story is so convincing that at one point, Kate begins to question whether some of it might be true. Maybe Jake had fallen in love with her. Maybe they were having an affair? But she banishes that thought too, almost as quickly as it floats to the surface. Jake would never do that. Besides, where and how would he have found either the time or the opportunity? They were always together.

No, it was Marisa who was the dangerous one, the unhinged one, the hysterical one. These were the hallucinations of a madwoman. She flicks through the remaining pages and her mood shifts from shock to pity. How unhappy Marisa must be to have done this. Not just unhappy, Kate corrects herself, but *unwell*. They needed to get her help and make her better. They needed to keep her stable for the remaining four months of her pregnancy. And they needed to do this privately, with the least amount of outside interference.

Kate checks her watch: 9:30 p.m. Annabelle and Chris should be here soon. She is about to put the diary aside and go downstairs when something falls out of the back pages. Kate retrieves it from the floorboards. It is a pressed daisy, its petals mottled and flattened, turning brown at the edges. It touches her, this little flower and the value someone had accorded it. She thinks of childhood daisy chains and she wonders, then, about Marisa's past and whether anything she had told them was true. Marisa had said that she was close to her parents, and that her own mother had suffered several miscarriages before giving birth to her sister, who was seven years younger. Kate and Jake had been moved by this story and reassured that Marisa, despite her relative youth, knew firsthand what infertility meant and the cost it exacted on a couple. Marisa had said that she and her mother had talked about it as adults. But perhaps that was invented too? Perhaps nothing they thought they knew about her, or the agency thought they knew about her, was true?

Bile rises in her throat. Kate slides the daisy back into the notebook and as she does so, the pages fall open again. She notices a small pocket inside the back cover, which expands when she pulls it to reveal a square of paper, folded over several times. When she unfolds it and spreads it out, Kate sees it is a prescription. She squints to make out the typed letters.

Risperidone, it reads, *1mg tablets*.

Kate looks it up on her phone. Her fingers are clumsy and she is short of breath as she taps on the search engine icon. Then the results come up: "Risperidone is licensed to treat the following conditions: schizophrenia, psychosis, mania." She checks the name on the prescription. It is made out to Miss Marisa Grover and dated six months before.

"Fuck," Kate says. The prescription is unused. They had done the embryo transfer just over five months ago, and when Marisa's behavior had become more volatile, Kate and Jake had attributed it—naively, she now realizes—to pregnancy hormones. Could it be that Marisa had been on these antipsychotic drugs but had stopped taking them so that they did not interfere with the pregnancy?

"Fuck," she says again.

The doorbell rings.

Jake's parents are here.

XXV.

Kate runs downstairs with the notebook still in her hand. The sound of the doorbell has agitated Marisa, who is now fully awake and sitting up, whimpering and asking Jake repeatedly what's happening.

When Kate walks past them, Marisa flings her arms around Jake's neck. "Don't let her hurt me, don't let her hurt me."

"I'm not going to hurt you," Kate says as calmly as her fear and fury will allow. "You hurt *me*, remember?"

Jake makes a shushing sound, although whether it is directed toward her or Marisa, she isn't sure. Kate opens the door. Chris is standing there in his familiar tweed jacket, a half smile on his face, and she experiences a rush of gratitude so acute she feels her legs buckle.

"Come in, come in."

He steps inside.

"Are you ok?" he asks, his voice low. "That gash looks nasty." He points at her forehead.

"Oh this—no, it's fine. Looks worse than it is. Where's Annabelle?"

"Parking. I thought I should leave her to it and come straight here. Sounded urgent from what you said on the phone."

On the porch, Kate reaches out and holds the sleeve of his jacket.

"Thank you, Chris."

He pats her hand. "Don't mention it. This is what family is for. We'll calm her down and keep her stable and your baby safe—don't you worry."

She tells him quickly about the prescription she's found and the diary and Marisa's current state of mind and he nods.

"Mmm. That makes sense. All right. We'll sort this out soon enough."

She leads him into the hallway, where he takes in the scene in one practiced gaze. Jake, still holding Marisa's head close to his chest, says, "Hi, Dad. Sorry about all this." Chris shakes his head and puts his fingers to his lips, motioning to Jake to stay quiet.

"Marisa?" Chris says, and his voice is kind but firm. "My name is Dr. Sturridge and I'm going to look after you now, ok?"

Marisa turns to look at him, her expression trusting. Her pupils are dilated, her skin waxy with sweat. Chris has crouched down to her level and is checking her pulse with his thumb and forefinger.

"We're going to take good care of you. Nothing for you to worry about. Now, first things first—how about another cup of tea?"

"Yes, please," Marisa says, her voice hoarse.

Chris signals to Kate, who goes back to the kitchen. She hears the doorbell ring again. Annabelle. Someone lets her in, and immediately Kate can hear Marisa shrieking. Chris is keeping up his calming patter, his voice a bass note to Marisa's soprano, and as Kate makes this second cup of tea, she hears the noise gradually subside until there is almost total silence.

She carries the mug up to the hallway. Annabelle is standing by the door, her hair wrapped up in a silk headscarf, a faded brown coat belted around her waist. She has no makeup on. Her face, denuded of its normal armor, looks defenseless, her pale lashes giving the impression of a mole blinking into the light. Kate realizes she must have been getting ready for bed. Despite it all, Annabelle had dropped everything to be here.

"Some things are more important," Annabelle had said on the phone. "We'll do anything for you and Jakey and the baby—you must know that."

Kate hadn't known but now she does. She smiles shakily at Annabelle.

On the hallway floor, Jake is carefully positioning Marisa's head on his rolled-up suit jacket. Chris is still holding her wrist, monitoring her pulse and looking at his watch to count the beats. Marisa is breathing long, heavy breaths. Her eyes are closed.

Jake slides away from her prone form and then comes straight over to Kate. He hugs her tightly, whispering into her ear how much he loves her and asking if she's ok over and over again and she starts to cry and tells him she's fine, that she just wants this to be dealt with and for their baby to be safe.

"It's going to be all right," Jake says. "Dad has it under control, don't you, Dad?"

"Yup," Chris says. "I've given her two milligrams of lorazepam and it seems to have taken the edge off. We'll wait an hour and then see what happens and giver her another dose."

"Should we move her . . . ?" Kate starts. "To the sofa or a bed or something?"

"No. Best leave her here rather than risk . . ."—he leaves a small gap—"disturbing her."

"Right," Annabelle says briskly. "The three of us have some talking to do. We have a plan," she tells Jake. "Kate and I have already talked about it, haven't we, dear?"

"Yes."

"First things first, I'm going to pop a bandage on that scratch." Annabelle reaches into Chris's medicine bag and takes out a bottle of antiseptic, some cotton wool, and a large square adhesive bandage. She walks over to Kate, takes her hand, and ushers her through to the sitting room, where she tells her to sit on the sofa.

Annabelle dabs at Kate's forehead with the antiseptic, which stings, and then she places the bandage on top and she does it all with such maternal tenderness that Kate finds herself wanting to weep again.

"Thank you," she says.

"Not at all, dear. That looks much better." Annabelle undoes the belt on her coat and sits on the armchair by the bay window. She slides her headscarf down and her hair looks wispy in the lamplight. "Jake, do you have any whisky? I think we all need a stiff drink."

Jake goes to the sideboard where they keep the drinks. It is just under the speaker and Kate is reminded of that Sunday, two months ago, when they had been playing music and Marisa had stormed in complaining it was too loud. It made sense now. An irrational kind of sense. *How she must have hated me*, Kate thinks, and she shivers.

"Cold?" Annabelle asks sharply.

"No, I'm fine. The whisky will warm me up."

She takes a tumbler from Jake, who passes another one to his mother. He pours himself a neat vodka and sits next to Kate on the sofa.

"Drink that up," Annabelle says. "It'll be good for the shock."

"Kate, you must have been terrified," Jake says. "I'm so sorry I wasn't here—"

"There's no time for that now." Annabelle speaks with level urgency. "While she's calm out there"—she gestures toward the hallway—"let's talk about next steps."

"Ok," Jake says.

"We think the best thing to do is take Marisa back to ours, don't we, Kate?"

Kate nods.

"We can keep her calm on the journey—Chris has all the necessary tablets and whatnot—and then we can put her up in the guest cottage. She'll be out of your home, which I think is absolutely necessary from what Kate has said."

Kate, realizing that Jake is several steps behind, brings him up to date as quickly as she can on what she found in Marisa's room, the contents of the diary, the prescription that hadn't been used for months.

"Christ," Jake says. "She's a fucking nutcase."

Kate winces. Annabelle draws herself up straighter, unimpressed by the swearing even in these extreme circumstances.

"Well, look—you both know it took me some time to . . . understand what you were doing with a surrogate whom you barely knew, but we are where we are. And I'm sure, with the right medical treatment, this woman—"

"Marisa," Kate interjects.

"Yes. I'm sure that she'll be right as rain. The main thing is we keep her safe and stable and away from you for the duration of this pregnancy. Once the baby is here, we can deal with everything else."

"She thought we were having *an affair*?" Jake is incredulous. "She thought *you* were a lodger?"

Kate touches the back of his neck, feeling the warmth of it against her palm. "Apparently so."

"How did we . . . I mean, how did she . . . How did this happen?"

Kate shrugs. The point is not that it was happening, she wants to shout. The point is what they do to salvage it.

She knocks back the remainder of the whisky and puts the empty glass on the coffee table.

She remembers her tooth on the hallway floor. She hasn't even thought what to do about that yet. Should she pick it up and put it in some ice the way you're meant to do with amputated limbs?

Annabelle's voice brings her back.

"Listen," Annabelle is saying, "if you have to pretend you're in a relationship with her, Jake, then so be it, quite frankly. It won't mean anything. You can say you and she need to be apart while you sort things out with Kate. Drag it out a bit; tell her your parents are looking after her until you can be together, if necessary . . ."

"Mum, come on. You can't be serious."

Annabelle fixes him with those blue, blue eyes. "I'm deadly serious. You got yourself into this mess. You have to do whatever it takes to get yourself out of it."

"It's hardly ethical—"

"Ethical?" She gives a short laugh. "You're going to talk to *me* about ethics, after everything she's put you through? This is my grandchild we're talking about."

Kate, sitting quietly on the sofa, is surprised by how together she feels. She sees that Annabelle is, in her own way, right. They have to do whatever is required. All of those traits in Annabelle that Kate had previously found so frustrating—her coldness to outsiders, her steely belief in the rightness of her own opinions, her clear-sighted ability to see straight through to a person's weakest point, and her borderline obsessive devotion to her son—were now coming to the fore in a positive way.

"What do you think?" Jake asks Kate.

"I think your mother is right."

And Jake—good, kind, solid Jake—agrees to go along with it, as both women had known he would. For all his good qualities, Jake is also weak. He is directed by stronger, prevailing winds and tacks his sail accordingly. It is partly why Kate loves him so much. She knows he will always support her because he relies on her to tell him where to go next. He is impressed by her, still, even after all these years. Now he needs Kate to steer the course. She knows exactly what they have to do, and so does Annabelle, and that is to protect their child at all costs.

XXVI.

Kate takes two travel cases from the basement and brings them up to Marisa's room. Then she folds up Marisa's clothes—baggy T-shirts, artist's overalls, ripped jeans, the odd-patterned sundress, bobbly and bleached pale by too many washes—and puts them into one of the cases. She finds a stuffed toy bunny with a stitched X for a nose on the shelves along with two books of poetry, and she puts these in too. She packs sketch pads and pens and a box of blunted graphite pencils, but the paints and the desk will have to stay behind. She goes to the bathroom to gather up Marisa's toiletries, which include a toothbrush and toothpaste, some Vaseline, a small pot of skin cream, hotel sample-size shampoo bottles, and, at the back of the cabinet, a half-empty box of risperidone tablets. She shoves these in too. Chris had indicated that he wanted to get her back onto the drugs as soon as possible.

"The risks to the baby are minimal and far outweighed by the advantages," he said. "If she carries on not taking them, then there can be more serious consequences."

"Such as?" Jake asked.

"Maternal suicide."

When the cases are full, she closes them and wheels them out of the room. Jake comes from downstairs to help her carry them outside. She keeps hold of the diary and of an address book she has found in the top drawer of Marisa's bedside table.

Kate and Jake pack the cases into the trunk. They have decided that Jake will travel in the back with Marisa, who will be able to stretch out and rest her head on his knees. Kate puts a tartan blanket and a flask of water in the footwell on the passenger side.

She kisses Jake briefly on the lips in the street and he holds her tightly. There is a single light in an open window in the block of flats opposite and a smell of weed in the air plus the low bass thrum of some indistinguishable music.

The two of them return to the house, where Annabelle and Chris and Marisa are waiting. Kate passes them in the hallway, making grateful eye contact with Chris, who nods, and then she goes upstairs to look on from the second-floor landing.

Chris has given Marisa the next dose of lorazepam and she is pliant and willing and childlike.

"We're going to take you to my parents'," Jake tells her, "to give you a bit of a rest while I sort things out with Kate."

Marisa looks up at him and smiles. "All right," she says.

Jake leads her gently outside by the arm, with his parents following. Moments later, Kate hears the Volvo engine start up and then fade into the distance. The house feels big and silent without any people in it. Her head is aching and she is suddenly very tired. She hadn't thought it would be possible to feel like this with so much adrenaline coursing through her body, and yet she is seized by an exhaustion so complete that the only thing she can do is stumble to their bedroom, roll onto the duvet cover, and close her eyes. She lies there fully clothed, her shoes still on from when she walked through the door when she got back from work. It is hard to believe that was just a few hours ago, she thinks as she drops into sleep, and that this was all it took for life to warp and snap into chaos.

When she wakes, it is early morning and she can hear the clattering sound of the rubbish-collection vans outside. She slams upright, heart skipping against her rib cage. Her mouth is throbbing. She takes two acetaminophen from the bedside table and gulps them down. She can live without a tooth for now, she tells herself. It wasn't one from the front.

She grabs her phone and sees several missed calls from Jake, followed by a series of text messages telling her they had arrived in Gloucestershire and all was calm but where was she, he was worried about her, please ring when she could.

She calls him and he answers immediately.

"Are you ok?" he says.

"Yes, yes, I'm so sorry. I fell asleep."

She can hear him exhale on the other end of the line. "Thank God. I was so worried about you. I was going to drive back down there but Mum told me not to. She said you would have gone to bed."

"I'm glad you listened. I'm so sorry," she says again. "How are you? How is everything?"

She hears Jake moving around, pacing the floor, and she imagines him in the Sturridge family sitting room where she had first met his parents, with the overstuffed sofas and the silver-framed photographs of christenings and graduations.

"It's under control," he says. "I feel weird about it."

"Why?"

"I don't know; it feels like we're exploiting her. We're kind of . . . lying to her, aren't we?"

Kate pinches the bridge of her nose. "Not as much as she's lied to us," she says, trying to keep her voice calm. "It's only until she's more stable anyway."

"Yes, you're right. Sorry. I know you're right. She's in the cottage, safely installed. The drive up was fine. She slept most of the way."

Kate ignores the disquieting thought that what Marisa really needs is proper psychiatric help. It's only until their baby comes, she reasons, dimly aware of her own mounting desperation. That's what they need to focus on.

"How's she been with your parents?" she asks.

"Um. I'm not sure she's registering who they are, to be honest. I've just let her think what she wants to think, said I'm coming back to London in a bit to talk things through with you."

"Good," Kate says. "But stay there as long as you need, won't you?"

"It shouldn't take more than a day or so," he says.

"Does everything seem ok with the baby?" Her voice cracks on this last word.

"Yes," Jake replies firmly. "Dad says there's nothing to worry about, so you mustn't worry either, ok? Everything is going to be fine. More than fine."

She allows herself to be pacified, even though she knows he can't be certain either way. In their bedroom, Kate opens the curtains with one hand, holding her phone with the other. The window is still open in the flat opposite, and there is a young man sitting there, leaning onto the sill to smoke a spliff. He catches her eye and gives a lazy grin. She smiles back shakily. *What if he'd seen or heard something?* she thinks. *What would happen then?*

She doesn't say any of this to Jake. Instead, she tells him she's going to have a shower and start sorting things out, although which "things" exactly she doesn't specify. They exchange *I love you*s and she promises to call him later.

Kate doesn't take a shower. She is still surfing the wave of jittery energy from the night before. She takes Marisa's diary and the address book down to the kitchen where she brews strong coffee and forces herself to eat a slice of toast. She hasn't eaten since yesterday at lunchtime. Kate sits at the table, looking out at the garden and the tower beyond it. The sun is low in the sky, partially blotted out by a tall magnolia tree. Along the top of one wall, she spots a magpie and automatically raises her hand to salute it, just as her mother had taught her she should in order to ward off evil spirits and bad luck. Then another magpie jumps up to join it, then another and another until there are four of the birds lined up next to each other on the wall. Their feathers glitter, white and black. One of them tips its beak into a shallow puddle of water that has gathered between the bricks. She has never seen four magpies lined up like this, on parade. She salutes the final three. What was that old folk rhyme? One for sorrow, two for joy . . . She can't remember how the rest of it goes, so she Googles on her phone.

"Three for a girl, four for a boy," she says out loud into the empty kitchen. "Huh."

A motorbike engine starts up somewhere beyond the wall and the mechanical scratch of it sends the magpies flying into the sky. She watches them go, darting into the air in a straight, disciplined line, and then she gets to work.

She flicks through the address book. She looks first for any family members, but there are no listings for the Grover surname and no one recorded as "Mum," "Dad," or Anna, her sister. The book proves to be scant on useful information. Marisa has used it mostly for doodles—intricate curlicues and looping flower petals and hieroglyphic eyes all folded in on each other so that the pages become more ink than paper. But there are a few names dotted about, here and there. Kate checks her watch. It's a little after 8 a.m. It is not a particularly friendly time of day to call a stranger, but it's not so unreasonable as to be actively rude.

She takes out her phone and dials the first number, attached to the name "Rosie Hodge." After three rings, a woman answers.

"Hello?"

"Oh, hi there. Sorry to disturb you so early."

"It's fine. I've been up since five with the kids. What do you want?"

"I was calling about Marisa Grover," Kate says and then she leaves a silence, waiting for the other woman to fill it.

"Who?"

"Marisa Grover. I understand you might know her. Your name is in her address book, you see."

"Can I ask what this is about?"

"Um. Yes. Marisa's been living with us and has been taken ill. Nothing serious, but I wanted to let her friends and family know in case they—"

"Marisa Grover," the woman says, turning the name over. "Wait a minute—do you mean the Telling Tales lady?"

"Yes, that's right."

"Ah, right. Well, yeah, I've commissioned her to do a few books for my kids over the years. She's very talented. Did you say she's ill?"

"Yes, but nothing serious," Kate repeats. "I've been asked to contact her clients and inform them there might be a delay in, um, their books arriving."

"Oh, ok, thanks. I wasn't waiting on anything from her."

Kate hears a child squealing on the other end of the line.

"Shush," Rosie says. "I'm coming now. You'll get your breakfast soon enough. Just calm down." To Kate she adds, "Hope she gets better soon. Thanks for calling."

"No problem."

In this way, Kate methodically works her way through Marisa's contacts. They are mostly former clients. A couple don't know who she's talking about. One is a school friend who hasn't heard from Marisa "for absolute yonks." A few more don't answer. Two go straight to voicemail. On the twelfth call, she dials a number for a woman listed as Jas.

"Yo."

"Hi there, sorry to bother you so early," Kate starts, easing into the now-familiar patter. "I was calling about Marisa Grover."

"Ris? Wow. I wasn't expecting that. Is she ok?"

"Yes, she is, she is," Kate says. "She's been living with me these past few months and she's been taken slightly unwell and I wanted to reach out to her friends and family to let them know."

"What's wrong with her?"

"Are you a friend or . . . ?"

"Yeah, I'm a friend. We were really close until a few months ago. Probably around the time she moved in with you. But hey, that's Marisa for you."

"What do you mean?"

"She gets deep and then she gets out. Hang on a sec, will you? I just wanna turn the radio off." The music that has been playing in the background cuts out. "That's better," Jas says. "Wait—I thought she moved in with that guy she was dating. Was it a house share or something? I thought they got their own place."

Kate stays very still, as if any movement will disrupt the flow of what Jas is saying.

"What was his name? It began with a 'J'—I remember because, you know, mine does too, so yeah, I remember that. *Jake*—that was it!"

"She did move in with Jake," Kate says.

"Yeah, that's what I thought."

"But she wasn't dating Jake. I'm Jake's girlfriend. Marisa was our surrogate. That's why she came to live with us. She's carrying our baby."

Jas goes quiet.

"I know it's a lot to take in, but I'd really like to talk to you properly if I could. You see, something's happened and it would be helpful to know a bit about Marisa's recent medical history . . . Her mental health, I mean."

On the other end of the line, the woman gives a low whistle. "What did you say your name was?"

"I'm Kate."

"Ok, Kate. I'll meet you. In a public place because, let's be real, I don't know who you are or if you are who you say you are, but if this is kosher, then, yeah, there is some stuff you should probably know about Marisa."

"I'll bring documentation," Kate says. "So that you know I'm telling the truth. You can choose where we meet. I'll come wherever."

"Thanks. Appreciate that."

"No, honestly, I appreciate you doing this. It will be really good to talk."

Jas laughs. "Man, you don't know what I'm going to tell you yet!"

"I'm ready," Kate says, and she means it.

They arrange to meet in a cafe near the Finsbury Park tube station in two hours' time.

The cafe is an old-fashioned greasy spoon. There is a man behind a glass-screened counter wearing a striped apron tied loosely across his stomach. He greets her cheerily in an Italian accent so pronounced that it sounds fake. She is his only customer.

"I'll have a cappuccino, thanks."

Normally she'd have a strong, black espresso but this morning she feels the need for something more comforting.

"I'll bring it over," he says, waving her away with one hand. "You make yourself comfortable, *bella*."

She chooses a table in the corner at the back and fiddles with the sugar sachets while waiting for Jas. Eighties rock emerges from a tinny wireless propped up behind the till. Jas had told her she was "short, blonde hair, and Black. You can't miss me."

She was right. When Jas walks in, the cafe bell tinkling as she opens the door, she is immediately recognizable: a small, compact woman with delicate features and a peroxide buzz cut. She is wearing an oversized camouflage jacket and when she turns to close the door behind her, Kate sees the word WARRIOR on the back, spelled out in sequins.

"Hey, Tony," Jas says to the man behind the counter, whose face breaks into a broad grin when he sees her. "I'll have my usual. Thanks, man."

She comes over to the table, shrugging off her jacket and placing it on the back of the chair.

"Kate, yeah?"

"Yes." Kate stands up and thrusts out her hand, which seems, immediately, overly formal. Jas shakes it with a wry, assessing look. Kate notices her nails are long and painted neon pink. The outer edge of her left ear is studded all the way up the cartilage with gold hoop earrings of diminishing size. Kate is briefly surprised that Marisa is friends with someone so cool and then admonishes herself instantly for thinking so.

Tony brings their drinks over in slightly grubby white cups accompanied by one individually wrapped thin ginger biscuit on each saucer.

"So," Jas says. Her nails clack against the handle when she holds it. "Why don't you tell me what's been going on?"

"First off, let me show you I am who I say I am," Kate says, sliding an envelope across the table. It contains the surrogacy agreement, a recent utility bill, a scan of her and Jake's passports, and some photos of the two of them together. She has also brought the baby scan but has kept it in her wallet. She isn't sure why.

Jas leafs through the documents and nods, satisfied.

"I also wanted to bring you this." Kate hands over Marisa's diary. Jas flicks through it, then looks up.

"What is this?"

"It's Marisa's diary or notebook or something. I found it in her room. She's been inventing this . . . this . . . *story* about how she and Jake are lovers and she's expecting his baby, but—"

Kate breaks off, embarrassed by how it sounds.

Jas speaks calmly. "But it's not her baby," she says. "It's yours."

"Yes," Kate says, relieved. "Yes, that's it exactly."

"Oh wow, I'm sorry."

She passes Kate some napkins from the dispenser and Kate presses them to her face, mopping up the tears that now seem to be on her cheeks. She takes a few breaths and then, having collected herself, she tells Jas everything: how they'd met Marisa, her increasingly odd behavior, the scene in the hallway, and the discovery of her prescription. Jas doesn't seem fazed by any of it.

"So where is she now?"

"Um, in the countryside," Kate says. "With Jake and his parents. We thought it was best she got away from me and had time to . . . recuperate. Jake's dad is a GP—well, a retired one—and so he's looking after her."

"You need to get her back on her meds as quick as you can," Jas says. "I've seen what happens when Ris forgets to take them, and it's not pretty."

Kate stops in her tracks. "Wait, so this . . . has happened before?"

Jas signals to Tony for another round of coffees. "We're going to be here for a while."

Jas leans back in her chair, clasping her hands in front of her chest. "The first thing you need to know about Ris is that she's a mistress of her own reinvention. She tells her own story, the way that she likes to believe it. You can't trust anything she says. An-y-thing," Jas says, drawing out the syllables for emphasis. "I love the girl, but she's damaged. Probably the most damaged person I've ever met, to be honest with you. That stuff about her parents she told you? It's bullshit. Excuse my language. Her mum abandoned her when she was seven years old and she doesn't talk to her dad anymore. She hasn't seen her sister in over twenty years."

"What about the miscarriages?" Kate asks, because this key detail seems of overwhelming importance. It was why they had trusted her.

"I don't know," Jas answers. "She never told me anything like that. Most of the time, when she's on her meds, she's fine. But she's got serious mental health issues."

"Like what?"

"It's not like I have the exact diagnosis. I mean, Ris and I were cool and that, but we didn't pry too much into each other's business. I think maybe she's a bit bipolar?"

The coffees are delivered to the table, along with two new wrapped biscuits.

"How did you guys meet?" Kate asks.

"You sure you want to know this?"

Kate nods. Jas leans forward and places her arms on the table. She has a tattoo in roman numerals on the inside of her right wrist.

"We met at a group for survivors of sexual assault."

"Oh God. Jas. I'm so sorry."

"Don't be. It's not your fault, is it?" She laughs, a deep chuckle. "I'm ok. Ris was raped when she was seventeen."

Kate thinks she might be sick. The caffeine mixes in with her adrenaline and she can feel the whoosh of blood pumping through her veins.

"That's horrific," she says. "Poor Marisa."

"Yeah."

They are silent for several seconds. Nearby, bacon sizzles in a frying pan and the smell of it fills the air, which becomes thick with grease.

"She sorted herself out as much as she could," Jas says. "It wasn't easy. It's a fucking miracle she managed to set up that business with the kids' books and that, but she did. The meds definitely helped. But sometimes she forgets to take them or she doesn't think she needs them and I'm guessing with you guys, maybe she worried they would harm the baby or something?"

There was that, at least, Kate thought. She is clutching on to the idea that Marisa had wanted to do her best for them.

"What happens when she doesn't take her medication?"

Jas looks as if she is about to say something and then thinks better of it. "Ris isn't a bad person."

"I know," Kate says.

"She'd get these . . . obsessions," Jas says slowly. "Like, she'd fixate on a man she'd been on a date with and imagine this future with him and it was all a bit much. She'd text them a lot and sometimes she'd follow them to work and that and I always told her to chill out but she never listened and the more I told her to chill out, the less she started telling me."

The cafe is filling up now. Some builders in dusty trousers and hard hats come and sit at the table next to theirs. They talk loudly and roll cigarettes while waiting for their lunches. Jas has to raise her voice so that Kate can hear her.

"I suppose we kind of fell out? When she told me about Jake, I said she was moving too fast but, you know, there's only so much you can do. She didn't want to hear it. And I had no idea what was actually going on. I had no idea about you."

Jas turns up the corners of her mouth. It is not quite a smile, but it is understanding. For the first time in eighteen hours, Kate unclenches her jaw and relaxes her shoulders. She is calmer now, knowing that there is someone else who can bear witness to Marisa's behavior, who can reassure Kate that she is not the one who is going mad.

"Thank you, Jas."

Jas starts putting her jacket back on. "I don't think I've done that much."

"You have; you really have. Is it ok if I keep your number and stay in touch? It's just useful, you know, having someone—"

"Sure," Jas cuts in.

"And you don't have any contact details for her family?"

Jas sucks air through her teeth. "Nah. And if you want my opinion, that would be the worst thing you could do."

"Ok, ok. So what we're doing now—keeping her safe and putting her back on her meds—that's what you think is best?"

Jas shrugs. "I can't really advise you. I'm not a doctor. But . . . have you thought of getting her actual medical help? Like, not just a guy you know who's a retired GP?"

Kate shifts in her seat. "Of course," she says. "But it's tricky. I suppose I wanted to keep it in the family. I didn't want her to feel . . . cast out by us."

Even as she says it, Kate wonders if it's true. But Jas seems satisfied.

"Yeah, I guess. Look after her. She'll calm down. You'll get your baby. And then—what happens next is up to Ris, isn't it?"

"Do you want to see her?"

Jas shakes her head. "No. I love Ris. Always will. But she won't want me to know what's happened. She'll be humiliated. Tell her I said hi. And when she's better, I'll give her a call."

Kate stands to say goodbye. This time, she hugs Jas, who is awkward in her embrace. Jas reaches into her pocket and is about to fish out a five-pound note, but Kate says, "No, I'll get these. Least I can do."

She watches Jas leave, a slight yet defiant figure. The sequined WARRIOR on the back of her jacket twinkles as she walks down the street. She turns left and disappears from view.

XXVII.

Marisa's eyes stutter open. She is lying in an unfamiliar bed, the duvet tucked over her, and a heavy quilted blanket at one end is weighing her legs down. She had always hated sleeping in beds with the duvets tucked in and made a point, on the rare occasions she stayed in hotels, to kick out the bed linen before going to sleep. But this doesn't feel like a hotel. Where is she?

Her head is aching and her throat is dry. The bed faces toward a window. Light is slipping through the crack where the blind has not been completely pulled down. She can hear birdsong and, beyond that, silence. The silence is strange. For the last few months, she had woken to a cacophony of traffic and thumping music that seemed to exist both inside and outside her mind. She couldn't do anything to rid herself of the noise. She'd tried stuffing her ears with cotton wool but that didn't work. She thought the noise was malevolent, part of a concerted conspiracy to force her out of her home.

This room is different. A shelter. She feels far away from the noise now, cocooned within these white, painted walls. Marisa shifts onto her side and notices a bookshelf built into the wall, lined with orange-spined paperbacks. The door has a brass handle and hanging from it is a lilac ribbon attached to a square of embroidered flowers.

Her stomach gurgles.

She closes her eyes. A scrap of the remembered past floats in front of the blackness. It is of a woman lifting a baby out of a cot and the baby is crying and it is all because Marisa has done something wrong.

She drifts back into blackness.

Hours, or maybe days, later, a man comes into the room. She wakes to find him holding her wrist, and his touch is known to her even though she does not recognize him.

"Marisa," the man says. "How are you feeling?"

She tries to speak, but no sound comes so instead she smiles weakly and concentrates on appearing polite.

"Better?"

She nods, although she can't remember why she is here or what she could be "better" from. Has something happened? Has she been bad?

"That's good," says the man by her bed. He is wearing a burgundy-colored V-neck over a checked shirt, the collar of which is gently frayed. "You gave us quite a scare. But there's nothing to worry about now. You're safe here with us. You're perfectly safe."

He smiles at her, reassuring. He passes her two pills, starkly white against the pink palm of his hand, and she takes them and puts them in her mouth obligingly as she wants to be good again and to be allowed home. She wants to show she is worthy of being loved. The man gives her a tumbler of water, the glass engraved with a pattern of diamonds that casts slivers of light across the white walls. She swallows the pills and the water feels cool in her mouth.

"Thank you," she says.

"You're welcome." He pats her on the shoulder. "Now you must rest. It's the most important thing you can do. There's no need to worry about anything else. Just rest."

Her head is heavy against the pillow. She closes her eyes. She sees herself crawling along a long, dark, gray corridor, the carpet scratching her knees.

When she wakes, it is dark outside. The silence is so thick she can almost taste it. No birdsong. She needs the loo. Marisa props herself up gingerly, sliding her legs out from the duvet. There are slippers on the floor. She puts them on her feet, bending down to do so, and when she sits up again, there is a rush of blood to her head. She waits for the faintness to pass, and then she stands, as though testing the solidity of the floor beneath her. She opens the bedroom door and is confused when she doesn't recognize the room on the other side. It seems to be a kitchen and a drawing room in one. She has never seen it before. A panicked, scrabbly feeling starts in her chest. Where is she? What is she doing here? Where are her parents? Why can't she hear Anna crying?

She reaches one hand out to the wall to steady herself and fumbles her way along the edge of the room. Somehow she finds the toilet and sits there, allowing her bladder to empty. She notices her belly is full and wonders why. She can't remember the last time she ate.

She flushes, then washes her hands. In the mirror, Marisa is shocked to see an adult face looking back at her. Straggly hair, pale skin, and puffy cheeks. She is slightly disgusted by the image. She goes back to bed.

A woman comes in. She is tall, with pinned-back blonde-gray hair and blue eyes the color of Arctic skies. She dusts the mantelpiece and the bookshelf and replaces the empty water bottle on the chest of drawers with a new one. She notices the blind is not pulled all the way down, so she walks over and rectifies it with swift, economic movements. She does not realize Marisa isn't asleep, that she's watching her through a sliver of sight line. The woman stands at the end of the bed, then turns to look at Marisa. The woman shakes her head, then leaves, taking great care to turn the doorknob as quietly as possible.

There are two pillows underneath her head. They feel expensive, stuffed with feathers rather than foam. She thinks of where the feathers come from, of whether they pluck young birds and leave them shivering. Or whether they wait for the birds to die, or perhaps they've been killed already and the feathers would go to waste otherwise? She imagines passing through a swirling, white tunnel of feathers, reaching out to try and catch one in her hand but they keep escaping her reach. The feathers blow and twist out of her grasp until they recede into the distance and then disappear and she is left floating in blankness.

"Marisa."

She hears her name being spoken as if from the opposite side of a chasm. The voice echoes toward her. She opens her eyes and stares into the face of a younger man. Light-blond-brown hair, sandy stubble. It is a face of notable symmetry, apart from one distinct eyebrow hair curling out of place. She knows this face and yet she cannot place it.

"How are you?"

Marisa looks at him, waiting for the answer to come to her. The man seems worried, a deep crinkle appearing just above his right eye, and then the worry passes and distills itself into a kind of sadness. His moods pass across his face like changing weather. He sits on the edge of the bed, causing the mattress to dip, and then he takes her hand in his and strokes it with his thumb.

"Marisa," he says again. "Do you remember what happened?"

For a few seconds, she doesn't. For a few seconds, she is still a child waiting for her parents to come and get her. And then, she remembers.

"Jake," she says.

The memories collapse around her, nuclear dust from an atomic mushroom cloud. The pregnancy. Her illness. The medication she'd stopped taking. The hallway. Kate, unconscious, her legs tied up with rope. Blood on the tiles. Jake. Her Jake. Except he isn't hers. He is Kate's and everything she had done in order to make that not the case now rises up inside her with such force that she has to lever herself out of bed and run to the bathroom. She kneels down in front of the toilet bowl and vomits.

She feels her hair being lifted and held back. Jake, she thinks again, feeling wretched that he is seeing her like this, that this is what she is reduced to.

Way back, years before she had met Jake, she had tried to ignore her illness. She had tried to ignore the manic episodes of work followed by the depression that hit her like a hammer blow, the times she heard voices speaking to her through the television and the microwave, telling her to do terrible things, that she wasn't important enough to live, that even her own mother had abandoned her. She had tried to deal with it silently, behind closed doors. She hadn't wanted to admit that she needed help. It went on for months. But when it became impossible for her to paint, she had to get help because the only other way out was to kill herself, and even in her darkest moments, Marisa knew that she would never be able to do it. She would fail even at that.

The doctor had tried different meds before arriving at the final dosage and type of pill that made Marisa feel better. Not wholly recovered but balanced out, her jagged edges smoothed down with sandpaper, her Technicolor imaginings dulled down to more manageable shades of gray. She was all right as long as she took her medication. She knew she couldn't cope without it. But sometimes, she would convince herself she could be "normal" again, and then she would spiral and Jas would have to fish her back out of the dark place and take care of her, and so it continued until she found a purpose beyond herself. She signed up with a surrogacy agency and realized, for the first time in her life, she could do something entirely good. Her mother had abandoned her. That was a subtraction of love. But Marisa could provide an addition of it for another family. In this way, her life would regain its natural equilibrium. In this way, she would feel once again that she belonged and was useful and loved, if not for herself, then at least for what she could do.

When she met Jake and Kate, she had loved them both. She had stopped taking the drugs because she was preparing her body for pregnancy. It was the *sensible* thing to do, she convinced herself. It was for the good of others. Besides, she had a stable family unit now. She was *better*.

She's so angry with herself. So humiliated by her own incompetence.

She lifts her head from the toilet bowl. Jake lets her hair go.

"Are you ok? Do you want some water?"

"Yes," she says, her voice croaky. "Yes, please."

He leaves the bathroom and comes back with a glass. She sips it slowly. Then he helps her up and she shuffles back into bed, careful now not to disturb the baby she has remembered she is carrying. She is appalled by what she has done. They are the actions of a different person, she wants to say, but Marisa can't speak anymore. She only wants to close her eyes. She rests her head against the expensive feather pillows and swims back into the tide of sleep. She doesn't hear Jake leave.

■ ■ ■

The next morning, Marisa rises feeling rested. She puts on a dressing gown someone has left hanging on a hook from the back of the bedroom door. It is soft and when she checks the label, she sees it is cashmere. She opens the blind. The window overlooks a long lawn, at the other end of which is a large redbrick gabled house. A sparrow pecks at a bowl on a wooden bird table. Roses climb the facade of the house, arching around the brickwork.

Marisa does not recognize either the house at the end of the lawn or the cottage she has been staying in, but the silence and the space make it clear she's in the countryside.

She walks into the next room. There is a U-shaped kitchen unit with a cooker that is an expensive make of the kind she had only ever seen in the pages of interiors magazines. Beyond the kitchen is a lounge, furnished in a neutral palette. There are blankets in a basket by the fire and an open dresser lined with mismatched crockery plates and a television that fits into a bookshelf so that you almost wouldn't notice it at first. The walls are hung with framed prints of flowers ripped out from long-ago botanical encyclopedias, the kind you could buy in a job lot from middlebrow antiques shops and secondhand booksellers.

Marisa decides to make herself a cup of tea and take it outside, to feel the morning sun on her face. She boils the kettle and searches in the cupboards for a tea bag. There is an open packet of Yorkshire Tea in one of them and half a jug of milk in the Smeg fridge. How thoughtful, Marisa thinks, for them to have put the milk there. She isn't sure who "them" refers to, exactly. There is Jake. There is the man who gives her medicine. And then the tall woman with the blue eyes. She must ask Jake who they are, and how long they are intending to stay here. Besides, Marisa thinks, where is Kate?

The clarity she had experienced the night before has gone now. She knows something happened with Kate, but she can't remember what. She knows she is Jake and Kate's surrogate, that she had stopped taking her medication, and that something had happened to worry them. But now she is taking her pills again. She is restored to a capable self. Now they don't need to worry. The baby is safe. This she knows in a deep, intractable part of her that no amount of outside interference can shake. The baby is fine.

She pours milk into the tea and walks to the door. It is one of those old stable doors that used to open in two parts, but someone has fused them together. She presses her thumb down on the iron lever and the door gives way. It opens onto a garden. The grass is twinkling with dew. She breathes in the cool outside air and tilts her face up to the sunshine, feeling its weak warmth graze against her cheeks.

For the first time in a long while, she feels safe.

XXVIII.

When Jake comes back to Richborne Terrace, he looks haggard. Kate makes him some hot buttered toast with raspberry jam and sits him down at the kitchen table, while she keeps up an inconsequential patter that she hopes will hide how concerned she is.

"Kate," he says after a while. "Stop. You don't need to make small talk with me."

She puts the plate of toast down in front of him and sits opposite. She hears it as a rebuke.

"Sorry," he says. His shoulders sag. His T-shirt smells of sweat. "Tell me how you are."

"I'm ok."

"The dentist was good?"

"Yeah." She had been to the dentist yesterday to be fitted with her new prosthetic tooth. They'd done a good job. The gash on her head had healed. She was sleeping better since her meeting with Jas, which she had told Jake all about over the phone while he was in Gloucestershire. He said it made sense, given what Marisa was like now that she was back on her medication—"So docile," he had told Kate, whispering so as not to wake his parents in the next-door bedroom. "It's as if she has no memory of this other person she was or of what she did to you."

Back in London, Kate had cleaned out Marisa's room. She had vacuumed the floor, washed down the walls and the window, which had sticky imprints all over the glass. She had thrown out the leftover takeout cartons and stripped the bed and left a scented candle lit in there for several hours. By the end of her efforts, the room seemed almost normal again and she could kid herself that nothing untoward had happened. The gothic horror of a week ago had receded into the distance and now belonged to another era.

She is not angry with Marisa. Neither of them are. They simply want her to be all right—this is what Kate keeps telling herself. That's why it makes sense to keep Marisa where she is, they agree. That's why Jake's parents are monitoring her progress and ensuring she stays at the cottage. It's for her own good, they decide. It's for their baby's protection. They have to do what they have to do.

"So what was she like when you left her?" Kate asks.

Jake shrugs. When he moves, he does so slowly, as though each muscle is a sandbag being hauled into place.

"She seemed kind of . . . fine. That's the strangest part of it. Back to the Marisa we met and liked and trusted, just like that." He clicked his fingers. "The power of medicine, I guess."

"And she can't remember most of it?"

"She remembers stopping taking the drugs almost as soon as she moved in but that's it."

"Bloody hell."

Kate has heard this before, in multiple phone conversations with Jake over the last few days, but she needs to have it repeated with him in front of her. She waits for him to continue.

"Says she wanted to prepare her body for the pregnancy, which I guess has a kind of twisted logic to it," he goes on. "To give her the benefit of the doubt, I think she was genuinely worried the drugs would damage the baby. Anyway, Dad was able to set her mind at rest on all that. Much safer to be taking them than not."

The toast she has made him lies half-uneaten on the plate between them. Kate can't remember ever having felt this distant from

Jake. When she catches his eye, there is none of his usual warmth there. He's just tired, she reasons. He's been through a lot. He's still in shock. He'll come back to me.

"Can I get you something else?" she asks.

"You know what I really want?"

"What?"

"A proper drink. Do we have any whisky?"

They do. She pours it for him and puts in one of those fancy square ice cubes they have in the freezer. No water.

"But she doesn't remember attacking me?" Kate asks when the whisky is in his hands.

Jake drinks, closing his eyes and leaning back in his chair as he swallows.

"Nope," he says.

"Convenient," Kate mutters under her breath.

"Honestly, Kate, I don't think she does. Dad says she's likely to get these, sort of, psychotic breaks."

Kate feels sick with the pressure of it all. The thought of her baby being this far away from her, in the belly of a woman with a history of psychosis and bipolar depression, is almost too much to bear. But she can't blame Marisa for her mental illness. The only person she blames is herself, for wanting a baby so much that it has led them here.

"Is it going to be ok?" she whispers.

Jake comes to her side of the table and puts his arms around her. "It is, my love. It's going to be fine. We're through the worst."

She presses her face into his neck, grateful for his tenderness.

"We've just got to get through the next few months as best we can," he continues. His breath smells of peat fires. "Mum and Dad will keep an eye on her and we can go and visit at weekends. We need to keep her away from stress, which I think means away from this house and away from us for the rest of the pregnancy."

"And she's ok with that?"

Jake nods. "She's had it explained to her. She understands. I don't think she particularly wants to come back. Too many uncomfortable truths."

Kate lifts her head and wipes a strand of hair away from her forehead. Her throat is dry. "You're right. I need to be strong."

"We both do," he says. "And we can be because we have each other, ok?"

They drive up at the weekend. It is a strange echo of the first time Kate met Jake's parents. Once again, she takes inordinate care with her clothes without wanting it to seem as though she had. Once again, she feels a nervousness in her chest that she tries to ignore. Once again, she rehearses possible conversations in her head. But this time, they are conversations with Marisa, not Annabelle and Chris.

Jake's parents have been in regular contact since taking Marisa in. They have been unwavering in their support. Annabelle has not complained about the situation once.

"Are you sure we're not imposing?" Kate had said to her on the phone a few nights ago. "I'm so sorry to have lumbered you with this."

"Not at all. Marisa is no trouble now. She's actually very pleasant."

"Oh good," Kate had said, surprised. "Thank you. I know you had your doubts about the surrogacy route, but—"

"Whatever I felt about it is in the past," Annabelle said, cutting her off. "It's family first and that's all there is to it."

Kate was unsettled when she ended the call but assumed it was just because she wasn't used to Annabelle being so helpful.

"That's the thing you have to understand about my mother," Jake said. "Family is everything to her. She sees you as family now."

When they get to the house, Annabelle opens the door and gives them a quick hug. She is wearing a flowing linen blouse. Her makeup is impeccable.

"You look fantastic," Kate says warmly. She knows she's trying to charm Annabelle. Now Kate owes her, and the debt will never fully be repaid.

"Oh," Annabelle says. "Really? Thank you."

There are no reciprocal compliments.

"Jakey, you look tired, darling," Annabelle says, leading them through to the kitchen where the table has been set with the "casual" crockery set and patterned paper napkins.

"I'm fine, Mum. How's she been?"

Annabelle leans against the oven, spreading her hands across the silver railing. "Marisa?"

Who else? Kate thinks.

"She's doing really well." There is an unexpected softness to Annabelle's voice. "She's been good as gold, really."

"That's a relief," Kate says. "Can we see her?"

She isn't sure why she asks. This is why they have come, after all.

Annabelle looks offended, as though she had expected more preamble, a little foreplay before the act itself.

"Of course," she says, her voice clipped. "I'd leave it for a few minutes. Chris is with her now, doing his thing. So," Annabelle says, looking at them brightly, "drinks?"

She makes them each a gin and tonic, one with less gin for Jake, who has to remind her he is driving ("Oh, you don't need to worry about that once you've had a meal," Annabelle says airily). They sit on the L-shaped window seat, the cushions made out of the same chintz pattern that dominates the sitting room. Kate sips her gin and tonic, frustrated by this social charade. She suspects Annabelle is rather enjoying her role as gatekeeper.

On cue, Jake launches into a little speech about how grateful they both are and how they couldn't have navigated this without her. Annabelle pretends she doesn't need to hear it, but she lets Jake carry on talking and Kate watches as she grows rosy and contented, fattened like a maggot by all the compliments.

When Jake comes to the end of his impromptu encomium, there is silence. Kate has just polished off the last of her gin when she realizes she is meant to speak. Annabelle is looking at her, her legs crossed and her eyebrows lightly raised.

"Yes . . . just to, um, second all of that. We're so, so grateful, Annabelle. To both of you. Thank you."

Annabelle lowers her head, as though graciously accepting an honor. "Please," she says. "I'll always be here for you, as you know. But it is nice to hear all of those things. We'll get through it. We'll get our baby—that's the main thing."

Kate bites her tongue.

At that moment, Chris walks into the kitchen through the French doors.

"Hello, hello," he says, shoulders sloping forward slightly so that she can see the bald spot on the top of his head.

"Shoes!" Annabelle says, and Chris obligingly unlaces his brogues and puts them to one side of the doormat.

He kisses Kate on the cheek and shakes Jake's hand. "She's doing very well. I've told her you're here and she's looking forward to seeing you both."

He smiles at Kate, his face benign.

"Thank you," she says, wondering if she will ever be able to stop saying the same two words over and over again to Jake's parents.

"No need to thank me. It's what doctors do, isn't it?"

The cottage is a single-story outbuilding, converted from a set of stables. To get to it, they walk past the rusting croquet hoops and the lopsided bird table. The cottage windows are small and meanly proportioned, the ledges dotted with moss. There is an untended pot of geraniums outside the front door, the stems overgrown and straggly. The air feels damp and oppressive.

Jake knocks on the door.

"Come in," Marisa says, her voice muffled.

They walk inside. Marisa is sitting on an armchair by an unlit wood-burning stove. She is cradling her belly—more pronounced now than it was even a fortnight ago. Her blonde hair falls in tendrils over her shoulders, partly shielding her face from them. She is wearing a cream shirt and white linen trousers. Kate realizes that Annabelle has lent her these clothes, and her stomach contracts.

When Marisa turns to them, she smiles in a way that Kate can only think of as beatific. The pain and rage that had been there before have gone. There are no dark circles under her eyes. Her face has lost its pinched quality and her cheeks have filled out. The Thomas Hardy milkmaid is back in abundance, Kate thinks, and although she should be relieved, she is also suspicious of the quickness of this transformation. In this light, Marisa looks slightly unreal, as though she is being inhabited by someone else.

"Marisa," Jake says. "You look so well."

She levers herself up out of the armchair and comes over to them. Her walk is still the same as it always was: ungainly, as though she had just dismounted from a horse. Marisa spreads her arms wide and before Kate can register what is about to happen, Marisa is hugging her. Kate feels the tautness of the other woman's pregnant stomach and smells lemon verbena coming from her freshly washed hair.

"Kate," Marisa says as she pulls back from the hug. "I'm so, so sorry. Can you ever forgive me?"

"Of course," Kate replies, remembering the time that Annabelle asked her the very same question at her birthday lunch at the Wolseley. How curious that they should use exactly the same phrase. "It's fine, Marisa. As long as you and the baby are safe."

"We are," Marisa says, still smiling, but she can't seem to meet Kate's eye. "I'm *so* much better now. Thanks to Chris and Annabelle. And to you two."

"We're so glad to hear that," Jake says. "You certainly look much better."

"Oh," Marisa says, biting the tip of one nail. "I'm sorry." She looks at Kate. "I must have been in a right state when you last saw me."

That's one way of putting it, Kate thinks.

"No, no," Jake interjects, batting away the idea. A blush creeps up the back of his neck.

"Come on in, won't you?" Marisa says, and ushers them to the sofa.

Marisa asks Jake about the drive and he goes into unnecessary detail about which route they had taken and why. Kate is not sure what she had expected but it definitely wasn't this. She knew Marisa was calmer now, but she had thought she would find her more disheveled and weak, perhaps still in bed recovering from her breakdown. To see her acting the part of hostess is eerie. The way she is speaking sounds fake, as though she's been programmed.

"Kate, can I get you a tea?" Marisa asks.

"No. No, thanks. I'm fine."

"I wanted to say . . . well, to explain, really," Marisa says, fiddling with the corner of a blue patterned cushion on the chair. "That what you witnessed is entirely out of character for me. I didn't want to tell you about my mental health history, for obvious reasons. I thought it would put you off."

"Yeah, well. It would have done," Kate says. She is frustrated and can feel a tension rising within her. She realizes now she had wanted some sort of showdown, a closure as dramatic as the event, and that this was being denied her.

Jake places his hand over Kate's, which she interprets as a warning to calm down. *How fucking dare he*, Kate thinks, and takes her hand back. It hadn't happened to him, had it? She'd been the one Marisa had targeted.

"I can understand that," Marisa says, looking at her vaguely. "It's why I didn't tell the surrogacy agency either. I thought I had it under control, and I did. But I liked you guys so much—loved you, even—and you were doing so much for me, asking me to move in and all that, and I just wanted everything to be perfect for you and I was feeling so much better, much more myself, and I felt that stopping the drugs would, you know, be beneficial to the pregnancy. I thought I'd be fine. I genuinely did. I'd been fine for so long."

"That's not the impression Jas gave," Kate says.

Marisa gazes at her, but any surprise she might have felt at this revelation seems to take too long to reach her.

"Oh. You've met Jas?" She smiles again and the smile, like everything else about her, is slightly off. "She's great, isn't she? But she has her own issues. I'd take what she says with a pinch of salt."

Jake clears his throat. He is cross with Kate—she can tell. They had agreed that the key thing was to keep Marisa calm, not to contradict her or make her feel bad. Their priority was the baby, he had said, not extracting the necessary penance. They had to let that go.

"Anyway, let's not dwell on the past," he says now. "The main thing is you're safe, you're back on your meds, and we're so happy you're able to rest here while you carry our baby to term."

"Yes," Kate says. "Exactly."

"You *are* happy staying here, aren't you?" Jake looks at Marisa and his face is so earnest Kate can only marvel at how well he is playing this.

"Oh yes, I am," Marisa replies. She rubs her belly in a circular motion. "The baby is, too—I can feel it."

"And you're eating well and taking the necessary supplements?" Kate asks.

Marisa nods. "I promise you that your baby is s-s-safe with me, Kate," she says, stammering in a way Kate hadn't heard before. "I'll go for all the scans at the local hospital—Chris has already arranged that—and of course, you're always welcome down here. Anytime."

"Thank you, Marisa," Jake says, giving an obsequious little bow of the head.

Kate twists her hands into her jeans pockets, picking at the denim seams. The gall of the woman, inviting Jake to his family home! She stands abruptly. Marisa, cow-eyed, stares at her.

"We'd better go, Jake. Your mother doesn't want the lasagna she's making to get cold."

They leave, and Jake, ever polite, tells Marisa not to get up. She stays seated and tells them she will see them soon and then she lowers her head again, letting her hair fall across one side of her face as they go. She waits pliantly for them to close the door behind them. They walk back to the main house, catching the smell of freshly baked lasagna on the breeze.

XXIX.

Over the next few weeks, Kate tries as much as possible to ignore her own mounting unease. She clears out the rest of Marisa's room and repaints it, going to her local hardware store for roller trays and brushes. She puts on old leggings and a cheap T-shirt and does it all over the course of a single weekend. She listens to podcasts as she does so—mother-and-baby interviews with successful bloggers-turned-authors who talk about creative stimulation and at-home crafting. She tries not to think of Marisa's empty gaze, the detachment she had noticed when they saw her. When the room is done, it smells fresh and new and looks brighter than before, and Kate is calmer for having done something tangible. The painting helped her to concentrate on the Marisa they now speak to every other day on the phone, who says all the right things about eating healthily and Annabelle giving her spinach from the vegetable garden and yes, she is fine, thank you, and no, they don't need to worry about her.

Jake is relieved. Kate is astonished by his ability to compartmentalize.

An unacknowledged distance is growing between them, as though they are sailing separately toward a horizon they will never quite reach. One month passes in this way, then two. Time assumes an elastic, gloppy quality and the seasons merge into one. She starts going to bed earlier, waking when the sun rises instead of sleeping in. She gets to work before anyone else is in the office, drafting press releases and arranging screenings weeks ahead of time. At one junket, she sits in on the day's interviews with the film's star and she stares out of the window, wondering if becoming parents will drive a further wedge between her and Jake. How will she know what to do? What if she cannot soothe her baby's cries? What if, deep down, her baby knows Kate is not its real mother?

She lets the interview overrun and a colleague has to knock on the door to tell the journalist their time is up. Kate apologizes to the actor, a man with speckled gray hair in his fifties who is still getting action hero parts.

"Just don't let it happen again," the actor says, his tone one of forced reasonableness.

In the past, she would have been mortified. Now, she no longer cares. Everything other than the baby seems trivial.

They make regular visits to Gloucestershire, where lunch with the parents is combined with an afternoon spent in the cottage with Marisa. They go for scans and checkups at the local hospital with Chris in attendance. They find out they are expecting a boy, which makes Jake cry and Kate laugh with delight at how real it all is. Once, they drive Marisa back to London with them for a catch-up with Mr. Abadi, but Kate spends the whole length of the journey being terrified that Marisa might hurl herself out of the back car door. Mr. Abadi, genial as ever, is pleased with the pregnancy's progress. When he asks them if they have any concerns or anything they want to tell him that might have happened in the interim since their last visit, all three of them shake their heads and fail to catch each other's eye. They drive back to Gloucestershire that same evening and Kate is relieved to hand Marisa back over to the care of Jake's parents. She feels bad for this, as if lacking some maternal spirit that should make her want to be next to her baby at all times, and she frets that it means she won't bond with her son when he arrives. She also can't shake the fear that their son will inherit Marisa's mental illness. Everything seems fragile, as though it could be taken away from her in an instant.

"You worry too much," Jake says when she tries to speak to him about it. "It's all going to be fine. The best thing you can do is relax and make sure you have plenty of sleep now before the baby comes."

It's not that he is dismissive, exactly, but more that in his eagerness to placate her, he makes Kate feel her fears are overwrought. Is she being hysterical? Or is Jake simply making her feel like that? She isn't sure anymore; she has lost faith in her own judgment. Their joint reliance on Annabelle and Chris also means that she feels outnumbered three to one. They are the family. She is on the outside.

As if to compound the feeling of exclusion, Annabelle calls one evening and delivers unexpected news. Kate listens in while Jake murmurs and says, "No, no, I understand . . . Yes, of course." When she asks to speak to Annabelle herself, Jake shakes his head silently and walks into the garden, pressing his phone to his ear, shielding his mouth with a cupped hand so that she can't even make out the words formed by his lips.

When he comes back inside, he tells her that Annabelle feels Marisa is "unsettled."

"Apparently, it's all sinking in—what she did, I mean," he explains. "And she's feeling so guilty about what she's done that she always feels she has to apologize when she sees us. To you in particular."

"Right."

"So Mum thinks it might be better if we eased off the visits. Spaced them out a bit."

"Ok."

"I honestly don't think it's Mum sticking her oar in," Jake says, as if reading her thoughts. "I think, as Marisa recovers, she's becoming more aware of what she put us through and she feels . . . a bit . . . awkward, I guess?"

Kate chews at a loose hangnail. It has been splitting off from her cuticle for days and the pain is both sharp and precise.

"Right," she says again.

"If anything, it's a *good* sign," Jake insists. "It shows she's getting better. We can worry less. And those trips to Gloucestershire are knackering."

"That's true."

"So we'll just go a bit less often—that's all."

Kate accepts it. She has to trust Annabelle, and she doesn't want to push it. One misstep and the whole edifice will come crashing down.

So Jake suggests a spa break. She laughs when he mentions it.

"A *spa* break?"

"Yes—why not?"

He looks at her, brow rumpled.

"Sorry, it's a lovely idea. I suppose it's just a bit out of the blue given . . . everything." She stops herself from saying what she really thinks. Spas and fluffy robes and cucumber-infused water belong to a past world. She isn't in the mood, she wants to say. That's the kind of thing unencumbered, romantically minded couples do in the first flush of a relationship, not a couple attempting to deal with the fact their surrogate has severe mental health issues.

"That's exactly why we should go," he says. "I'll take care of it. Some time away will do us good before our baby boy comes. Who knows when we'll get the chance again after he's here?"

"You're right," she replies, allowing herself to be convinced.

He books a spa an hour's drive from London. They are offering a weekend package deal, which includes what the website describes as "two mini-treatments"—facials and massages at twenty-five minutes each. Anything else is "extra."

"Do they feed us?" Kate asks, only half joking. "Or is that extra too?"

"All meals included," Jake replies, not taking his eyes from the bright-white flicker of the computer screen. "Vegan and macrobiotic options."

"No alcohol, I'm guessing. Maybe we should take our own?"

"Ha."

Jake double-clicks on the superior double-room option, then enters his card details.

"Congratulations," the screen flashes up. "We look forward to welcoming you for your stay at Charlton Manor."

"Terrible font," Kate says, pointing out the flouncy gray copperplate. Jake is a font geek.

He laughs. "The worst."

Charlton Manor is set on the edge of a large lake and as they drive to the car park, Kate sees a heron separate itself from the reeds with a sudden unfurling of wings and beak, its brown-gray silhouette stark against the dusty sky.

She recalls a drawing on the wall in Mr. Abadi's office, the corners of the paper misshapen by four small bulges of Blu Tack. It was of a stork, flying with a baby tucked into a polka-dot handkerchief sling knotted around its beak. The lines were firm, black and adult, but a child had clearly colored it in with scribbles of yellow and red and blue pencil. *THANK YOU FROM THE TRAYNOR FAMILY* was written across the bottom in block capitals.

The drawing had stayed with her, and afterward she had looked up the significance of storks as harbingers of birth. She found an ancient Greek myth involving the goddess Hera who grew jealous of a beautiful queen and transformed her into a crane. The heartbroken queen sought to retrieve her child from Hera's clutches, which is why the Greeks depicted the bird with a baby dangling from its beak. Later retellings mistakenly identified the bird as a stork. In Egyptian mythology, she learned, storks had been associated with the birth of the world, but again this was an error: it had been a heron in the original legend.

Storks and cranes and herons. She is about to say something about it to Jake but doesn't. She decides that this weekend she will try not to talk about anything baby related.

The spa lobby is a paean to faux beige marble, every surface unnaturally shiny and veined with pink. A uniformed man whose name tag says JAMAAR takes details of their car number plate and asks whether they would like a morning newspaper. They are offered a detoxifying juice consisting of carrot, orange, and ginger that fizzes in Kate's mouth with a fermented quality.

"Lovely," she says, wincing.

Their room is frigid. It overlooks the internal courtyard rather than the lake and there are no biscuits on the tea tray, only herbal tea bags. The double bed is overstuffed with cushions, arranged in a pyramid of descending size order. The en suite bathroom is small and windowless and hanging on the back of the bathroom door are two of the requisite white, fluffy robes, each one embroidered with CM in the same curlicued copperplate. Instead of slippers, they are provided with unforgiving plastic flip-flops that are cold and heavy against her feet.

"Shall we go for a sauna?" Jake asks.

"Sure."

She wants to stay in their room, lie on the bed watching TV, and for him to hold her close and be affectionate but she puts on her one-piece bathing suit without a murmur. The suit is an old one, bought cheaply online a few summers ago. It has red-and-white stripes, the material bobbling at the edges. It's a bathing suit she wears for function rather than form and she regrets bringing it now, wishing instead she had chosen something that Jake would find more appealing. She doesn't usually think like this. It had always been obvious to Kate that Jake found her attractive. Although he paid attention to her clothes and liked her style, he would compliment her when she least expected it—coming out of the shower in the morning or on her way back from the gym, her hair stiff with sweat. But now she can't remember the last time he noticed her physical appearance.

They sit and sweat in the sauna, heat prickling against her skin. She supposes this is the kind of thing they won't be able to do when they have a baby, at least for a few years. An older man is in there with them—bare chested, his flesh loose, slabs of his skin overlapping each other like some geological curiosity. Kate has always found it odd how most British people are uncomfortable making eye contact on public transport and yet will quite readily strip half-naked and sit in a confined, airless space to sweat with strangers. The man levers himself upright, his bones creaking as he does so. He pushes open the door and a welcome gust of fresh air breezes across Kate's reddening face.

Jake ladles more water on the stones without asking.

"Are you ok?" she asks eventually.

"Yes, of course," he says too quickly. "Why?"

"Oh, nothing really. You just seem to have something on your mind."

He looks at her then and the corners of his eyes crease up in that familiar way. "Sorry, no. No, there's nothing wrong. I guess I'm just a bit . . . you know, distracted."

She reaches out to massage the back of his neck. "That's understandable. I am too. But everything's ok. Marisa's fine."

"Yes, she certainly seems better," Jake says. "Her cheeks are pinker."

"What?"

He glances at her. "I just meant . . . on FaceTime."

"I didn't know you were FaceTiming Marisa without me."

"No, no." He shakes his head. "I was FaceTiming with Mum, I mean, and Marisa was there."

"Oh." Kate removes her hand and lets it rest on her lap. "Annabelle knows how to FaceTime? That's . . . unexpected."

She had lost count of the number of times Annabelle had launched into spontaneous disquisitions on the evils of modern technology and the incomprehensibility of "newfangled" modes of communication.

"Yeah, I think Marisa showed her how to do it."

The sauna door opens again, and two giggling women with blonde highlighted hair walk in and splay themselves out in matching black bikinis. The women are tall and angular, flat chested and narrow waisted, with the long, lean limbs of fashion models. Kate gathers her towel closer around her stomach. But, she wants to say, Marisa is hopeless at that kind of thing. Her phone has needed upgrading ever since they've known her. She glances at Jake and his face has closed up again, like a blind coming down over a shop awning. The sauna heat continues to rise.

That night, she sleeps well for the first time in months. The room is quiet and, once they had worked out how to turn off the air-conditioning, stays at an ambient temperature. When she turns on her side to face Jake in the morning, he smiles at her.

"Hello there." He rests his hand on her cheek. "Sleep well?"

"Mmmm," Kate says. "Really well."

"It's because we sweated out all our stress."

"If that's actually the reason, then we should totally look into getting a sauna at home."

He grins. "Do a basement extension like everyone else on the street, you mean?"

It had been a source of shared amusement between them how much building work their neighbors engaged in. Kate had joked that having a Portakabin outside your front door was the new status symbol.

"Great idea. Months of disruption that will make us properly stressed just in time for the sauna that has been causing us the stress by being built."

He kisses her, holding her close and letting his hands slide down to her back. They have gentle, quick, uncomplicated sex and then he gets up to fill the kettle from the bathroom tap and puts it on to boil.

"Herbal tea?" he asks as she props herself up against the pillows. "Or would you prefer an herbal tea?"

"Um, ok, let me think. I'll have an herbal tea, please. But only if it's really weak and doesn't taste of anything."

She watches him walk around the room, naked apart from those silly flip-flops, and she marvels at his lack of self-consciousness. He has a good body: tall and broad with a pronounced rump and the merest hint of a thirtysomething paunch, but he appears unaware of his physicality in these moments in a way that a woman never would be. A woman, Kate thinks, would be worried about her flabby belly or her wide thighs or the fact that her breasts are saggier than she'd like and she would assume she was being monitored by the male eyes in the room. Yet Jake treats his body as his own.

Jake's phone beeps. He picks it up, unhooking it from the sleek black charging device on the bedside table. He becomes instantly absorbed in its screen and doesn't notice the kettle boiling. Kate wraps her robe around her and finishes making the tea. She hands him a cup, which he takes from her without raising his head.

"What's up?" she asks, getting back under the duvet.

"Oh, sorry, thanks," he says, drinking the tea. "It's . . . annoying . . . It's a work thing."

He taps rapidly at the phone screen, typing out text with his thumbs. When he sends it, the phone makes a swooshing sound and he returns to the room and to her.

"Kate, I'm really sorry, but . . ."

Instinctively, she fears the worst. Her stomach plummets.

"There's an issue at work—this deal we've been doing with the oil company . . ."

Oh, is that all? she thinks, relieved. She nods as if she knows what he's talking about. She is sure he must have told her but she never fully listens when he mentions work because much of the technicality washes over her. It is so removed from her own existence that she doesn't feel she can understand it or offer anything useful to the conversation. Besides, Jake always has work issues, so there's nothing to worry about. It's just more of the same.

". . . and I'm going to have to go back to London to get to the office," he finishes and she realizes she has glazed over again without meaning to. It's like asking someone for directions and not focusing on their answer and then being too embarrassed to ask again.

"Of course," she says. "I understand."

He lifts her hand to his mouth and kisses her knuckles. "Thank you. I'm just sorry it's ruined our break."

"It hasn't! There's only so much sweating you can do in one weekend anyway. It's fine. I'm ready to go."

"No, no, you shouldn't have to come with me—stay here and make the most of it. We've got the room for another night."

He is already gathering up his belongings from around the room, rolling up T-shirts and his pajama bottoms into the executive case she had given him once for Christmas.

"But what about the car?"

"I'll go and deal with this and come back to pick you up tomorrow," Jake says. "We can stop somewhere for a pub lunch on our way back to London. Get some calories into you after this forced deprivation."

She settles back against the pillows. Admittedly, it does sound tempting.

"That's a hassle for you," she says weakly.

"It's not. It would make me feel better if I knew you were here, having a nice time."

He disappears into the bathroom and she can hear him putting his shaving cream and face wash into his toiletry bag.

"I won't have as nice a time without you."

"Nonsense," he says, coming back to the bed and nuzzling her neck. "I saw you eyeing up that man in the sauna yesterday. You were undressing him with your eyes."

"He was already undressed!"

"Ah!" he says, wagging his finger like Columbo. "So you admit it."

She laughs and wraps her arms around his neck, drawing him close.

"I'll see you tomorrow?" Jake says.

He's probably right: staying here for a bit longer on her own would enable her to relax properly. Plus, she had her facial booked in for 3 p.m.

"Ok," she agrees. "Sounds like a plan."

Jake leaves half an hour later, saying he'll call her, and she waves him off quite happily, before stretching out across the double mattress and falling back asleep.

She sleeps for two more hours and is shocked, when she wakes, by the time. It has been difficult to rest at all in the last few months.

Kate wraps herself tightly in her robe. One of the nice things about the spa is that you don't have to get dressed: you can just wander around in your dressing gown. The dining room, when she reaches it, is full of similarly robed guests padding up to the brunch buffet with hair scraped back and a dazed expression on their faces as though they are members of the same peculiar cult.

She eats a bowl of Bircher muesli, accompanied by the obligatory decaffeinated coffee, and then finds a quiet spot to read the paper. Her phone is on airplane mode in her robe pocket. The spa discouraged use of any mobiles in communal areas so she sneaks off to the loo to check it surreptitiously, expecting to find a message from Jake saying he'd got back to the office safely. There is nothing. Maybe it's just taking a while to get through, she thinks, and slips the phone back into her pocket.

She goes for her facial and is asked to fill in a lengthy form detailing the ins and outs of her medical history. There, at the end of a series of questions about blood pressure and skin conditions, is the inevitable "Are you, or is there any chance you could be, pregnant?" She ticks the box for "no" and resists the temptation to write ". . . but it's a long story."

Her therapist is called Kasia, a neat, diminutive woman with soft brown eyes, wearing a black uniform with a Nehru collar. Kate is led down a long corridor and ushered into a treatment room, where generic panpipe music is playing and the air is softly scented with herbs and citrus. Kasia leaves the room so that Kate can get comfortable, and as she lies back onto the massage table, she notices that the towels are heated. She closes her eyes and, when Kasia starts sweeping the tips of her cool fingers in circular motions across her cheeks and up to her forehead, she feels herself falling asleep.

Afterward, her skin glows when she looks at it in the bedroom mirror. She lies back on the bed and lazily flicks on the television. She checks her phone—still nothing from Jake. It's unusual, but not worryingly so. She places her mobile on the bedside table and resolves not to look at it for at least another hour. She refuses to be the kind of girlfriend who texts anxiously just because she hasn't heard from her boyfriend. She had never been that kind of woman before, and she is determined not to be so now. She has noticed that, since everything happened with Marisa, she is more likely to catastrophize even the most trivial occurrence. There's nothing to worry about, Kate tells herself. Just be normal.

She watches a cooking show where chefs from different parts of the country compete to make dishes in a banquet and then she watches a quiz where celebrities she doesn't recognize compete to make fools of themselves and then she makes herself a cup of tea and contemplates going for a swim.

She looks at her phone. Still no text. She's cross now and impatiently grabs it from the charging port and finds Jake's name in her recent calls. The phone rings. Once. Twice. Three times. He picks up on the fourth.

"Kate?" he says. "Are you ok?"

She feels immediately silly. "Yes, yes, fine. Just, you know, I hadn't heard from you."

"Oh . . . sorry. I didn't want to disturb you. Are you having a nice day?"

He seems distracted and she imagines him hunched in front of his computer screen, analyzing a spreadsheet of numbers. But then she hears a whooshing sound in the background. Then another. Cars.

"Wait—are you driving?"

"Um. Yeah. Yeah. But don't worry—you're on speakerphone."

"You're not in the office?"

"No. But I just was there, I mean," he says. There is a ticking sound and she realizes he must have turned on the indicator. "And now I've got to meet a client."

"Oh, I hadn't realized you'd driven all the way in. I thought you'd go home, then get the tube."

"No time," he says curtly.

His tone is unconvincing.

"Where's your client meeting?"

"Sorry, what was that?"

"Your client meeting," she repeats, enunciating the words even more clearly. "Where is it?"

"It's, erm, God knows. I had to put it in the satnav. In the countryside somewhere. One of those billionaire second homes—you know what it's like."

She doesn't know what it is like, Kate wants to say, but she stops herself. She's letting her thoughts run away with her. There is no reason to be suspicious.

"You still there?" Jake asks, tinny on the other end of the line.

"Yeah, still here."

"You know I love you, don't you? There's nothing to worry about, ok? Sorry I didn't call earlier but I've just been busy."

"Ok," she says.

"I'll text you later. I promise."

When the call ends, she switches her phone off and leaves it in the room while she goes for a swim. She tells herself she won't check it again until tomorrow, and this time, she doesn't.

XXX.

"Do you really think it's a good idea to leave it so long between visits?" she asks Jake. It is a weekday evening and he is working out in the garden despite the freezing temperatures.

"I think . . . we have to be . . . guided by what Marisa feels . . . comfortable with, to be honest," he says, panting between words. He is using a new set of complicated straps, holding one black loop in each gloved fist, hanging back at a forty-five-degree angle, and then pulling himself back up with a grunt. Jake had wrapped the straps around an iron bar he'd installed over the weekend with large nuts and bolts in the brickwork above the garden doors. The event had required a lot of noisy drilling and afterward, she had swept away the fine sandy drizzle of stone from the patio.

"Are you enjoying your new contraption?" Kate asks now, raising her voice so it can be heard from the warmth of the kitchen. She pours herself a generous glass of Malbec from an already opened bottle on the counter.

"Yup," he says, his voice straining. He turns around and pushes his feet through the straps, then flips into a plank position. His biceps bulge, like a mouse wriggling to escape from a python's stomach. He launches into rapid push-ups. "Body weight. Is. Key," he says between breaths.

She puts on her parka and goes outside to sit on the bench, sipping her wine while watching him. Jake's borderline obsession with exercise had always amused her but now she finds it unsettling. Since the spa weekend, there had been a few more unplanned absences—late nights at the office and a work conference one weekend that necessitated an overnight stay. Before the fertility treatment, he regularly had business trips that took him away for several nights at a time, but he had stopped going on these in order to support her and be around for appointments. Over the last few weeks, he's resumed his old routine, but she remains suspicious. Anxiety clouds her thoughts like condensation on a mirror. Does he really need to be away so often? Why is he working out so much? Why has he turned off the tracking app he used to have on his phone?

After the push-ups, Jake shrugs himself into a graying hoodie with HARVARD written in an arch across the front. He had never been to Harvard but the hoodie is so old now that he can't remember where it came from. He comes to sit next to her and she feels the heat and smell of his sweat, mossy like a forest.

"Don't worry about the visits," he says, mopping his face with a towel. "Let's go down this Saturday if you're stressed."

"I'm not stressed. I just . . ." She lets the thought hang. I just worry that I'm losing you, she wants to say. I just worry that you're having an affair. I just worry that my desperation to be a mother has driven you away and there is no "just" about it.

"The main thing, as we've agreed," he says, as though speaking to a child, "is to keep Marisa calm and happy and—"

"And stable—yes, I know." There is a swell of frustration in her chest.

Jake stops mopping and looks at her. "You *are* stressed. Mum was right."

Her throat contracts. "I'm sorry, what?"

"I just meant—"

"So you've been talking to your mother about me?"

As a couple, they rarely argued. They were good at talking things out. She had never understood it when other couples admitted they argued vociferously, and she claimed it as evidence of their passion. But now she is furious. She can sense herself about to say something irreversible.

Jake is silent.

"I *said*, have you been talking to your mother about me?"

He glares at her and she is shocked by the anger she sees in his face. "Yes, for fuck's sake—of course I've been talking to her. She's my *mother*. She's worried about me—about us."

"How kind," Kate says. "But I don't need her concern."

She stands, holding the wineglass so tightly she wonders if she might snap the stem.

"You see, this is just what I mean," he says, still sitting on the bench. He has clenched his hands at either end of the towel around his neck. His knuckles are white. "I can't say anything without you flying off the deep end."

"Are you serious?"

"Yes! And Mum's noticed it. She's worried you're too involved, too obsessive, that it's not good for Marisa—"

"I'm the *mother*," Kate screams.

A window slams in the housing estate opposite and then, all at once, the stairwell lights snap on simultaneously as they are programmed to do at the same time each day. The garden is pitched into a ghoulish half-light.

"Of course I'm going to be involved!" She notices with surprise that she is still shouting. "Obsessive? Bullshit. Our surrogate attacked me! She had a breakdown and thought you were together! I think I've earned the right to be concerned, don't you?"

"Jesus, Kate, keep your voice down. The neighbors will hear."

"Oh, fuck off," she says, walking inside the kitchen and slamming the wineglass onto the table so that red drops stain the wood. She knows, instinctively, what Annabelle will have been saying about her: that she's unhinged, that this drive for a baby has made her lose perspective, that Jake must be careful. No wonder he wants to get away from her. She tortures herself, briefly, with an image of the kind of woman he might be sleeping with—young, that goes without saying, and easy, uncomplicated, quick to laugh, a body without a crease.

She remembers a phone conversation with Annabelle a few days before. She usually called Jake and only tried Kate if she couldn't get hold of him, so Kate had answered, saying, "He's not here, I'm afraid, Annabelle."

"What? Oh, no, Kate. I was calling to talk to you, actually."

The older woman's voice was clear on the other end of the line, vowels tinkling against consonants like ice cubes in a gin and tonic.

"Ok. How . . . nice," Kate said, checking her watch to see how long would be polite to wait until she could draw this unwanted interruption to a close. "Is everything ok? Is Marisa ok?"

"Yes, she's thriving," Annabelle said, and Kate felt it as a rebuke. Why couldn't she just have said "fine"?

"I wanted to see how *you* were," Annabelle continued, placing emphasis on the "you," as though it were an unparalleled act of kindness on her behalf.

"That's . . . nice," Kate repeated. "I'm pretty good, thank you."

"Really?"

She could hear Annabelle breathe in noisily and the sound of a door closing in the background and she wondered if Chris had walked in or out of the room. Or maybe it wasn't Chris at all, Kate found herself thinking—maybe it was Marisa.

"Yes, why wouldn't I be? I mean, aside from the huge stress of this entire situation." Kate gave a sharp burst of laughter. She had meant to be funny, but the joke landed more bleakly than she'd anticipated. "No, but honestly, Annabelle, that's so sweet of you to check in. Thank you."

"I've been worried about you," Annabelle said, her tone unchanged, almost as if Kate hadn't said anything. "I love my son, but I'm also aware that he's been a bit . . ."—she pauses meaningfully—"distracted, shall we say?"

Kate didn't know how to respond. There was no reason Annabelle should have known about Kate's suspicions. Unless, she thought with a lurch, Jake had been talking to her about their issues? Unless—her stomach turned—he had confided in his mother about an affair?

"He's been *such* a support to Marisa," Annabelle was saying, "and it's clear how well they get on, and of course he's been a wonderful support to me too, as he always is. But I do hope he hasn't been neglecting you, dear Kate."

Annabelle was one of the only people who could use the word "dear" as a weapon.

"No, no, not at all," Kate said, ignoring her own disquiet. "He's been great."

"Oh," Annabelle said, with a light note of surprise. "Oh, *good*. I'm so glad to hear it."

Reflecting on that phone call now in the grip of her own anger, Kate refills her glass and steps back outside. Jake has not moved from the bench. She sits back down beside him. She knows that the only way to prove Annabelle wrong is to be calm. She's being ridiculous, Kate tells herself. Jake isn't cheating on her; he's simply traveling for work. She refuses to become as deluded as Marisa was. She is the stable, reliable one, after all.

"I'm sorry for shouting," she says. "I just don't want Marisa's needs taking priority over mine. She's carrying my son, after all." Kate pauses. "I am the mother," she repeats.

Jake, immediately contrite, draws her in close.

"Of course you are," he tells her, kissing the top of her head.

"You've been away loads," she says.

"I know. I'm sorry."

She expects him to say more but he doesn't, and after a few minutes of silence she unfolds herself from his arm and sits up, tilting the wineglass to her mouth so that the liquid hits the back of her throat.

"Look, let's go down this Saturday," he says.

"Really?"

"Yes—why not? I'll let Mum know we're coming."

"Ok, great. Thanks."

He turns to smile at her. "It'll set your mind at rest."

She had always thought that was such an odd phrase: to set one's mind, as if it were clay that needed to be fired into a state of stasis.

"I'm sure it will," she replies.

The visit is cleared with Annabelle and they head to Gloucestershire that Saturday, listening to a podcast series on Jake's plugged-in phone on the drive down. Kate is tense, made even more so by her efforts not to show it. Her face is drawn and a speckled patch of gray hair has sprouted along her part. She has never had to dye her hair before and is curiously reluctant to do so now. *Let it grow*, she thinks to herself. *What does it really matter?*

Jake, by contrast, looks well rested and glossy with good health. He's been taking a new herbal sleep supplement that he swears by and getting up early each morning to do a session with the straps before going to work. He has ordered a three-day juice cleanse for next week. He's never done anything like it before, so of course, she can't stop herself from wondering if he's trying to look his best for someone else.

She is already planning the unhealthy take-out meals she will eat in deliberate protest. Pizza one night, a cream-laden curry the next, perhaps rounded off with a double cheeseburger with fries. Kate, who has always been a conscious eater, a woman aware of the importance of getting her five-a-day, a person who owns a blender in which she used to mix together kale and celery and coconut water, is now struck by the absurdity of expending so much energy on things that made no perceptible difference. Spending time on herself is the last thing she wants to do.

The podcast episode comes to an end. Unthinkingly, Kate picks up Jake's phone to find some music to listen to. She knows his security code but when she taps it in, the screen remains locked. She taps it in again and the same thing happens.

"What are you doing?" Jake asks. He reaches out with one hand and grabs the phone from her, keeping his other hand on the wheel.

"What?" Kate says. "I was just trying to play some music. I thought I knew your code."

"I had to change it when the phone updated."

That makes no sense, Kate almost says. She watches out of the corner of her eye as he keys in the new code and she memorizes the number. She can't believe that this is what it's come to. Where had her trust in him gone?

This is the question she is turning over in her mind when they clamber out of the car and walk into the redbrick house. Annabelle ushers them briskly through to the kitchen.

"I'm afraid I haven't made anything special. It was such short notice," Annabelle says pointedly. "So I've just got some veg soup on the go."

There is a burnt-orange Le Creuset on the stove, the lid rattling and emitting a steamy, earthy smell. Annabelle has pinned her hair back, and a pair of reading glasses hangs from a gold chain around her neck. She puts them on as she takes the lid off the saucepan and stirs the contents.

"Delicious," Jake says. "Exactly what I feel like."

"Lovely," Kate adds. "Sorry to put you to such trouble."

"Oh, it's no trouble," Annabelle says in a way that suggests the opposite. "Chris is off buying some wood for the fire and various bits and pieces. Feeding an extra mouth means we're running through groceries rather rapidly."

"You must let us know how much we owe you," Kate says. Sweat trickles down her neck. She is still in her coat.

Annabelle looks at her sharply. "It's not a question of *money*," she says.

"Oh, I . . ."

Jake presses his hand into Kate's lower back. She falls silent.

"We really appreciate it, Mum," he says. "Thank you."

Annabelle sighs. "Nonsense."

She peers into the saucepan, the steam clouding her glasses. Kate takes off her coat and hangs it in the hallway. She slips her phone reluctantly into the pocket—Annabelle doesn't like them to have their mobiles at mealtimes.

When she returns, Jake and his mother are speaking quietly. They stop as soon as she walks in.

"What were you two talking about?" Kate asks.

"Oh, nothing," Annabelle says, getting a seeded loaf from the bread bin and slicing it with practiced ease.

"Can I do anything?"

"No, I've done it all now. It's just soup," she repeats.

"Shall I grate some cheese?" Jake asks.

"Actually, that *would* be helpful." Annabelle reaches out to squeeze Jake's shoulder. "Thank you, Jakey."

Kate leans against the wooden dresser, forgetting, as she does so, that it wobbles precariously if any weight is put on it. The plates clatter within. She steps away, standing awkwardly on the flagstones with her arms crossed in front of her as Jake busies himself grating cheddar into big yellow mounds. No matter how much time she has spent in this house or how long she has notionally been a part of this family, Kate always feels so out of place: an interloper from an alien race.

She fixes her eyes on the opposite wall, which has a calendar hanging on it, every month accompanied by a photograph of a different European city. Annabelle is rigorous about noting down all appointments and visits in black marker pen. The square for today has *J & K to visit* in the top left-hand corner. Tomorrow is *Meeting with vicar*. Monday is *Cleaner*. Typical of Annabelle not to use the cleaner's name, Kate thinks. She probably doesn't even know it.

She scans her eyes back toward the beginning of the month and notices, with surprise, that the letter *J* is repeated several times. She tries to remember how often she and Jake have been able to visit, but she knows they haven't been at all this month. So why is Jake's initial there?

"Right, I think we're almost there," Annabelle says, lifting the pot away from the stove and onto a woven mat on the table. She catches Kate looking at the calendar and the two women's eyes meet.

"Too many 'J's," Annabelle says, straightening the butter dish. "My fault for naming two children Jake and Julia."

"Haha, right," Kate replies. Doesn't Julia live in Hong Kong? she wants to ask. Unless these were scheduled phone calls, but that seems unlikely. Before she gets the chance to say anything else, there is a gust of cool air from the back of the kitchen and Marisa walks in from the garden.

"Hi, everyone."

She is pink cheeked, hair tied back by a velvet scrunchie, belly neatly rounded.

"Marisa!" Kate says, her voice slightly too eager. She goes to hug her, but Marisa steps back and kisses Kate on the cheek instead. Her face is cool and windblown. She smells of peanut butter.

"It's so good to see you," Kate says. "How are you feeling? Is everything ok?"

"Let the poor girl get inside," Annabelle says, ladling soup into small bowls, each one circled with the word BOWL and a pattern of polka dots.

Kate looks at the soup, swampy and filled with lumps, and is pierced with loathing for Annabelle. She closes the door behind Marisa and the kitchen is sucked back into its own heat.

Marisa bends down to remove her Wellingtons. Jake rushes to help her, holding her hand for support as she levers off each shoe using the cast-iron boot remover Annabelle keeps by the back door. Marisa is wearing a high-lace-collared shirt underneath a woollen navy top. Other than the gold glasses chain and the lack of cashmere, her outfit looks exactly like Annabelle's.

"Righto, everyone come and sit down or the soup'll get cold."

This fucking soup, Kate thinks.

Jake, satisfied that Marisa's boots have been dealt with, gives Kate a peck on the lips and ushers her toward the table. It is as though Jake is parenting them both, absentmindedly treating them like toddlers he must get to sit down on time. She takes her usual seat, which is the only chair that doesn't match the rest of the furniture—it is an old dining chair, padded with cracked leather, whereas all the others are stripped pine. When Annabelle had first allotted Kate the chair, she had made a big fuss of how it was "the throne" and reserved for "very special guests." If that were actually true, Kate thinks now, then surely it should be given to Marisa?

"Are we not waiting for Dad?" Jake asks.

Annabelle rolls her eyes. "He was meant to be back half an hour ago and I'm not waiting any longer. I can heat some up when he finally makes an appearance."

"This smells so good, Annabelle," Marisa says. Her voice is softer than Kate remembers it. She turns to Jake. "How was the drive?"

"Fine, fine. Uneventful." He smiles at her.

"Good," she says, taking a slice of bread and buttering it slowly. "And how is work, Kate?"

"Work? Um. Yeah. Good."

"Good."

Annabelle is still rushing around the kitchen asking if they have everything they need and fetching the salt and pepper and wondering if anyone wants a glass of wine. No one does. They wait for her to sit, and when she does, she exhales loudly to show this has been an extraordinary imposition on her time but she's not one to complain. She wipes her brow with the back of her hand.

"Start, start," Annabelle says, flapping her hands.

Marisa seems distant, her gaze vague. Kate imagines it must be the drugs. She asks her whether she's feeling tired. How is her appetite? Can she feel the baby kicking? Marisa smiles and gives monosyllabic answers, inviting no further discussion.

"Goodness, Kate," Annabelle says, her spoon hovering. "You only ever ask Marisa about the baby! Let the poor girl eat her lunch before it gets cold."

Kate is so stunned by the rebuke that she pushes her bowl away. She has eaten half of it. The soup, after all the attention paid to it, had tasted like stale dishwater. She glares at Jake, wanting him to step in and say something, but he doesn't. Instead, he catches his mother's eye and Kate realizes this is a topic they've discussed.

She gets up from the table.

"Excuse me for a moment," Kate says. "Nature calls."

She walks into the hallway and finds Jake's jacket hanging up on a hook by the front door. She reaches into the right-hand pocket until she feels her fingers graze against the edges of his phone. She slips it out and taps in the code. Her pulse quickens as she opens Jake's text messages. She scrolls through them quickly and sees nothing but messages from Annabelle and colleagues. No unknown names or numbers. There is a rush of relief. Then she checks his photos. It's mostly pictures of Kate in the garden from last weekend and a bookcase they were thinking of buying. But then, an unfamiliar scene catches her eye. She taps on the small square and it expands to fill the screen. It is a picture of Marisa on a sofa that she immediately recognizes from Annabelle and Chris's drawing room. Marisa is smiling, her pregnant stomach bulging. She is sitting next to a man whose hand is placed protectively on her baby bump. The man is Jake. Kate can't remember having taken this photo. It must have been Annabelle, she thinks, on one of their weekend visits, but it's weird that she can't immediately place the image. Unless, she thinks . . .

"Kate!"

She jumps. Jake is calling from the kitchen. "What are you doing?"

"I just—sorry. I was checking the . . . weather. I'm going to the loo now."

When she walks back into the kitchen, she notices Annabelle has reached across the table to rest her hand on Marisa's arm.

"We were just saying, Marisa's been doing some painting, haven't you, Marisa?" Annabelle says, glancing up at Kate.

"Yeah, I've been loving it." She nods her head gratefully at Annabelle. "It's so nice to be doing something creative again without it being a work commission, you know?"

"You're very talented," Annabelle declares. To Jake she adds, "I'm going to get a gorgeous still life she's done framed and hang it in the hallway. It'll look perfect there. Just above the umbrella stand."

"I'd love to see it," Jake says. "We both would."

Marisa shakes her head prettily. "No, honestly, I'd be too embarrassed. It's not ready yet."

"I understand," Jake says, leaning back in his chair and stretching out his arms with a groan. "It's artistic prerogative. You must only show your work when it's ready."

Kate stares at him. Maybe he hasn't been disappearing to spend time with some unknown young woman. Maybe he's been sneaking off to see Marisa.

She pushes the thought to the back of a shelf in her mind.

"I'll make the tea," Kate blurts.

She stands. Waiting for the kettle to boil, she steals a glance at Marisa and Annabelle. They look almost identical in their navy tops and their light, pinned-up hair. The similarity is so pronounced that Kate wonders why she has never properly noticed it until now. She looks away. Heat from the kettle has steamed the window. Her vision blurs and when she makes the tea, her hand shakes as she pours.

XXXI.

After that, Kate decides to stay away from the redbrick house in the country as much as possible and Jake handles the day-to-day dealings with Annabelle. Being around Annabelle has always made Kate question her own strength of mind, and she feels drained by every encounter. If Kate doesn't interact with her, Annabelle loses the power to hurt her, Kate reasons.

Jake tells her that she's taken his mother's comments out of context, that she's in danger of losing perspective by "fixating on every tiny perceived slight," and that she needs to give herself space "for her own peace of mind." Jake says all this kindly, insisting he is on her side, and she nods silently, not wanting to make the situation harder than it currently is. She needs the baby to get here safely, and then she can decide what to do.

She calls Ajesh. They haven't seen each other for months. After he brought Jake to her thirtieth, they had hung out as a threesome a few times, but something about it didn't quite work. It always felt as if one person never fully belonged, as though different lines of intimacy could never be triangulated.

Kate hadn't really noticed when they fell out of each other's lives. In the early days of her romance with Jake, the relationship between the two of them had seemed the most important thing in her life, and a lot of her friends had fallen by the wayside. She only became aware of what had happened when it was already too late: at work, her younger colleagues still partied while her contemporaries were having babies at just the same time as she was having to contend with infertility and surrogacy, and she found she had no time or inclination to keep up with WhatsApp groups and shared voice notes and regular coffees after yoga or evening glasses of Pinot. She fitted in with neither world. She was an unreliable friend, and perhaps a resentful one. She had never got the knack of cultivating a closeness to other women.

Ajesh was different. He had no desire to settle down and had never had a girlfriend who lasted for longer than six months. His own unpredictability meant that Kate didn't feel judged for her failure to return phone calls or emails. He would dip in and out of her life at irregular intervals, having just returned from a hiking trip around Bhutan or an Ayurvedic retreat in Somerset.

Now, hearing his voice for the first time in ages, she realizes she is lonely and longing for his flirty irreverence. Everything else has become so serious. She wants Ajesh to remind her she exists as her own person, that she is fun and not just insecure and preoccupied with fertility and motherhood.

When she meets him for coffee on the South Bank, she tells him about her dealings with Annabelle, without going into detail about anything that had happened with Marisa. She likes Ajesh but she doesn't fully trust him and she and Jake have agreed that the fewer people who know about Marisa's breakdown, the better. So she explains that Marisa is staying in the countryside with Jake's parents, so that she can get regular fresh air and be out of London and so that they can maintain a closeness to her without overstepping any boundaries. She brings him up to date on Annabelle's antics.

"Mate, it's not good for you to be around toxic people," Ajesh says. They are sitting on the outside terrace of the Royal Festival Hall so that Ajesh can smoke.

"Want one?" he asks as he rolls himself a thin cigarette. It is windy and yet he licks the paper with practiced ease, not losing a single wisp of tobacco. At university, Ajesh had always been the best person to roll joints at a party. He would call them "dense but chic," which got shortened to "DBC" in their friendship group.

"No, thanks."

Almost as soon as Kate has said it, she changes her mind, wanting suddenly to be the younger her, the one who existed before babies and dysfunctional surrogates. "Actually, go on."

He passes her the cigarette and lights it for her. She inhales and the nicotine hits the back of her eyes, thudding through her synapses. She is light-headed and her thoughts unfurl themselves, like sea anemones.

"Wow," she says. "I'm out of practice."

Ajesh laughs. "You know it's not weed, don't you, fam?"

"Yeah, ok, I'm not a complete loser."

"Never said you were. You were always the coolest out of all of us."

"As if."

"Seriously. Jake got very lucky with you."

He looks at her steadily.

"You've been through a lot, Katie," he says. "And Annabelle sounds like a right bitch. So, y'know, fuck her. The most important thing is that you'll be a mum in a couple of months and that's great. So, so great."

She takes a second drag and then a third.

"It's all gonna be ok," he says.

"Do you really think so?"

"More than ok. It'll be brilliant. You'll be an amazing mum. Jake will be the world's cutest dad. You just need to get through this rough patch and you'll be golden. Trust your old uncle Ajesh."

She smiles at him. Ajesh has always had this ability to make her feel special, as though she can handle anything. It's nice to be reminded of it.

"You're so sweet."

He leans back, turning up his collar and folding his arms. He is wearing a suede coat, a gray cashmere scarf, and black jeans half tucked into oversized army boots.

"Of course," he says, casually blowing a smoke ring. "What are friends for? You better make me godfather—that's all I'm saying."

"It's a deal."

She returns home feeling lighter than she has in months. When Jake gets back from work, she goes to greet him at the door and kisses him, holding him tight, pressing the bulk of him against her. She is determined to make it normal again. Things are a little easier between them after that—at least for a little while.

When they are eight months pregnant, Annabelle surprises them by suggesting a baby shower.

"I thought it would be nice," she says over the phone. "You know, they're *very* popular."

"Oh," Kate replies. "Yes. Um. Ok."

In truth, she can think of nothing more horrible than a baby shower.

Even Jake thinks it's ridiculous.

"It's the most un-Mum thing I've ever heard," he says when Kate tells him. "She didn't even believe in Valentine's Day when we were growing up. Said it was an American invention."

But they agree, of course, because it's Annabelle and they have to play nice.

This time, the car is packed full with six blue helium balloons and a cake with blue icing and the words BABY BOY emblazoned across the top in fondant copperplate, all of which Annabelle had ordered online to be delivered to them in London because no shop in Gloucestershire had been deemed of a sufficiently high standard.

"She's gone mad," Jake jokes as they turn out of Richborne Terrace and he struggles to see out of the rearview mirror because of all the paraphernalia in the back. "It's finally happened."

The baby shower felt dangerous in its presumption. Last week, Kate had told her work about the pregnancy and it had been difficult to explain to her colleagues that yes, she was having a baby, but no, she wasn't actually *having* it.

"Wow," her assistant Monique had said. "That's so cool."

"Really?" Kate asked, taken aback. She'd anticipated lots of questions and maybe even some mild disapproval, but everyone was immediately supportive and accepted the situation with a matter-of-factness that left her slightly deflated.

"Yeah," Monique said. "It's so badass being a woman who knows what she wants and just, y'know, goes out and gets it."

"It's a bit more complicated than that," Kate said gently. "But thank you. That means a lot."

Even then, Kate had worried she was speaking too soon, that it might not happen the way it was meant to, that Marisa could change her mind about handing their child over, or that she could have another psychotic break. But she couldn't hope to explain any of this to the outside world.

A baby shower was the last thing she felt like.

They arrive at the farmhouse shortly after midday.

"Jesus," Jake says. "I can't believe it."

Kate follows his eyes and then she sees it: a banner hung across the front door, silvery-blue letters hanging from a string spelling out ABOUT TO POP.

She starts to laugh and then Jake joins her and for a few seconds, they are unable to stop themselves. It feels good to know they can still share this. She is wiping tears from her eyes when Annabelle opens the door.

"What on earth is the matter?" she asks them. "Are you all right?"

"Yes, yes," Jake says, collecting himself. "Hi, Mum. Great banner, by the way."

Kate chews the inside of her cheek to stop herself from breaking into laughter again.

"Oh, that." Annabelle waves her hand. "Just a bit of fun. Your father found it in the village shop—can you believe it? The stuff they have in there!"

"Catering for every conceivable occasion," Kate adds, sotto voce.

Annabelle looks at her in that way she has, as though only just remembering her existence. "What's that?"

"What a lovely occasion," Kate says more loudly as they walk into the house.

Annabelle is in a diaphanous floor-length dress that seems to be made up of several intertwined pieces of fabric gathered up and tied in a ropelike construction at her neck. She looks like an imposing Greek goddess, the kind they built forty-foot statues to in the Acropolis.

"Come in, come in. I've set everything up in the living room. Marisa's so excited about seeing you, the darling girl."

Kate stops in her tracks. She glances at Jake. He looks away and lowers his head and she knows he has heard it too. *The darling girl?* Kate thinks. Annabelle has never been so casually affectionate with her.

Jake reaches out to take Kate's hand. She does not give it to him. They walk into the living room where Chris is ensconced in his usual armchair.

"Ah, here we all are," Chris says, rising to greet them both.

Marisa is sitting on the flowery sofa to one side, wearing a bright-blue smock dress Kate has never seen before. She stays seated when Kate walks over to her.

"Sorry," she titters. "It takes quite a lot of effort to stand up from a sofa these days."

Her pregnant belly sticks out half a foot in front of her, a mountainous beacon of her indisputable womanhood, announcing itself proudly to the room. She proffers her cheek to be kissed by Jake and then by Kate, whom she grabs by the hand and says fervently, "It's *so* good to see you. Baby will be here any day now!"

Kate nods, teeth gritted, and although she wants to be aloof toward Marisa, she also can't help but be drawn, ineluctably as though to an edge of a waterfall, to the baby bump. She places her hands on the solid warmth of it. Without warning, there is a thumping beneath her left palm.

"Oooh, someone wants some attention," Marisa laughs. "He's been kicking all night. Barely had a wink."

Kate's heart beats faster. It is as if her baby has given her a sign that he knows she is here. His mother. The real one.

"I remember Jakey was just the same," Annabelle says. "Quite the little kicker, wasn't he, Chris?"

"Mmm."

"We were *sure* you'd be a rugby player," Annabelle continues, fiddling with her earring and gazing into space.

"Can I feel?" Jake says, kneeling down beside Kate. Reluctantly, Kate shifts to one side and he places his hands on Marisa's tummy. Kate watches as those familiar knuckles and close-cut fingernails rest on another woman's body, and then she turns away and asks Chris if she could have a drink, and he says of course, how remiss of me, and he pours her a gin and tonic that is at least a double measure and probably a triple.

"Did you bring the cake?" Annabelle asks.

"Yes," Kate says automatically. "And the balloons. Honestly, Annabelle, you shouldn't have gone to so much trouble."

"You really shouldn't have," Marisa says. Kate smiles at her but Marisa turns away. Jake is still kneeling next to her, touching her stomach.

Marisa smiles, and her face has that unlined, faraway quality that makes Kate think again that the real Marisa is buried deep underneath the surface of this conscientiously pleasant one, as though she is wrapped in protective plastic. She is saying and doing all the right things, and yet something doesn't quite fit.

Jake fetches the provisions from the car. The room is soon filled with blue floating orbs. The cake is placed on the coffee table in the center of the room. Annabelle claps with satisfaction, then disappears, reemerging a few moments later with a tray bearing a bottle of champagne in an ice bucket and five glasses.

"You'll have a glass, won't you, Marisa?"

Kate gives an audible whimper. She hadn't meant to, but she is so appalled by the idea of Marisa drinking alcohol while pregnant with their child that she isn't able to stop herself. Marisa turns to look at her, eyes swiveling slowly round like a lizard.

"No, that's ok; thanks, Annabelle. I'll stick to the elderflower."

"You sure? One glass can't hurt."

"She's said she doesn't want one," Kate says, her voice loud.

Annabelle purses her lips. She pops the champagne bottle in silence and when the cork flies to the other side of the room, Chris says, "Watch it!" and they all laugh, apart from Kate, who seems to have lost the capacity to find anything funny.

With the gin and tonic finished, she accepts the champagne from Annabelle and sips it, reminding herself to take it slowly. Although she wants to numb the awkwardness of this day, Kate also needs to keep her head clear. She tries to speak but it feels as though a piece of lint has got stuck in her throat. She looks at Jake and his parents and at Marisa, the four of them so physically alike: all blond and strapping in their own ways, those blue eyes of Annabelle's mirrored by Marisa's, Jake and Chris's shared florid cheeks and strong jawbones. They are poster children for a new Aryan nation, she thinks, while she is the dark, difficult one in the corner.

"Well, this is nice," Annabelle says, crossing her legs daintily at the ankle. "I think a toast is in order."

She raises her glass, with her long, elegant arm.

"It's been a long journey to this point, but I wanted to make a toast to our baby boy. We can't wait to meet him."

The casually spoken "our" lashes Kate's heart like a jellyfish sting. She readies herself to raise her champagne flute, but Annabelle hasn't finished yet.

"And to Marisa," she continues, winking—actually *winking*—at Marisa. "Thank you for giving these two such a precious gift. It hasn't been an easy road for you, as we know . . ."—there is a loaded pause—"but you've come through it and we're all so lucky you came into our lives."

"Hear, hear," Chris says.

Jake lifts his glass to cheers and smile with the others, while Marisa sits resplendent on the overstuffed sofa cushions, beaming like the pope on his balcony. Only Kate doesn't raise her glass. No one clocks it.

"I hadn't realized Marisa was making herself so indispensable." Kate tries to sound breezy, but the words are shrewish in spite of herself.

"Of course she's indispensable," Annabelle says. "You wouldn't be having a baby without her!"

"No, no, no," Marisa murmurs softly. "I haven't at all. I'm so grateful you've had me to stay here—truly."

"It's been lovely to have you around," Annabelle replies. "And you've been very helpful with all the village fete preparations—"

"That was nothing . . ."

"Nonsense. There are not too many people patient enough—or talented enough, for that matter—to draw posters and flyers. The vicar was *thrilled*."

Chris, topping up Kate's glass, says waggishly, "And we all know how important it is to please the vicar."

Marisa and Annabelle erupt into peals of laughter.

"Sorry," Annabelle says, waving her hands in front of her face. "It's too complicated to explain."

Jake, the corners of his mouth twitching vaguely in a way that could, if necessary, be construed as a smile, reaches forward for the cake knife.

"Shall we cut this thing?" he says abruptly.

Cut their fucking throats, Kate thinks.

"Yes, yes, go ahead," Annabelle replies. "The plates and napkins are just there."

Kate watches as Jake slices decisively through the cake. The point of the knife enters at the top of the "B" for "Baby" and thuds when it reaches the solidity of the tray beneath. He slides individual triangles of cake onto each plate and hands them out. The cake is overly sweet and fluffy, more air than sponge. The icing is the fondant kind that has the texture of wallpaper paste. The sugar jolt hits Kate squarely between the eyes and her head aches as it does when thunder is about to break.

Of all the things she had imagined might happen when they asked Marisa to be their surrogate, this is a scenario she could not possibly have anticipated. The fact that Marisa had stopped taking her meds and had deluded herself into believing she was in a relationship with Jake before attacking Kate in the hallway of her own home was almost easier to handle than this charade. Kate sees how Marisa comes alive under the beam of Annabelle's attention, and how Annabelle, too, is transformed, appearing younger and increasingly vital in her movements. And Chris, also, seems more involved—leaning forward in his chair to hear better, asking Marisa if she's comfortable enough or if maybe she needs another cushion.

Kate tries to catch Jake's eye, but she can tell he is avoiding her. She sees his mouth moving and realizes he has joined in the conversation. There is a rushing noise in her head and she can't hear what anyone is saying. She tries to steady her breathing but her lungs feel as though they are being wrung out like a sponge. There is an oil painting on the wall behind the sofa of a clifftop, waves crashing against the gray stone, and she focuses on the brushstrokes until the panic subsides. Her legs buckle when she stands. She steadies herself by reaching for the back of the chair.

"Goodness, we haven't drunk that much, have we?" Annabelle says, watching her.

"Are you all right?" Jake asks.

"Yes, fine," she lies. "Just going to the loo."

She makes her way out of the room into the welcome coolness of the hallway. In the bathroom underneath the stairs, she splashes her face with water and holds her hands under the cold tap. She dries them on the monogrammed towel hanging by the sink. Kate opens the lavatory door and she can hear the four of them talking, their voices slipping toward her like skimming stones across water. She feels as she did as a child, when her parents had friends over for dinner and she was meant to be in bed but instead would creep to the edge of the staircase, poking her head through the banister to see what was happening in the dining room below. Sometimes her mother would find her and brush her off and Kate would pad back to bed in her bare feet and be unable to sleep, tormented by the fact that she was not involved in all the fun happening downstairs.

Annabelle appears, without warning, in the hallway.

"There you are," Annabelle says. In the half gloom, she gives the impression of having grown several inches. Kate steps back.

"We were wondering where you'd got to."

Annabelle is unsmiling, her formidable profile turned to its three-quarter point. The silk of her dress shimmers in the half-light like melting ice.

"Sorry," Kate says. "I hadn't realized I'd been so long."

"I'm going to get some more elderflower for Marisa," Annabelle says. She sweeps past Kate into the kitchen, but Kate follows, unwilling to let her go. She wants to say something but she isn't sure what. She is so angry at this woman, so repelled by her interference, that she has to cross her arms to stop herself from lashing out.

Annabelle opens the fridge door and takes out a bottle of Sanpellegrino, then reaches to the cupboard for a glass, which she fills with ice from the rubber tray. She moves with grace, her arms expanding like a bird's wings, and she pays no attention to Kate, who stands in the doorway, one foot on the kitchen flagstones, one foot on the hallway tiles. Before she can stop herself, the words burst out of her.

"Annabelle," Kate starts. "If you think you can unsettle me with this little power play you have going on, then you're very much mistaken."

Annabelle stops what she's doing. The half-poured bottle of Sanpellegrino hangs from one hand. Her face is immobile, denuded of expression.

"I don't know *what* you're talking about, Kate."

"Marisa. I'm talking about Marisa. You seem very . . . *cozy* with her all of a sudden."

Annabelle gives a quiet exhalation of laughter. "You seem to have forgotten that she's been living here for months," Annabelle says, her voice level, each word delivered with cool precision. "Because *you* couldn't cope with the mess you'd got yourself into—"

"That's not the case—"

"Do me the courtesy of letting me finish." Annabelle slams the water bottle onto the table. She is angry, her lips pale and drawn, the veins in her neck sticking out. Kate has never seen her angry, she realizes. She has only ever seen Annabelle in a state of controlled passive aggression, tracking other people's tender points from the sidelines like a sniper but never once demeaning herself by showing uncontrolled fury. Until now, that is. Now she is incandescent. And Kate, who finally has her attention, is no longer sure what to do with it.

"Chris and I did everything we could, putting ourselves in God knows what sort of danger, and we nursed that poor girl back to health—"

"That poor girl?" Kate asks, incredulous.

"Yes. That poor girl. Who you took advantage of because of your *demented* obsession with having a baby."

Kate, shocked, feels tears begin to form. "That's not true."

"Yes it is. Jake's told us how impossible you've been, how he doesn't feel he can ever satisfy you." Annabelle is getting into her stride now, the words delivered like the staccato gunshots of a firing squad. "It must have been quite obvious Marisa wasn't in a fit state but you insisted on moving her in with you to keep an eye on her and then you act surprised when it all got too much for her. I mean, honestly, Kate. What were you thinking?"

Kate hangs her head. Annabelle is right. She should have known. She had pressured Jake into doing it. She had wanted to believe in Marisa's perfection so badly that she had ignored any signs to the contrary.

Annabelle does not comfort her. Instead, she takes two long steps toward her so that she is inches away from Kate's face. Her voice drops to an almost-whisper.

"That child isn't yours anyway," Annabelle says, the words delivered in a fine spray of spit. "Not biologically. It's quite clear to everyone else that Marisa and Jake are far better suited than you two ever were."

"What . . . ?" Kate shakes her head, as if to rid it of the buzzing noise.

"Well, just look at them, dear," Annabelle says, her lips twisting upward in a strange little smile. "They're two peas in a pod, aren't they? You must have noticed!"

Kate steps backward, so dizzy that she is sure the kitchen floor must have dissolved underfoot. Her back thumps against the wall and the impact causes the pages of Annabelle's calendar to flutter. She remembers seeing the initial *J* there on multiple different days.

She hadn't allowed herself to think about what it really meant, but somewhere, in the unacknowledged grimy pit of her, she had known.

"He's been spending an awful lot of time with her," Annabelle says, as if reading Kate's thoughts. "You can't be that dense, Kate. Come on. He's been down here most weeks and the two of them have been getting on like a house on fire."

"But I thought she didn't want us here . . ."

Annabelle tilts her head in a pose of sympathy. "She didn't want *you* here, Kate. Jake and I had a long chat about it and decided it would be best. Marisa felt so guilty about what had happened and seeing you made her feel even worse, so I told him quite sensibly to keep you away. He's been as good as his word."

Kate remembers the spa weekend and Jake's early departure. The photo on his phone. All those unexplained absences for work. He was here all along. With Marisa. Easily manipulated Marisa. How thrilled Annabelle must have been when she saw how pliable Marisa was; how smoothly she could inveigle her way back into Jake's life with Kate out of the way; how much sway she would hold over the life of her grandchild. And Jake, trying, as ever, to do his best to keep everyone happy, had gone along with it. Good, cowardly Jake.

Kate presses the palm of each hand against the wall, wanting it to break open and swallow her. Annabelle is still speaking.

". . . and it's been lovely to see. Marisa is so easy to talk to, don't you find? It's only a matter of time until Jake realizes . . ."

She stops then, as if aware she has gone too far. Annabelle doesn't need to complete the thought. Kate can do it for her. It's only a matter of time until Jake realizes he should be with Marisa, the mother of his child. It is only a matter of time until Kate loses everything.

Kate turns her head to one side, pressing her cheek against the clamminess of stone. She shuts her eyes, tears leaking out. She wishes she could stop crying, but she can't. She wishes she could drown Annabelle's voice out but she can't. She wishes she had the strength to stand up for herself, but she feels consumed by what Annabelle is saying. She had never been good enough or charming enough or blonde enough or fertile enough or sweet enough to be Jake's equal. Annabelle's words are confirmation: she is not worthy of Jake and not worthy to be the mother of his child or, indeed, a mother at all. Annabelle has known this from the very beginning, scenting her weakness like blood and chasing it until Kate had nowhere left to run. Yes, she thinks, yes—you're right about it all. I don't belong here. I never have.

She slides onto the floor. She has no more energy. She can't fight this anymore. For the briefest of moments, Kate imagines her total erasure. How much simpler everything would be if she ceased to exist.

Ignoring her, Annabelle busies herself around the kitchen, calmly finishes preparing Marisa's drink, then smooths her hair behind her ears, a warrior queen readying herself for the final assault.

"Marisa and I have become close because that girl hasn't got a mother," she says, standing over Kate like a shadow. "It should be perfectly clear . . ." Annabelle pauses, checking she has Kate's total attention. "Or maybe you can only see that kind of thing when you've had a child yourself."

Annabelle takes the glass of elderflower and walks past Kate, her dress swishing as she goes. Kate sits on the floor a moment longer. And then she feels a sharp twinge in the side of her belly. It is a deep, muscular ache and it reminds her of those interminable scans she used to have during her fertility treatments, the way the consultant would sweep the ultrasound wand from side to side, angling it to get a better view of each ovary. The sensation was unlike anything else she had ever experienced. It was less the presence of pain and more a hollowing out of it.

Yet she feels it again now. But this time, the throbbing rises upward, through her stomach and up toward her chest, fizzing into her shoulders, and then when it reaches her throat, she finally recognizes it for what it is. Power. She sees with sudden, certain clarity that she is strong precisely because of the pain she has withstood. She levers herself upright.

Fuck Annabelle, she thinks. That woman is not going to get away with it.

She walks back down the corridor and into the living room, where Annabelle is bending to leave the sparkling elderflower on the side table. Marisa isn't there. Jake and Chris turn to look at Kate as she enters. Annabelle keeps her back to her.

"Are you all right?" Jake asks.

"Where's Marisa?"

"In the bathroom," he says. "Are you ok?" He looks worried.

Kate ignores him. In her mind's eye, she sees a gun cylinder spinning and clicking and the safety catch sliding off. She imagines lifting the sight up to her eye and pointing the barrel directly at Annabelle's forehead.

"Annabelle," she says. "I'd like you to tell everyone what you just told me in the kitchen."

Annabelle straightens and sighs audibly. "Oh, for goodness' sake. What is it now? I don't know *what* you're talking about, Kate."

Annabelle swivels on her heel and faces her, and Kate is astonished by her composure. Annabelle's face seems to have become younger and less lined, as though the viciousness of a few minutes ago has invigorated her.

"You know exactly what I mean."

Annabelle shrugs and lifts her hands, palms facing upward in a gesture of supplication. "I honestly have no idea. I just know that everything I do seems to annoy you in some way and I'm on the verge of giving up altogether. Apparently, nothing I do can ever be good enough. You see"—Annabelle shifts on her feet, directing her next comment to Jake—"this is exactly what I've been telling you about."

So there had been countless conversations about her behind her back, Kate thinks. She can imagine it all now: how Annabelle, with her evangelical zeal for "family first" and the genetic importance of lineage, would have plotted carefully to exclude Kate and bring Marisa into the fold. Annabelle had no doubt told Marisa all sorts of things about Kate's unfit mental state while at the same time emphasizing Marisa's delicacy to everyone else.

"What's she been telling you?" Kate asks Jake, her chin jutting upward.

He opens his mouth to speak but no words come out. He looks like the small boy his mother still wishes he were. Annabelle's power over him is more firmly embedded than Kate had ever imagined.

"Annabelle," Kate says. "It's over."

"What nonsense—?"

"And if I have anything to do with it, you'll never see your grandson." The words gather and brew and boil over. "I won't let you get near him, you poisonous old witch."

Annabelle takes two steps toward her, hands knotted into fists, teeth bared. For a moment, Kate thinks she's going to punch her but Chris leaps to his feet, knocking his drink to the floor, and rests his hand lightly on Annabelle's elbow.

"Come now," he says, trying to sit her down as if to avoid an unsightly fracas.

Annabelle bats away his hand. "Leave it," she says, spitting out the words. Chris sits back down and his face looks as crumpled as his shirt. He raises his eyebrows at Kate and she knows this is his way of apologizing, but it's not enough. None of it is enough to compensate for how malicious Annabelle has been.

"You told me, in the kitchen, that Jake and Marisa were better off without me," Kate says. "That Marisa's the biological mother. That I've been impossible and it's no wonder Jake's been spending so much time here behind my back."

A beat of silence. Kate's cheeks are hot. Chris, lifting the glass from the floor, suspends his arm midair. Jake walks toward her, his face pale.

"Kate, I—"

"I don't want to hear it right now," she says.

He stands awkwardly in the middle of the room, and she keeps staring at Annabelle, refusing to look away from that blue, blue gaze. Annabelle blinks. Kate thinks she's going to cry, but then Annabelle tilts her head to one side, showing off the white vulnerability of her neck. She is looking out of the window to the front garden and the driveway and the fraying patch of woodland and then the room is filled with a strange sound, like a rustling of leaves or a rushing of water, and Kate realizes with horror that Annabelle is laughing. Her laughter is loud and potent and jarring against the quiet. Annabelle looks back to Kate and her eyes are unmoving. They are silvery, glinting, dead-fish eyes. She is laughing but the laughter does not reach the rest of her face and this makes her more frightening than she was before.

"What utter nonsense," Annabelle says. "Jake, I've been trying to tell you for some time I've been worried about Kate's mental health, haven't I? What further proof do you need?"

"Mum, that's not—"

"I just can't believe that you've invented this ludicrous . . . conspiracy," Annabelle continues. "And you're lashing out at me—*me*! I've done so much for you, even if I haven't always understood you. I . . . I . . . just don't know what more I could have *done*." Annabelle's eyes are moist now, welling with self-pity.

Oh, she's good, Kate thinks. *She's very good*.

Annabelle wobbles backward, as though she is about to faint, but she collects herself just in time to ensure she collapses onto the sofa, where she leans against the cushions, pressing the back of her hand against her forehead.

"Mum, please don't do this," Jake says.

"Annabelle, there's no need to get so upset," Chris adds.

But neither of them, Kate notices, move toward her. Kate bends closer to Annabelle so that there can be no escaping what she is about to say.

"I am perfectly sane, Annabelle," she says, her voice breaking. "How fucking dare you suggest otherwise."

Annabelle is clutching her necklace now, pushing her head farther into the sofa cushions, trying to turn away from Kate's face, as if it is Kate who she needs protection from rather than the other way around.

"Chris," Annabelle is whimpering. "Help me, please. I don't know what she's going to do to me."

Then, out of nowhere, a voice.

"She's not going to do anything to you," the voice says.

Annabelle flinches and her eyes flicker to the left. A shadow passes over her face. When Kate looks over her shoulder, she sees Marisa standing in the doorway.

"What was that?" Kate asks.

"I said that you're not going to do anything to Annabelle," Marisa repeats. "Because I heard exactly what she said to you back there."

Marisa's face is calm. She is lit up from behind, golden hair glowing.

"In the kitchen," Marisa explains. "I heard exactly what Annabelle said to you."

On the sofa, Annabelle goes very still.

"I came out into the corridor. You can hear everything there. It's why we always close the kitchen door, isn't it, Annabelle? To keep the draft out."

Marisa's voice is flat but clear, like a teacher wanting to make herself heard at the back of the class.

"And you did say all those things, Annabelle," Marisa says, mouth twisting. "I'm sorry, but you did."

Annabelle doesn't speak. Her necklace glints in the half-light.

"You said that Jake and I had been getting close and that we were going to be together with the baby. You said the baby was mine and that I was better suited to Jake."

Annabelle emits a low noise, halfway between a growl and a sob.

"But the truth is, Jake has been coming here on his own because you told me Kate didn't want to see me after what I did. You *told* me that."

"I did no such—" Annabelle starts.

"What the hell?" Jake says, reaching for Kate's hand. She allows him to take it. "Mum. Is this true? You told me Marisa was the one who couldn't bear to face Kate out of guilt."

Annabelle says nothing. The skin around her mouth puckers.

"I'm sorry about that, Kate," Marisa says, head bowed and unable to look at her. "Annabelle told me it was better that way. She told me you weren't . . ."

"It's ok," Kate says. And then again: "It's ok."

Relief surges through Kate like a cold wave. So Jake had never betrayed her. He had been doing it to protect her. She turns to meet his gaze. His face is so stricken that she knows Marisa is telling the truth.

Jake shakes his head. "I would never . . ." he starts, then stops, then starts again, his voice hoarse. "I wouldn't do that to you . . . I was just . . . trying to manage it all . . ."

He lapses into silence. She rests her head against his solid, comforting shoulder and exhales.

"I know," she murmurs. "I know that now."

"Jakey," Annabelle says, "don't listen to this rubbish. She's talking nonsense. I never said—"

"You can't dismiss *both* of us as mad," Kate replies. "You might just get away with one. But two begins to look a lot like carelessness." And then, looking straight at her, she adds, "Don't you think, dear?"

On the sofa, Annabelle is withered, her cheeks sunken. Her eyes radiate anger.

"You're not exactly perfect yourself, Kate. Look at the lengths you went to so that you could get your baby—ignoring this girl's mental breakdown; refusing to call in proper medical help. You knew quite well what you were doing."

Kate has no response to this. Annabelle's words pull on a twisted thread of truth she refuses to untangle.

"Besides," Annabelle says, looking at Chris now. "Marisa's drugged up to the eyeballs. She doesn't know what she's saying."

Chris says nothing. He looks ashamed.

"I know what I'm saying," Marisa says, coming to stand next to Kate. She knocks one of the helium balloons out of the way as she does, and then this woman who has caused Kate so much angst and sadness, who has also given her so much hope and optimism, who has scared her and mystified her in equal measure, does something wholly unexpected. She takes Kate's other hand in hers.

"None of that is true, Annabelle," Marisa says. "You know that, don't you?" She talks slowly. "This is Kate's baby. It always has been. It always will be. Jake and Kate are the parents."

Kate squeezes Marisa's hand so strongly it feels as though she might never let go and then Kate begins to cry again. Jake lets go of her hand and places his arm around her shoulders. Finally he speaks.

"Mum," Jake says, his voice tight and throttled. "This is outrageous. I came up here without Kate because you told me it was the best way to protect her and protect our baby."

Annabelle turns to her son. Her hands are clasped in her lap and she raises them, palms cupped, beseeching.

"Oh, Jakey," she says. "I thought that's what you wanted. You and Marisa were getting on so well, you see, and I . . . well, I . . ."

"You what? You lied to all of us," he cries. "I've always defended you, always done what you wanted."

His voice is cracking. He sounds so helpless that Kate wants to speak up for him. But this is something Jake has to do for himself.

"You've gone too far this time," he says. "Too far. How could you? How *could* you do this?"

"Now, steady on, old chap," Chris says, and his mildness is absurd. Kate wants to take Chris by the shoulders and shake him.

"This is why your daughters don't talk to you," Jake is saying to his mother now, his voice rising to a shout. "This is why they can't fucking stand the sight of you. They always said to me I'd see it one day, that you're a raging narcissist who treats us all like fucking chess pieces."

"Shush, Jake, shush," Chris says. "There's no need to bring all that up. You know how much it hurts your mother."

"I don't care," he shouts, and then he is kicking the coffee table so that it upends and the sickly blue cake lands in a messy glop on the red-threaded rug. "She's hurt me! She's hurt us! She's hurt Kate in the most unimaginable way . . ."

Kate tries to grab his arm but he frees himself from her grip, walks to the shelves by the fireplace, and before she can stop him, he slams his arm onto the sideboard and with one violent sweep, he clears the surface of all its silver- and wooden-framed photographs. They clatter and smash to the floor. All the shared moments of grinning, gap-toothed toddlers and sepia-tinted weddings and first days at school and a long-ago family summer holiday spent on a boat near the Scilly Isles, the wind whipping their cheeks pink, a younger Annabelle's hair tied up in a patterned silk scarf, her smile fixed and lipsticked as though nothing would ever go wrong under her watch.

Chris and Annabelle are huddled together on the sofa, Annabelle softly sobbing into a handkerchief, Chris shaking his head with confusion. Outside, it has grown dark. Kate takes Jake by the hand. He is sweating and has a faraway look on his face. She strokes the back of his neck and sees him come back to her with a flick of a switch. They tell Marisa to pack her bags. They are taking her back to London with them. They leave the room.

Annabelle makes no protest. She and Chris stay seated, their features gradually obscured by the falling dusk, two flawed people, fitted into each other's failings like ivy burrowing into the loosening gaps between brick. You couldn't cut back the ivy without risking the house falling down. But the stone would crumble eventually, weakened by the insistent force of the plant pushing its thickening stem into every soft place. And then there would be collapse, a cloud of imploded stone. That is how it would end.

Kate closes the door to the living room behind her. Marisa, who has been packing her things in the cottage, reemerges with her wheeled suitcase in tow and Kate hugs her tightly. No further words need to be said. They understand each other now.

The three of them get into the car. Kate sits in the back so Marisa can take the front passenger seat. She watches as Jake slots the key into the ignition and pulls out into the driveway. There is a waxy moon in the sky and condensation on the windscreen. He turns the heating up and the radio on. She does not twist her head back to look at the redbrick house as they go. She lets it disappear and recede in her mind, imagines a watery tide rising up to claim it, sees the white pediments and the gray roof tiles and the sooted chimney turrets overlapped by a deepening sea. She lets it sink. She breathes.

She watches the two people sitting in front of her. Two blond heads, side by side.

Kate's limbs are heavy. She could fall asleep now if she wanted and she knows Marisa and Jake would talk quietly so as not to disturb her and that Jake would dial down the radio volume and take extra care not to judder the car when he brakes and she knows that he would wake her up when they arrived back home and the three of them would walk into the house and have a cup of tea together around the kitchen table and talk about everything that had happened that day.

It would feel safe.

It would feel right.

It would feel like family.

XXXII.

At the birth, they had played 1990s hip-hop.

"Most people choose Mozart," Mr. Abadi said with a curious smile. "They want something calming."

"Marisa says she wants music that makes her feel strong, like she can do anything," Kate explained. "It's her idea. And we like it, don't we?" She turned to Jake, sitting beside her in the now familiar chrome-framed chairs of Mr. Abadi's office.

"We do," he replied, grinning.

Mr. Abadi gave an amused twitch of the head. "We aim to please," he said, making a note with his gold pen in the medical records.

So it was that Leo Christopher Sturridge made his entrance into the world accompanied by the frenetic vocals of Busta Rhymes rapping "Thank You." When Jake and Kate were invited to cut the umbilical cord and when they heard their baby cry for the first time and when the midwife handed Kate her son, it was Snoop Dogg. Jay-Z accompanied the moment when Jake took Marisa's hand and squeezed it tightly, tears falling down his face. As Kate held her baby, Marisa looking on with a tired smile, the playlist segued into TLC. The whole thing was stupidly beautiful.

"Hello," Kate said, peering into her son's mottled, querying face as Jake cupped the baby's velvety head with his hand. "We've been through a lot to get to meet you."

On the bed behind them, Marisa rested back on the pillow, her body sweaty and bloodied with exhaustion.

Kate turned to her.

"Thank you," she said, her voice cracking. "Thank you so much."

By the time Kate held Leo to her bare chest in the next-door room, the music had stopped and there was a calm so solid it felt like certainty. She and Jake craned forward to hear Leo's tiny sniffles and squeaks, each noise signifying the barely credible fact of his existence. The baby's fists were scrunched shut and the creases of his fingers and nails struck her as something prehistoric and inexplicable. She was astonished by him, at once so miraculous and yet so fully theirs.

As soon as Mr. Abadi had delivered him, as soon as Leo had emerged into the clinical light of the theater, Kate had recognized him as hers. They had been linked forever, she saw now. She simply had to wait for her son to be born. It didn't matter which strands of whose particular DNA had gone into creating the infinitesimal nuance of him. He was hers.

Jake kissed her gently. Soon he, too, would hold Leo close, pressing his skin against the baby's newness, but she wasn't ready to give up her son just yet. She felt fiercely that she would never be able to let him go, not fully. She felt a momentous current ricocheting through her blood cells. She was stronger than anything on earth, capable of everything it would take to protect her son. She was fizzing—crazed, even—with motherhood.

"He's got dark hair," she said. It was true—Leo's head was dusted dark brown, so that when she lowered her lips to his face, and her hair fell forward, she and her son were a perfect match.

At weekends, they walk along the riverside path. Today, it is sunny and windy, one of those London days that looks deceptively warm from inside the house. Jake has the baby strapped to his chest in a sling and Kate, wrapped up in a parka and hoodie, walks alongside, holding his hand and checking occasionally to see whether Leo is dropping off to sleep. He's ten months now, and they've almost got him into a routine. Leo mewls gently.

"Sh-sh-sh," Kate says. "You know you want a nap, poppet. Come on, have a nice, little sleep."

She cajoles him in a soft voice, the same one that she uses when Jake is at the office and she spends long hours chatting to Leo as if he understands. For two days a week, she works from home and often she will find herself treating Leo like a particularly receptive colleague. As long as she keeps her voice light, as though she is reading from his favorite storybook, Leo is entranced by whatever she says.

On Friday, Leo had been sitting in his high chair, pompous as an emperor with a plastic spoon in his chubby fist, seemingly indignant at having a bib around his neck, his face smeared with mashed carrot, and she knew he was about to lose it. She could tell from the particular tension in his neck, the slight flare of his nostrils, that he was gathering up his efforts for a momentous caterwaul.

Quickly, she launched into a singsong rendition of her thoughts from that particular day.

"So we're organizing a junket, Leo, and you'll never guess what one of the film's stars asked us to do." She waited. Leo, attention diverted from his threatened tantrum, widened his eyes as if to say, Please, continue.

"Well, she wants us to repaint the entire hotel suite. Says the smell of tired hotel rooms triggers her. I know! Crazy, right?"

Leo banged his spoon against the plastic tray.

"You and me both, mate," Kate said. "So I said no, and then she threatened to pull out altogether and so now"—she lifted Leo out of his high chair and scooped him close to her—"I don't know what to fucking do; yes, yes, that's right, poppet, I don't know. Mummy doesn't know."

Leo's mouth split into a smile. She laughed then, and he rested his head against her clavicle. There was no better feeling.

The first few months had been brutal, of course. Although Kate had known all about the sleep deprivation in theory—had longed for it, even, during all those years of trying—nothing could quite prepare her for the reality. But it was true what those blissed-out new mothers said, the ones she had once found so annoying—she genuinely wouldn't have it any other way. Leo was a gift so precious that it was only logical to be expected to work for it. Take away my sleep, she wanted to say. Take away my individuality, my job, my nights out, my ability to read a book, my trendy clothes—take all of it and see if I care. There was no sacrifice too great, no lack that she wouldn't willingly suffer. She had her baby. Finally, after so much time and so much suffering: he was here.

As for Jake, he was an attentive, sweet-natured father who got up to do night feeds, tucking the baby into one arm with a bottle and checking his emails on his phone with his other hand. He was proud of the technique. Seeing him like this made her love him more.

She liked the fact their home was now filled with baby paraphernalia and toys: fabric books that crinkled to the touch, bears in waistcoats, brightly colored play mats and foam balls and tinkling rattles. They had turned Marisa's room into the nursery, installing shelves for baby clothes and muslin cloths and nappies. Before she left, Marisa had given them a mobile of elephants and beach balls to hang above Leo's cot. She had painted it herself. It caught the light in the mornings, and Leo followed the movement of the shapes and the shadows they cast on the ceiling.

Marisa had moved in with Jas after they got back to London. It had been agreed between the four of them: they all knew it was a good idea for Marisa to have her own space, and Jas's flat was only a short drive away from the clinic. Jas had a beat-up VW Golf and offered to take Marisa to appointments whenever necessary. Kate and Jake covered the rent, topping it up when they could, and, in this way, they got through the last weeks of the pregnancy.

"Don't worry," Jas had said to Kate when she came to pick Marisa up, packing her belongings into the back of the car. The suitcases were battered and tired-looking, which made Kate sad. "I've got her. I'll look out for her. Make sure she's taking care of herself."

"I'm just anxious about her after the birth," Kate said, arms crossed as she stood in the street. "I want her to be ok."

"She will be."

"I just . . . I feel so bad about what happened. Did we do the right thing?"

Kate wanted Jas to absolve them of the discomfiting thought that maybe they had prioritized the baby over Marisa's needs. What Annabelle said had lodged inside her like a splinter.

"She wanted to do this for you, remember?"

It wasn't absolution. But it wasn't condemnation either. Kate gave a tentative smile.

"You're very kind to do this, Jas."

Jas glanced at her sharply. "Ris is my friend. She'd do the same for me."

As it turned out, Marisa had surprised them all. During their regular phone calls, Kate got the sense that Marisa had gradually rediscovered her strength. Standing up to Annabelle had given her back confidence in her own judgment.

"I feel like, for the first time, that I can do this," Marisa said one evening.

"You can," Kate said. "Our baby couldn't be in better hands."

"Thank you. But I meant more generally, like . . . I don't know; I feel I can do life again. I know how to *be*. Does that sound weird?"

Kate shook her head. "No. It sounds powerful."

A few months after Leo was born, Marisa went traveling. She called them before she left, and Kate put her on speakerphone as

Marisa told them her plans. She was going to fly to San Francisco and make her way down the Pacific Coast, before wending her way to Mexico and backpacking through South America.

"I've always wanted to do it," she told them. "And I've saved so much money on rent, thanks to you guys, that now I can."

Kate was taken aback by how emotional she felt. "Look after yourself, won't you?" she said, a grizzling Leo on her chest. "You're very special to us."

There was a static pause on the line and the sound of Marisa swallowing hard.

"Thank you, Kate." Her voice was faint. "That means a lot."

"And please tell us how you're getting on," Jake added. "Let us know you're still alive."

She laughed. "I will."

Marisa had been as good as her word. Every month or so, a postcard would slide through their letter box: an image of the Golden Gate Bridge or bronzed divers in Acapulco or Christ the Redeemer spreading gray stone arms out across the mountains. On the back, Marisa would always write the same thing: *Still alive! Having a great time. Love to you both and kisses to baby Leo.*

The gaps between the postcards got longer as time went on and then they stopped altogether. Kate was secretly relieved. It was difficult for the three of them to know how to be with each other, after everything that had happened. It was necessary to maintain a distance between them now for the good of everyone involved.

But she still wanted to know that Marisa was safe. Every now and then, Kate would meet Jas for a coffee at the cafe in Finsbury Park to check in on her.

"How's she doing?" Kate would say, and she wouldn't have to refer to Marisa by name for Jas to know who she was talking about.

At one of these catch-ups, Jas told her that Marisa was dating an Australian yoga instructor she had met on the Machu Picchu trail.

"He sounds great," Jas said. "Really down-to-earth and kind."

"But she hates yoga."

"I know!" Jas snorted. "That's what I love about it."

Landscapes change and shift, Kate thinks, as she and Jake and Leo walk along the river. She watches their reflections distort in the shimmering windows of the smart new apartment blocks. This is their story now, not Marisa's.

They would tell Leo when the time was right, when he was old enough to understand.

"Mummy and Daddy had help to make you extra special" is what they would say. What happened after that, and whether Leo would want to make contact with Marisa, was beyond Kate's control. She tries not to think about it. She is his mother, she keeps telling herself. She would do anything to protect him. She has come to realize that the ferocity of this kind of love is enough to drive you mad, that the tragic flaw of parenthood is that you equip your child to leave you. But what if you never want to let them go? And then she thinks, inevitably, of Annabelle.

"Penny for them," Jake says.

She laughs. "Does anyone actually say that?"

His eyes crinkle. "I do."

They have reached the edge of Battersea Park. The sun is low in the sky, casting a misty light over the surface of the Thames. On the river, two long rowing boats sweep past, eight silhouetted people sitting low in the water, their bodies flexing and straightening in unison. The dipping oars make a light splashing sound as they enter the water.

Kate checks on the baby, whose eyes are flickering shut, his small fingers slowly unfurling. She speaks softly when she replies.

"I was just thinking about a mother's love."

"Wow. Ok. Deep."

She brings her hand up to her forehead to shield her squinting eyes from the sunlight as she looks into Jake's face.

"It's not that I've forgiven Annabelle, exactly . . ." she starts.

"I should hope not," he says.

"It's more that I think I can understand a bit better."

He turns his head to the river. "You're a more generous person than I am."

She places her hand on his cheek, bringing his face back to hers, and she stretches up on tiptoes to kiss him on the mouth.

"I understand why she loves you so much. I couldn't stand it if I felt Leo was being taken away from me by someone who didn't like me."

Jake smiles, but his face is shuttered.

"Let's not talk about it," he says. "I want to have a nice afternoon."

"Ok." She snuggles closer to him, winding her arm around his waist. "I love you."

"I love you too."

Kate always thought that, out of the two of them, she was the angrier one. And she had certainly been furious with Annabelle for a long time after the baby shower. But when Leo was born, it seemed such a waste of energy to keep the fire of her outrage burning. Jake had been horrified by Annabelle's schemes, and horrified by how unwittingly he had taken part in them. He now understood why his sisters barely spoke to her—Annabelle had meddled in their lives so much that they couldn't take it anymore. Toad had developed an eating disorder. Millie was a workaholic. Julia had married an abusive man simply to placate their mother.

"Mum thought he was 'the right sort,'" Jake explained. "You know, double-barreled surname, country shooting weekends, public school—that kind of crap. They're divorced now. But it's why all three of them have moved so far away. I should have told you, but

I could barely admit that was the reason to myself. And I suppose I didn't want you to think badly of Mum. Which is stupid, I know, because no one thinks more badly of her now than I do. I'm sorry. I'm so sorry."

He had apologized repeatedly to Kate for his "weakness" and his "disloyalty" until she told him to stop. She couldn't take the constant rehashing of the past. It was pointless.

"Annabelle can be very convincing," she said to him. "You stood up to her in the end. We all did. And that's what matters."

Besides, she asked, hadn't Annabelle and Chris helped them when they most needed it? Did it matter what the ulterior motive had been? When they were in crisis, and had feared losing everything, it was Jake's parents who had shown up. She is grateful for that, in spite of everything.

Annabelle had sent a pair of blue knitted bootees when Leo was born. The envelope was addressed to Jake, and when he opened it, he threw the card away unopened and stuffed the bootees in the kitchen drawer where they kept the spare batteries and elastic bands. The bootees are still there in their plastic gift box, long outgrown. Whenever Kate catches sight of them, she is moved, in spite of herself, that Annabelle had remembered their due date.

She knows not to press the issue with Jake. It is his pain to carry and his to reconcile, not hers. In time, maybe they will allow Leo's paternal grandparents back into their lives. For now, though, there is no need. They are complete, the three of them. A perfect family, just as they are.

They reach the Peace Pagoda at the edge of the park. Its two layered roofs remind Kate of a Victorian lady lifting her skirts. Kate had read somewhere that the pagoda was presented to London as a gift by a Japanese monk who, after the atrocities at Hiroshima and Nagasaki, had vowed to spend the rest of his life building shrines to peace. She looks at the golden Buddha shining out from the center, its clean brightness like a fresh, new coin. Peace, she thinks. She understands it now. She rests her hand against Leo's head and feels the sleeping warmth of him.

"Shall we go home?" she asks.

"Sure," Jake says.

The baby is swaddled in his sling. Jake's arm is around her shoulders. They walk back to where they came from, and the golden Buddha watches them go.

Acknowledgments

Thank you to Carina Guiterman, an editor who always makes me feel seen, supported, and understood before I even have to explain anything. I so value your insights, humor, and style—which is even noticeable over Zoom.

At Simon & Schuster, my thanks to the ever-patient Lashanda Anakwah. It's rare for me to meet someone as efficient as I am, but Lashanda, you're way ahead of me. Thank you.

Thank you also to Elizabeth Breeden and Hannah Bishop for all their hard work. Books would not be read were it not for the efforts of marketing and publicity teams and I'm forever grateful.

My agent, Nelle Andrew, is my champion in more ways than I can enumerate. I count myself incredibly lucky to have her in my corner—in life as in books.

Emma Reed Turrell, you are everything I've ever needed in a best friend—and more (and yes, that is a Leanne Hainsby Peloton reference).

If you've read this far, you'll know that *Magpie* has a plot twist. This meant I was very strict with myself about who I confided in, but Lisa Albert was one of the first to give me encouragement, as was Dolly Alderton. Thank you both. To my LA family: Andrea Remanda, Joan Harrison, Michael Janofsky, Bonnie Garvin—thank you for supporting both me and my writing in so many ways.

Thank you to my parents—my father, Tom, for the medical

advice on correct drug dosages, and my mother, Christine, for her kindness in always being one of my first readers.

Thank you to my most cherished friends. I couldn't do life without you.

Thank you to all the women who have shared their stories of fertility with me. I am honored every single time you choose to tell me the paths you have traveled. I see you.

And finally, thank you to Justin. During the course of writing this book, we went through a lot. Every single day of it, you made me feel loved. You still do. Thank you for that—and for showing me that the happiest plot twists in life come after we get the pacing right.

London, November 2021

About the Author

ELIZABETH DAY is the author of the novels *The Party* and *Paradise City*. She is an award-winning broadcaster based in the UK and the host of the podcast *How to Fail*, a celebration of the things that haven't gone right.